Between the Lies

Alison Oburia

OMNIFIC PUBLISHING
DALLAS

Omnific Publishing
10000 North Central Expressway, Dallas, TX 75231
www.omnificpublishing.com

First Omnific eBook edition, October 2012
First Omnific trade paperback edition, October 2012

The characters and events in this book are fictitious.
Any similarity to real persons, living or dead,
is coincidental and not intended by the author.

Library of Congress Cataloguing-in-Publication Data

Oburia, Alison.
Between the Lies / Alison Oburia – 1st ed.
ISBN 978-1-62342-909-6
1. Bulgarian Mafia — Fiction. 2. Money Laundering — Fiction.
3. Romance — Fiction. 4. Pacific Northwest — Fiction. I. Title

10 9 8 7 6 5 4 3 2 1

Cover Design by Micha Stone and Amy Brokaw
Interior Book Design by Coreen Montagna

Printed in the United States of America

To Dmitry, who inspired this story.
Wherever you are now, I hope you are safe.

Prologue

The color photo of the catastrophic damage to the café in Brindisi made Josef smile. Two bodies in black bags. Shards of glass everywhere. Even the sagging, burned remains of the awning that had draped over the wrought iron table left no doubt this was the result of a bomb. Normally staid and sophisticated, he couldn't help the childlike grin on his face as he smoothed the aging newspaper. He absorbed every detail, particularly the shocked looks on the faces of the Italian townspeople gathered behind crime scene tape in the background.

What made Josef happiest, though, as he examined the photo and other news clippings in the stack, was that even five years later the police and international investigation teams had no way, no reason, to connect him with this act of terrorism.

Over the years, he'd become a collector of sorts: he liked amassing mementos of his conquests — secretly, of course. In this case, the bomb had been intended for a nosy photojournalist; his new bride had simply been in the wrong place at the wrong time. The deaths of Sergio D'Antonio and his wife, Marisol, were eventually attributed to anti-Catholic protestors who had vowed to get the pope's attention. The group naturally denied any involvement; the investigation was soon shelved for lack of evidence, and no one was ever arrested.

Josef's gaze dropped to a lower part of the article he'd printed from the Internet. There he saw pictures of Mr. and Mrs. D'Antonio, both in their early sixties — he a handsome native Italian and she an American with a freckle-covered face and a head of loose reddish-brown curls. It was a shame, Josef mused, for such a pretty woman to have lost her life because of her new husband's recklessness. If D'Antonio had backed off his investigation when he'd received the warning three weeks earlier, the couple could have continued to enjoy their honeymoon on Italy's southeastern coast. Ah, but that was five years ago. Bloody water under the bridge.

He moved on to reminisce about the sniper attack on a defense minister in Albania…the poisoning of a pair of embezzling brothers in Greece…the auto "accident" of an acquaintance who'd challenged him in Latvia…

The intercom call caused Josef to quickly shuffle the photos and papers back into the lower drawer of his large mahogany desk. "*Da,*" he said abruptly as he locked the drawer and asked the assistant to show in his guest.

Josef adjusted his tie as he came around his desk and extended his hand, his smile wide. "Good morning, Senator," he said in his best English. "I am Josef Aleynekov, Minister of Finance for the great Republic of Bulgaria. Welcome to my country. I am glad you have accepted my offer and look forward to working with you on some, shall we say, mutually beneficial proposals." He gestured to the American to be seated. "Shall we begin?"

Chapter 1

Sunlight from the tall windows illuminated the dust that floated above Cari's hands. She continued to pick absently at her fingernail; it was going to need either filing or a bandage soon. The conference room's sterile beige walls and pale wood furniture blended with the monotony of the discussion taking place around her. Only the clock's ticking behind her had become more pronounced in the last half hour, and she tapped her foot against the carpet, hoping if she increased her rhythm, the clock would do the same. This meeting wasn't going well at all. The bearded man at the end of the long table droned on to the point that she was barely listening. His final statement caught her attention, though, and she raised her eyes to meet his.

"The committee has agreed, Miss Lopez, that your proposal will need to go through a substantial revision before you submit it again."

Cari smiled politely as Dr. Henrik Swanson, one of her four doctoral committee members, folded his hands over the thick document in front of him: the product of the last two years of her life. Nervously tucking an escaped curl behind her ear, which immediately fell back toward her cheek, she glanced at each of the solemn faces gazing at her.

She wasn't surprised, really. She had the toughest collection of professors possible to decide whether her dissertation topic was worthy. One of them, she was convinced, was never going to give his approval. But he could be overruled if she could just pinpoint the right topic to persuade the others. Something within the realm of accounting that she would spend a year or longer researching. She had to really embrace the topic, live and breathe it twenty-four seven, and make it the best damned thing the St. Eustachius University faculty had ever read.

But that was the problem; she hadn't found a topic she wanted to work on. What she'd submitted to the committee had been chosen because it was readily available, not because it was challenging or insightful. Her research hadn't revealed anything new or amazing. Even *she* had found the whole thing tedious. Couple that with her perfectionism—whatever she wrote had to be flawless—and she was starting to feel that she'd never finish this beast. Her shoulders slumped.

"Cari?" The distinguished Dr. Renate Kruger glared at her colleagues and touched Cari's arm gently. "Let's talk in my office, shall we?"

Chair legs scuffed against the carpeted floor as they all stood. Cari thanked the committee graciously, holding her growing frustration—and budding tears—at bay. She couldn't let them see that she was defeated...yet. She wrapped her sweater around her and followed her advisor out of the room.

Over in the faculty office area, Dr. Kruger gestured to the well-worn chair in her small office as she scooted around piles of papers and books on her desk. Wisps of graying curls framed her face; she was an attractive woman in her early sixties, well-respected on campus as well as across the field of accounting.

"You're in year three of your dissertation, Cari," she began, her German accent soft and soothing. "You know the department limits you to five. I hate to remind you that you're running out of time, but I know you can do this. In order to finish, you've got to follow my advice."

"I know. KISS. 'Keep It Simple, Stupid.'"

"Let's put it in a better light. How about 'Keep It Statistically Simple'? It doesn't have to be perfect or grandiose. The graduate with the best dissertation will sit next to the graduate with the worst. No one's going to care if your work wins any kind of award. Honestly, few people beyond you and your committee will likely ever even read the thing."

Cari sighed, sinking deeper in to the cushioned chair. Her eyes cast downward as she focused on a small container of colorful paperclips at the edge of Dr. Kruger's desk. "I just wish I could find some new angle, something that will drive me to want to know more."

"How about we meet again in three weeks, hmm?" The professor's warm eyes caught the glow of the lamp on her desk as she peered at Cari over her reading glasses. "In that time I want you to come up with two or three ideas, as well as some brief research that will justify doing a dissertation on them. You know I'll support you, Cari, but I won't be able to bend the rules on the time frame, okay?"

"Yeah, thanks, Dr. Kruger." Cari gave a half-hearted smile, gathered her notebooks and backpack, and made her way home.

After waiting for twenty minutes at baggage claim in the Seattle-Tacoma airport, Tristan Saunders hobbled to a row of chrome and black leather chairs and sat down. He pulled his luggage toward him, draped his coat across his lap, and pressed the familiar numbers into his cell.

"Gemma, I'm at the airport. I thought you were going to pick me up."

His sister. He loved her dearly, but she could be forgetful. Tristan thought flying in from London for the first time in four years would have been cause for her to remember, but, well, that was Gemma.

He continued leaving his message. "Look, love, I'll catch a cab to your place. I hope you'll get this message by then, and one of you can meet me there. I'm calling from the new mobile I purchased when I landed, so don't ring my BlackBerry."

He ended the call and grabbed his luggage awkwardly, piling as much as he could onto the largest piece with rollers on the bottom. Leaning on his cane, he made his way to a queue of cabs waiting outside.

The hour's ride to Gemma and Ethan's island flat was pleasant; the endless green of the trees, curving roads, and occasional glimpse of Puget Sound were different from London's busy cityscape, but the weather was quite similar: overcast with a constant mist in the air. This was Tristan's first visit to this part of the States. He and Gemma had been born and raised in London, but she'd met Ethan during a semester studying art history in Madrid. He was American, and she'd gladly given up Europe in favor of living in the States. They'd started out in his native Missouri, but a few months ago relocated to Bainbridge Island, Washington.

The last time Tristan had seen them was their wedding. Since then, he'd spent much of his time in various former Soviet Bloc countries, most recently Bulgaria. His work with Carson World Financial involved investigating money laundering—and Bulgaria, like many former Communist countries, was rife with corruption. The government had stabilized, but the influence of organized crime was pervasive—and dangerous. The relative safety of the United States was welcome relief. Tristan could already tell that his three-week stay would be over too soon.

The cab driver pulled up to the curb at Gemma's flat and pulled Tristan's bags from the trunk. A passenger with a cane and a heavy limp must have brought out his Good Samaritan, and Tristan tipped him generously. He couldn't have managed without the man's help.

As the cab drove away, Tristan began to move his luggage piece by piece, step by step, to the base of the outdoor stairway. It figured Gemma and Ethan lived on the second floor and there was no lift. Tristan left the three bags at the bottom and began his slow ascent to apartment 5203.

After knocking twice and trying both of their mobile phones again, Tristan returned to his luggage. He could manage his briefcase and carry-on one at a time, and with nothing else to do, he decided to bring what he could up to their doorway. The heavy rolling suitcase would just have to wait. Tristan moved it to the wall under the overhang and, for the fourth time in forty minutes, climbed the steps to his sister's front door.

His right knee brace didn't allow bending, and he briefly considered remaining standing or sitting on the steps. Despite the hours he'd spent in various airplane seats, the ache that grew as his pain meds wore off convinced him that a horizontal position for that limb would be best. He really needed food to take another pill. Bad planning on his part, he realized; he'd have been smarter to eat before leaving the airport. He eased himself to sitting using his cane and the wrought iron railing across from their door.

It was getting on toward three in the afternoon, and he still had no word from Gemma or Ethan. Their flat was in one of probably six or seven buildings, all angled in different directions to give tenants views of the rolling landscape and Puget Sound at the bottom of the slope. The area was pleasant, the only sound the seagulls nearby. No cars, no mothers with baby strollers, no one walking a dog. The quiet was soothing; Tristan closed his eyes and let himself relax.

"Um…hello?" Cari wasn't sure what to say upon finding some-one sleeping on the doorstep of her next door neighbors' apartment. Given the suitcase at the bottom of the stairs and how this man was dressed—tan slacks, pinstripe shirt, and an expensive-looking overcoat—he didn't seem like he was homeless and had chanced upon their little landing to take a nap. Nor did he seem dangerous, like she'd need to call the police. Maybe he was just lost; Gemma and Ethan weren't due back until tomorrow. This man must simply be at the wrong apartment and not know it.

"Hello?" she said again, a little louder this time. "Can I help you?"

The man slowly opened his eyes and… *Wow*. Cari had never seen eyes so light; they were almost gray, like a wolf's.

"Oh, bloody hell," the man groaned after glancing up and then shutting his eyes tight.

Cari furrowed her brow. Was she that horrible to look at?

He arched his back and ran his hand through his dark hair, finishing with a hard rub against the back of his neck. "Sorry 'bout that." He winced, but then gave her a quick half-smile.

"Are you, um, at the right apartment?" Cari asked. "Whose place are you visiting?"

"What? Oh, I thought I was at Gemma and Ethan Stonecipher's. Am I not?"

British accent. Just like Gemma's.

"Yeah. I mean, yes," she sputtered, embarrassed to feel so awkward. "You're at the right place but, um, they won't be home until tomorrow."

"Well, that's just grand." He ran his hand across the back of his neck again. Then he looked up. "Sorry. I'm being rude."

"Are you…related to Gemma?"

"Oh, my apologies, yes. I'm a bit disoriented. Long flights to get here. I'm Gemma's brother, Tristan."

"You've just arrived from—"

"London, yes. And Gemma was supposed to meet me at the airport." He smiled and shook his head, snickering lightly. "My little sister never was the best about remembering things."

"She did know you were coming, though, didn't she?"

"Oh, yes. I spoke with her a week ago and let her know when I'd be arriving."

"I talked with her last night, and all she told me was to be on the lookout for something at her door today." Cari laughed. "I was expecting a package, not a person."

He dropped his head and groaned. "Gemma…"

"I'm sorry?"

"Nothing. Private matter between siblings." He reached for the railing, picking himself up slowly, keeping his right leg stiff. As he stood, Cari noticed a cane in the crook between the wall and Gemma's apartment door.

He must have seen her gaping mouth and smiled. "Knee surgery a few months ago. Still wearing a brace while recuperating."

"Oh. So traveling from London was—"

"Uncomfortable, yes, to say the least." He smirked. "Say, you don't happen to have a key to—"

"Their apartment?" They were getting good at finishing each other's sentences. "Yeah. Let me grab it from my place." She turned and tried to get her own key to work. Feeling a sudden burst of nervousness, she dropped it on her doormat. She recovered as best she could, turned to smile at her neighbor's handsome guest, and shoved the key into place, bending it slightly. A few jiggles dislodged it, and Cari was finally able to open her door. "Be right back."

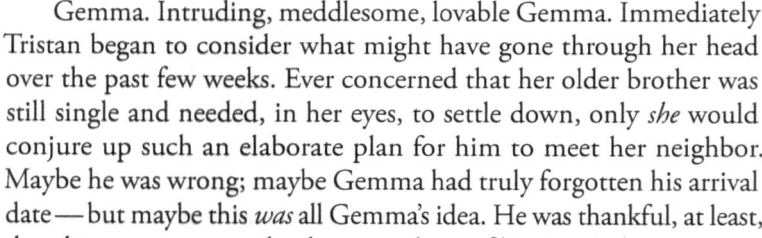

Gemma. Intruding, meddlesome, lovable Gemma. Immediately Tristan began to consider what might have gone through her head over the past few weeks. Ever concerned that her older brother was still single and needed, in her eyes, to settle down, only *she* would conjure up such an elaborate plan for him to meet her neighbor. Maybe he was wrong; maybe Gemma had truly forgotten his arrival date—but maybe this *was* all Gemma's idea. He was thankful, at least, that this woman seemed to know nothing of his sister's devious ways.

And Gemma *did* know Tristan's type. The woman who now helped him into his sister's flat was quite pretty. Reddish-brown ringlets cascaded down her back while shorter curls framed her face. Her brown eyes, surrounded by long eyelashes, brightened each time she smiled. And freckles! This woman had more freckles than he'd ever seen. She didn't appear to wear much makeup; it didn't seem she needed to. She had an almost olive complexion and a natural beauty to her; Tristan imagined she enjoyed spending time outside.

It wasn't just Cari's looks that intrigued Tristan, though. Her willingness to assist a stranger indicated she was nothing like Melanie, his ex-girlfriend whom his parents had despised. But did this woman know anything about *him?* She didn't even seem to know Gemma had a brother. All part of his sister's plan, he surmised. She wouldn't want to scare off a "suitable" woman with tales of all he'd been through recently. And, for Tristan's sake, she'd want to be sure the woman was right for him as well. Maybe if Gemma had met Melanie, she'd have steered him away from her. Instead, Tristan spent a year of one-sided compromising—his—trying to make something of the relationship. He'd actually been relieved when Melanie moved out. While Tristan had been clinging to the idea that happiness was having someone to come home to between trips to Bulgaria, she'd been expecting someone who could devote the level of attention to her that she demanded.

Tristan had to stop this thinking; he had no proof that he was being set up with Gemma's neighbor. This woman could very well be married with three children. Right now, he needed to focus on getting settled, finding food, and taking some pain meds.

"Here you go." The woman returned, smiling lightly, key in hand.

"Thank you, ah…I'm sorry; I don't know your name."

A quick blush crossed her cheeks. "Oh. Um, I'm Cari."

"Well, Cari, I'm delighted to meet you." Tristan nodded properly toward her. He unlocked and opened the door. Before entering, he turned back to her. "And you say Gemma and Ethan aren't due home until tomorrow?"

"They're in LA. Ethan's at a conference and Gemma is with him, visiting all the boutiques she can find, I'm sure."

Tristan let out a quick laugh. "Yes, that would be Gemma. Let's hope for Ethan's sake she takes home more ideas than purchases." Gemma had started a successful online business—upscale baby clothing and décor—when she and Ethan lived in St. Louis, even securing a few celebrity clients. When they'd moved, Gemma added a brick-and-mortar shop in the tourist-rich downtown area of the island. Tristan knew she enjoyed traveling with Ethan when his work brought him to bigger cities where she could gather new merchandise and inspiration.

As Tristan crossed the threshold into the apartment, Cari suddenly disappeared. He found her at the bottom of the stairway, and before he could protest, she began hauling his remaining suitcase up the steps.

"Oh, no!" he called down. "That's too heavy!"

"And there's no way you can get it up these stairs on a bad leg, right?"

She had him there.

"But, really…" He hated being stuck like this. Ethan wouldn't be home until tomorrow, and Tristan would surely injure himself further if he tried to handle that task himself.

"Not a problem!" She returned to the top of the steps quite quickly, then engaged the rollers along the bottom of the suitcase and headed toward the Stoneciphers' flat.

He held the door open and studied her as she walked past. This lovely young woman, with no ring decorating any finger on her left hand, was currently the only person he knew and could talk to in the entire United States. He wasn't going to ignore that. His mind began to wander in a new direction: the limited time he might have to get to know her before his meddlesome sister returned. And why not? Cari lived next door, she seemed genuinely friendly, and Tristan was going to be staying with Ethan and Gemma for the next three weeks. It would be rude to disregard the kindness she'd shown him already.

Tristan hobbled into the kitchen and opened the refrigerator. Nearly empty, certainly no fresh eggs or milk. Mustard and whipped cream were not meal-makers, and frankly, he needed to eat.

When he turned, Cari was at the front door, but she seemed to linger rather than heading back out.

"I'm so terribly sorry, but, well, Gemma and Ethan seem to have left me in a bit of a spot. There appears to be nothing edible, and I'm here without transportation until their return tomorrow."

Cari tipped her head shyly. "Uh…I could get you something from my apartment next door," she offered with a shrug. "I'm not much of a cook, but if you like macaroni and cheese, you're definitely in business."

There was no time like the present — and Tristan liked his present company. "That's very kind of you, but actually, I don't believe I've eaten a decent meal since —" he glanced at his watch " — the day before yesterday. Might I impose upon you to be my dinner companion at a local restaurant? My treat, of course, but I'd obviously need you to drive."

Wow, Tristan thought. He hadn't been this forward since…well, ever. Melanie had been a co-worker for two years before their first date. And now, here he was asking a complete stranger out to dinner in a town he'd been in for all of three hours. Whether Gemma planned this or not, she'd be proud of his bold efforts.

"Oh, um," Cari stammered, "that would be great. But you don't have to pay for me." She smiled. "I think I could use a night out after today. And we'll stop at a grocery store on the way home for a few items Gemma'll need and a bottle of wine for me for later."

"Wine?" Tristan raised his eyebrows. "Are you celebrating or commiserating?"

"Commiserating, definitely commiserating." She waved her hand and shook her head. "But that's just…stuff. Sorry, just had a day that—" She stopped. "Never mind." Cari straightened her posture and gave Tristan a refreshing smile. "Are you interested in any particular type of restaurant? I mean, we have everything from McDonald's to five-star fare."

"How about…" He sized her up. She didn't seem the McDonald's type unless she was in a hurry. The other extreme would be, well, *extreme* given they'd just met. "How about something casual, perhaps? I'd prefer not to have to change these slacks. The brace underneath can be difficult to deal with."

"Cairo's is good. They've got international cuisine. A lot of it's Egyptian, but you can get fish, chicken, or a steak prepared any way you want. And their desserts are phenomenal."

"That sounds perfect." Tristan sighed. "And I'm starved. Would we be able to go soon? I hate to inconvenience you; you've been a godsend to me already."

"I skipped lunch, so I'm ready when you are." She flashed a radiant smile. "Do you need a few minutes to unpack or anything? I just want to slip next door real quick. I can meet you between our doorways in five, if that's okay."

"Meet you in five, then," he replied. "And thank you."

She raised her eyebrows in surprise. "For what?"

"Coming home."

Chapter 2

"Your vehicle is…lavender?" Tristan asked as they approached Cari's Hummer.

Cari beamed, giving her car a gentle pat on the hood. "More periwinkle, really."

Tristan snickered. "I'm sorry. I've just…never…"

"Yeah. It took a little getting used to. It was my father's idea. He found it online and got it as a gift for me when I turned twenty-one. He wasn't quite ready to let go of his little girl, and there's certainly no hiding *this* beast."

Tristan climbed carefully into the passenger side and placed his cane next to his thigh by the door. The huge front seat and spacious floorboard seemed perfect for his outstretched leg. Cari smiled; if she'd owned some little MiniCooper, he wouldn't have been able to maneuver into it. They were only a mile from their destination, but she was still glad the short trip would be comfortable for her guest.

It was a Thursday, so Cairo's wasn't too packed when they arrived. The casual atmosphere seemed appropriate; the background noise and expansive view of the water would have provided a distraction if their conversation had lagged at all. But the sights and sounds around them were never needed to rescue them from any down time, because there was none.

They were led to a table just off the main walking path, which allowed Tristan to extend his right leg without worry of tripping passers-by. Once seated, they both took a minute to look over the menu. Cari wondered if the food would be to an Englishman's liking. She already knew what she would order, but took her time reading each entrée's description and thinking, *Is this something he might like?* And, *Do they serve it this way in England?*

Tristan spoke, interrupting her thoughts. "Do you want a glass of wine with dinner?"

"Hmm?" Cari looked up. "Oh. Um, no, designated driver and all that. You go ahead, though, if you'd like something." She smiled. "But I can't have you getting drunk," she warned. "I may have been strong enough to get that massive suitcase up the steps, but if you pass out, you'll be spending the night in my car."

He laughed and nodded. "I believe I shall pass on any alcohol this evening." He reached into his jacket pocket and pulled out a prescription bottle. "I need this instead."

"Pain medication?"

"Yes. Many hours cooped up in various airplanes, even in first class, isn't good for my knee as it heals."

"Why'd you have surgery? Sports injury?" Cari cringed inwardly at her intrusive question, but so far they'd gotten along well enough, so it couldn't hurt to ask.

"Actually—" he looked up at her from his menu "—my knee had a close encounter with a metal pipe. The pipe got away with no damage whatsoever, but my kneecap didn't fare so well."

"Ouch!" She winced. "How did that happen?"

Before he could answer, their server arrived, and the two took a moment to order Diet Cokes and their meals: for Cari, the chicken curry, and for Tristan, grilled salmon on a bed of couscous and olive leaves.

As they were left alone again, Tristan leaned back and let out a sigh. Cari was ready for his answer to her question, but instead he changed the subject.

"So," he began, "why will you be commiserating later this evening over a glass of wine? Or is it something that will result in an empty bottle and a hangover tomorrow?"

His eyes never left hers. They were almost hypnotic.

"Well, I'm a doctoral student at St. Eustachius University—it's a small school over in Seattle—and I was told today that I basically need to start over with my dissertation." Their drinks arrived, and Cari took a long sip of hers, worried that this topic of discussion would dead-end quickly.

"Wow. How far along were you?"

"About a hundred and thirty pages." She sighed. "And two years of work."

"Christ, that's got to be devastating."

Cari sat back and stroked the arms of her chair, watching her hands as they moved. "Yeah."

"So...can you start over?"

He seemed genuinely concerned.

"I mean, you're not going to give up, are you?"

"No, I guess not." She shrugged. "Problem is, I have no idea what I want to research. Starting from scratch wouldn't be a problem if I could just identify something, anything, that I can attack with a vengeance."

Tristan leaned forward, elbows on the table and fingers laced together in front of him. Suddenly his demeanor seemed eerily like Dr. Kruger's. "Okay. Let's brainstorm."

"What? You're fresh off a plane, probably exhausted and dealing with jet lag, taking pain medication, and yet you're ready to help me figure out a dissertation topic?"

"Sure." He gave her a wide smile. "Why not? Now, what's your field of study?"

"Accounting."

He stifled a short laugh. "What area?"

"Um, international mostly, but my dissertation can be on anything as long as it's accounting-related."

"But your interests lie in international accounting or perhaps even global economics?"

"Yes..."

"And you've got to be under a time constraint now, I assume. So it would be best to find a topic you'll want to devote all your energy to, right?"

"Okay, Tristan, either you teach at a university or recently finished your own doctorate. Which is it?"

He smirked. "PhD in accounting."

Cari couldn't help but laugh. "You're kidding me! Really?" Suddenly this chance encounter with her neighbor's handsome brother took a dramatic, and wonderful, turn.

Tristan grinned, holding his hands up in surrender. "Absolutely. Graduated four years ago."

As they nibbled their salads, Cari grilled Tristan on his dissertation. He graciously answered each of her questions in detail and asked about her interests as well, following up on his idea to brainstorm with her. Cari now found the idea of a whole new dissertation topic much more appealing; she was actually excited at the thought of starting fresh.

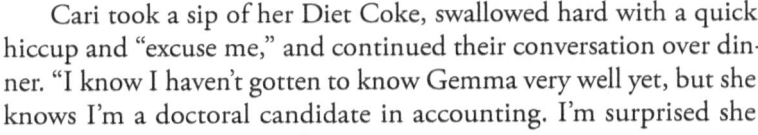

Cari took a sip of her Diet Coke, swallowed hard with a quick hiccup and "excuse me," and continued their conversation over dinner. "I know I haven't gotten to know Gemma very well yet, but she knows I'm a doctoral candidate in accounting. I'm surprised she didn't mention you to me."

Ah, Gemma. Tristan knew all too well why his sister hadn't told Cari about him. He loved his sister's persistence at playing matchmaker, and he was convinced now that she'd arranged this whole "chance encounter." She'd tried to set him up with women since they were in college, but he'd always balked at the idea. And even though he'd met a few of them, his nervousness inevitably sabotaged any chance at a relationship. If he'd known that Gemma had a single, attractive next-door neighbor who was working on her PhD in the same subject he'd studied, he would have canceled the trip. Accounting he knew and embraced; women, on the other hand, scared the hell out of him.

Maybe Cari was the same way, and Gemma was taking double precautions by telling neither of them about the other. *Good thinking, Gemma*, Tristan thought.

A few times during their meal, Tristan could feel Cari trying to steer the conversation back to his knee injury, and he finally decided to tell one of the stories he'd made up. He feared the truth would jeopardize their developing friendship. She seemed to accept readily that he'd fallen off scaffolding while painting the shutters on the upper floor of his parents' home—an adequate explanation as to how his knee had made painful and unavoidable contact with two very thick metal pipes.

But he hated always having to lie. His knee was just one of the injuries he'd been slowly recovering from over the past three months. However, being nearly beaten to death by the Bulgarian mafia wasn't something one shared with a new acquaintance over a pleasant dinner. Hell, he'd even lied to Gemma and his parents.

Because he continued to be a wanted man, Tristan hoped staying quiet might just keep his family and friends safe. He still had vital information that he'd not shared with anyone after completing his investigation of an international money laundering scheme. Information he'd told Bulgarian Minister of Finance Josef Aleynekov he was willing to take to the grave. Information that, if kept secret, would keep Aleynekov and his "colleagues" in business, under the UN's radar or any new investigator's probing.

Tristan just hoped Aleynekov would eventually be willing to trust that he'd keep his mouth shut. He wondered if the Bulgarian had sent some of his hired mafia hands after him to the States, all the way to Washington even. All Tristan knew was that Aleynekov's people wouldn't hesitate to follow through with their threats: they knew where his parents and sister lived, and they had worldwide connections.

But Tristan was a threat to them too. The information he had could bring down the entire government of the former Soviet Bloc nation, something they wanted to avoid at any cost. That kept their delicate relationship at a precarious balance: Tristan let them stay in business; Aleynekov and his colleagues let Tristan—and his family—stay alive.

Chapter 3

Tristan had to be the most intriguing man Cari had met in a long time. She chose to push to the back of her head the reality that his home was in England and his visit with Gemma and Ethan would only be for a few weeks. And it was a visit with *them*, not her. Of course she couldn't stop a little voice from musing that perhaps now was perfect time to get to know Gemma and Ethan better. Cari could only hope—especially after the wonderful time she and Tristan were having—that maybe her neighbors (and Tristan) would want to include her in some of the things they'd be doing while he was here.

Their trip to the grocery store was…interesting. Tristan had discovered that Cari blushed easily, and he seemed intent on finding ways to embarrass her as they cruised the aisles of the Safeway market. To observers, they must have seemed like a young couple enjoying each other's company. Any time another shopper came within earshot, Tristan would ask a question or make some comment sure to turn her cheeks beet red.

As they wandered down the wrapping paper and greeting card aisle, Tristan followed a few paces behind Cari, leaning on his cane. Then without warning, a loud serenade began—the chorus of "I Think I Love You," the Partridge Family's famous tune.

Cari stopped, hands frozen in place on the cart, and turned slowly around. There stood Tristan, holding open one of those musical greeting cards and singing in perfect tune with David Cassidy and awful, metallic-sounding music.

"What on earth are you doing?"

He was all smiles as he closed the card, returned it to the shelf, and selected another. "These are bloody brilliant!"

"Tristan!" Cari wheeled the cart back to him and whispered urgently. "This is not a karaoke bar!"

"And you're blushing again." He grinned broadly. "This is fantastic!" He turned back to face the rows of cards, eagerly searching for another.

"I'm heading to the next aisle. Follow me or stay here. Your choice."

"Oh, come on," he called as she began to walk away. "I'll find one with a duet in it! You'll sing with me, won't you, Cari?...Cari?"

Before he could possibly embarrass her more, Cari laughed and waved. She continued around the corner.

As she scanned dryer sheet options along with two other women, Tristan's voice and another tin-can song wafted over to them. This time, it was Player's classic one-hit wonder "Baby, Come Back."

"Is that for you?" one woman deadpanned.

Cari blushed. "Yes. Excuse me while I go kill a visiting Brit."

She scurried back to the card aisle, and Tristan was ready for her, the next card already in his hand and a devious grin on his face.

Cari hesitated. She could see a zebra on the front wearing sunglasses and a Mohawk.

Tristan lowered his eyebrows and gazed seductively at her as he began to sing "Wild Thing."

"You're incorrigible!" she said with a laugh.

"And you're still a lovely shade of red, so if you think I'm going to quit, you're wrong." He was obviously enjoying himself, and Cari had to admit, she was too. As he closed the card, stopping The Troggs' famous tune mid-line, he sported the most adorable smile, dimples and all.

When Tristan turned to find yet another card and Cari shook her head in frustration, he dropped his shoulders and finally stepped away from the shelf to join her again in their shopping. "What?" he asked with childlike wonder as he hobbled up next to the cart. Cari didn't respond, but she knew Tristan could see the grin she was trying to suppress as she gestured for him to follow her.

In the fruit section, he offered seemingly innocent comments that nonetheless continued to make her blush. Once again, there were other shoppers conveniently nearby to hear him.

As he picked up a small bunch of bananas, he furrowed his eyebrows. "I don't know what's so funny about 'Is that a banana in your pocket or are you just happy to see me?' I mean, honestly—"

Before he could finish, Cari decided to beat him to the punch. "I know! Cucumbers are *obviously* the better produce for that joke."

That stopped him short. Cari didn't wait around for his reaction but did catch a sly smile of acknowledgment. Her comment, however, did not yield the desired result: she'd wanted to see if she could embarrass him. So far the score remained about ten to zero in his favor.

The comment that finally convinced Cari to really fight fire with fire, though, occurred near the pharmacy.

"Darling?" Tristan called rather loudly. "Is it the ribbed condoms you liked last time?" When an elderly woman waiting for her prescription looked over at the two of them, mouth slightly open, he winked at her. "Got to practice safe sex, right?"

It was time for Cari to play along.

"Oh, Tristan," she cooed, sauntering up to him and gliding a single finger slowly down the front of his shirt. When she got to his belt, she tugged it a little. "Let's skip the condoms for once, huh? I want to really *feel* you tonight." She put on a girlish pout and stared up into his now very wide eyes.

But Tristan recovered quickly, turned to the woman, and pumped his fist. "Yesss!"

With that, Cari backed away, threw up her hands, and just had to laugh. "You win. There is no embarrassing you. I surrender."

Tristan cocked his head and eyed her seductively. "Wow. You surrender that easily, do you? This *is* my lucky night!"

"Tristan!"

Once they were out of the pharmacy and on the way to the checkout line, he laughed. "You play the game well. I nearly lost it when you did that thing—" he ran his finger partway down his chest "—and kept a straight face."

"That poor woman!" Cari blushed again. "Maybe I should go apologize."

"Poor woman?" he scoffed. "I heard the pharmacist take her husband's order for some, ahem, enhancement medication. She'll be the one 'getting lucky' tonight, not us."

"Does that mean you didn't get the condoms?" She pouted again, and he laughed.

"I'll be right back!" he said with a quick wink.

"No! Tristan!"

But he was gone, hobbling back to the pharmacy before Cari could stop him. When he returned, he held an item behind his back and gave her a look full of the devil.

"You didn't!"

Suddenly, people in line around them watched with voyeuristic interest.

"I did! And you are *so* going to thank me later," he said seductively.

Then he threw a package of dental floss on the conveyor, and the two of them lost themselves in laughter once again.

Chapter 4

Tristan hadn't laughed that much in...he couldn't remember when. It felt good to finally be relaxed, not always looking over his shoulder, wondering if he was safe.

And where had this brazen side of him come from? Were the pain meds having some strange side effect? It was like he was someone other than the staid, nervous, boring Tristan he'd been all his life. Even when things were good with Melanie, he couldn't recall ever being so...God, what was it?...*free*. Had he really made sexual innuendos with this woman he hardly knew? And done so *repeatedly?* Thank heavens she hadn't slapped him. Christ, what was he thinking?

The meds had never caused such behavior before. Maybe it was some subconscious knowledge that, because he was visiting from the other side of the world and would be gone in a matter of weeks, he *could* be somebody else; he could adopt a persona just for the hell of it. Soon he'd be back in England, back to being dull, serious, shy Tristan once again.

But he wondered: had any of this change been because of Cari? There was something...something enlightening...about her that he couldn't deny. In his real world, Tristan never would have had the confidence to speak to a woman like her, and certainly not in the way he did. But today, he'd had to depend on her out of happenstance. Or was it fate? Either way, he'd found her so easy to talk to, so interesting to listen to.

Tristan's thoughts circled back to Gemma. Could she have foreseen his amazing transformation? She knew him better than anyone, but even during his occasional drunken stupors in college, she'd never witnessed *this* side of him. Tristan didn't even recognize *himself* tonight.

It was just refreshing, so refreshing, to simply laugh until his ribs hurt.

"That was the most, um, interesting trip to the store I've ever had." Cari giggled as they drove out of the grocery store's parking lot.

"I am so sorry! You've got to believe me that I'm normally a very shy person."

Cari gave him an incredulous sideways look.

"No, honestly, I am! I don't know what got into me. You must think I'm a total git." He paused, running his hand across the back of his neck like he always did when he was embarrassed, then added in a quieter, more repentant tone, "You're not going to have to find a new place to shop, are you?"

She brushed loose ringlets from her forehead as she broke into another fit of laughter. "No, of course not. But I hope to never run into that woman from the pharmacy again. I don't know what would embarrass me more: the commentary she witnessed or knowing what her purchase was."

"Well," Tristan mused seriously as Cari kept her gaze on the road ahead, "I'm happy for her. No need to 'go without' if there's medical help available."

Cari closed her eyes for a moment, quickly shaking her head from side to side. "No, no, no, no, no! I do not want the image of their impending activities invading my head, thank you!"

Tristan stifled a snort of laughter as he, too, tried to delete any such thoughts before they emerged in his mind's eye. "Absolutely. So! New topic, then?"

"Yes, please, I beg you!"

Cari's laugh was euphoric, lightening Tristan's heart and sweeping away the worries that had weighed heavy for so many months.

"Um…I'm trying to think, trying to think." And he honestly was, but their outing at the market was blocking everything. "I know. I wanted to ask you two things," he finally said. "And I'll understand perfectly if the answer is no to the second one."

She looked over at him curiously. "Okay, shoot."

"Well, I was going to ask if there is any way for me to get this leg some exercise. A park, maybe, or just somewhere I can walk? I'm not looking for a treadmill, at least not tonight. The weather's too pleasant, and I've been cooped up too long over the past few days. And my second question—" he hesitated, hoping he wasn't pushing beyond her comfort level "—I wondered if you'd mind driving me there and…perhaps…joining me for a short walk?" Tristan winced, prepared for Cari to respond with a polite "I can't" or "Maybe some other time" or, worse, "My boyfriend and I have plans later."

"Sure."

He let out a silent sigh of relief.

"Actually," she continued, "we wouldn't have to drive anywhere. There's a nice walking path that circles the apartment complex. Would that work for you?"

The smile that suddenly appeared on Tristan's face felt way too big. He looked out the passenger window so she wouldn't see how elated he was. Besides, he knew his face was red—like a schoolboy's reaction to getting the pretty girl to walk to class with him. "That sounds perfect."

The remainder of their short ride was quiet but for an occasional question from Tristan or a tour guide's comment from Cari about the scenery they passed. He tried to reach Gemma and once again got her voicemail. Surely she'd listened to his numerous messages by now, but he'd chosen not to mention that he'd met Cari; two could play this game of being elusive.

He just hoped she wouldn't call Cari. They were doing fine on their own.

Actually, they were doing great on their own.

While Tristan's first impression of Cari had been that she was simply an attractive woman, in the few hours they'd spent together, he'd found her to be intelligent, funny, sensitive, outgoing…amazing. Did Gemma know all of this about Cari already? If not, Tristan had every intention of making sure she found out. He and Cari hadn't discussed their personal lives; he hoped she wasn't seeing anyone and might be available to spend time with him during his visit—assuming she wanted to, of course.

They arrived back at the *apartments*—it was time Tristan tried using American terminology—a little before seven. The sunset on Bainbridge Island was breathtaking; the misty overcast afternoon had melted away, and the sky was a mix of gold and pink swirls of cloud cover. The forecast called for storms later, but for now all was calm. As they made their way up the stairs with their few bags of groceries, Cari holding most of them since Tristan needed to hold the railing and his cane, he confirmed their plans for taking a walk, still amazed at his newfound boldness.

"So, we'll put our packages away and meet here again?"

Cari turned back toward Tristan as she climbed the last few steps. "Yeah. That sounds good."

She handed him the two bags she'd carried for him, and they each inserted their keys to unlock the apartment doors.

"Stupid key," Cari muttered as she struggled to remove hers once her door was open.

After a few more vigorous tugs, it pulled free. She grumbled some more as she entered her apartment. Even in her frustration, she was entrancing.

Tristan quickly unloaded his parcels—bananas, eggs, milk, some salad items and dressing, and a bottle of the same wine Cari had purchased as a gift for Gemma and Ethan's anticipated arrival tomorrow. He put everything away and took quick inventory of the apartment, touring each room without being invasive. To the left of the front entrance was an alcove with three doors, one along each small portion of wall. The first led to a room that faced the parking lot. It was just big enough to house a small built-in desk, a futon, and some bookshelves...or a crib in the future. The middle door, immediately in front of him, was the guest bath, and the third opened to a larger bedroom—Gemma and Ethan's, of course—with another, more spacious bath around the corner.

The long, thin kitchen was across from the alcove of doors, its entrance just after the open countertop that separated it from the living area. Once in the kitchen, Tristan opened a set of bi-fold doors at the end of the cooking space to find a small pantry to the left and a stackable washer and dryer next to it.

The spacious living area had a small fireplace in the far corner, matching its twin in Gemma and Ethan's bedroom on the other side of the wall. The décor showcased Gemma's eclectic interests; antiques harmonized with modern art throughout the space. Along the short back wall, French doors opened to a terrace that had another single door to the left connecting to the back bedroom. Tristan took a moment to look out over the walking trails that meandered back into the trees. In the distance he could see the tips of some snow-capped mountains. Gemma had bragged about the view when they'd first moved in; now Tristan could see why. He wondered if Cari's flat next door was a mirror-image of the same design.

The pain meds had once again done their job, and his knee felt much better. He rolled his suitcase into what he assumed would be his room and sat down on the chair by the desk. Dropping his trousers and quickly unfastening the knee brace, he sighed at the instant release around his thigh and calf. He'd had that damned thing on for nearly two days straight.

He got his pants back on and belted, maneuvering much of the transition from a sitting position. Flexing his knee carefully, extending the range of motion with each bend, felt wonderful, and after a moment of applying gentle pressure to his foot, he stood and slowly began to bear weight on it. Yes, this was good. With his cane, he could definitely get some good walking in; something his physician in London said he needed to be doing regularly.

Once again, they met between the doorways. Cari had changed into a sweater, low-slung jeans, and sneakers. She'd also grabbed a lined windbreaker and tied the sleeves around her waist, prepared for the usual drop in temperature as the sun went down. Tristan had exchanged his trench coat for a more casual jacket, and the two started down the stairs for their walk.

"You're bending your knee!"

"Took off the brace. Feels great to be able to move it again. I'd had it on during the flights to keep it safe, and then I kept it on because it hurt so much." He smiled as they turned down the sidewalk that led to toward the fountain. "Those pills have helped tremendously, as did my meal. Thank you, by the way, for recommending that restaurant; the food was quite good."

Cari smiled, and she and Tristan walked in silence for a few minutes, passing the fountain and following a tree-lined path that wound around to a small, manmade lake that Cari's apartment building overlooked. Small lights lined the winding sidewalk, creating what — on any other occasion, Cari told herself — might be considered a romantic setting.

"So, have you been to the States before?" Cari could only think of silly things to ask. The path they'd chosen went in a nearly one-mile loop around the apartment complex. She hoped their ability to talk so comfortably would return as they strolled.

"A few times. But Washington is new to me." He tilted his head. "It's very, uh, *green* here, isn't it!"

"Yeah." Cari laughed. "That's the first reaction most people have when they visit." She inhaled deeply and smiled, looking up toward the canopy of trees. "But you've got to admit, it is gorgeous."

"And it's serene," Tristan added. "I don't know if I'll be able to sleep. It's so quiet. I may have to find a movie that has a lot of city scenes with the noises I'm used to."

"Do the pain pills help you sleep?"

"Not really, but having only slept for short periods over the past few days — all of them sitting upright — I really shouldn't have trouble. I got a bit of rest this afternoon..."

"Before I woke you?"

"But I'm glad you did. My back couldn't have taken that position much longer."

Tristan favored his right leg as he walked beside Cari. She noticed that his limp had lessened considerably since they'd started, and the cane now seemed more a precaution than necessity.

"This trail goes for almost a mile. Is that okay? It'll loop back around to where we started."

Tristan sighed with a smile. "This is exactly what I needed, both mentally and physically. Thanks."

The two fell into gentle conversation. He told her more about Gemma and growing up in England; she shared her upbringing in a suburb of Seattle. Tristan enjoyed music; in college he and some friends had even formed a band that had played at a few weddings. He could play the violin, guitar, and piano, and he'd composed some original songs, although he quickly clarified that they had horrible lyrics. Cari explained that her interests leaned toward outdoor sports. She loved to snow ski and wasn't too bad at snowboarding either.

"All right," Tristan stated matter-of-factly. "Let's go into lightning fill-in-the-blank, shall we?"

"Excuse me?" Cari was caught off guard.

"Well," he mused, "I'm only here for three weeks and, other than Ethan, you're the only American I know. So…" He gazed at her with a brilliant smile. "I want to learn as much as I can about a typical American in the limited time I have."

"Oh." Cari shrugged, a little uncomfortable. But that pesky little voice in her head cheered that Tristan wanted to know more about her. "Um. Okay. How do we do this?"

"Well, I'll ask you a variety of questions, and you have to answer as quickly—" he tilted his head down to look her in the eye "—and honestly as you can."

"Your goal isn't to make me blush more, is it? 'Cause I don't think my blood cells can stand much more racing to my face!"

"No, no. I promise." Tristan put his free hand to his chest, swearing his oath.

"Okay. But I have to warn you, my life is pretty boring, especially compared to you and Gemma being raised in a big city like London."

"You let me decide that, hmm?" And he gave Cari that smile she was quickly becoming addicted to seeing.

"Favorite movie of all time."

"Oh. Um. Crap." She was already tumbling over her own thoughts. "Um…"

"There's no prize attached to any of your answers, you know," he teased.

"Well, how about you tell me *your* favorite movie to get things rolling?"

"Oh, turning things around already, hmm? Okay…let me think…"

"What about 'answering quickly'? Not so easy, is it!"

"Point well taken. All right. Favorite movie of all time. *Bourne Ultimatum.*"

"Really! All three of those Bourne movies were good. Why that one in particular?"

"I like American movies, first of all. But seeing all the European scenery in a movie like that makes it, I don't know, more familiar since I've visited nearly every country there. Plus, I like the intrigue, the good guy outsmarting all the bad guys." He hesitated for a moment and added, "And I've learned some things from those movies too."

"Learned some things? Like what?"

Tristan dropped his eyes to the path in front of him. "I guess I fancy myself a James Bond-Jason Bourne thinker."

He gave Cari a sideways glance, but she just smiled.

"Whenever I watch movies like that, I try to imagine ahead of the character what the best move or decision will be. You know, just in case I ever have to escape from evil villains bent on world domination."

They both laughed at that. He was embarrassed, she could tell, but she appreciated his openness and honesty.

"Well, if I'm ever a damsel in distress—decked out in my best Dolce and Gabbana evening gown, of course—I'll look to you to rescue me with your clever one-upmanship over the bad guys."

Tristan seemed relieved that Cari hadn't made fun of his quasi-hero worship of adventurous fictional movie characters. "All right. Your turn," he groused. "No more stalling. You've had plenty of time to consider your answer."

"Okay. I guess it's a tie between the nineteen sixty-nine version of *Romeo and Juliet* and *Pay It Forward.*"

"The first one I've seen, but I'm not familiar with the second. But tell me your reasons for both."

"Well, *Romeo and Juliet*—it's the classic romance. Plus," she added shyly, "when I saw it in high school, I thought the boy playing Romeo was so handsome. Never have forgotten those eyes." Cari had to make sure not to look at Tristan, whose eyes were much lighter but equally entrancing.

"So you're a romantic, then, are you?"

"To my bones, yes. I love that stuff. Even the corniest movies can bring me to tears when the guy and girl finally get together. It's pathetic." She shrugged her shoulders. "But it's me."

"Interesting…"

He left his comment at that and made her wish she could read his thoughts.

"Now, the other movie, *Pay It Forward,* was amazing in how the story came full-circle."

"Full-circle?"

"Yeah. It kind of starts with one scene, then it seems to move in all sorts of directions, but by the end of the movie, you're back to the start and you see that all of these in-between disconnected scenes really weren't so disconnected after all. The circle—the meaning of the movie—is complete."

"Hmm…"

"And it makes me cry buckets at the end, too."

"Why is that? Or do you cry at anything?"

"I can't tell you or it ruins it. You have to see it. It's important to *not* know what all the disjointed puzzle pieces mean during the movie, even though you can't help but put them together as little light bulbs go off in your head."

"And do you have this movie?"

"Yeah. I can loan it to you while you're here."

"Maybe the four of us can watch it together."

"That sounds like a nice idea." She looked away quickly, feigning interest in something beyond the trees so he wouldn't see what she knew were reddened cheeks. Heaven knows what he'd think if he saw her blush at this! She certainly didn't want him to know how easily her face flushed just being near him. As good looking and smart and funny as he was, there had to be some gorgeous woman in England anxiously awaiting his return. That's why Gemma had never told her about her brother: he was obviously involved with someone else.

The attempted Q&A session never materialized as they were still discussing the first question when they returned to the apartments. Tristan was slow to climb the steps, and Cari guessed he'd soon be propping up his leg again. At the top of the stairs, she felt a sudden loss for words, almost as if they'd just finished a first date and didn't know what to say as they parted. Tristan wasn't speaking either.

"Thank y—"

"That was ni—"

"No, you first," he said.

"I was just going to say it was nice to go for a walk. I don't do that very often, and pretty as that trail is, I really should."

"And I wanted to thank you for accompanying me. If you'd like to go on more walks any time soon and don't mind having me tag along, my leg could definitely use the exercise."

"Oh! Yes. Sure." Cari knew she sounded flustered; internally she was doing excited backflips. "Well…good night," she added sheepishly as she dug out her key and Tristan moved toward Gemma's door.

He flashed her a smile. "Good night, Cari. See you tomorrow, then."

Cari looked at him, grinning and hoping the dim lighting hid the blush she was sure had just reappeared on her face. She turned again to her doorknob as he went inside and closed his door. This blasted key had been giving her trouble for the past few days, and she promised to make a note to call the complex's office in the morning as soon as she was inside. She needed someone to check the key before it broke off complet—

"Shoot!" And then it happened. Key went in; only half came back out. "Shoot, shoot, shoot!" It was eight thirty at night. The office was closed, and Cari was locked out of her apartment. "Shoot!" she added once more for good measure.

Chapter 5

"Hi, is James Bond home? 'Cause I need the help need of an international spy."

Lame! She laughed to herself.

"Hi, I'm Cari, local damsel in distress."

That was even more lame.

"So…miss me?"

Oh my God, Cari thought. *How pathetic can I get?*

As she plucked with her stubby fingernails at the broken key in the doorknob, she contemplated clever one-liners she could use if she eventually had to knock on Tristan's door. Her best scenario would be to somehow get the key to engage internally and allow her entrance into her apartment, but the more she tried, the more she realized she'd need some strong and really skinny tweezers if there was any hope of getting the key to turn or come out.

She probably had some kind of tool in her glove box that might work…but her car keys were sitting on the kitchen counter. She could call her father, see if he wouldn't mind a late-night drive to visit his daughter and help her out of a jam…but her cell phone was next to the car keys.

Ugh. She was in trouble.

Cari spent a few minutes more on her knees, peering at the stuck key and contemplating any other possible options. Bottom line: she needed help — either a locksmith, for which she'd need a phone, or a tool that would allow her to solve the problem herself. After sitting on her legs in tight jeans for ten minutes, it also occurred to her that she now also had to pee. Badly. A chill went down her spine as a quick breeze hit and the rumbling of a distant storm startled her. Wonderful. The night was barreling down Misery Lane at a fast clip.

Pushing herself up from her uncomfortable position—and working to get the pins and needles in her legs to subside—she waddled over to her neighbor's apartment and tapped her knuckles on the door. She still hadn't decided what to say.

It took a minute before she sensed any movement inside the apartment, and she worried that she'd once again woken her visiting neighbor. She heard the rustling of Tristan peering out the peephole and turning the key.

"Hello." He was, of course, surprised to see her and only opened the door partway.

Instead of saying something stupid, Cari simply held up her broken key and gave Tristan a pitiful "help me" look.

While she could see fine in the dim light from the small bulb overhead, Tristan looked out from a much brighter area and had to open the door a little wider, leaning forward and squinting before he realized what she was showing him.

"What happened?" Now he pulled the door wide and stepped out.

Cari noted his loose gray T-shirt and darker gray sweatpants. He'd probably been going to sleep or at least finally stretching out and relaxing for the night. She could hear the television in the background; sounded like a news channel rather than a movie.

"The key broke off in the door, and I've been trying to get it out, but it's just no use." Cari shrugged. "Can I just use the phone to call my dad?"

"Mind if I take a look at the doorknob first, just in case I'm able to fix it?"

"Oh. Yeah. Sure." Cari hadn't really considered that Tristan might be more successful than she'd been. She backed up and leaned against the railing so he could walk the few steps over to her door.

Tristan crouched, extending his right leg gingerly, and jiggled the doorknob. He tried to pinch the broken portion of the key with his fingernails, and then attempted to push against the key while trying to turn the knob—everything Cari had already tried to no avail.

She didn't tell him that, though. If nothing else, Cari was glad to see she'd done the same things Tristan did and, twisted as it sounded, he'd not had any better luck. She was justified, if that was the right word, in finally conceding that she needed help.

"Might Gemma and Ethan have something like a set of long tweezers?" Tristan posed.

Ah-ha, Cari thought, they were still thinking along the same lines. "I don't know. Maybe they have a junk drawer in the kitchen or something in the bathroom medicine chest."

He returned to the doorway of his apartment and gestured for Cari to follow. "Let's see what we can find. Why don't you check the kitchen, and I'll check both bathrooms." Without waiting for her response, he turned toward Gemma and Ethan's room.

Instead of going into the kitchen, though, Cari bee-lined it to the guest bath. Noting his quizzical look, she called, "Sorry! Gotta go before I burst!" She heard him chuckle as she closed the door.

A few moments later, in the kitchen and feeling oh-so-much better, Cari opened what she assumed would be the junk drawer—the spot in their kitchen that mirrored where she kept odds and ends in hers. *Bingo!* But as she moved birthday candles, refrigerator magnets from local restaurants, little fuzzy things for the bottoms of chair legs so they won't scrape the floor, and a nearly depleted rubber band ball, Cari discovered only one small Phillips screwdriver, the kind used to gain access to the battery compartment of a remote control. No flathead to be found, and definitely no tweezers.

"Nothing," Tristan reported as he entered the kitchen. "If Gemma owns a pair of tweezers, they're probably with her in California."

"Thanks for looking anyway." Cari paused. "Well, I guess I should call my father. Do you mind?"

Tristan shifted to one side and allowed her access to the phone on the countertop. Then he nodded and left the kitchen.

"Hello. You have reached Ron Lopez. I, um, can't come to the phone so please leave a message. Okay? Thank you."

Bless his heart, Cari's dad had recorded that simple message six times before he was satisfied that it sounded professional enough. As owner of a small but successful hardware store in eastern Seattle, he always wanted to make a good impression, even on the home voicemail.

Just as Cari was about to leave a message, it occurred to her: he'd told her he was going hiking with a buddy in the Olympia National Forest. "Take care, Cari. We're going to be in the middle of nowhere," he'd said a few days earlier. "I'll call you when I get back home on Sunday."

Okay. She couldn't reach her father, and he was her only relative within a six-hour drive. Her final option, then, was a locksmith. She wasn't looking forward to paying probably seventy-five dollars for the service call and repair, but she was stuck. She needed to get into her apartment.

Cari started searching the lower cabinets and pantry for a phone directory. Next to the laundry detergent, behind the bi-fold doors, she found what she was looking for. She placed the thin book on the counter, turning to the "L" section.

There were three local locksmiths, if you could call them local. One was easily an hour's drive from her apartment, and the other two were probably forty-five minutes away. It was doable, of course, so she didn't complain...until she got a "disconnected" message on the closest one and price quotes of one hundred thirty dollars and one hundred fifty-five dollars from the other two. Evidently night calls to non-vehicle locks on Bainbridge Island cost extra.

Tristan returned to the kitchen, prescription bottle in hand, and opened a few cabinets until he found a drinking glass, which he filled with tap water. He looked over her shoulder and pointed to the price quotes she'd written down in the margins of the phone book.

"Tell them you'll call them right back," he whispered as she considered the cost of the third locksmith.

Cari raised her eyebrows, and Tristan nodded in a "go ahead" way. She said goodbye to the Lucky Locksmith Company's operator.

"What?" she asked as she laid the phone on the counter.

"Why don't you stay here? It's the least I can offer after all you did for me this afternoon. You can sleep in Gemma and Ethan's room and call the complex's office first thing in the morning. They've got someone on staff who can help, don't they?"

Cari contemplated this very tempting notion: she wouldn't be putting anyone out by staying there, it would save her a lot of money, and she could get to sleep sooner.

"Are you sure?" She scrunched her face.

"Absolutely!" he responded with a smile. "You know Gemma would insist on it. And, best of all, you can have that glass of wine you wanted even sooner." He went around her to the fridge and pulled out the now-chilled bottle.

"But you got that for Gemma and Ethan." Boy, did Cari want—no, need—a glass of wine.

"So trade your bottle for this one in the morning."

She could have thought of that but her brain was a few steps behind, contemplating the whole staying-with-her-neighbor's-handsome-brother thing.

"Do you have classes or work tomorrow?" he asked, the issue regarding Cari staying the night evidently resolved.

"I teach a ten o'clock class and need to put in some office hours, but Fridays are pretty light."

"Will that allow you time to get the lock fixed, yourself ready for work, and to the campus in time?"

"The staff here is pretty good about keeping tenants happy. Someone should be there by eight, and I'll call right away. If it comes down to it, I can go to class like this." Cari looked down at her T-shirt and jeans. Not the most professional look, but certainly more conservative than her students' usual attire.

Then she remembered something more crucial than what she was wearing. "Of course, I have no ID, no car keys, no money to take a taxi…" Being stuck here and having to cancel class was unfortunately a possibility, Cari realized. But she chose to remain optimistic that she'd get a chance to shower, change, and make it to class. She wasn't going to worry at this point. It would all work out fine.

Tristan proceeded to uncork the bottle and pour a glass of wine for Cari. He then refilled his ice water, reminding her that pain pills and alcohol were not a good combination. With drinks in hand, the two wandered into the living room where, sure enough, CNN was on. He gestured for her to sit before selecting a spot for himself. Cari had done a few "chick movie" nights with Gemma over the past few months, so she slipped off her shoes and plopped down in her usual place on the very comfortable sofa, pulling her feet up under her as she did.

As Tristan settled in at the other end, suddenly Cari noticed a blanket tossed over the back of the sofa and a throw pillow on his end of the coffee table. It had just the right size dent in it where his lower leg had probably been resting. They were now like bookends on the sofa, and Cari had to make a quick decision: move to the small chair (that honestly didn't look very comfortable) or stay put on the same piece of furniture as this person she didn't know very well. She stared uncomfortably at the TV as she waited for the heat in her cheeks to go away.

Tristan picked up a folded section of newspaper and a pen and placed them on his lap. "Is this all right? CNN, I mean?" he asked.

"Oh, of course. Any big world news we need to be aware of?" Cari glanced, only half interested, at the television. She suddenly felt even more awkward that she'd disturbed his first bit of relaxation in days.

"Just that some foul weather is apparently headed toward us, and we're in for a stormy night. How bad does it get here?" He didn't seem nervous, just intrigued.

"Sometimes it rains so much you think you should be building an ark. Winds can get kind of nasty, but if it's typical, it should be calmer by sunrise and just a bit drizzly all day tomorrow."

Tristan nodded, satisfied with her impromptu weather report, and scowled at the newspaper he was holding.

"I'm usually pretty decent at crossword puzzles, but I'm struggling with a few four-letter words."

Cari raised her eyebrows and smirked.

"No, it's that I've got the whole bloody thing filled out except for words that are merely four letters long, and I'm getting frustrated."

"Throw one at me. Maybe I'll know the answer." She shifted against the pillow behind her and repositioned herself, perking up for the intellectual challenge ahead. Besides, having her feet under her, like she had outside her door, had caused more lower-leg numbness. She turned to keep one leg bent sideways and let the other move to the edge of foot-friendly coffee table.

Tristan looked up from the paper with a smile and began. "Number five across, 'Spontaneous, on a…something.'"

"Whim?" she offered.

"Thought that was it too. Won't fit. Second letter has to be an 'a' to work with 'local' going down."

"And you're positive 'local' is correct?" She just wanted to be sure. When she was growing up, Cari and her father had sometimes worked on Sunday morning puzzles together. Although he fancied himself a puzzle master of sorts, he made a lot of errors.

"Yes, other words crossing it match as well."

Cari thought for a second, then blurted, "Lark!"

"Hmm?" Tristan looked up, evidently having moved on to another clue.

"'On a lark' means to do something spontaneously, doesn't it?"

"Oh, right. Perfect. Thank you!" He immediately focused his attention on scribbling the letters onto the newspaper.

"Does that help you fill in any other missing words?" Cari suddenly wished she had a puzzle of her own to work on. She sipped her wine as she waited for his response, but he remained focused on the paper.

"Okay. This must be an American thing, and I'm just not grasping it. 'April must-do.' Starts with an 'f.' Spring cleaning was my first thought, but I can't think of short words that have to do with that, let alone any that start with 'f.'"

"American thing it is. We have to 'file' our taxes in April. See if that'll fit."

"God, you'd think someone who studies accounting could have conjured up that one! I feel like an idiot," he groused as he filled in the missing letters.

"Glad I could help," she replied. "Next?"

"There are two others, and they're connected, so if we get one, we should be able to guess the other. Fifteen down is 'Congressional fear,' and eight across is 'The best you can get.' They share the second letter down and third letter across."

"And do you have any letters already?"

"The third letter of 'Congressional fear' is a 't.' Does that help?"

"Yup. 'Veto' should fit there."

Tristan rolled his eyes and wrote in the word. "This puzzle is not very foreigner-friendly."

Cari grinned. "So…does that help with the other word?"

"How about 'aces'?" He looked at her for confirmation. "That's the best you can get, right?"

"Does it work there?"

He wrote in the letters and smiled. "Yes, it does. Good. Thank you. I was not going to sleep well with any clues unsolved."

"I'm like that too, but my addiction is Sudoku. You know, those number puzzles?"

He raised an eyebrow tauntingly. "And are you any good at them?"

"I like to think so. I can handle the mediums easily and do pretty well on the difficult ones. But I'm like you; I hate it if I can't solve it."

"Well, I should have saved the one here for you."

"Did you get it right?"

"Yes. I find those puzzles good for developing logic strategies."

A double flash and rumble outside let them know the predicted storm had found its way to the greater Seattle area. Moments later, rain pattered against the French doors that led to the patio.

"Should we check the weather? See what's coming?" Tristan reached for the remote on the cushion between them.

"Yeah, sure. The Weather Channel's on forty-nine."

Sure enough, the radar showed a line of severe storms heading their way and likely heavy rain for much of the night. Cari took a few more sips of wine, glad to be indoors, even if it wasn't her own apartment. Sleeping on her doorstep would have been extremely unpleasant and, well, a little scary. She shifted her back deeper into the pillows behind her as she felt a chill.

Tristan noticed her shiver, despite her efforts to minimize it, and pulled the blanket from the back of the sofa. He opened it and draped it across her lap, scooting the bottom of it toward her so she could wrap herself up if she wanted. Before she could protest, Tristan put his leg down from the coffee table, stood up, and limped toward Gemma's bedroom. "I'll be right back. I saw she had another blanket across the bottom of the bed."

"Thank you!" Cari called as he disappeared around the corner.

Soon Tristan was back on his end of the sofa, leg propped on the coffee table once again. "So, tell me about the classes you teach," he said as he unfolded the blanket across his legs.

Cari pulled the hair elastic she'd had on her wrist — she wore one as a pseudo-bracelet most days out of habit and convenience — and began to finger her hair, gathering it into a ponytail. A few curls couldn't make it, and she nervously pushed them away from her face. They fell forward as soon as she put her hand down.

"Well," she sighed. "I teach one course, but I have three sections of it. It's a consumer awareness class that all students, including anyone who transfers in, have to take before they graduate. Helps them learn how to budget their money and stuff. Two of my sections are all freshmen. God, they're so young and naïve! Tomorrow's class, though, is nearly half juniors and seniors who either didn't start at St. Eustachius, didn't pass it the first time they took it, or postponed the course until now."

"Are the dynamics of this class different from the other two?"

His question made Cari think he'd probably taught undergraduate courses himself during his doctoral years. "Oh, it's like night and day!" she scoffed. "Some of them have real attitudes and feel that because this is a freshman-level course, it should be a blow-off class."

"Sorry, 'blow-off class'? You mean they think it should be easy?"

"Yeah. And so when they don't make As on assignments, or worse, receive zeros when they don't come to class or complete homework, they can get really disrespectful. You know, threaten to go to one of my doctoral committee members or another faculty member to complain."

"And do they? Formally complain, I mean."

"Not yet, but there's one student, Ashley, who gives me the most trouble. Her family donates a lot of money to the university, and other faculty members, especially doc students, have felt pressured to change her grades. You can bet if she complains about me, I won't have any backup at all."

Tristan just nodded. "It's amazing the power money has. It can make the most honest people do things they don't want to." His gaze became distant for a moment.

"Tomorrow's class is kind of low-key. Just going over some notes to prepare them for the pairs project they have to complete by the end of the semester. A few of them — Ashley and her cohort in crime, Celine, being two — still have to present the last project I assigned. They're late, of course, but I'm sure they'll still expect full credit."

"And this class goes until…?"

"Eleven twenty. Then I need to put in an hour or two in the adjunct office. I'll mostly be going through some old articles I had for my former dissertation topic and filling the recycling bin." Cari took a big gulp of wine, and Tristan laughed. "Thanks for the wine, by the way. It's relaxing me nicely."

"You're quite welcome. Perhaps one of the next few nights, should my knee be pain-free, I'll join you."

Cari nodded, raising her glass in a mock toast, and sat up slightly. "Hey! Would you like to come to my class tomorrow? I mean, if you want to. You could get more of those 'American experiences' you said you want. You might find American college students are different than British students, you know?"

Tristan smiled. "That sounds wonderful. Thank you for asking. I wasn't exactly excited at the thought of sitting around here until Gemma and Ethan got back. That will entertain me quite nicely while I await my sister's return."

"And," she spoke hesitantly, "perhaps you could be an impromptu guest speaker, should the project stuff get done quickly?"

Tristan seemed to blush a little. "Well, I don't know that you'd want *that*."

"Sure! The students love it when I change it up a little. Letting them hear about accounting and world economics from British guest lecturer Dr. Tristan…um…I'm sorry. I don't know your last name."

"Saunders. But I've never been so formal. Even when I taught a few grad school courses, I had the students call me Tristan."

"Well, tomorrow you may be Dr. Saunders. These students need constant lessons in respect. Anyway, they'd probably want to ask you about what you do and how a basic understanding of accounting and economics will benefit them. You know, something like that."

"Let's just hope the projects take up the entire class," he said with a smirk. "But I promise, if they have any questions, I'll answer them in a very 'learning is important' kind of way. Would that be all right?"

"Perfect. Thanks."

Tristan couldn't imagine speaking to a class of college students without having prepared first, but Cari had asked so nicely, and he was pleasantly surprised by her invitation. He'd take whatever happened, but secretly hoped he could be a silent bystander, watching *her* teach and seeing the students present their projects.

They decided to check out what was on American cable television on a Thursday night while the storm continued to brew outside. Tristan discovered the British news station and made note of its channel, but he moved on and found a Jimmy Stewart classic, which they settled in to watch.

Cari was curled up on her side now, her head resting on the end of the sofa and the blanket pulled up to her chin. Her wine glass was empty, and Tristan chanced some quick peeks out of the corner of his eye to notice that she was falling asleep. *Rear Window* was not enough to keep her awake.

"Cari?" he whispered. "Do you want to lie down in Gemma's room?"

"Hmm?" she moaned, moving her head only slightly.

"You're falling asleep. Do you want to go to Gemma's room?"

This time he got no response. He looked over now without worrying about being caught: she was soundly asleep.

She wasn't a snorer—and even if she had been, Tristan would never reveal such information to her or anyone else. No, she slept peacefully…except for her left foot. Peeking out from the end of the blanket, her toes flexed back and forth almost rhythmically, like she was keeping time or counting something or playing some song in her head. It was an endearing quirk, while it lasted, and he laughed quietly when a half hour later, her toes began moving again.

Maybe it was wrong, but he was thankful that Cari's key had broken off. They'd had a very nice evening together indeed. Tristan leaned over to the lamp beside him and turned it off. A quick press on the remote silenced the television as well. The light from a full moon, peeking for a moment through the heavy clouds, shone in through the French doors and lit the raindrops on the glass like a thousand shining diamonds.

He shifted downward on his end of the sofa so he could lay his head back comfortably and put both feet up on the coffee table, and he drifted off to sleep.

11:45 p.m. Saunders at sisters home. he & sister went to dinner, store, & walked @ apt complex. lights out in apt. no sign of sisters husband. will report more in a.m.

His text sent, Ben Pritchard's work for the evening was complete. He moved his car to a darker part of the parking lot that would still allow him a view of Gemma Stonecipher's front door. Despite the wind's rocking the vehicle and a storm that bordered on dangerous, Ben positioned the driver's seat as far back as it would go and settled into a peaceful sleep.

Chapter 6

When Tristan awoke around half past seven on Friday morning, he found his "sofa mate" buzzing around the kitchen, preparing a pot of coffee as quietly as possible. As he stretched his arms upward and let out his typical morning growl, he could tell he startled Cari.

"Oh! I hope I didn't wake you," she said as she peeked over the breakfast bar.

"Not at all. How long have you been up?"

"Um, since five fifteen or so?" She scrunched her nose as she spoke, something Tristan had noticed last night—something that made her eyes light up.

"Did you not sleep well?" Perhaps he'd tossed and turned, causing her to get up before she would have normally. He was petrified that he perhaps he'd snored, not that he'd ever been known to, but after spending the night with someone—not in *that* sense, of course—one would obviously worry. Like Cari and her wiggling toes, Tristan wondered if he, too, had some quirk he did in his sleep.

"Oh, I slept fine," she assured him. "I'm just an early riser. Used to bug my parents—my mom at least—when I was growing up that no matter what day it was, I was up before dawn. My dad never really minded; he liked to hike or go fishing and would take me with him so my mom could sleep in. My parents split up when I was in eighth grade, and during my high school years, it was pretty common for me and my dad to have a hearty breakfast by five a.m. on Saturday mornings." As she talked, Cari checked out Gemma and

Ethan's kitchen cabinets, finding coffee mugs and a container of sugar. "How about you? Sleep well?"

"God, yes," he said through another upper-body stretch. "The sound of the rain put me right to sleep."

"And it's still raining now. Did you notice?" Cari walked out of the kitchen, leaving the coffee maker to do its job. She peered through the French doors to look outside.

Tristan stood, tested his leg—it was working well, though there was some stiffness and a dull ache—and joined her there. "Will it linger?"

Cari sighed. "Probably until noon anyway. I hope you weren't planning on getting a suntan 'cause that's nearly impossible around here, unless you go to a tanning salon."

Tristan laughed. "No. I'm quite content being a stereotypical pale Brit." He turned back toward the sofa and began to fold the blanket he'd used. Cari's was already folded and draped over the small chair.

She passed him and returned to the kitchen. "Coffee's ready. Do you want some?"

"I'll get some in just a minute. Help yourself, though," he said as he ambled into Gemma's bedroom with the blanket.

When he returned, Cari held her coffee in both hands, letting the steam warm her chin between sips. Tristan could tell she was watching as he poured himself a cup; she looked away suddenly to stare out over the breakfast bar when he turned to lean against the counter across from her. They were quiet, uncomfortable, for a moment, as if they'd been lovers and now faced the dreaded "morning after." She blushed slightly when she glanced up at him.

"I've got to have my morning coffee. I'm glad Ethan had some I could make."

"Yes, Gemma has always been a tea drinker."

"She's branched out, though. You'd be impressed. She can order a double mocha latte espresso thingy at Starbucks with the best of 'em."

"Double mocha latte espresso?" Tristan laughed openly. "Is there such a thing? And if there is, why on earth would someone ever knowingly serve a person as active as my sister a drink with that much caffeine!"

Cari smiled brightly. "That would be dangerous for the general population, wouldn't it!" She chortled. "No, what I meant was she can order those complicated coffee concoctions like a pro. I'm simply a regular-coffee-with-sugar-and-cream type. Starbucks intimidates me."

Tristan raised his eyebrows and smiled right back. "You're afraid of a coffee shop?"

"Yeah," she began as she shifted from one leg to the other. "I mean —" she faltered "— you know, you walk in there to order a coffee, plain and simple, but you're faced with, like, fifty different options, none of which easily translates into just 'coffee.' It's overwhelming!"

Tristan stifled a laugh as Cari gave him a look of utter despair.

"Sometimes I can just tell the people behind the counter are rolling their eyes and grumbling to each other about me. You'd think I'd asked for something weird." She stood taller and continued. "Give me Maxwell House from my own kitchen — or my neighbor's — and I'm totally content." She lifted her cup proudly.

Tristan nodded and raised his cup as well. "Would you like some breakfast?" he asked after another sip of coffee. "I make a fantastic scrambled eggs on toast." He peered into the bread box on the counter. "Let me amend that: I make a fantastic scrambled eggs on a plate."

Cari considered his offer, looking at him intently. "Are you sure you don't mind? That *would* be wonderful. Thank you," she finally responded. "I'll set the plates out while you cook."

Tristan couldn't help but feel that this was…right. The two of them waking up together, sharing breakfast. He'd had plenty of mornings with Melanie, but not like this. Cari made him feel comfortable, at home.

As soon as it was eight o'clock, Cari got on the phone with Sheila, the complex's office manager. The woman sweetly apologized for the inconvenience, gave Cari the emergency number — which she hadn't known existed until now — for future reference (she'd leave a copy of it for Gemma and Ethan too), and promised to send the maintenance man up as soon as he arrived. Meanwhile, Tristan and she enjoyed the eggs and coffee. He also had a banana, noting the benefits of the potassium it contained.

When Tristan said he could make a "fantastic" breakfast — God, she loved his *fahnTAHstic* accent — Cari had no idea that it would actually be the best scrambled eggs she'd ever had. He wouldn't reveal which spices he'd stolen from Gemma's cupboard to season the eggs as they cooked; he'd merely winked and shooed Cari away with the spatula while he hovered over the frying pan like a mad scientist.

Once they finished eating, Cari took care of washing the dishes and cleaning the kitchen while Tristan retreated to the guest bathroom to shower and shave. It caught her off guard when she realized this was likely what Gemma and Ethan's life was like in this apartment: enjoying making and eating meals, taking turns keeping the place cleaned up, just feeling totally comfortable...*right*...with each other. She immediately stopped herself; she couldn't get caught up in romantic thoughts about a guy who would be back in England in a few short weeks.

The maintenance worker—Rudy, a young man with a Russian-sounding accent—arrived at eight forty. He was able to dismantle the doorknob and let Cari in so she could shower while he worked on the broken lock. She hated that her front door would be literally wide open while she was getting dressed, but she had no reason to distrust the man. He'd always been pleasant to her. It also seemed he had a crush on Gemma; whenever he was around, he watched every move she made. Not surprising, given his apparent newness to the country and Gemma's pretty smile and cheery disposition toward everyone she met.

"I feex yoor lock, missy, and I gets new keh fyor you. You like?"

"Can you get me two keys? I'd like to have a spare."

"Yes, missy, I get you all kezz you needs, but I geeve zhem to Sheila in office if you no here, yes? To keep you safely, yes?"

Cari nodded and told him that would be fine. As she went to get ready, she locked both her bedroom and bathroom doors "to keep herself safely" while Rudy worked. She was also comforted knowing that James Bond was only a distressed damsel's scream away, should she need him.

Today she wanted to look like the college professor she intended to become in another year or so, but she knew she was trying to impress Tristan as well. The gray wool pants and tailored gray-and-white striped shirt looked good; it showed off her figure without looking too casual.

By nine twenty, Rudy had finished, provided Cari with two new keys, and departed. Cari collected what she wanted to bring to the university and met Tristan at their usual spot between doorways. His slacks nearly matched hers in color, but he'd paired his with a solid black dress shirt. In a word, he was striking. The dark color made his eyes seem even lighter than they'd been last night.

As they drove, he let Cari know he'd finally been able to reach a very apologetic Gemma. And he announced that he intended on making her worry a little bit longer about how his first day in Washington had been.

"But, Tristan, she's your sister!"

"Bloody right she's my sister, and she didn't even tell me she wouldn't be there when I got off the plane!" he retorted. "I'm going to enjoy torturing her for a few days, get her to appreciate her brother a little more."

Cari could tell that underneath it all, he just wanted to tease Gemma a little so she'd grovel for forgiveness. That would be worth seeing. Getting to know her neighbors better, even the temporary one, seemed that much more likely with every conversation she and Tristan had.

On the way to the campus, Cari gathered vital information so she could properly introduce Tristan to her students: He'd graduated with a PhD in accounting and economics from the University of Manchester. His concentration was international economics and his dissertation, which of course had some complicated title too long to remember, had to do with the impact of war on a country's ability to maintain financial stability. He told Cari he'd actually lived in Croatia for a year, collecting data and doing a good portion of the writing. Her students would be bored with such information, but Cari was instantly fascinated and hoped to hear more about how he selected and researched his topic.

After a half-hour's drive, Cari steered her car into a side street nearest the main entrance of St. Eustachius University and parked. She smiled as she exited the car, proud to be a part of the small but prestigious school. Through the campus's arched entry was an enormous oak tree surrounded by a rich lawn. As spring approached, students would flock to the area to read, study, or chat with friends. Facing the grassy commons were three of the university's colleges: Education, Engineering, and Business, each housed in beautiful, ancient, red-brick buildings. Cari and Tristan took the sidewalk to the right, leading to the accounting building, newer in both age and style.

As they walked, Cari explained what she knew of the school's history. St. Eustachius University had been founded in the mid-eighteen hundreds as a monastery. It was named for the patron saint of difficult situations and, ironically, hunters, as well as victims of torture. In 1927, it was converted into a boarding school for the Pacific Northwest's Catholic community. Then, about thirty-five years ago, the day-school closed and a four-year liberal arts university was born.

Although the campus hosted just over four thousand students, their programs were strong and faculty members well-respected around the country and the world. Cari liked the cozy atmosphere: small classes and the opportunity to be a person, not a number or faceless entity among a swarm of students. The downside was that everyone knew everyone else's business, or at least it seemed that way some days.

Cari had gotten her undergraduate and master's degrees at Cal State, enjoying the freedom that came from living so far from home. But the fact that St. Eustachius University offered such specialized classes in accounting and international economics was enough to move her back to the Seattle area, albeit to the quieter Bainbridge Island, when she decided to pursue her doctorate.

Coming here also gave her her first real opportunity to teach at the university level. Her father was convinced she was a professional student since she'd not held a "real" job yet. She'd waited tables at local restaurants while at Cal State ("Is this what an accounting degree teaches you? How to count your tips?"), and now she was one of about a half-dozen adjunct instructors teaching undergraduate classes to help pay their way through the PhD program. It was a good deal: it gave her experience in the field she wanted to pursue, provided opportunities for her to get to know the professors better, and gave her the inside scoop on the latest and most respected research she could use as she wrote her dissertation. The professors were decent people — well, most of them anyway — who truly wanted to see their doctoral students succeed.

On the way to her classroom, Cari peeked in to Dr. Kruger's office to introduce Tristan and was surprised — and pleased — to learn Tristan had used an article she'd written in his dissertation. Dr. Kruger smiled shyly, thanking him for his kind words, and wished them well with today's class.

They entered room 113 a few minutes before class was to start. Cari didn't really need prep time today since the "lesson" was simply a review, distribution of some handouts, and student presentations. The stark cream-colored room had long tables set in a U-shape so all the students could see the whiteboard on the wall between the room's two entrances. On the left side was a podium connected to a base that held an old-fashioned overhead projector; modern technology was hard to come by in the building, and was usually claimed by the full-time professors before any doc student had a chance. As her pupils entered, Cari glanced around the room. All but one of her sixteen students was present; missing was a senior who was seriously in jeopardy of failing the course—again.

Cari placed her notebook on the end of the table closest to the podium and gestured for Tristan to take the seat next to where she'd be. Across from him sat Kevin Lamb, a junior with tousled red hair and a meager attempt at a goatee. He eyed Tristan intently, clearly interested in knowing who he was. Kevin had been quite obvious about his crush on Cari, and she tried hard to avoid eye contact with him. She didn't allow him to visit the adjunct office unless she knew another grad student would also be there. She'd never want anyone to interpret anything inappropriate between them.

An empty chair separated Kevin from two other sets of eyes that were locked on Tristan. Ashley and Celine stared as if he were something edible. Cari could tell he'd noticed as he nudged her and mouthed, "They're here! Better give them an A." She stifled a laugh and stood to greet the class.

"Hi, all. Glad to see you all on a rainy Friday. We don't have too packed a schedule," she said as she wrote a short agenda on the board, her usual procedure. "Before we get started, though—" she turned to face them "—I have a guest to introduce."

Cari took a deep breath, and she and Tristan looked at each other for a moment. She wanted to be sure not to embarrass him or herself.

"This is Dr. Tristan Saunders. He has a PhD from the University of Manchester in England."

An audible gasp came from Celine and Ashley, who suddenly sat up straighter. Ashley even stuck out her ample chest, but Tristan's gaze remained toward the front of the room.

"His degree is in accounting, the same as what mine will be," Cari continued. "And he works for Carson World Financial, an international accounting firm. He's visiting the US for a few weeks, and I thought he might like to see an American college classroom. If we have time at the end of class," she added, looking at him for confirmation, "he'll answer any questions you might have about the work he does and how studying accounting can lead to an interesting career." Tristan smiled and nodded nervously in response.

Celine and Ashley still looked like the might have a few questions *now*, but Cari quickly got the class started. She took several minutes to go over notes and readings that would be helpful to the students as they studied for their next test, clarifying content and taking questions. Then she handed out the guidelines for their pairs project, going over expectations and responding to comments and concerns.

"Now, we still have four budget projects that need to be presented. Are you all ready?" Cari looked at each of the three students who had yet to turn in their work (Mr. Failing Senior was the fourth) and got positive nods from each. "Who first, then?"

"I'd like to go!" Ashley shouted. No one dared challenge her request. She stood, picked up the poster board leaning against the wall behind her chair, and sashayed to the front of the room, her eyes never leaving Tristan's face.

Ah. Another student crush. Not surprising given his handsome face and sophistication.

She flipped her long hair over her shoulders and balanced the poster on the table. "Here's my budget presentation…" She proceeded to describe the two pie charts she — or someone she paid — had created to explain her earnings and expenses, as well as her plan for being financially stable after she graduated.

That was the main goal of the course: to get students to realize that their parents weren't likely going to support them too long after they'd earned their degrees. The university wanted students to understand that much of the money they spent as college students had been given to them; after graduation, they'd have to earn money before they could spend it. Ashley, however, seemed to miss this concept completely.

"Right now, my parents keep my Visa debit account with at least fifteen thousand on it." When she heard a general intake of breath from her peers, she pouted. "Well, you know, in case of emergencies!"

"Yeah, like that 'emergency' trip to Milan back in October?" Kevin muttered loudly.

"I had to see the latest bikini designs! You don't just buy them off the rack! Aspiring swimsuit models have to work hard, idiot!" Ashley retorted, shooting a quick glance at Tristan as she spoke.

"Now, now," Cari said above the giggles and side remarks. "Continue, please, Ashley, and there's no need for insults. Okay?"

"So," the girl said with a huff. "Out of that fifteen thousand per month—" and another class-wide gasp escaped from her peers "—I spend about six thousand on basic expenses. You know, gas for my BMW, membership at the gym and tanning salon, maid service, and stuff like that." Ashley made sure she looked at Tristan as she mentioned "bikini model," "BMW," and "tanning salon," along with the details of her expense account.

Cari watched him; he was all but looking through her. He was paying attention to what she was saying, but not even remotely responding to her obvious attempt at making herself look attractive. She offered lots of desirable bait, but he wasn't biting. Cari worked hard to keep herself from smiling.

"I looked at last month's Visa bill," Ashley said directly to Cari, making sure it was noted that she'd fulfilled one of the requirements of the assignment, "and I spent five thousand three hundred on clothing, shoes, and a new purse. That was below average, though, 'cause my family bought me lots of stuff for my twenty-first birthday." Another glance over at Tristan, like she wanted him to know she was of legal drinking age. "And the rest of it went toward food. Um... thirty-seven hundred?"

Cari nodded to let her know her math was correct.

"You spend nearly four thousand dollars a month on food? But you're a stick!" Monty, a sophomore, called from the back of the room.

"I eat healthy."

"So do I, but I spend, like, a hundred a month. Where you buying your salads and tofu?" The class giggled.

"The yacht club mostly, why?" She seemed oblivious to the sarcasm.

"Shit..." Aaron, Monty's equally frugal roommate, mumbled under his breath. He shot a glance toward Cari and added a humble "sorry."

Tristan smirked.

Cari nodded at Aaron in a you're-scolded-but-forgiven way and returned her attention to Ashley. "And your financial plans for independence are...?"

Ashley perked up. "I'll be living on my same limited allowance until I turn twenty-two," she said, giving everyone a look that begged for pity. "And then my trust fund will be available to finance my *career* as a model." She looked at Tristan again and did a small curtsy, indicating that she was done with her presentation and waiting for applause. A couple of students and Cari clapped a few times, half-heartedly.

"Thank you, Ashley," Cari said with a genuine smile. Poor girl. Cari had heard plenty about Ashley Hunsinger: that the only reason she was in college was because her parents wanted her to land a marriage proposal from some young, brash, and equally wealthy young man with "the fourth" tacked on to his name. She'd probably live her life like her mother did, with regular visits to the plastic surgeon, mostly to keep her husband from too many affairs. Cari had seen pictures of Mrs. Hunsinger at various big-wig things at the university; her face was so collagen-filled it looked painful, like she'd been stung by bees — all puffy-cheeked with little facial expression. Mr. Hunsinger, a third generation oil baron, was quite debonair, but rumors were rampant about college professors and students he'd slept with.

The other two presentations, from Celine and a studious young man named Gordon, both went well and were more on target with the goal of the project. As much as Celine wanted to run in Ashley's social circles, her presentation indicated that their friendship would probably cease once they graduated. Celine planned to pursue a master's degree in communications — she wanted to be the next Katie Couric — but would not have an inheritance to lean on to get her bills paid. Nor would she be jet-setting around the world to go bikini shopping.

"Okay." Cari sighed as Gordon returned to his seat. "We've got about ten minutes before I can realistically release you from class so…" She clasped her hands in front of her nervously and glanced quickly at Tristan. "Does anyone have a question for Dr. Saunders?"

As expected, Ashley and Celine shot their hands up immediately. Cari prayed they'd ask appropriate questions.

"All right. One of you go first," she replied hesitantly.

"Are you single?" they asked in unison.

Cari wasn't sure who blushed more: Tristan or herself.

"Uh…yes, I am," he mumbled.

"Oh, God! Talk some more! We love your British accent," Celine cooed.

"So…" Cari interrupted the giggles coming from the two girls as well as a few of their followers, "does anyone have an *accounting-* or *budget-* or *class*-related question for Dr. Saunders?"

Only Ashley raised her hand this time. Others looked from her to Cari, waiting for the latter to respond.

"Ashley, is this an appropriate question?"

"Yes, *Miss* Lopez." Her condescending manner wasn't lost on Cari. "*Dr.* Saunders, since you have your PhD and Miss Lopez doesn't, why don't *you* teach some courses here? I bet you know lots more than she does, and I, for one, would sign up for every course you teach. I'm sure I could get you an interview with the university president."

"Well," Tristan started. He coughed and cleared his throat. "I believe Ms. Lopez is doing an exemplary job. Frankly, I'm quite impressed, and if I were an undergraduate here, I would be signing up for all of *her* classes." His eyes remained on Cari the entire time he spoke.

If Cari had been blushing before, she was certainly five shades deeper into crimson now. It didn't help that every one of the students saw Tristan's gaze and Cari's red face. They responded with a class-wide "Ooooh!"

"All right, everyone," Cari quickly interjected, taking control. "You've got your instructions for the pairs project. You can work with someone in here or from one of the other sections I teach. Start thinking about the topic and your method of presentation. Three weeks will come and go quickly, so I suggest you get started deciding some basics soon. Have a good weekend!" She waved, and the class quickly gathered their things and headed out.

Ashley lingered, making sure she was the last one to leave, which didn't surprise Cari at all. "Here's my father's business card. I can guarantee you that if you want a position on the faculty here, the Hunsinger family will make it happen." She winked slyly at him and swished her hips out of the room.

It was quiet for about ten seconds while Cari gathered up her notes. Then Tristan burst out laughing. "Good God, that girl's a living nightmare!"

Cari pondered yelling "Yay!" but held back. "She's a powerhouse in this class and is definitely Daddy's Little Girl on this campus."

"I can see how she could intimidate professors." Tristan shook his head. "And it wouldn't surprise me in the least to hear that she's slept with a few of hers already."

"She likes to dig at us doc students. Her dad does too, and at first he was against her taking this course from me. But Dr. Kruger told him that having doc students teach the 'lowly freshman courses' wouldn't damage the students too badly and of all the adjuncts, I was the best she had. Of course, she was really just trying to get him off her back."

"No. You're good!" Tristan countered. "I see that you enjoy teaching. These projects are real-world. I only remember lots of papers stuffed with mindless theoretical research. I meant it that I would have enjoyed my undergraduate coursework if I'd had instructors like you."

Cari smiled at his kind words. "Well, I do like teaching this course. Other adjuncts have heard about my project-based syllabus, and a few are going to try it next semester, so I must be doing something right!"

Cari had gathered her belongings and now headed toward the door. Tristan grabbed his cane, delighted to find he didn't need it at all, and followed her out, flicking off the lights as they exited. They turned toward the lift at the other end of the hallway.

"Oddly, the adjunct office has the only fast copy machine on the floor," she said as they rode the one floor up. "So there are constant interruptions from people coming to make hundreds of copies or to pick up things they sent from their computer. And it's loud! But eventually, you learn to ignore all the distractions."

The adjunct office on the second floor was not far from the lift, and Tristan surveyed the room as they entered: it was decent sized—probably the equivalent of three professors' offices—but it certainly wasn't designed to accommodate many people. Against one wall were two bookshelves framing a huge copy machine. A sink and a pot of what smelled like either old or cheap coffee took up space on a countertop to the left, and a round table with some torn leather conference room chairs around it filled the center of the room. In the back corner was an attempt at a "living area" with a seventies-style gold plaid sofa and mismatched but surely comfortable easy chairs facing a battered coffee table. Tristan smirked as he realized a childhood query was finally answered: *this* was where his grandparents' furniture had gone when they'd died.

Cari explained how the adjuncts had posted office hours so that, for the most part, no more than three of them were here at any given time. Fridays she usually had the place to herself, which was nice; Tristan had hoped to chat about academics a little after seeing her teach. She told him she generally spent Friday office hours getting papers graded or plans written while her mind was still academically engaged. She was better off getting everything done before leaving campus so her weekends would be free and clear. Tristan immediately had some ideas for how she might spend that free time: with him, with or without Gemma and Ethan.

A tall, distinguished man in his fifties — with salt-and-pepper hair and a neatly trimmed goatee — stood at the copier. He turned toward Cari and Tristan and a slow smile formed on his face.

"Hello, Dr. Lassiter," Cari said shyly.

"Ms. Lopez." He bowed his head, his voice deep and thick. "And who have we here?"

"Oh, this is Dr. Tristan Saunders. He's visiting from England, so I invited him to sit in on my class today." She spoke as though she was unsure Tristan's presence was allowed. "Tristan, this is Dr. Jonathan Lassiter," she said, gesturing toward him now. "He teaches accounting and international economics to the graduate and doctoral students. He's also on my doctoral committee." Cari's voice was quiet; she seemed in awe of him and barely looked at him as she spoke.

Suddenly, it was Tristan who was in awe. "Dr. Lassiter? Author of *Theoretical Constructs to Post-War Economics?*"

The man nodded slowly, his smile growing wider. "You've read my book, have you?"

"Read it! I referred to it significantly in my dissertation, sir." Tristan extended his hand and shook the professor's enthusiastically. He was face to face with the inspiration for his research. If Tristan were to name his hero, it would be Dr. Jonathan Halstead Lassiter. "It's a great pleasure to meet you, sir!"

The two fell into easy conversation about their common interests, and Tristan felt bad that he was ignoring his gracious host. Before he could apologize, though, Cari flapped her hand at him and she dropped into an easy chair across the room, pulling out her laptop. She smiled and winked at him. "Go. Talk. I have to get some work done anyway, and you're stuck here until I'm finished."

Just as Tristan and the professor walked out, fellow doctoral student Jazmyn Riley walked in. She stopped, backed up half a step, and craned her neck to see down the hallway for a moment before returning, her eyes wide. "Who was that and is he single?"

Cari gave her friend a sideways smile. "My next door neighbor's brother, visiting from England."

"Good Lord, tell me he doesn't have an accent to go with that face."

"Yep." Cari knew her blush had once again surfaced.

"Kill me now. I am a total sucker for British accents," Jaz said. She dropped her backpack on the large central table. "So…single? Available?"

"Like I said, visiting from England." Cari looked at Jaz. "Besides, you're not single."

"Well, I'm not married, and I'm not dead, either." She glanced back at the doorway. "Dang. You'd better snag him while he's here, girlfriend. Or is he stupid?"

Cari laughed. "Far from it. He's got a PhD in accounting and works for Carson World Financial."

"Dang."

"Pull yourself together, Jaz. Tell me how the budget project went in your classes."

The women spent a few minutes comparing student presentations and upcoming assignments. Jaz and Cari had started the doctoral program together and become fast friends. They'd designed the semester's new curriculum, and students were showing real gains over previous semesters' students on the department's standardized midterm exams. It looked promising that the department would adopt their ideas permanently.

After a pause, Jazmyn looked at Cari warily. "And…how did the dissertation proposal—?"

"Nope. Starting over."

"Crap. Got any ideas?"

"Tristan—the British guy you were just drooling over—has offered to help. Dr. Kruger wants a short write-up after spring break with possible topics."

"Nice." Jaz's wide smile was back. "Good luck focusing on research with British boy around."

"I'll do just fine, thanks," Cari said as she straightened her shoulders. "I'm not interested in him beyond getting his help with my dissertation. He'll be gone in three weeks, and I figure an outsider's point of view—you know, someone who's got an international perspective and real-world experiences—is just what I need."

Tristan could not stop talking about Dr. Lassiter as he and Cari drove back to the apartments. "He took me to his office, and we talked about *my* work for nearly an hour," Tristan reported. "And he'd actually read a series of articles I wrote about anti-money laundering. Wow. I mean, I've read a lot of things he's written, but I never…" Tristan trailed off, as he could hear himself gushing. Cari had remained quiet, nodding and smiling as she focused on the road, but seeming genuinely pleased that he'd enjoyed his morning.

"And he's on your doctoral committee as well, right?" Tristan beamed.

"Yeah."

"Cari, do you have any idea how prestigious a PhD is from a university with Jonathan Lassiter on the faculty?"

"I guess." She seemed distracted. "I guess I just don't know him like you do, so I can't appreciate all of his *importance*." Now she sounded sarcastic.

"You don't like having him on your committee?"

She exhaled in a huff. "No. It's fine. I'll get the damned thing done if it kills me."

"Does he challenge you to be more than you are?"

Cari shot Tristan a glare that shocked him. "Look. He's *your* hero, and I'm glad you got to meet him. Let's just leave it at that."

But there was no way Tristan was going to let the conversation drop. Something bothered her, and it had to do with Jonathan Lassiter.

"I want to understand," he coaxed gently.

Cari kept her gaze straight ahead. Tristan leaned forward to get her to look at him, and when she finally did, her eyes were wet around the edges.

"Talk to me, Cari."

"Jesus, Tristan. Let it die, will you?"

Now he was feeling put off. He'd done nothing to bring on her ire, but even in the short time he'd known Cari, he'd gotten the impression one had to do something really horrid to make her this upset. "Was he the reason your proposal wasn't accepted yesterday?"

"No." Her grip on the steering wheel tightened. "*I'm* the reason my proposal wasn't accepted."

"I think you're only giving me half-truths here. Granted, we're all responsible for the research and writing we do, but I think there's more to your situation than you're letting on. I'm trying to understand what has you so completely ready to tear that steering wheel in half."

She released one hand to brush it haphazardly over her hair, a physical manifestation of her anger and frustration — at him or Lassiter, Tristan wasn't sure yet. Cari gave him a long, cold stare, then turned her eyes back to watch the road, a single tear finally spilling from each eye.

"Damn it!"

Cari continued to struggle, and then it hit him.

"Did he expect favors in return for a positive review of your proposal?"

More tears. Tristan's hero was a villain in disguise. Nearly a minute passed before Cari finally nodded.

"And you said no."

"Of course I said no!" she shouted as she turned to look at him. "Did you sleep with your professors to get your PhD? I mean, geez, if that's the norm, then, hell yeah, let's just turn around, and I'll go take care of things right now!"

"Cari —"

"Don't patronize me, Tristan."

"I'm not patronizing you. I've just walked into a situation that I have a feeling I'm the only one who knows about. Am I right?"

She glared at him again, this time in a you-didn't-seriously-ask-that way. "What am I supposed to do? Tell someone at the university that one of their most esteemed faculty members is a lecherous SOB? What proof do I have? He's made innuendos — lots of them — making it very clear to me that he would continue to give my proposals a 'no' as long as I gave *him* a 'no.' But I have no emails or text messages or voicemails or witnesses to back me up. If it's me versus him, I lose."

So, Tristan realized, unless Cari could get Lassiter to withdraw from her committee or somehow be overruled by the others, she'd likely never complete her degree.

A tapping on the window woke Ben Pritchard. It was daylight; Ben swore under his breath. He'd overslept.

He rolled down the window and squinted at two men in uniform.

"Sir, are you a resident of this complex?"

Ben knew he had to think quickly.

"Yes. Um. I mean no. My sister is Gemma Stonecipher, but she's not home. I fell asleep waiting for her."

"And her apartment number is?" the shorter security guard asked.

"Um. She's in fifty-two-oh-three." Ben pointed to show that he knew the building. So far so good, he thought.

"Sir, can I see some ID, please?"

He shifted to get his license out of his back pocket. He didn't have to be Tristan Saunders—Gemma could easily have a brother named Ben Pritchard, and these goons would be none the wiser. As one guard scrutinized his ID and the other talked on his cell, Ben stole a glance at his watch. Ten seventeen. Shit. He shifted the car's seat back to upright and looked for the Hummer Tristan and his sister had been driving last night. It was gone—damn it—and Ben had no idea where.

"All right. We've confirmed Mrs. Stonecipher's address, but I'm sorry, sir, without her being here, I've got to ask you to leave or go in her apartment."

"I don't have a key," Ben said with a shrug as his license was returned. "I'll head out and call her later. Thanks." Willingly leaving the apartment complex should end of their investigation. The two officers tipped their hats as Ben started his car; they were letting him go.

He'd have to re-park somewhere outside the complex later so he could watch for Saunders's return. For now, he was hungry and drove to the nearest sandwich shop he could find. All Josef Aleynekov had asked was that Ben keep an eye on this guy. A few hours missed here and there wasn't going to be anything he needed to know about; Ben would get his pay as long as he filled the guy in daily on what Saunders was doing.

After getting a bite to eat, Ben decided to drive around Bainbridge Island—get a feel for the area and keep an eye out for Gemma's purple car. He would definitely spot it if it was anywhere around town, and he'd return to Cedar View Apartments by late afternoon. No worries.

After a strained ride with little more conversation, Cari and Tristan retreated to their flats just after one o'clock. He hated that he didn't have a decent reason to stay with her, but he didn't want to impose, especially since he hoped to see her later when Gemma and Ethan returned.

Once inside, Tristan pulled out his BlackBerry. Certainly there would be work-related emails and likely a note from his parents, checking to be sure that he'd arrived safely. Of the seven messages, five were from Carson World Financial — and all could be handled by his colleagues — and two were from Mum and Dad. Tristan also had one text message. Odd. Most people contacted him via email.

He clicked on the text.

My associates tell me your sister is quite beautiful.
I am hoping you had nice dinner with her. It would be shame if
she got hurt. You keep her most safely if remember
importance to keeping secret. Josef

Sister? But Gemma wasn't even home yet. Then Tristan realized who Aleynekov was referring to.

As soon as Tristan Saunders had left his office, Dr. Lassiter closed his door, panic setting in. By late afternoon, he'd decided what to do. He pulled out his cell phone — this was one call he didn't want traced back to the university. He dialed the lengthy international number and waited. The call was answered on the second ring.

"Hello, Josef. It's Jonathan Lassiter. I'd like to talk to you about a visitor I had at my office today."

Chapter 7

Ben Pritchard trolled the streets of Bainbridge Island, looking for Gemma Stonecipher's Hummer. He had an address for some small shop she had down on Winslow, but every time he drove by it looked closed, and the vehicle was never there. He decided to park at the Safeway a mile away. Surely no one would bother him if he just sat in his car for a while.

He also needed to stop by the post office up near his apartment in Poulsbo to check the box Josef used to send him packages. If there was anything there, he'd likely have to make some "deliveries" to out-of-the-way places in Seattle and the surrounding islands: hiding unopened envelopes under park benches, on specific shelves in a library, in back seats of cars conveniently left unlocked. This job paid well, but it was weird some days and honestly boring as hell. Ben knew one thing, though: he wasn't spending another night in his car. He'd be in his own bed tonight.

Not long after parking, he felt his cell phone vibrate in his jacket pocket. He opened it and found a text message from his rival—and his enemy—Chameleon.

I saw u tracking her. Back off if u no whats good 4 u

Oh, the asshole wants to play, eh? Fine.

U no damn well when it comes 2 an attack-n-capture, no 1 can beat my skilz. U back off. Shes mine - I'll have her w/ me as soon as I get rid of that hunk of meat by her side

Chameleon didn't respond; then again, Ben hadn't expected him to. Deep down, he and the others like them knew not to mess with each other's territory or prey. Besides, Ben wasn't bragging when he said he was the best. He'd proven it many times, and Chameleon certainly knew he wouldn't hesitate to show him personally. It'd be no skin off his back if that jerk was out of the picture. His latest target was quite a beauty — and feisty, he was guessing. He'd prefer to have her all to himself. It'd be a bonus if she put up a fight, and Ben would enjoy every stinkin' minute of it.

He checked his watch — twelve thirty. Time to get to the post office and then back to Cedar View Apartments to see if that car was back yet.

Tristan had to think quickly. He now knew Aleynekov had spies watching him, watching Cari. The Bulgarian — and his associates — obviously didn't realize she wasn't Gemma. That was good news for Gemma…Luckily, they didn't know Cari's name — not yet, anyway. They knew Tristan, they knew Gemma and Ethan's address, but as far as Tristan could tell, that was all; Cari's identity and Tristan's new cell phone number were unknown to them. He could only hope whoever was spying hadn't noticed Cari entering her own apartment instead of Gemma's. Tristan would know soon enough if Aleynekov sent another text.

As he pondered this new situation, Tristan had to admit he wasn't surprised. After nearly three months in hospital, he'd gone home to visit his parents briefly, spent a week at his flat in London, then taken off for the States. If he were Aleynekov, he'd have been suspicious too when Tristan hadn't returned to work at Carson World Financial. He certainly looked like he was on the run.

What Josef Aleynekov didn't know — and the reason Tristan was still alive — was the location of the documents Tristan had retained when he'd discovered Aleynekov was not only laundering money from the Bulgarian government but also double-crossing his colleagues. If the government officials, or the UN for that matter, found out about Aleynekov's thievery, he'd be jailed — if he were caught, of course. Tristan had read enough about the mafia to know that the others in Aleynekov's business posed the most danger to him. They wouldn't just kill him if they found out what he'd been doing; they'd make sure he and his family suffered. They'd use nightmarish methods of torture. These people showed no mercy and no remorse.

Tristan had contact information on each of the mafia men involved, and Aleynekov certainly knew the implications should any of them be told of his double-cross. Ultimately, Aleynekov wanted those documents safely in his own hands and Tristan Saunders six feet under. Once Aleynekov had the papers, Tristan would be a walking target and dead within days of some "accident."

Tristan's boss had granted him an indefinite leave of absence from CWF, given the extent of his injuries and the fact that he'd received them "in the line of duty." When he did return, he certainly wouldn't be doing international work for a while and would likely be desk-bound in London. He'd been wanting to visit Gemma and Ethan for over a year and decided now was likely his best opportunity for an extended holiday. But here he was, more than five thousand miles from Bulgaria, and he still couldn't escape what had become a dangerous occupation for him.

How had he gone from being a simple accounting auditor to a man with deadly enemies?

Tristan peeked discreetly out the front-bedroom window, trying to spot anything suspicious. Seeing nothing, he went to the back of the apartment and opened the French doors to the balcony. He walked out and leaned over the edge of the railing. He hoped he appeared to be merely taking in the scenery as he calculated the distance to the ground and whether he could jump down safely without reinjuring his leg. Although there was grass below, the drop was probably five meters — not a safe move for anyone.

But then he looked to his right: Cari's balcony was less than a meter away. He could easily climb over to her flat, or she could come to his, thus avoiding the front doors and anyone possibly spying from the car park.

He went back inside to think. His main concern now was Cari. If Aleynekov believed he was not acting in good faith on his end of their bargain, he could — and would — force his hand by doing something to her. Aleynekov surely knew Tristan didn't care about being beaten again, just as he knew injuring or killing him would result in vital information being revealed to his enemies. No, if Aleynekov wanted to control Tristan, it would be through threats against people he cared about. And the Bulgarian would be proactive, rather than reactive. That meant Cari was in danger now, and if Tristan didn't act quickly, she might face kidnapping and torture at the hands of Aleynekov's associates.

But Cari wasn't his only worry; Ethan and Gemma would be walking into danger as well. While Tristan wasn't sure yet what to do about Cari, he knew he had to stop his sister and her husband from returning home. Gemma had informed him that they were taking a rental car up the coast rather than flying home, hence their delay in getting back, but that was good news now. He immediately opened his phone and punched in the familiar numbers.

"Gemma, love, where are you at this point?" he asked when she answered, noting that it was nearly half past one.

"Tristan! Oh, darling, I'm so sorry to let you know, but it seems we won't be home until tomorrow. We only left LA this morning and took the coastline for much of the way. It's just beautiful, Tristan. The Pacific Ocean is so much different than the Atlantic!"

"Where are you right now?" he interrupted.

"Tristan, you sound angry. I know you expected us sooner. I promise we'll make it up to you — "

"No, everything's fine," he lied. "I just need to know where you are and what roads you're going to take to get here."

"Well, we just passed through San Francisco and are heading to Interstate Five. Do you want to talk to Ethan?"

"Yes, please, Gemma, if you don't mind."

There were a few seconds of muffled conversation before Tristan heard Ethan's jovial voice.

"Tristan! Glad to know you made it safely to the States. I think you figured out your sister's ulterior motive for not being there when you arrived. Ouch, Gemma!"

Tristan snickered. "Yes, Ethan. Tell Gemma I've met your neighbor, and she's quite lovely, thank you."

"I had to agree, you know. I mean, Cari's a great girl and did seem like the type you'd go for."

"Oh, Christ. Not you too, Ethan!"

"Yeah, man. Sorry."

At the thought of Cari, Tristan's words turned serious. "Ethan, I need to know where you are and how you're getting here."

"Tristan, is there something wrong?"

"Right now I need you to talk to me like everything's all right so Gemma won't know, but, yes, I've got a situation that I believe puts you two and Cari in danger."

Ethan began to play along immediately. "No kidding? Tell me more!" he laughed into the phone.

"You can't come home."

"Really? That's intriguing. Can you elaborate?"

"No, not yet anyway." Tristan ran his hand across the back of his neck and opened his laptop. Ethan provided their Wi-Fi password, and Tristan quickly logged on. He brought up a map of the western coast, trying to figure out where they might meet.

"Did you want us to stop somewhere for souvenirs, perhaps?"

"Yes, thank you!" Tristan sighed. He scanned the map. "I'm not sure where yet, though, and since you're still quite a distance from here, that'll give me time to figure things out and get back to you."

"So," Ethan asked enthusiastically, "what's happening up there?"

"You know that 'accident' in Bulgaria? It wasn't what I told everyone. I've got people associated with money laundering out for my blood, and they'll hurt my family and friends to keep me quiet."

"Jesus, Tristan, that's amazing!"

"The man hunting me down sent a text today saying he's got spies watching Cari and me. I've got to get her out of here or they'll take her, maybe even kill her, to get what they want from me."

"Hey, Tristan, I'm going to head back over to the interstate and stop for gas in about ten minutes. Can I call you back? The signal's not too good here and you're breaking up."

"Absolutely. Thank you, Ethan. I'm going to go see Cari next door and try to get us out of here."

"Okay, man, I'll call you back in a few."

Chapter 8

Tristan had tried to sound calm on the phone, but Ethan could tell he was scared as hell. Tristan hadn't shared much about his lengthy hospital stay, but the car accident he'd been in was severe enough to have left him in a coma for a week and in a hospital in Sofia for nearly three months. Ethan couldn't imagine what the car must have looked like to have left *him* that mangled.

But now Tristan was saying it wasn't an accident. So, maybe someone had run him off the road? He was lucky he'd survived.

When they stopped for gas, Ethan told Gemma his stomach was a little upset, and he escaped into the back of the truck-stop restaurant. He reassured her that he'd be fine and to wait in the car for him — they didn't want to open the door to having the rental vandalized by being away from it too long.

Once alone, Ethan purchased a map of Oregon and headed to an empty booth. He spread out the map and quickly calculated a midpoint along I-5. There were three small towns along the highway: Grants Pass, Canyonville, and Roseburg were at about the halfway mark and seemed to have the most east-west roads running through them. Along the coast, which would mean slower travel, Gold Beach, Bandon, and Coos Bay seemed possibilities. He opened his cell and called Tristan.

"Hey, man. We've got about three minutes before Gemma will come looking for me at this hell-hole truck stop. I've got a map of

Oregon. What do I need to know without Gemma around? We can fine-tune details when I'm back in the car."

"Christ, Ethan. It's insane. In short, a Bulgarian mafia boss wants me dead because I found out he was double-crossing his so-called friends. Until he can get his hands on the information I gathered, he needs me alive, but I think he's getting tired of this cat-and-mouse game and is ready to force my hand by threatening Cari."

"Why Cari? You just met her."

"He thinks she's Gemma."

"Shit."

"Yes. Exactly. So, I've got to get her out of here and would feel better if we could all hide out together until I can figure out this mess."

"Any ideas?"

"I've looked at a map online. You're right that we'll have to meet in Oregon. I was figuring somewhere between Eugene and Medford."

"We're thinking alike, brother," Ethan assured him. "I've got some ideas. Let me call you back once I'm back on the road. Have you talked to Cari yet?"

"Heading to her flat right now through — "

"Go across our balconies."

"That was my plan. How about I ring you after I've spoken with her and have a better idea of when and how we'll leave. By the way, have you got a vehicle I can use? I don't want to take Cari's if I can help it."

"Yeah. The keys are in the top drawer of the dresser in the bedroom. You should find some cash there too — take it all. I've got a black Lexus parked in the covered area to the side of our building, bay number seven twenty-two."

Tristan held the phone to his ear as he walked to the bedroom and opened the drawer. Sure enough, he found an envelope shoved in the back with a few hundred dollars. He continued to move clothing around, searching for the keys, but came up empty.

"I found the cash — thank you. It'll help me avoid a paper trail. There aren't any keys, though. Might they be in another drawer?"

"No, not likely. Gemma must have moved them without telling me." Ethan huffed in exasperation. "Okay. Not a problem. There's another set taped to the back of the headboard."

Tristan laughed.

"Yeah, yeah. Hey, you know your sister! I have to hide seconds of things like that because sometimes even she can't remember where she put them."

Ethan heard Tristan's shuffling as he moved through the apartment. "Got them. Thanks again, Ethan. I'll call you soon."

Tristan had liked Ethan the moment he'd met him. The way he was so willing to help right now only confirmed his belief that Gemma had married a great man.

He returned to the balcony and scanned the area to see if anyone was watching, flexing and extending his leg as he stood there. It felt so much better — little pain and no limping. He was glad that if he had to run, possibly quite literally, his knee had healed enough to handle it. In one motion, Tristan spanned the short distance between railings and landed noiselessly on Cari's balcony. He approached the French door, knocking gently and hoping she wouldn't scream, finding a man at her back door.

No answer. He cupped his hands and peered through the glass — not something he'd do normally, of course, but he had to gain entry as quickly as possible in case someone was watching from a distance.

A sheer cream-colored curtain covered the glass, but Tristan could see Cari lying on her side on her bed, a light blanket over her. His eyes immediately looked toward her feet. Sure enough, her left foot was moving slightly. Once again he was caught in the moment, enjoying watching her as she slept.

He tapped lightly on one of the panes and whispered as loudly as he dared. "Cari, it's me Tristan. Cari? Cari, wake up. I need to talk to you."

She awoke with a start and, thankfully, muffled a scream behind the hand she clapped to her mouth.

"It's okay. It's Tristan. I need to talk to you. It's very important."

She rustled her hands through her hair as she stood and padded over to the balcony door to unlock it. "Sheesh, Tristan. You scared me to death!"

"I'm so sorry." He bowed slightly as he entered her bedroom. "It's vital that I speak to you, and I didn't have a number to ring you."

"Didja think about knocking on the *front* door?"

"That's what I need to talk to you about. I'm afraid I've put you in a serious situation, and it was dangerous for me to be seen at your front door."

"What?" She was still waking up and obviously confused. "Come here." She gestured for him to follow her. She plopped into an overstuffed chair in the living room and immediately pulled her legs up in front of her, placing a throw pillow across her lap and resting her arms on top. Tristan sat near her on the end of the sofa. "Now. What's going on?"

Tristan sighed and began to tell her the real reason he'd had knee surgery. "As you know, I work for Carson World Financial. About six months ago, the UN was informed by a Bulgarian government staffer—basically a whistleblower—that a number of high-up government officials were involved in an Eastern European money laundering scheme. The UN hired CWF to investigate the allegations, and I was sent with two other auditors to Sofia.

"At first, it appeared that maybe a few million dollars had been misallocated but nothing more. Then, one afternoon, I discovered documents that showed that nearly five hundred million dollars designated to development and infrastructure had somehow been moved out of the government's control, in small increments, without the proper protocols. I investigated further and found the recipients to be fabricated corporations—businesses that didn't really exist. Naïve as I was, I met with Bulgaria's Minister of Finance—his name is Josef Aleynekov—and he appeared stunned by the news. He asked to see the documents and wanted to know who else was aware of the missing money. He was so persistent that I began to suspect his desire for information wasn't so he could bring the thieves to justice."

Cari's eyes were intent on Tristan's, wide and unblinking as he continued.

"Aleynekov thanked me and ushered me out of his office, telling me again that he needed me to provide the proof so he could launch an internal investigation. Well, I knew not to do that and headed to my flat in the city, ready to report to my boss my suspicions that Aleynekov might be involved. My job then became to find out where that missing money was."

Tristan realized this was the first time he'd talked about that day without all the lies and made-up stories about a horrible car crash or a devastating fall from scaffolding. He was scared to tell Cari the whole truth, but she was now inextricably involved.

"That night, as I entered the building where I'd rented a flat on the fourth floor, I found the lift broken. Not surprising, really; it was often out of service. So I made my way up the stairs, and at the landing between the third and fourth floors, two men came out of the shadows, each carrying meter-long metal pipes. Before I could react, one of them hit me in the abdomen, and I crumpled to the ground.

"As I struggled to breathe, the other man looked down at me and simply said, 'Stop looking for the money.' Then the two of them hit me repeatedly with those pipes—my back, my head, my legs. I couldn't lose consciousness fast enough. It hurt so badly."

Cari gasped, bringing her hand to her mouth.

"I woke up in hospital a week later in more pain than I would have thought possible. Doctors told me a colleague had found me by chance; the lift evidently had been dismantled only while the men attacked me. I had four broken ribs, a broken collarbone, two skull fractures, a broken nose and cheekbone, one shattered kneecap and the other not much better, damage to my spleen and liver, and a collapsed lung."

Cari sat, seemingly transfixed, and Tristan turned his gaze to his hands clasped in front of him as he leaned his forearms on his thighs.

"It's amazing you survived," she whispered.

"No." He looked straight at her. "The point was they *wanted* me to survive. I was a message to my company that if they continued to look for the missing money, more employees would end up like me… or worse. The man who reported the situation in the first place? We believe he's dead, probably at the bottom of some lake."

"Are you sure he wasn't able to get away?"

"Yes." Tristan paused. "Suffice it to say there was fairly conclusive evidence that he's dead." He didn't dare tell her the man's severed foot and identification papers had been mailed to his wife. The bottom line was that the mafia meant business. They were evil, cut-throat (often literally), despicable people who would stop at nothing to protect their interests.

And now, because of Tristan, Cari was their newest target.

Jenny Allen liked spying on people. She was good at it—good at guessing people's motives, reading their demeanor, and gauging how they'd react under pressure. Being an enigma was also part of the job; she was invisible to most and a mystery to anyone she spoke to.

Right now, she had three "subjects" to watch: the first she'd slept with, the second she lusted for, but the third—the one she was currently watching—might be her next conquest just for the hell of it. She'd kept a keen eye on him from her dark-windowed car at Cedar View Apartments. Her report was due soon, and she wanted to include details that would please the Bulgarian mafia boss. She'd observed Apartment 5203 over the past few days and made some inquiries about its occupants. It seemed Ethan Stonecipher and his wife were in California, even though Tristan Saunders had come to visit them. Bad communication between siblings, perhaps?

Jenny hadn't yet seen Dr. Saunders; juggling three cases meant she couldn't give any one of the men her full twenty-four-seven attention. She'd received information via text from Bulgaria that Saunders had arrived and was staying at his sister's apartment. Aleynekov didn't mention that Saunders was in the apartment alone, so it seemed no one else knew the Stoneciphers were away. Being one-up on her associates as they tracked Saunders's movements in the States would earn her brownie points for sure.

She'd simply called the offices of Barclay-Bradshaw in Seattle and asked for Ethan. Marissa, the receptionist with a way-too-perky voice, let spill that both Stonecipher and his wife were in California, and he wasn't due back until Monday. If Marissa had been Jenny's employee, she'd have been fired on the spot—or mysteriously killed—for revealing personal information like that; instead, Jenny gave a friendly "thanks so much" before hanging up. Her smile was bigger than the Cheshire Cat's. Having up to three days without Saunders's family in the way, she might be able to secure what Aleynekov was so desperate for all by herself.

Yes, she'd stay out of contact with her boss and colleagues a little while longer. No need to let others know. If this worked out, she'd get full credit and maybe even a personal reward from the mafia boss himself: time alone with Alexei back in Bulgaria. She flipped open her phone to make some calls and solidify her plans.

Rudy looked at the car keys in his hand. He'd been able to slip in and out of the Stoneciphers' apartment as soon as Miss Cari and the man with the limp had left. It wasn't really stealing if he put them back later, right? He was just doing what that pretty Bulgarian girl, Evgenia, had asked. She'd been a mystery he wanted to unravel since he'd first heard her thick Eastern European accent a few months ago at a bar; they'd spent the evening discussing "life back home." She didn't speak Russian, and he didn't understand Bulgarian, so their conversation had been restricted to very broken English. He didn't mind, though; it gave him practice and he got to spend time with the most beautiful woman he'd ever seen.

Now, after she'd finally agreed to go out with him, they'd simply borrow the expensive Lexus and return it later. Rudy's car was a piece of junk; Evgenia said she knew the Stoneciphers and that, since they were away, they'd never find out. Rudy would be rewarded, Evgenia told him. Her seductive smile had let him know he'd like how she thanked him, and he was looking forward to tonight.

He shoved the car keys into his pocket, checked his watch—a little after three o'clock—and headed to Building Two to fix a leaky faucet.

At one o'clock, Ben had just finished delivering two envelopes and picked up one of his own with five thousand dollars cash inside—man, this new job was sweet!—when he got a text from his boss.

> I am disappointed at mistake you make. Woman with Saunders is not sister. You will make better with me by find out about Carolina Lopez. I pay you much money to do this. Do not make me angry again.

What a jerk! This foreign guy gives him nothing but a man's name and his sister's address. How was Ben to know the woman coming and going from the apartment wasn't actually his sister? Whatever. What was Josef going to do? Fire him? The guy lived in another country, for Christ's sake. Right now all Ben wanted was a beer, so he drove toward the pool hall near his apartment. Likely some of his friends would be there, having knocked off early on a rainy Friday afternoon.

When he got to Zimm's, sure enough it was already crowded and noisy, and it wasn't even happy hour yet—that's when the good stuff happened. Friday was always Ladies' Night, and Ben hoped to run into that hot blonde with ice blue eyes he'd seen here the past few weeks. Man, he'd been having dreams about this woman with a Lara Croft body and an attitude that shut down any overconfident SOB that dared approach her. He didn't even care that sometimes she had some beauty queen of a guy hanging at her side. Yeah, the guy seemed like he could handle himself in a fight, but he was way too pretty. They seemed "together," but Ben had never seen them making out or anything. They just seemed protective of each other, and they didn't mingle.

Last week, Ben had definitely noticed her looking at him. She'd even winked when he made a fantastic play at the pool table, pocketing three balls in one move. He'd been going to approach her that night, despite the warning glare from Pretty Boy, when she suddenly got up and left with him. She'd looked over her shoulder as she walked out, though, and her eyes told Ben she'd be back — for *him*.

If she showed up tonight, Ben was going to let her know he'd been watching her too. He'd tracked her and discovered they had, let's just say, some common traits: a take-no-prisoners attitude, rock-solid determination to go for what they wanted, and deadly aim with a gun. Yeah, turned out she was his competition, but tonight he planned to get her to be with him...in more ways than one.

Ben downed his first beer and started right away on the next, his eyes never turning away from the front door, waiting almost impatiently for her to arrive. Then a few guys from his old neighborhood came in, and he got distracted, caught up in the latest news from Redmond. At about four thirty, his friends Keith and Tom suddenly dropped their jaws at what was evidently right behind him. He turned and found himself face to face with the she-devil he'd been waiting for.

"You planning on puttin' your balls in any pockets tonight, handsome?" She was the essence of seduction in a creamy silk bustier and jeans she must have poured herself into.

"Why?" he responded as he drank her in. "You offerin' yours? I mean, I don't know that they'd fit, but I'm sure as hell willing to try."

"Well, aren't you straightforward," she cooed. "I was talking about your excellent pool skills, and you turned it into a come-on."

"Have I offended you, then?" Ben knew he hadn't but played along. "How about I buy you a drink as an apology, eh?"

She must have expected that and immediately turned to the bartender, who had been listening intently to their conversation. "Vodka, straight up."

Then she turned back to Ben, moving closer. Keith and Tom had the good sense to find someplace else to stand around like idiots, leaving Ben to his fantasy come true.

"So, what's your name, pretty lady?"

"I'm not sure I want to tell you yet. Maybe I'd like you to give me a pet name right off, hmm?" She now stood between his legs as he sat on the barstool. When he rested his hands on her hips, she didn't pull away. "So...you'll need to know a little about me to figure out a good name."

Ben smiled, and she responded by putting her forearms on his shoulders, hooking her fingers behind his neck.

"What do you want to share with me first?" he whispered.

Before he knew it, she was full-out kissing him. Ben returned the favor enthusiastically. When they pulled away from the kiss, he could see in those ice blue eyes a whole lot more she wanted to share — things they'd need a much more private place for, and they both knew they needed it now.

Ben threw a twenty on the bar, and they were out the door. They got in his Camaro and she nearly had him undone, literally and figuratively, before they were out of the parking lot. His apartment was only a few blocks away, and once inside, it was mere moments before they were satisfying each other in his bed. Her name could have been Fred, for all Ben cared. She was way too good to be true.

Chapter 9

Assassins are out to get…me? This is insane, Cari thought. "Let me try to call my dad. He has lots of friends who are police officers and he ca—"

"No." Tristan's voice was emphatic. "You'll only endanger him too. We have no idea who's watching us and, believe me, even upstanding citizens—including the police—can be bought."

"But what else can we do? You've got me frightened, Tristan." She wrapped her arms across her abdomen, trying to mentally grasp what had happened to Tristan…what could happen again.

"We need to leave here," Tristan said softly. "We need to escape from whoever expects us to keep up a regular routine. If we stay here, we become more and more an easy target. I'm not afraid of Aleynekov coming after me, Cari. It's you he'll try to hurt."

"But I'm just your sister's next-door neighbor. How did I get pulled into this?"

Tristan pulled his BlackBerry from his back pocket, pressed some buttons, and handed it to Cari, showing her a message he'd received.

"He thinks I'm your sister…" Her voice was barely audible as tears welled up in her eyes.

"Yes. Right now, that's to our advantage, though. He doesn't know anything about you, only what someone has told him. Whoever has been watching us must not know what Gemma looks like and didn't follow us to your university or they would have figured out who you are, name and all. But it's only a matter of time."

"If they find out who I am, would they go after my dad too?"

Tristan didn't answer, and Cari felt her mind begin to spiral toward panic. She got up and walked quickly into her bedroom. "We've got to get out of here. My car can get us wherever we need to go. And my dad…I've got to find a way to warn him." She grabbed a duffle bag from under her bed and turned to her dresser, pulling out items and tossing them in, barely paying attention to what she packed.

She was about to take off to somewhere undetermined, and her father was hiking. If these people found out her name, they could find him too — he might come home to an ambush. She'd have to leave him a message at home; he'd never bothered to get a cell, figuring he was always either at the house or the hardware store.

But what if they went there and got the message before her father? She could call one of his friends at the police station…but now Tristan had her scared that anyone could turn against them. Her mind whirled and she'd nearly emptied her jeans drawer into her duffle bag now, unable to control herself.

"Cari. Stop." Tristan gently took her hands in his and backed her to the side of her bed, sitting her down. He crouched in front of her, still holding her hands in her lap. "I need you to listen for a minute, okay?" Cari nodded numbly. "I've already been in touch with Ethan."

"Oh, God!" she said with a gasp. "They can't come here!"

"I know," Tristan responded calmly as he let go of her hands and stood up. "Ethan and I are going to talk again in a few minutes. He and Gemma are going to meet us halfway between here and San Francisco, which is where they are now."

"Oregon…"

"Right. We're both looking at maps to figure out a best plan." He stepped back and leaned against the door frame, releasing a heavy sigh.

Cari's mind now started to think logically, thank heavens. If she was part of this, she needed to be helpful, not full of panic and indecision. Suddenly, she recalled scenes from the movie *The Pelican Brief.* Julia Roberts' character was chased by assassins too. Cari mentally reviewed the things she'd done to remain anonymous to her killers.

"We need cash. We can't use credit cards they can trace to us… Wait." Her thoughts continued on a coherent path. "I have a cousin who lives in southern Oregon, along the interstate. Would it be safe to go there? I mean, if we're being followed and have to be gone for a few days, we're going to need some place to sleep, right? Wouldn't it help if we were able to avoid hotels and restaurants as much as possible?"

Tristan seemed to light up. "Where does your cousin live?"

"It's a little town south of Eugene. Canyonville. It's right along I-5. He grew up there, and I've visited every other summer or so since we were kids. He's like a brother to me—I'm sure he and his wife would want to help us if they can."

Tristan nodded. "You're on to something. Do you have his number? Can you ring him right away and see if they could possibly accommodate four people on short notice? I'm not sure I'd tell him you've got Bulgarian mafia after you, though..." he added with a sideways grin.

Cari forced a smile, willing everything to be all right. "Yeah. I'll call him right now. Do you want to get back in touch with Ethan too, ask him what he thinks about staying with my cousin?"

"Got it." He sighed. "Let's get on the road soon, though. Every minute's delay worries me."

"Ann! Can you get the phone?"

"Sorry, hon. I'm elbow-deep in potting soil!"

Damn, Mark Stoddard thought. He had gotten busy right after work and was in the middle of hauling two-by-fours from his truck. He hated getting interrupted as he counted the boards. But after gently dropping the wood on the grass, he jogged to his cell where it vibrated on the top step of the porch.

"Hello?"

"Hey, Mark, it's me, Cari."

"Hairy Cari? How're you doing?" He lit up at the sound of his cousin's voice. She was the little sister he'd never had—his summertime partner in exploring the woods.

"I'm doing okay. How's Ann?" Her voice didn't seem normal. It sounded strained, uncomfortable.

"She's good, she's good. She's getting the business ready, and we're both working hard to make sure we stay ahead of the bills. You know how it goes." He paused. "So, what's caused you to call me out of the blue like this? Everything okay with your family?"

"Yeah. Um, Dad's great. He's found himself a hiking buddy—some guy who sells fence supplies to his store. The two of them are out wandering some trails this weekend."

There was silence.

"Um, Mark? How would you and Ann like four houseguests for a few days?" Her enthusiasm sounded forced.

"Sure. No problem." Mark knew this was not just a social call. "When we talking?"

"Well…tonight, actually. I'll be leaving my apartment in just a bit, and my friends would be arriving from San Francisco."

"Cari, what's wrong?" Mark had to get to the bottom of what had her so nervous—scared, even.

"It's too hard to explain over the phone, but I promise, Mark, it'll only be for a few days. You'll be a real life saver. I know I'm imposing on you two."

"Carolina, you are *never* imposing! Hell, I should be mad that you haven't made a trip down here to see us in almost a year. Now, what do you need? Sounds like there's trouble, and you know I'll grill you big time when you get here, but what can Ann and I do to get ready?"

Mark heard her sigh of relief clearly through the phone. "God, Mark. Thank you. Um, well, Tristan and I will be traveling south, and I've got your number, of course. Is it okay if I give Tristan's sister Gemma and her husband the number as well, in case they get lost?"

"Sure! So…Tristan, huh? You finally got a good guy in your life?"

"No. It's not like that. I just…well…it's complicated. I'll explain everything when we get there, okay?"

"Yeah, baby, it'll be good to see you. And don't hesitate to call if you need us to do anything."

They hung up, and Mark went out to the garden where Ann was planting some flowers, all part of getting a local landmark ready to reopen.

"We've got company coming. You think we could use the family business for *family* for a few days?"

Ann smiled. "Sounds like Canyon Creek Bed and Breakfast will be opening a little sooner than expected."

Cari knew she was an anxiety attack waiting to happen. Crazy thoughts kept invading her head. *Why? Who* are *these people? How did they find Tristan here on tiny Bainbridge Island? Are they watching us—can they see into our apartments?* She quickly moved to close all the drapes and turn off any extra lights; she was more comfortable moving around in dim lighting than risk being seen packing. She could hear Tristan in her kitchen, still talking with Ethan on his cell phone.

Focus, Cari.

She had some Visa gift cards her father had given her at Christmas. She'd planned to save them until she found something special. Now, though, that two hundred dollars on anonymous credit cards was going to come in handy. She had about thirty dollars in her purse, and she'd check with Tristan to see if it would be all right to withdraw more cash from an ATM before they left the island.

She returned to packing, removing the unnecessary items she'd hastily stuffed in her duffle bag and replacing them with three days' worth of clothing. The positive side of her hoped she'd be safely back home by then; the negative side worried her life could be over before she needed everything she brought.

"I'm so sorry, Cari, so sorry that you've been dragged into this hell." Tristan looked exhausted as he leaned against her bedroom door. She gave him a half-hearted smile.

"So…am I okay to just throw some stuff into this duffle bag? I talked with Mark and he said yes to us all coming to his place."

"His last name isn't Lopez too, is it?" Tristan's eyebrows furrowed a bit.

"No. It's Stoddard. His mom and my dad are siblings. That's good, right?" She glanced at the window. "They won't be able to guess where we're going, then."

"Right. That's what I'm hoping. I just don't know how many people Aleynekov has watching us or at what point he's going to figure out you're not Gemma. Once he does, it could be mere seconds before he's got people on your trail, finding out everything they can about you. But it's unlikely they'd trace you to a cousin in another state; at least not quickly anyway."

Cari shivered.

"God, Cari." Tristan moved toward her, his hands tucked in his back pockets. "I'm sorry I'm frightening you." He ducked his head to look her straight in the eye, needing her—pleading with her—to hear his words. "I'll keep you safe. I promise. Okay? Do you believe me? I'll keep you safe."

Cari nodded, sniffed, and wiped her eyes before any tears could fall. "Tell me what I should pack."

Tristan helped Cari finish packing only what he felt she might need, turning away when she tucked some underthings beneath a second pair of jeans. He had her grab her laptop and all the ID she had in her apartment: bills, passport, and mail. If anyone broke in, they'd be hunting for family members' names and addresses.

After feeling fairly certain no one was watching, Tristan climbed back over the balcony. Cari handed him her things, and she followed, taking his hand so he could help her as she crossed the span.

Tristan had barely unpacked, so it was easy for him to gather his things and transfer them to a gym bag he'd found in Ethan's closet. But now he and Cari had a problem: how to get out of the flat and into Ethan's car without being seen. Again Tristan cursed that Gemma and Ethan lived on the second floor.

"Wait!" Cari lit up. "I'll be right back!" Before Tristan could stop her, she was back out and across the balcony. He stood by the French doors as she disappeared into her bedroom. When she came out and relocked her back door, she held a black canvas bag. "Rope ladder!" she said, smiling brightly as she passed it to him.

Tristan's eyebrows showed his curiosity, and she laughed. "From my dad's hardware store. He sells a lot of fire safety stuff. As soon as he saw there was only one way out of my apartment, he brought me a fire extinguisher and gave me this so I'd have some way to escape out the back in case my front door was blocked."

"Your father is very protective," Tristan said appreciatively.

She shrugged. "Yeah. I told him it was silly to worry like that but, hmph, who knew I'd actually need this thing?" She climbed back over and together they set up the ladder, draping it down the balcony's side.

They stared at each other with a who-should-go-first? look and quickly determined it was wiser for Tristan to climb halfway down so Cari could pass their belongings. It was still daylight but hazy; Tristan hoped that would provide some cover for them. Cari took off as soon as she hit the ground, and Tristan was relieved to see that they could reach Ethan's car without passing in front of the building. If someone were watching the front doors and stairway, they'd not see them running to the covered parking area.

After stowing their things in the trunk and closing it gently, Tristan looked up to see Cari standing by the driver's side, holding out her hand for the keys.

"But I think Ethan will be expecting me to drive his car," he protested.

"And you've driven on American roads how often?" she challenged with one eyebrow raised.

Good point, Tristan quickly realized. He tossed her the keys and circled over to the passenger side. Well, Tristan thought, at least this *felt* like he was driving back in England. As Cari backed out of the parking space and headed to the street, he was pleased to notice that the windows of Ethan's car were tinted dark enough to mask them from anyone's watchful eyes. At least he hoped so.

Chapter 10

R udy was ready an hour early for his date with Evgenia, still not quite able to believe his run of good fortune. Evgenia had told him about the maintenance position at Cedar View, and she even contacted the apartment's main office to recommend him for the job. He'd called her a few times to thank her and ask her out, but he'd always gotten her voice mail. Yesterday she'd finally returned his calls, and she was certainly friendly on the phone. They talked for a while, and she readily accepted his invitation to dinner. Rudy wasn't sure if she was looking for friendship, or just a good time, but given her beautiful body and sparkling eyes, he was ready and willing to deliver both.

She'd called again this morning to solidify plans for their date. Her seductive voice had melted him as she insisted the Stoneciphers, friends of hers, wouldn't mind him borrowing their car. Tonight he planned to give her the impression he was going to be promoted to management, that soon he'd have a nice car too. Evgenia looked like she came from money — lots of it — and Rudy would do anything he could to earn her affection.

It actually startled him how quickly he'd agreed to her plan about the car. Up to now, he'd been very professional about the people he'd met at the complex. Most of them scoffed at his friendliness — or his accent — but a few had been very kind, especially Gemma Stonecipher. In return for her friendly demeanor, he'd always been quick to respond to her needs, putting her maintenance requests before anyone else's. He liked her, more than he should, he realized. Now that he'd met Evgenia, perhaps he could get over his crush on Mrs. Stonecipher.

He looked again in his mirror, making sure his hair was the way he wanted it and his clothes looked good. His apartment was in order—including his bed, in case they ended up back here after dinner. He felt the keys to Ethan's car in his pocket, and his wallet held his first American credit card. Yes, he would be making a very good impression.

"So, you gonna tell me your name?" Ben asked.

The woman with the gorgeous eyes lay across his chest, her arm draped over his stomach, her warm body snuggled close.

"How about Delilah?" She smiled and kissed his chin, weaving her fingers into his hair. "And you can be Samson."

Ben pulled her closer and kissed her passionately. Delilah was the most beautiful woman he'd ever seen, and he felt like the luckiest man alive. They'd been perfect together in bed. He reached for his bottle of beer on the nightstand; Delilah had offered to get two cold ones from the fridge between "rounds."

"Mmm-mm-mm, Delilah, you are amazing. You know that?" Ben played with her golden hair as it fell in soft waves down her bare back.

"Maybe it's because you bring out the best in me."

Her smile was intoxicating. And those eyes, they were mesmerizing. She moved her hand back down to his chest, tracing light circles and figure-eights across his skin and softly kissing his shoulder. Her gentle, soothing touch relaxed him. Having her here, holding her... it was heaven. Ben closed his eyes and let sleep take over.

Evgenia left Ben "Hawk" Pritchard's apartment fully satisfied—a rarity. She wasn't usually one to give in to lust, knowing she needed to stay in control at all times. But this extremely sexy man had most definitely pleased her. She might just need to find a few more opportunities to sleep with him. Maybe.

But she had a job to do, just like he did. He just didn't know they were on the same trail. While he slept—aided by the bit of muscle relaxant she'd put in his beer—she was eager to take care of another situation. She had to make sure Tristan Saunders didn't take off. She grabbed Ben's keys and drove to her place. She put on a simple floral dress, freshened her makeup, and combed her hair, adding a light blue ribbon to give her that sweet-and-innocent look for tonight's date.

She had no interest in the Russian immigrant, but he was unknowingly, and enthusiastically, a part of her plan. Stupid fool. She glossed her lips and headed to the apartment complex to meet him at Ethan Stonecipher's car. Saunders had likely received a text from Aleynekov by now, so he knew he was being watched. That also meant he was a flight risk. Her goal: Keep Saunders on Bainbridge Island by taking away his most likely method of escape.

Tristan and Cari made their first and only stop at Cari's bank to withdraw a few hundred dollars. By three o'clock, they were heading south to I-5 in Tacoma. Their trip to Mark and Ann's place in Canyonville, it turned out, would be almost exactly the same distance as the trip from San Francisco. Cari hoped the coincidence was a good omen—that meeting Ethan and Gemma there was the right thing to do.

Just outside of Bremerton, Cari called Mark to tell him she and Tristan were probably six or seven hours away and that Ethan and Gemma would likely arrive a little before them, given the stop they'd had to make. Tristan called Gemma to convey the same information and gave her Mark's phone number.

Cari designated Tristan the co-pilot, in charge of selecting music on the radio or from Ethan's small CD collection in the console. The weather was pleasant—mid-fifties and overcast but no rain—so at least the driving conditions wouldn't add to her stress. Still, there were times they rode in silence, just letting music fill the space between them.

"Might you be willing to allow me the opportunity to drive?"

They'd been on the road for about an hour and would remain on I-5 until they reached Canyonville. There was surprisingly little traffic for a Friday afternoon, and this section of the Washington interstate didn't have much road construction to impede their progress.

"Yeah, I guess," Cari said. With at least another six hours of driving to go, she probably would want a break—or two. "There's an exit coming up in three miles. How about I pull off there and let you have a try? If you don't feel comfortable, though," she cautioned, "I can take back over!"

Driving was a little disconcerting for Tristan at first, but teasing Cari about how Americans drive on the *wrong* side of the car and the *wrong* side of the road was worth it. He adjusted quickly, and Cari soon settled into her seat and searched Ethan's CD collection.

"The Decemberists okay?"

"Sure."

She inserted the CD and adjusted the volume so as not to drown out their conversation. Tristan smiled to himself; that's just what he would've done.

"Tell me about your cousin." Tristan looked quickly at Cari. She sat with her left leg tucked under her right, turned slightly toward him.

"Oh," she stammered. "Um, well, Mark's like a brother to me. Neither of us have any siblings, so we kind of adopted each other growing up." She smiled. "He's a great guy; you'll like him."

"What does he do for a living?"

"He's a guidance counselor at Canyonville High School. He coaches most of the sports there too. He loves coaching and connects so well with the kids. He's the reason more than fifty percent of the school's athletes receive major scholarships to universities around the country."

Tristan was impressed. "He writes letters of recommendation and all that?"

"That's the final thing he does. But mostly he's a phenomenal coach. He runs the school's football, basketball, and baseball programs, and they've won state championships for their division a bunch of times. A few years ago, they were 'triple crown' winners, bringing home first place trophies in all three sports he coaches. Recruiters know his reputation for developing strong, dedicated athletes, and he expects them to do well in school too—lets them know a career in sports is fleeting; they have to have a backup plan. Universities seek out his students, and he makes sure they're ready to excel."

"And he's married, yes?"

Cari tilted her head and smiled again. "Yeah…Ann is so neat. She's drop-dead gorgeous, but the nicest person you'll ever meet. And hard working too! She can take apart just about anything and put it back together better than it was."

"Really!"

"And she's so talented in everything," Cari continued. "There was this old bed and breakfast—well, actually it was a really nice home that was converted to an inn back in the fifties—and she and Mark bought it last year so she can renovate it and attract some of the tourist trade that visits the casino there. She understands mechanical stuff and, with a little help from a friend who's a professional electrician, brought this decrepit three-story mansion into the twenty-first century. I haven't seen the place, but Mark and Ann made their Christmas cards with a picture of it on the front, all snow-covered and draped in garlands and red ribbons. It was beautiful." She paused for a moment. "That's where we'll be staying, I'm guessing, since they sold their house to help pay for the business. I really hope we're not putting them out by bombarding them like this."

"We'll pay for our stay, I promise," Tristan said.

"If they'll let us," she said with a smirk. "No, it's more…you know…" She glanced away for a moment.

She was worried they might be endangering their hosts, Tristan knew. And possibly their home and business too.

They stayed silent then, just letting the music fill the car as they looked out at the road ahead. The highway meandered to offer an occasional glimpse of snow still clinging to distant mountain ranges. The sun moved behind the trees in the west as they headed into early evening. The drive was soothing, even if the purpose for it was not.

Evgenia parked Ben's car at the far end of the lot, not wanting anyone to see what she'd been driving, especially her "date."

Time to play Little Miss Immigrant again. She smiled slyly.

As she approached the covered bays where Ethan Stonecipher's car should have been, she saw Rudy scratching his head and pacing back and forth, scanning the parking lot.

"Where eez care fyor date, Rudy?" she sputtered shyly in her Bulgarian accent.

"I do not know. Meester Eetan eez no homes today, but care here yesterday, and I am having kezz here." He held up the keys to prove he'd done what she'd requested. "Care eez no here."

She swallowed her anger. This idiot could foul up something as simple as making sure *that* car didn't leave? She walked quickly toward the front of the Stonecipers' apartment building and she saw the blue Hummer. Her eyes narrowed.

"You stayings here, Rudy. I will walking to Gemma's 'partment to seeing if she eez home."

She hurried around the corner of the building and climbed the steps. But rather than the Stonecipers', she knocked on Carolina Lopez's door. Her car was here; she was either inside or gone with Saunders.

After a second knock and no answer, she quickly picked the lock—these apartments were way too easy to break into. A quick perusal let her know the Lopez woman wasn't there and, further, she had packed hurriedly: toothbrush and hairbrush gone, bathroom cabinet left open, one dresser drawer askew, and some socks on the floor.

Yeah, the woman was most likely with Saunders, and they were long gone.

Shit.

She got out her cell and began to dial as she headed back down the stairs. As soon as she heard the deep voice on the other end of the line, she spoke in fluent Bulgarian. "*They're gone...I don't know, maybe an hour or two ago?...Ne! Ne! I've got this under control!...Of course I'll be able to track him. As soon as I know more, I'll let you know...I've never let you down!...Da...Ciao.*"

As she walked back to Rudy, she concocted a quick Plan B—and a quick end to this useless idiot in front of her.

"What do you mean 'what happened to Tristan in Sofia wasn't an accident'?" Gemma turned in the passenger seat to face Ethan.

"I don't know much, hon, just that something's wrong, and we're going to meet him in some little town in Oregon."

"He did get a chance to meet Cari, though, right? I was so hoping they'd hit it off and maybe—"

"She's with him."

"What?" This was exciting news indeed!

But then Ethan looked over with worry in his eyes. "She's part of what's wrong. They're evidently both in danger and had to get away as fast as possible. They've got my car and are heading south to meet us at Cari's cousin's house."

"Danger? God, Ethan, Tristan's a bloody accountant! What did he do, cook the books on a client or something?" Gemma scoffed at the idea her perfect brother would do anything unethical.

"Like I said, I don't know, but I can tell he's scared, Gemma. Scared for Cari more than himself."

She couldn't help but be pleased to learn she'd see Tristan and Cari together, to see for herself if they made a smart match. But under these circumstances? She turned her gaze to the road ahead, sipping her Diet Coke and hoping whatever was wrong was easily fixed.

The portion of I-5 in southern Washington had few exits. Tristan and Cari finally hit civilization again an hour north of Portland and stopped at the first promising intersection. Luckily, Tristan was agreeable about American fast food, and after a quick stop at Burger King and a refueling at Chevron, they were back on the road.

Cari had taken over the driving again, and her cell phone sat in the console between them. He picked it up.

"We should program our numbers into each other's phones, don't you think?"

"Oh, yeah, of course!" She glanced quickly to offer assistance, but he was already finding her address book and soon had the numbers punched in. He then pulled out his personal cell and his BlackBerry and programmed her information into both. As he stared at the BlackBerry, Cari couldn't help but ask if he'd received any more messages from Aleynekov.

"No, thank heavens. Nothing so far." He turned that phone off and put it in the glove compartment, but placed his other cell next to hers in the console. "Hopefully that means his assistants haven't yet deduced that we've left town. I'm just afraid they'll soon find out your identity; God knows they've been able to figure out nearly everything else. I just wish I knew how many people have been watching me and for how long."

"How did they know you had a sister in the States?"

Tristan glared at her. "This is the Bulgarian mafia. They have unlimited resources worldwide and unlimited money to keep anyone on their payroll. Obviously they figured out when and where I would be traveling and had someone in place on Bainbridge Island to watch me as soon as I arrived." He ran his hand across the back of his neck roughly. "God! I am so sick of this."

"So…" Cari said shyly. "What can you do to make it stop?"

"That's what I've been trying to figure out—particularly since I've realized I'm putting others in danger."

He sounded so frustrated, so angry at his current lot in life.

"You have something Aleynekov wants, right?"

"Yes. Information that would ruin him, including lists of other members of his inner circle who have no idea he's cheating them." He sighed and looked nervously out the side window. "Aleynekov could kill my parents at a moment's notice if I do anything to make him suspect I'm going back on my word to keep silent about what he's been doing. He could have Gemma and Ethan killed—or you."

Cari glanced over at Tristan; he stared at her, and she could see the pain in his eyes. He wasn't worried about himself.

"I'm sorry, Tristan…but…" She hesitated. "What keeps him from just killing you? Then you wouldn't be any more trouble to him."

"Before I left the office to meet with Aleynekov, when I began to suspect he was involved in cheating the Bulgarian government, I made copies of all of the bank account information and the list of major players in Eastern Europe who are part of this giant spider web of money laundering. I knew I couldn't trust him or others in the Bulgarian government, but I also didn't know if my own company might have spies. That night I was attacked. While I was in hospital, I had the copies sent to the States to be hidden, with instructions on what to do if anything happened to me.

"I'm willing to keep quiet about all of it; the documents are sealed and are to remain that way unless I'm found dead. Aleynekov knows if he kills me, that information will be sent to his colleagues, who will hunt him down and kill him."

"So…couldn't you anonymously send this stuff—this information you have—to one of the mafia people on that list? Let them take care of Aleynekov and leave you out of it."

"I've wondered about that. It's too simple. He could still have me killed anyway, out of spite. I think Aleynekov must have his own backup plan, should he be killed or even feel threatened—a plan that would implicate me, I'm sure, and send even more mafia after me and my family. We'd never be free." He paused to look out the passenger window. "I wouldn't want to join that world, but I would in a heartbeat if it meant my family and friends would be safe."

Cari looked at him open-mouthed, and he smirked sadly.

"Like I've told you already, Cari, anyone can be bought. Even me."

Chapter 11

Cari just stared straight ahead. She couldn't look at him. What did he mean "anyone can be bought, even me"? Had he done something unethical or illegal to cause all of this?

He'd told her before they left that his company had chosen to protect its employees over facing the mafia. Everyone but Tristan had been sent back to London immediately after his attack to keep them safe. Once Tristan had recovered enough, he and the Bulgarian accountant with CWF completed their report—with no mention of wrongdoing by Aleynekov or any other government official.

Tristan had lied on that report, and Cari wondered the extent to which his colleague knew that. And Tristan had all these account numbers and names of criminals? Certainly he hadn't included *that* in his report! He made it seem like this was some kind of secret agreement between Aleynekov and himself, that Aleynekov's government colleagues and employees knew nothing about it. So, did that mean he'd made a deal? Had he been bought?

Or had he made a deal not realizing the price he'd pay in return?

Cari knew she couldn't—and shouldn't—pry. Truth be told, she was afraid to ask questions. If the mafia was after her, she'd rather keep herself as much in the dark as possible. But now she was on the road with this man...this...criminal? If they found him, they'd find her too. What had she gotten herself into? Even more worrisome, what had she just gotten Mark and Ann into?

Cari continued to focus on driving and on keeping her emotions in check. *No crying. Absolutely no tears. Don't let on that you doubt him.* She began to wonder if she could escape. Maybe at the next rest stop, she could just leave him there…

She needed to know more. Everything seemed so far-fetched, so unbelievable—she wasn't sure what, if anything, he'd told her was true.

But she knew she'd seen pain in his eyes, not callousness. She'd seen fear, not brazen disregard for her or his sister or the others. Cari wanted desperately to trust Tristan. Something told her he'd meant it when he said he'd keep her safe.

Or was that a lie too?

She vowed to make her decision at the next place they stopped.

Tristan stole glances at Cari. She'd become pensive, quiet, and he was sure she was still grappling with the realization that she was on the run from unknown enemies. There was nothing he could say or do to comfort her. He still wasn't sure how or when Aleynekov's associates would figure out that they'd left Bainbridge Island. Part of him wanted to check his BlackBerry, but a stronger part wanted to live in ignorance just a little while longer. If Aleynekov had sent a message, it would still be there later.

Tristan was tired, physically and emotionally. He rested his head against the doorframe, letting the steady hum of the tires relax him. He'd taken one of his pain pills to ward off the dull ache he could feel starting in his knee again. For a moment he regretted having left the brace back at Gemma's flat.

Eyes closed, his thoughts wandered through the past thirty hours—had it only been that long since he'd met Cari? It seemed far longer. Didn't matter, really; he felt a connection to her and, despite the circumstances, was so very glad they were together. He winced. How selfish that he was relieved to not be alone again as he ran from the very real demons of Bulgaria.

As he relived the mere hours he'd spent in the nearly constant companionship of his sister's lovely neighbor, his memories took a more…what was it?…intimate turn? He could see more now in their conversations and eye contact than simple friendship. Their dinner at

Cairo's was now their first date; their banter at the market was that of lovers, not new acquaintances; and their walk behind her flat had had a romantic feel as they'd shared simple details of their personal lives. When she'd knocked at his door because of her broken key, he'd felt honored that she'd come to him for help. Tristan liked being someone Cari could count on, someone she could trust.

And then watching her sleep, her toes maintaining their quirky rhythm…He liked imagining what was going on in her head. Perhaps he'd have the opportunity to find out. He began to compare Cari to Melanie. When word had gotten back to CWF in London of his attack and hospitalization, Melanie and he were pretty much over, but still, he thought she'd cared for him at least enough to want to know how he was doing. Instead, his calls to her went unanswered, and messages were never returned. A colleague finally revealed that Melanie had announced she wanted nothing more to do with him or the dangerous situation he'd put himself in.

But Cari was different. He was drawn to her intelligence, her caring—her fear for Gemma and Ethan's safety took precedence over any concern for herself. Tristan hated that she'd been caught up in all of this. He vowed to keep his promise to protect her until he could figure out how to stop Aleynekov.

He was finally resting. Good. Cari couldn't help but worry about Tristan; he'd had so much happen to him, and clearly it wasn't over yet. Cari needed time to think, to plan what to do.

She stole glances at him while his eyes were closed, afraid of what she'd somehow gotten pulled into, afraid of what Tristan still wasn't telling her.

Her goal was to get just north of Salem before stopping to use the restroom. By then, they could either split up—by mutual agreement or because she'd peeled off without him—or get back on the road to Canyonville. If she did decide to abandon him, at least he had more options there than at some desolate rest area. He could make his way back to Portland's international airport, if nothing else. Maybe he could fly to some nowhere island and hide out for a year or so. Of course, that didn't solve the problem of the mafia knowing where his family—and she—lived. God, this became more complicated the more she thought about it.

She looked over at her sleeping companion again as she checked the car's GPS. Then she turned up the volume on the music just slightly, allowing the Eagles' *Hotel California* to numb her mind for a while. Funny how the final line of that song hit her...that "checking out" didn't mean freedom. From what she'd seen in movies about the mafia, checking out meant dying.

Josef snapped his cell phone closed and tossed it on his desk. He stood and walked over to the tall windows of his office. He straightened one of the braided satin tassels on the brocade curtains, remnants, as it were, from the Communist regime that had ruled Bulgaria for more than forty years. As he stared out over the snow-covered park across the street, he let out a low, furious grumble. How could Evgenia let Saunders get away? *I should have known not to trust a woman.*

It was early Saturday morning in Sofia. The weekend cleaning staff would show up soon, but for now he was alone. Josef liked to be in his office before the workers, and during the week, he would stay until the last one left each day. His employees considered him dedicated and hard-working, but, no, it was simply to ensure that no one could ever access any computer or file that would connect him to any of his *personal* business interests.

He walked across the thick Persian rug to where he kept his vodka and poured a glass. Should he contact Nikos and put him in charge instead? No, he decided quickly; despite the current situation, Evgenia was far more experienced and had the hardened heart necessary to complete the tasks assigned. Nikos was loyal, but Josef wasn't sure he had the stomach for the tough stuff — assassination orders — yet.

In time, though, Josef felt his young protégé would be ready for bigger and more important responsibilities within the family business. Someday his son would be his successor. As much as he relied on Evgenia, he certainly wasn't going to put her in charge. She knew quite well that her job was to do as she was told, and she knew the consequences if she failed him.

As Josef returned to his desk and sat in the overstuffed Italian leather chair, he decided to let things play out for a day or so. Evgenia had already begun trying to redeem herself, informing him that she'd tracked Saunders, and he was traveling toward Portland. His destination was not yet known, but Evgenia was investigating likely possibilities. Josef had also sent another Bulgarian associate, Grigor Matveyev, to the US to work with her and Nikos to find out more about the woman. This Carolina Lopez was now part of their little "family issue." Josef thought for a moment. He could at least let the Brit know that he was aware he'd left Bainbridge Island with his pretty neighbor.

Josef smiled as he composed his text, knowing the impact it would have on Saunders's psyche and sense of security. While the purpose of the message was to keep the man aware of his obligation to stay silent, Josef couldn't help his grin. He so thoroughly enjoyed frightening his prey.

Tristan woke with a start as the car slowed. Quickly sitting back up, he glanced around as they pulled into a Pilot gas station at a busy intersection just off the highway. He glanced at his watch: a few minutes after eight p.m.; he'd obviously slept well.

"Where are we?"

"Southside of Salem." Cari unbuckled her seatbelt as she spoke. She didn't smile or look at him as she shut off the car, and her voice was stiff, simply informational. "We need gas. Can you take care of paying? You just stay in the car; they pump the gas for you in Oregon. I've got to go to the bathroom."

He rubbed his hand through his hair vigorously in an attempt to wake up. "Um, yes, of course. Go ahead. I'll go inside after you come back out."

Without another word or glance, Cari walked with determination toward the small store. Tristan got out and moved to the driver's seat, cash in hand to pay the attendant. His primary thought was of the caffeine his body desperately needed.

Within minutes, Ethan's car was once again ready for the road. Cari came back with a few Diet Cokes and a sandwich. She stood outside the car, unwrapped her food, and took a few bites. She made little eye contact with Tristan. Something was wrong.

Before going into the store, Tristan grabbed his phone as well as the BlackBerry. He smiled at Cari when he caught her glancing his way. "Be right back."

After cleaning his hands as thoroughly as possible in the wash-
room, Tristan purchased a small sandwich and a hot, if not acidic,
cup of coffee. He sat at a small booth for a moment to check his
messages in private. Sure enough...

Where you go, Dr. Saunders, that you drive far from sister's
home? My associates watch you all times. Remember that your
silence is what keep family and pretty Carolina Lopez safe.

Tristan cursed under his breath. How did Aleynekov know? How
were his associates aware of where they wer— *God! I'm an idiot!*
Tristan grabbed his purchases and ran out of the store.

But where was Ethan's car? And where the hell was Cari?

Chapter 12

Cari pulled into a parking space by the little restaurant two driveways down from the gas station. An orange neon sign proclaiming "Jami's Fried Chicken — Voted Best in Oregon" flashed in the building's window, and a distinct, oily scent made its way through the vents of the car. She laid her head against the back of her hands as they rested on the steering wheel, and she began to sob.

She'd never felt so lost. Her life had been normal: going to work, keeping her apartment clean, calling and visiting her dad, teaching courses, and writing her dissertation. She had little to no social life, planning for plenty of time in her post-dissertation future to entertain the possibilities of falling in love and getting married. But now? Who knew what the next hour would bring, let alone the next year or two.

Fear still told her to drive and drive and drive; the farther she could get from Tristan Saunders, the safer she'd be. But her heart had pulled her into the restaurant parking space, the car somewhat hidden behind shrubs but with a clear view of the gas station. She watched for Tristan, still unsure whether she could actually abandon him.

But then it occurred to her: all of his belongings, including his passport, were in the trunk. She couldn't be this heartless. Tristan would have no way to get home to England without proper ID. She had to go back, let him have Ethan's car; she could catch a bus or something and go somewhere that no one would find her. Or maybe she could just wait here until Mark could come get her.

Cari looked out over the steering wheel. She watched as Tristan hastily dumped a bag and drink into the trash can and began to scan the gas station's parking lot. Growing more frantic, he ran one hand through his hair and punched numbers into his cell. He was either pissed as hell or in full panic mode; between her doubts about him and his distance from her, Cari couldn't tell which. As her phone began to buzz beside her, she figured out who he was calling. A heartless person would have let it go to voicemail, a scared person would have thrown the cell out the window, but the brave person in her answered on the second ring.

"Hello, Tristan."

"God, Cari! Where are you?" His voice was full of panic. "Are you all right? Just tell me you're all right! Please, God, tell me you're all right!" He sounded more frightened than she was.

"Tristan, calm down. I'm fine. I just...I just needed to thi—"

"Where are you?" he interrupted, terror in his voice. "God, Cari, you can't be out on your own. They're tracking us! Christ, Cari, Aleynekov knows we've left the island!" He paused long enough to draw a deep and ragged breath. "Just come back, Cari. Please, please, just come back to me!"

Her heart dropped to her stomach. They hadn't escaped at all.

Cari opened the car door, phone still to her ear, and got out. "Tristan, I'm right here. Look to your left. I'm in front of the little restaurant with the yellow sign."

His head jerked her way, and he broke into a staggering run, his limp suddenly pronounced as he struggled across the two parking lots. She met him at the other corner of the restaurant, ready to talk, ask the questions she needed answers to. But then he surprised her.

"You're safe. They didn't take you," he said as he threw his arms around her and pulled her into a nearly suffocating embrace. He buried his head in her shoulder, his breathing erratic and his body shaking.

Cari wrapped her arms lightly around him, not knowing what else to do.

"Oh, God, Cari, I thought they'd taken you...I thought they'd taken you."

Cari Lopez had wondered whether Tristan was one of the good guys. Now she had her answer. "I'm fine," she whispered, rubbing her hands gently up and down his back. "I just got scared, that's all."

He faltered a bit, and they separated. He dropped hard to the curb and extended his right leg, his breathing still heavy. He wiped his eyes with the back of one hand and reached for her to sit beside him with the other.

Cari crouched, her knees pulled up to her chin, and looked sideways at him. He was broken, hurting. Without hesitating, she put her arm across his back and leaned her head on his shoulder for a moment. They sat in silence as he regained his composure.

"I'm sorry I scared you," she said softly. "All this stuff—and what you said about 'being bought'—it's just so unreal. I wasn't sure for a while if I was willing to take on all this danger with you." It was all she could offer. She'd never imagined that he'd interpret her hasty departure as anything other than her ditching him. Had he thought she'd been kidnapped? Cari shuddered.

"I…I checked my BlackBerry," he began, his body slumped and his head down. "I got a text from Aleynekov. He knows we're not at Gemma's anymore."

"But what would make him suspect you didn't just get on a plane or something? How does he know I'm with you?"

"He said he knows we're heading south, that I'm in a car. He mentioned you by name, Cari. By name! He knows who you are now." Tristan ran his hand across the back of his neck and turned to look at her, his eyes boring into hers. "I think he's tracking the GPS in Ethan's car. We've got to dismantle it somehow."

"God, Tristan, how do these people do this?" Cari shifted and sat on the sidewalk now. She found she was shivering, but not because of the temperature. She rubbed her arms with her hands. "How did they know we'd be in Ethan's car?"

"I don't know; they probably had already been tracking him and Gemma before my arrival. They're smart, Cari. We can't underestimate them." He stood and limped over to Ethan's car, and Cari followed. "Would you open the hood, please?"

Cari unlocked the car and did as he asked. She had no idea what they were looking for, and it soon became apparent that Tristan didn't either. As they stared, like idiots really, at the various engine parts, a middle-aged man in a plaid shirt, faded jeans, and a Texas Rangers baseball cap called over to them.

"You all havin' trouble?"

Tristan looked up and evidently decided to take a risk. "You don't happen to know how to disengage a GPS, do you?"

"What's the matter, it ain't workin' for you?"

Cari shrugged. "It's sending us funny information," she said, eyes wide. "Do you know what we can do to dismantle it?"

"Well, no, but it can't be too hard. Lemme have a look-see." After examining the GPS, as well as the engine, he removed his cap and scratched his head. "Have y'all just tried turning the thing off?"

Tristan stood beside the man and shook his head. "Is it not just something that can be unplugged or removed?"

"Nope. Cars these days are all computerized, you know? All them wires and parts are interconnected." He smiled up at Tristan. "Outside of taking a hammer to the thing, I think your best bet is to just turn it off until you can get to a dealer."

Although momentarily tempting, Cari knew smashing it was probably not an option. They needed the car to continue functioning. Tristan thanked the man, shook his hand, and gave him twenty dollars for his help. The man hemmed and hawed about how it was nothing. They waved to him as he entered the restaurant and finally faced each other again.

"So…I guess we keep the GPS off and take our chances," Cari said with a sigh.

Tristan waited for her to look up at him. "I know I'm putting you at risk by staying with you, but I fear you're at greater risk if we separate. There's no fixing the situation until we find out how Aleynekov knows we're not on the island." He paused, taking a deep breath. "Are you okay? Am I all right to keep traveling with you?"

Tristan's gray eyes were radiant. He could have asked her to lick the pavement at that moment and she would have done it, no questions asked. All the doubts she'd had about him were gone. Her fears remained, but they were about the people threatening them, not Tristan.

Cari gave him a weak smile. "Yeah. I'm good. I still have questions, and I'm going to want you to answer them as much as you can, but, yeah, I'm okay for now. How about I drive again?" She glanced at his knee. He was putting most of his weight on his left leg.

"You don't mind?" He winced.

She could tell he wasn't physically up to maneuvering the gas and brake pedals with his knee obviously sore. "No, no, not at all. Besides, next stop should be Canyonville. Are you ready to go?"

He hesitated and gave her a small smile. "Might I trouble you to go back to the petrol station again? I seem to have discarded my dinner and coffee in my earlier panic."

"Oh, God. I'm sorry! Yes, of course. But let me treat this time since I caused all this trouble." Cari closed the hood, and they got back inside the car.

As they buckled their seatbelts, Tristan reached across and held her hand for a moment. "You, Cari, are no trouble at all. I'm just so very relieved that you're all right."

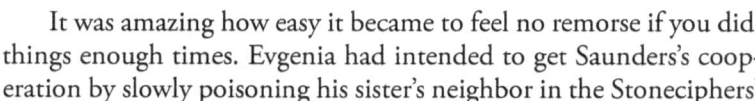

It was amazing how easy it became to feel no remorse if you did things enough times. Evgenia had intended to get Saunders's cooperation by slowly poisoning his sister's neighbor in the Stonecipers' apartment as he was forced to watch, then dispose of her hapless Russian suitor later, but her plans had changed.

When she'd discovered, two hours earlier, that Saunders and Lopez had escaped, she was furious. Her job had suddenly become one of tracking rather than simply watching. Luckily that was a task she could take care of before returning to Ben's apartment. Soon enough, she'd know where they were. But she still had the immigrant to deal with, so she jumped immediately into the second act of the night's performance.

"You haves vodka in 'partment, da?" Evgenia let her Bulgarian accent return.

Rudy's smile blossomed as he nodded; he seemed to believe she'd forgiven him.

"Forget missink care. We staying here, da? Why not we go haves drink?" Evgenia approached him with swaying hips and a sensuous smile. "I likes you, Rudy. I wants getting to know you better."

She linked her arm in his, and they headed to his studio apartment, attached to the management office. This would only take an hour, maybe less.

Ben woke up, and it took him a minute to focus on the clock radio beside the bed. It was eleven thirty, but he couldn't tell if that was a.m. or p.m. A glance toward the still-dark window let him know he'd slept soundly for a few hours. He rolled over and found Delilah snuggling the pillow beside him, fast asleep. He also realized his head was banging—he never got hangovers! What was up with this shit? He padded over to the bathroom for some much needed Advil. When he returned to bed, he wrapped his arm around Delilah's waist and fell back to sleep.

As Cari steered Ethan's car back onto the highway, Tristan couldn't help but hate the fact that his companion was still driving after all these hours.

"You look tired, Cari," he said. "Are you sure you don't want me to drive so you can get some rest?"

"No, I'm okay," she responded—and then yawned. They both laughed. "All right, co-pilot. Keep me awake! How about we play that game we started last night?"

"Game?"

"You know, um, what did you call it? Lightning something?"

"Oh!" Tristan smiled. "Lightning fill in the blank. Do you want to start, then?"

"Sure. And we can ask anything, right?"

Tristan wasn't quite ready to answer *any* question, but nodded anyway, his willingness to trust her superseding his fear. Inappropriate questions weren't her style.

"Okay. This is something I always ask my students on an information sheet at the beginning of each semester. Just like I tell them, I'm not looking for you to reveal anything illegal or immoral."

Now she had him worried. Perhaps he was wrong to trust her after all.

"Tell me something about yourself that a stranger wouldn't know unless you told them." She took a deep breath and exhaled loudly.

He gave her a sideways look. "Now I understand the preface about 'nothing illegal or immoral.' Have you gotten responses from your students that required that caveat?"

"Oh, yes. And believe me, you don't want to know what some American college students are doing behind the closed doors of their dorms!"

"I can only imagine." Tristan looked ahead at the darkness. The highway was busy with what seemed to be state-to-state travelers rather than larger trucks. He'd spotted a number of California license plates whizzing by as Cari maintained a speed just a bit above the limit. "Something about me, hmm?" He smirked. "You'd better be thinking of *your* response to that one because I'll be asking you the same thing in a moment."

"I already know my answer. I have several to offer; I have to do this with my students so they're less afraid to respond honestly."

"Right. Thanks for adding to the pressure," he scoffed. "All right, here's a simple one: I'm a fiend for M&Ms."

"What? What does that mean?" she asked with a laugh.

"I love M&Ms, both plain and peanut, and whenever I worked in the London office, I'd steal them from my colleague's candy dish. She hasn't a clue as to why her supply gets depleted so quickly."

"You thief!"

"I know, I know. But I would also occasionally leave a replacement bag in her desk drawer — no note or anything. Then I'd watch her reaction as she discovered it. I'm afraid she thinks she's gone bonkers, finding M&Ms missing one day and replaced the next. Poor woman. I do feel bad, but it's really quite humorous to watch her."

Cari laughed heartily, and it warmed Tristan to provide an escape from their worries, even if only for a short while.

"All right. Your turn," he challenged.

"Well, my revelations are much more boring," she began. "There are three things I always tell my students to spark their imagination. First is that my uncle has been in three Olympic games; he medaled once too. Won a silver."

"Really? What sport?"

"Luge. And let me tell you, that is one scary sport to watch in person. It's like watching a race car go by, but it's a human body with no protection other than a helmet and a skimpy sled. And you only get to see a split second of it — they go by that fast."

"Interesting. And the other two?"

"You want two freebies, eh? You've got to give me one more first, pal."

"All right. And this one does not include any thievery or other blatant disregard of the law." Tristan paused and lowered his voice as he continued. "I like to relax by playing music." This was something private he didn't reveal to just anyone. But, for whatever reason, he wanted Cari to know.

"And how do you do this?" she asked in barely a whisper.

"I play the violin. My parents were both very accomplished musicians, so they made Gemma and me take all sorts of music lessons from a very young age — violin, harpsichord, piano, and even electric guitar in my teen years. Gemma is quite talented playing the classics, but I prefer to come up with my own creations. I just get lost in the music and let it guide my hands. It's invigorating and relaxing all at the same time."

"Wow. I always wished I could do something artistic," Cari mused. "My parents must have wanted a boy because I was signed up for soccer when I was three and softball when I was seven. I even learned to play lacrosse in high school. I could handle any kind of sport, but I probably caused many parents and classmates permanent ear damage when I sang 'Tomorrow' from *Annie* one year."

Tristan choked back a laugh. "And when was this?"

"Fourth grade, I think. I'm evidently tone-deaf because I thought I'd belted out the best rendition of that song this side of Broadway, but when I asked my parents if I could try out for the next school musical, I found myself on a county-wide soccer team that had practice every other day. They made sure I never got a microphone in front of my mouth ever again. Gee...now you've gotten an extra for free!"

"Well, I haven't heard the two you were going to share yet," Tristan reminded.

"Fair enough. I'll spill, given how much you made me laugh with your M&M fetish," she replied. "The other two things I tell my students are that I'm allergic to strawberries, and I got engaged at the top of the Eiffel Tower."

Engaged? Cari had no ring on her hand...but she was engaged?

Chapter 13

"Mark? A car just pulled up. I think it's Cari's friends." Ann backed away from the window overlooking the parking lot.

Mark came down the stairs and met her at the front door. They walked out onto the porch and down the brick pathway that led around to the small parking area beside the house. He took her hand, as usual, and they watched a lithe, dark-haired woman in a flowered sundress get out of the passenger side of the convertible sedan. A tall, thin man with close-cut strawberry-blond hair got out of the driver's side.

"Are you Mark?" the woman asked in a raspy British accent as she extended her hand. "And Ann, right? I'm Gemma Stonecipher, and this is my husband, Ethan."

The men exchanged handshakes, and Gemma pulled Ann into a hug with a quick "Lovely to meet you." Ann had been around plenty of women who would hug you while planning your demise, but Gemma was the real deal, and Ann liked her immediately.

"I'm not quite sure why we're here, but thank you anyway for your willingness to accommodate us on such short notice," Ethan said grimly. "Tristan and Cari are driving my car, and they should be here within the hour—if they don't have to make any unexpected stops."

"So there *is* something wrong?" Mark asked. "I felt it as I talked to Cari, but she didn't say much. What can you tell us?"

"It has something to do with Bulgaria and the work Tristan did there," Ethan replied. "He's evidently gotten somebody mad enough to threaten him while he's visiting here."

"Jeez. What does he do that he was in Bulgaria?" Mark asked with raised eyebrows.

Ann stepped forward, smiling, before Ethan could respond. "How about we head inside? We can talk more in a minute." She turned toward Gemma. "So you were traveling up from California?" The two women headed toward the inn's front porch.

"Come, let's get your things." Mark stood by Ethan as he unlocked the trunk, and soon they were lugging three suitcases up the steps as Ann held open the door. "We'll meet in the living room in a minute," Mark said as he winked at Ann.

They entered the foyer, and Mark led Ethan up the grand staircase to the second floor as Gemma followed Ann through the large and (Ann hoped) welcoming living area to the kitchen. She glanced back to see the woman taking in everything; this place was Ann's pride and joy, and if her guest's wide smile was any indication, it seemed she was making a good impression.

In the kitchen Ann had laid out a tray with fruit, cheese, and a variety of crackers. Next to that on the island counter, she'd placed wine glasses, tumblers, and coffee mugs.

"Can I get you and Ethan something to drink? I have both red and white wine from a local winery, soft drinks, coffee or tea…oh, and juice if you'd like."

"Ah, after being in a car all day, I think I'd fancy a nice glass of white wine, if that's all right?" Gemma's eyes lit up; if she was tired, she surely wasn't showing it.

"Pinot grigio or chardonnay?"

"Chardonnay sounds delightful, thank you."

"And for Ethan? I've got some bottled beer too; sorry, I forgot to mention that."

"That may be just what he'd like. But let me wait a moment and ask him."

"Sounds good." Ann poured the chardonnay for Gemma and some pinot grigio for herself. "I can have Mark get something for the two of them when they come back down."

Ann added delicate charms around the stems of their wine glasses to tell them apart. Without saying a word, Gemma took both glasses as Ann lifted the tray, and the two women headed back into the living area.

"Have you done all the décor?" Gemma asked as she placed Ann's wine glass on a coaster. She moved slowly around the room with her glass, taking time to study the framed artwork, furniture, and window treatments.

"Yes. Most of it's new, but I've tried to keep with the style of when the home was built, just after World War I."

"It's lovely, just lovely," Gemma cooed. "Looks like you've added touches from different decades as well, though, haven't you!" she said. "Ethan will love this." She gestured toward some nineteen fifties memorabilia in a large glass shadowbox on the side wall.

"Come, have a seat," Ann said as she tossed off her flats and curled up on one of the overstuffed chairs to the left of the fireplace. Gemma pulled one leg up under her as she sat on end of the sofa closest to Ann.

"...took nearly a year. You wouldn't believe the mess the original electricians left when the house was built. It's amazing this place didn't burn down long ago," Mark was saying as he and Ethan walked into the living room. "Hey, hon, beers cold?"

"Yeah. I didn't get you two anything, I'm sor—"

"Oh, no, no, Ann. I'll get them! Come on, Ethan, I'll show you the kitchen. You and Gemma can have free rein of the house while you're here..." The two men vanished around the corner and through the kitchen door.

Ann turned to Gemma and they were quiet for an awkward moment. "I didn't talk to Cari, but I know Mark's really worried. She's your neighbor, right?"

With that, Gemma perked up. "Yes. I think she moved in just a month or so before we did. It's such a relief to have someone so quiet living next door. My brother—he's just arrived from London—he's quiet too. Did she happen to mention him?" Gemma asked hesitantly, unable to resist. "You know, how they're getting on?" Her eyes sparkled and she leaned forward, awaiting Ann's response.

"Nothing more than that she was traveling with him from the island and the four of you needed to meet here. We were hoping you'd know more. Care to fill us in on what's going on?"

Just then Ethan and Mark reappeared. Ethan took a seat next to his wife on the sofa, and Mark dropped into the chair opposite the fireplace. "I'm sure they'll have a lot to tell when they get here," Ethan offered. "So far all I've gotten from Tristan is cryptic information about how the car accident that landed him in a hospital in Bulgaria wasn't an accident and the two of them — and Gemma and I — are in some sort of trouble."

"Cari sounded scared as hell even though she was trying not to let on," Mark noted.

"Tristan didn't sound much better," Ethan added. He then explained what they'd initially been told about his Tristan's car accident months earlier.

"We were glad when he decided to come stay with us on extended holiday," Gemma said. "I thought it would do him some good, help him recover before returning to work." She glanced over at Ethan as she spoke. Then she turned to Mark. "We had no idea that he was, or is, in any kind of trouble. And now Cari too? I'd wanted them to meet, given all they have in common, but certainly not like this!"

"Well," Ann offered encouragingly, "there's no use us worrying until we know what's going on. And that won't happen until they get here. For now," she said with a smile, "I want to get to know you two. How do you know Cari?"

Gemma launched into a story, and after a few anecdotes about Cari's propensity for sports and Tristan's shyness, the air felt much lighter around them. Ann thought she could see why Gemma had wanted to match her brother with Cari; they did seem to have similar interests.

According to Gemma, Cari had never really had a long-term relationship, partly because the guys she'd gone out with were easily intimidated by her intelligence and drive. Not many twenty-seven-year-olds were completing their PhDs in accounting. If Tristan was all Gemma made him out to be, he could very well be the perfect match for her.

"How long have you been married?" Ann asked, changing the subject after refreshing their glasses of wine.

"It was four years in February."

"Really? Us too! What day?"

"The twenty-second."

Mark let out a laugh. "You're kidding. What time of day? I need to know how many hours apart our weddings took place."

"You're joking!" Gemma giggled. "That's amazing! What's the likelihood of that? We were married at one o'clock in St. Louis."

"No way!" Mark continued to roar. He calculated mentally for a moment. "Given the time difference, we got married at the same time!"

"Well, this is meant to be," Gemma chirped as she raised her glass. "Maybe Tristan and Cari would like that date as well. You know, if my matchmaking works out…" She winked at Ann and smiled, reaching across the end table between them to clink glasses in a silent toast.

"How did you two meet?" Ann asked.

"We met in Spain five years ago," Gemma began. "We were both taking the same 'summer abroad' course on art history." She ran her hand up and down Ethan's leg, patting it occasionally. "It consisted of daily visits to museums. Whereas I could grasp the artist's mood and use of color and shadows, Ethan understood the historical aspects of the paintings and the events that inspired them. We started walking together on the tours, and in the evenings we'd share our very different notes." She paused and smiled at her husband. "We both earned As in the course, and he proposed before we left Madrid."

"Enough mush," Ethan said, giving Gemma a quick kiss on her forehead before turning to Mark. "What's your story?"

"I was a stalker," Mark offered with a shrug, and they all laughed. Ann smiled, shaking her head with a "not really" look at Gemma. Mark loved telling their story, so she always let him.

Mark took a swig of beer and winked at his wife. "This lovely woman is an honest to goodness beauty queen. We both attended the University of Oregon but didn't know each other. When the Miss Oregon pageant was held on the university's campus, I got a job as one of the security guards." He smiled at Ethan. "Hey, who was I to turn down the opportunity to protect a bunch of gorgeous women in bathing suits?" He chuckled and gave Ann a nod.

"Well, as soon as I spotted Ann, I knew she was the girl for me. And she was more than just incredibly beautiful. She was a double major in interior architecture and mechanical engineering. Damn smart, she was. So…I made sure I was stationed wherever I knew she was most likely to be. I got to talk to her a few times, and we hit it off pretty good."

"A charmer is what he was!" Ann added.

"Anyway, Ann didn't win Miss Oregon. She came in third and was totally robbed, I'm tellin' you."

"But I walked away with more flowers than the winner did that night," Ann added. "Mark gave me three dozen roses at the end of the competition, and when I went back to the dressing room to change, there were nine dozen — yes, nine dozen *more* — waiting for me."

"I told her a dozen wasn't nearly enough, but maybe a *dozen* dozen might convince her to go out with me."

"And I did, of course. I'd been hoping he'd ask me. Mark was amazing and clever and smart and handsome and funny and romantic—"

"And I haven't changed a bit," he added, raising his beer and laughing.

"Ah, but you have, my dear. You've gotten even better." Ann turned to Gemma and Ethan. "If it weren't for his daily encouragement, unquestioning faith in me, and lots of hard work, this wouldn't have come to be." She gestured to the room around them. "He's helped me every night and every weekend, even though he's working full time and coaching sports year-round! This has totally been a joint effort."

"Here's to the Canyon Creek Bed and Breakfast, then!" a voice called from the entry hall.

"Hairy Cari!" Mark jumped up, placed his beer on the table, and hustled toward his cousin.

"Sparky Marky!" Cari responded as she held out her arms.

He pulled her up into a hug and spun her around. "God, it's good to see you, baby!"

"You too, Mark."

Behind her appeared a tall, attractive man carrying two duffle bags. He placed them at his side and extended his hand to Mark.

"Tristan!" Gemma squealed, and with quicker-than-lightning moves, she was in his arms.

"The gang's all here, it seems," Ethan said with a shrug and a smile.

Ann followed Ethan to join the others and exchange handshakes and hugs. Then she turned her attention to getting their newest arrivals much needed drinks. Beverages in hand, the party meandered upstairs to find their rooms. The bed and breakfast had been the home of a wealthy doctor with many children. There were seven bedrooms: two on the first floor that had been made into an owner's suite, four on the second floor, and one large dormer room with a private balcony on the third floor.

Mark and Ann directed Gemma and Ethan one of the larger rooms on the second floor. The two smallest rooms shared a bathroom, and Cari would sleep in one of those. Tristan would take the room on the third floor. Once everyone had seen the various rooms and their adjoining bathrooms, Tristan turned to Ethan and whispered something.

"Don't worry, Tristan, we'll work it out," Ethan responded.

When Ann gave them a questioning look, Tristan sighed. "I don't want Cari staying by herself." Mark raised an eyebrow, and Tristan immediately put his hand up. "No, I'm not suggesting she and I share a room. I just don't want her staying alone."

Ann watched Cari. She seemed to agree with Tristan and stood almost stoically by his side, her face full of worry.

Gemma and Tristan exchanged glances, and she nodded. "Cari? How about the two of us take the room with the two beds?" Gemma asked. "It'll be grand. Reminds me of my schoolgirl days having a friend for an overnight stay! I'm sure Ethan can live without me for a night or two, right, love?" She turned toward Tristan, keeping her tone light. "That would work, wouldn't it!"

Tristan nodded, his lips pursed. Ann decided she, and the rest of the group, needed to know what was going on — immediately. Once they had the bags appropriately delivered, they'd all return to the living room to get caught up. Ann intended to start the conversation once again, this time with a question about what had put the inn's visitors on the run.

Chapter 14

The six soon reassembled in the Stoddards' living room. Tristan shared the sofa with Gemma and Ethan, and Cari now sat where Mark had been. When Mark returned from the kitchen with drinks for the newcomers, he dropped to the floor at Ann's feet. Cari held her glass of wine in both hands, still too overwhelmed by the day's events to drink much of it. She listened to the voices swirling around her.

"I'm hoping to have a handle on all of this in the next day or so," Tristan said. "I'm sorry I've dragged everyone into this; I just couldn't risk staying where we were. Aleynekov has someone watching me. That's certain. But whether we've been tracked here is anyone's guess until I get another text from him."

"Have you tried texting him back?" Mark asked. "You know, try to get a sense of how much he knows?"

"Yes, well…" Tristan sighed. "Aleynekov is trickier than that. He's got my number, but I don't have his."

"But he's a bigwig in Bulgaria!" Gemma piped in. "Can't you —"

"Ring him at his office?" Tristan replied. "I've thought of that too. The soonest I can try is Sunday night our time, when it'll be Monday morning in Sofia. Otherwise, I have no way to reply. The number he sends from isn't shown." He looked at Mark and Ann. "I know we've put you in a spot, troubling you like this. I promise we'll be on our way as soon as we can — probably Monday afternoon if I'm able to convince Aleynekov I'm not doing anything to give him any concern."

Ann put her hand up, as if to protest. "We're glad we're able to help. Don't worry. You all should stay until you feel safe to head home."

Cari caught Ann's eye and smiled, feeling some relief at her generosity.

"So," Ethan asked Tristan, "you think my GPS has been tampered with? I've only had that car for a month."

"I don't know. I think it should stay off until we can have it checked and know it's safe, though," Tristan said. "After receiving that text message, I can't imagine how else he knew where we were going."

Mark assured them he had a friend who could look at it tomorrow, and Ethan nodded with a weak smile.

Tensions were high, of course, and even the drinks couldn't relieve them from...what? So many questions remained. Cari knew Tristan was not about to believe they were out of the woods yet; if Aleynekov had figured out this much, he certainly had the capability to do even more. The problem was, Tristan knew Aleynekov by sight, but it didn't appear that Aleynekov himself was following them. It seemed there was likely more than one person in the US keeping tabs on them.

As it neared one a.m., the group had put everything in the kitchen, and Ann said she'd take care of further cleanup in the morning. Mark and Ann said good night at the foot of the stairs as the guests went up to their rooms.

Gemma was quiet as she and Cari unpacked, but Cari caught a couple of sideways looks. She couldn't read what Gemma was thinking, but surely it could keep until morning. They left on the nightlight in the bathroom and each selected a bed. Gemma immediately snuggled under her covers.

Cari felt a little restless, though, and decided to check her cell phone for messages. If her father had called, she'd need to call back first thing in the morning to say she'd made an impromptu visit to Mark—something that wouldn't necessarily worry him. Sure enough, a text message was waiting...wait. A text? Her father wouldn't know how to do that, and even if he did, he'd have had to borrow a cell phone.

Tristan was impressed with the comfortable retreat Ann had created in the third-floor room. He'd put his duffle bag in the dresser, not willing to unpack it outside of basic toiletries. He now sat on the king-size bed, completely awake, nerves making him edgy. After taking a few seconds to see that there were no new messages on his

BlackBerry, he shut it off and pulled his cell phone out of his back pocket; suddenly Bold Tristan surfaced, and he began to type.

> Cari, it's Tristan. I wanted to be sure your cell phone accepted text messages. Please text me back so I know it does. Thanks.

Couldn't hurt to make sure of something like that. It was a practical gesture. When his phone vibrated, he found himself nervous, hoping the message was from Cari.

> Hi, Tristan. Yes, I can get and send texts. I hope you're able to get some sleep tonight. Gemma is already in Dreamland, but I'm still wide awake. My nerves are on edge after today, I guess.

Wide awake? Tristan was encouraged.

> I can't sleep either. Maybe it's due to my getting rest while you drove today. Thank you, by the way, for driving those last few hours when it was certainly my turn.

He waited, hoping she was awake enough to want to keep texting.

> I could tell your knee was hurting. I'll expect you to treat me to ice cream to make up for it.

How could he refuse? He smiled at the prospect.

> Wow. You drive for hours on end, and all you want in return is ice cream?

Her response was almost immediate.

> Well, I'll be ordering chocolate fudge and nuts on top, so it could get pricey! Besides, I got to drive the fanciest car I've ever been in. Buy me an ice cream, and we'll call it even.

In their exchange, something occurred to Tristan that he had to share.

> You are amazing! I've never met anyone like you.

Tristan's fingers typed before his mind could catch up. Then he accidentally hit "send" before he could explain. Part of him was embarrassed, but he also wondered what she'd make of what he wrote, even if it wasn't what he intended.

Tristan thought she was amazing? Because of what she put on ice cream?

Cari furrowed her brow. That came out of the blue, and so did the butterflies in her stomach as she reread Tristan's text. She'd turned off the table lamp, crawled into bed, and propped up the pillow to lean on when his first message had come in. Now she repositioned her pillow, glanced over at Gemma, who was fully asleep by the sound of her breathing, and read the message again. She tried to remember what she'd sent that would have prompted this mysterious comment. *Stay cool*, she reminded herself. *Don't assume he's flirting*. Though she had to admit that would be pretty nice. She thought for a moment before composing her next message. A nonchalant response would be good, just in case.

> Chocolate fudge and nuts are pretty normal
> ice cream toppings in the US.

It was agonizing to wait for another message. Was he regretting what he wrote? Was his response that complicated? Or was he not really wanting to text anymore? The butterflies were quickly turning into a flock of seagulls, flying aimlessly in her stomach.

> What I meant is that you have got to be the first person
> I've ever received text messages from
> who uses full words and proper punctuation.

Oh. He wasn't flirting after all. Cari blushed. Now she was glad she'd not sent anything coy.

> Wow. I hadn't thought about it, but you're right.
> I think you're the first person I've texted
> who does this too. Pretty sad, isn't it?

It was nice to have full-word texts; it kind of felt like they were actually talking.

> It's a relief. I hate getting texts with abbreviations
> I don't understand; and I'm too embarrassed
> to ask what the sender means.

They were kindred spirits on this one, Cari realized. She yawned as she typed her response. Gemma rolled onto her back, let out a deep sigh, and began to snore. Softly, but it was definitely a snore Cari heard.

> I'll make a solemn oath to you, Tristan.
> I'll never use abbreviations or code words when texting you.
> Oh, and did you know your sister snores?

Tristan laughed out loud at Cari's message, remembering sharing a room with Gemma on childhood vacations. She'd keep him up to all hours with the odd sounds she made.

> Ah, yes. You might want to try telling her
> in a deep British accent to roll over.
> If that doesn't work, we'll look for a store
> that sells ear plugs tomorrow.
> I know she can get pretty loud when she's exhausted.
> I hope you're able to get some rest!

Poor Cari. He'd forgotten that in addition to preventing her from being alone, sharing a room with Gemma would jeopardize the sleep she surely needed at this point. Two minutes later, another text arrived.

> It worked! It startled her a little, I think, but she's
> sleeping on her side now, facing away from me.
> Thanks! I owe YOU ice cream for that valuable bit of advice!
> I'm finally starting to feel tired, so I'm going to try
> to get some sleep. See you in the morning. Good night.

Tristan responded with a quick "good night," and after he silenced his phone, he held it for a few minutes. "See you in the morning," she'd noted, and he smiled. Being here, safe in this little town — at least for now — brought him the first relief he'd felt since Aleynekov's first text message arrived. He lay in his bed, facing the moonlit balcony, and sighed. He had plans for tomorrow that had nothing to do with Bulgaria: he'd buy Cari some ice cream, and if possible, get to know Mark. He needed to find out more about Cari's engagement.

"So, Ann," Mark said as he snuggled with his wife in bed, "what do you think of this guy Tristan?"

"Do you mean what do I think of him for Cari?"

Mark squirmed.

Ann smirked in the dark. "Let's just see what happens, hmm? At least Cari's here so you can be all protective of her!" She smiled up at Mark and tickled his chest. "But...I think Tristan's sister would like nothing better than to see a romance blossom between those two. How about you do some guy stuff tomorrow with Ethan and

Tristan, and I'll take Cari and Gemma with me. Let's get to know our guests a little better. Sound good?"

"You are the smartest person I know." He kissed her forehead. "Damn, am I glad I married you! Love you, hon."

"Love you more." She pulled his arm so it wrapped even tighter around her waist, nestled her head under his chin, and closed her eyes for a good night's sleep.

Chapter 15

en woke with a start. His alarm buzzed softly beside him, letting
him know it was six thirty in the morning. He gathered his
senses and realized it was Saturday. He hit the "off" button — hard.
As he turned over, however, Delilah sat up in bed, smirking beside
him with a pair of handcuffs dangling from her index finger.

"I, uh, found these just under my side of the bed." She smiled
devilishly. "Are you a cop, or are these simply for nocturnal escapades?"

Ben sat up beside her, bunching his pillow behind his lower
back. "Well, I hope to be in law enforcement someday. The CIA's
my goal, but, no, those are my *personal* property." He wiggled his
eyebrows at her, and she smiled, her ice blue eyes sparkling, even in
the dim morning light. "I like to — " he took them from her hand
" — practice my interrogation skills. Have you committed a crime? I
have ways to make you confess, you know."

"Well, maybe I *have* committed a crime. Maybe I murdered a
man last night. What would you do to get me to confess?" She lay
back down, twisting her hands into her hair.

Ben threw the covers back from his legs and quickly straddled
her, trapping her in the middle of the bed. "First, I'd cuff you. You
are my main suspect, you know. And I don't want you getting away
from me." As he spoke, he gently put one of the cuffs around her
right wrist. She playfully tried to wriggle free from him, but that
only increased his interest in their game. He slowly brought both her
wrists above her head, looped the cuffs around one of the wrought
iron headboard poles, and attached the other cuff to her left wrist.

He made sure they weren't too tight, of course, but she was definitely not getting away.

Over the next half hour, Ben teased and tickled, kissed and caressed Delilah's body as he questioned her. "Care to tell me where you were last night?" he asked as she squirmed under his touch.

She groaned slightly in pleasure. "I went to see an acquaintance. He was supposed to do something for me, and he didn't."

He began to nuzzle her neck. "And did you get angry?"

"Yes…yes. I was angry." Her hips swayed beneath him as he continued to move his hands on her.

"And what did you do to relieve that anger?" he asked, adding kisses across her shoulders.

She moaned pleasantly and moved toward his mouth. "You can't get me to confess that easily."

But Ben was having a very positive effect on her, of that he was certain. "So, you're not going to cooperate, eh? No problem. I've got other ways to get you to talk." Ben slipped off of her and repositioned himself beside her, but not before biting her gently. She inhaled deeply at his touch. "I'm going to need to search you. See if I can find evidence of a murder weapon."

He began at her neck, moving his hands in massaging motions slowly down her body, and then he stopped, a sly smile on his face. "I forgot to read you your rights, ma'am."

"Forget the damned rights. Don't stop." She lifted her hips slightly, urging him to continue.

"This is my interrogation," he said firmly. "I follow the law." He started to move his hands again as he looked down at her. "You have the right to remain silent," he stated authoritatively, then he leaned in and whispered, "but I'm really hoping you won't be." And without warning, he began to touch her in places he knew she wanted him to. "You got a murder weapon hidden somewhere on you?"

"I'm not telling," she gasped. "You'll have to search me to find out for sure."

He eased his massaging, and she opened her eyes, disappointed. "I'm still waiting for you to tell me what happened," he chided as he touched her more innocently.

"You're mean," she snarled as she writhed, trying to entice him.

Slowly, he resumed his teasing. "Now talk."

She moaned at his touch. "I don't remember what happened."

Ben moved down and began to kiss and blow on her skin. "I don't believe you." His teasing continued.

"Okay, okay!" she begged. "We went to his apartment..." Ben began massaging her more vigorously and kissing her again. "He poured glasses of vodka for both of us..." Her breathing quickened as Ben continued to tease her skin. "I put some window cleaner in his vodka...He didn't see me do it..."

"Window cleaner? What would make him drink that?"

"I was, um, pretty good at keeping him preoccupied...kind of like you're doing now, but without handcuffs. He said it tasted really bitter but he didn't know why. Then I promised him I'd keep going if he kept drinking."

"Very clever. What then?" He was on top of her once again. "Tell me everything."

She tried to lift herself up to kiss him, but he wouldn't let her. "He'd already swallowed most of his drink...so then I told him I'd poisoned him." She gasped as Ben nuzzled her neck. "I pointed a gun...I had a gun...and I...I made him write a suicide note in Russian..."

Ben stopped and looked at her. "Russian?"

"Um..."

She arched her back to make contact with him and her words came out in gasps, but he lifted up from her slightly. Her story was really intriguing at this point; he wanted her to finish describing this "murder" she'd committed.

"Yeah...he's Russian and I...I know Russian too...so...I made him write the note, said I'd kill his family if he didn't do what I said. And I made him drink a lot more...so when the police find him... it'll look like a suicide...There, I've confessed! Please, please..."

Ben closed his mouth on hers and made love to her, their bodies moving in harmony once again until they were both satisfied and exhausted.

"If you're not a mystery writer, you should be," Ben told her as he reached up with the handcuff key to release her wrists. "You did great coming up with that story so quickly."

Once again, this man had pleasured Evgenia beyond her dreams. He was amazing. She thought about what he'd revealed to her: that he wanted to be a CIA agent. If that happened, Josef would certainly find him useful in the future!

And how sweet that he felt she was clever enough to be a mystery writer. Evgenia smiled in spite of herself.

After more fun in the shower with Ben, she headed back to her apartment. They'd agreed to meet at the shooting range at ten. She had definite objectives to meet today, but would need to convince him to want to join her — without letting him know the true nature of her plans.

As soon as she got home, she turned on her computer. She had to check Saunders's location, hoping he wasn't yet aware of her ability to track him. While the program loaded, she packed a small bag with her usual items: dark clothing, a few grand in cash, two versions of her passport, various fake IDs and credit cards, two P-9 semi-automatic pistols, and plenty of ammunition. Evgenia had slipped the handcuffs from the morning's dalliances into her purse and added them now to her travel bag.

She checked the tracking program. Sure enough, they'd reached Portland, but then she looked at the time stamp on the location map. *Shit.* The satellite hadn't updated in more than twelve hours. Saunders was money-smart, not tech-smart, as far as she knew. Had he discovered how she was tracking him?

She certainly wasn't going to contact Bulgaria or any of her colleagues until she knew more. She'd just have to keep checking her laptop and watch for a satellite update. In the meantime, she'd be on the road. At least her contacts at the airport in Portland were sure that neither he nor the Lopez woman had left the country.

Personally, she was hoping he was still traveling with the little neighbor. Evgenia wanted to meet her in person, see if she was more than just a traveling companion. And if she was? God help her, this would be fun! Evgenia had some unfinished...business with Saunders, and ideas for revenge were beginning to swim in her head.

She arrived ahead of schedule, found a spot, and began shooting a few rounds. Her ribbed white tank top and skin-tight jeans seemed to cause a few of the other shooters to miss their targets. She loved the attention her body could attract.

"Hey, beautiful. Didja dump that loser from last night?"

She turned to find that lanky college kid known as Chameleon—Kevin Lamb. He eyed her like she was a piece of meat; she returned the stare to his body, and as she let her eyes linger on his crotch, she smirked.

"Actually, we spent all night and this morning in his bed. Thanks for asking!" She winked and smiled as he turned beet red and returned to firing, hitting someone else's target.

She'd finished a few rounds by the time Ben showed up, and College Boy was clearly and firmly put in his place when Evgenia kissed Ben deeply. This maneuver accomplished two goals: it got rid of Lamb and gave Ben the impression that she was definitely with him. Getting him to travel with her would be easy.

Ben took the space Lamb vacated, and the two spent the next forty-five minutes firing round after round. She glanced over occasionally, noting that he was probably nearly as good a shot as she was, and she complimented him often. She was glad she'd recommended him to Josef.

As they loaded up their gear and sat at a picnic table with some bottled water, she put on her giddy girl routine. "Hey, what's your name, anyway? I mean, I know just about every inch of you, and yet I never even asked your real name!" She giggled to add to the false euphoria.

"I'm Ben Pritchard. And I'm guessing your name isn't really Delilah, although I must admit that after last night, I think it suits you perfectly." He wriggled his eyebrows, and she dropped her eyes momentarily to look at her hands.

"I'm Jenny Allen. It's very, very nice to meet you, Ben," she said as she extended her hand.

He placed a lingering kiss on the back of her fingers. "The pleasure is…and was last night and this morning…*all* mine, I assure you." They gazed at each other flirtatiously, while internally she found the whole scene nauseating. Yeah, he was fantastic in bed, but Jenny wasn't looking for a boyfriend, just someone to help her find and eliminate Tristan Saunders.

"Hey!" She perked up, allowing her hand to remain in his. "Are you free today to do something totally unplanned?"

Ben sat up a little taller. "What do you have in mind?"

"Well…" She lingered and looked to the edge of the table shyly. "I thought maybe we could take a drive. Just, you know, go where the road takes us. My dad sent me birthday money to spend as I please so, whattaya say, Ben?" She let her smile consume her whole face. "Dare to be daring with me?" Then she dropped her voice and looked at him through her eyelashes. "And later, we'll find some nice hotel somewhere and…hmm…think of *some* way to spend the evening."

He continued to hold her hand and put his other on her cheek. "I'd like nothing better, Jenny, than to spend more time with you." He leaned forward and kissed her gently.

You know, if I were into this shit, he'd be a pretty good catch, Jenny thought as she kissed him back.

She admitted sheepishly that she'd hoped he'd say yes and already had a bag packed in the trunk of her car. They drove back to Ben's apartment, where he threw a few things into a sports bag, and soon they were headed out of town.

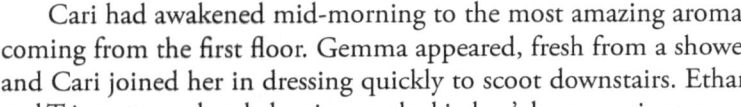

Cari had awakened mid-morning to the most amazing aromas coming from the first floor. Gemma appeared, fresh from a shower, and Cari joined her in dressing quickly to scoot downstairs. Ethan and Tristan were already leaning on the kitchen's large granite-topped island, sipping coffee and stealing pieces of fresh-cut fruit from a beautiful crystal bowl between them. Mark had his head in the fridge, while Ann gently flipped the thickest French toast Cari had ever seen.

"You find the cream cheese, hon? It's next to the parmesan on the top shelf." Ann never took her eyes off the long griddle straddling the stove top.

"Ah. Got it. Different brand this time. I was looking for the red package. My bad!" Mark pulled out two containers and began to put the contents into a large metal bowl on the counter next to Ann. Cari watched the duo moving about the kitchen in harmony.

"Anything I can do to help?" she and Gemma said at nearly the same time.

"No, no. Just help yourself to coffee, tea, juice, or ice water. If you don't see something, just ask!" Ann was a multitasker extraordinaire. Running a bed and breakfast was the perfect role for her.

"I've got yours ready, babe," Ethan announced before giving Gemma a quick peck on the lips. He handed her a steaming cup of tea, and she let out a little raspy squeal of delight as she took her first sip.

"This is wonderful!" She held her cup to her chin and closed her eyes for a moment.

Cari added creamer to her coffee and went to stand near Tristan. "Good morning," she said shyly.

"And good morning to you. Did you sleep well?" He winked and shot a glance toward Gemma.

"Perfectly!" she responded in a deep British accent, only loud enough for Tristan to hear. He smiled and raised his cup to hers.

The six of them soon sat around the beautiful antique dining room table. Ann had designed the eating area to have the one large table as well as four smaller, more intimate tables along the lace-covered windows. Cream cheese, apricot, and strawberry-stuffed French toast was presented on plates adorned with fresh orange curlicues, sprigs of parsley, and a sprinkling of confectioner's sugar.

Conversation was congenial, if sparse, as they ate. Toward the end of their breakfast, Ann spoke up. "Mark and I thought that today, perhaps, we'd make it a guys' day and a girls' day. I'm going to Roseburg for some groceries and maybe to putter around some of the shops up there, and I thought Cari and Gemma might join me?" She raised her eyebrows encouragingly, and Cari nodded eagerly. Happily, Gemma did the same.

"And I," added Mark, "have some things I wanted to get done around town. Thought you guys might enjoy walking a bit after your travels yesterday. What do you say? And if you're up for it, we can go to the school gym — shoot some hoops or whatever." He shrugged, glancing around the table.

"Personally, a good bit of exercise today is exactly what this knee could use," Tristan said.

Cari was glad he looked so at ease. She caught his eye, hoping to silently ask if he'd gotten any further messages from Aleynekov. She'd text him later if they weren't able to talk this morning. The last thing either of them wanted to do, she knew, was remind everyone why they'd all descended on the Canyon Creek Bed and Breakfast.

After helping with the dishes and cleaning the counters after breakfast, Cari refilled her coffee before returning upstairs for a shower. She hadn't had a chance to talk to Tristan, but if he was okay with her heading off with Ann and Gemma, she assumed they weren't in danger...for now.

An hour later, the three women pulled out of the parking lot in Ann's SUV, waving to the men as they left. This would be the first time in two days that she hadn't been with or near Tristan, Cari realized. She missed him as soon as they were out of the driveway, and it made her sad.

Spending the next few hours without Cari nearby worried Tristan. He wasn't certain, and neither was Ethan, that they weren't still being tracked even with the GPS disabled. He also hadn't checked his BlackBerry since last night and knew he needed to. Tristan wanted to live in relative normalcy for as long as possible, so every minute he postponed checking for messages was precious.

"All right, guys!" Mark approached Ethan and Tristan in the driveway and clapped them on the back. "Ready to walk to the hardware store? I've got some hinges on the basement door that need replacing, and this'll give me a chance to show you around our humble little town."

Ethan looked at Tristan, who nodded approvingly, and the three went back inside to get ready—and Tristan grabbed his cell phone, along with his wallet. A quick check of his BlackBerry revealed no new texts, and he turned it back off with a sigh of relief. Five minutes later the men were walking up the sloped side street next to the Canyon Creek Bed and Breakfast.

Canyonville's downtown was located along a single main road that paralleled the interstate. As they arrived, one block up a small hill, at Main Street, Tristan quickly scanned his surroundings: a small market, what looked like some city offices, and the Canyonville Community Center were all to their right, and a bank and a few small stores to the left. At the corner directly across from where they stood was Ken's Sidewalk Café, and to the left were Dennis's Hardware Store and Gordon's Pharmacy. It was quaint, really, how the stores were probably named for their owners. Farther to the right was Canyonville Elementary School, as well as what seemed to be additional small businesses located along side streets and down the road.

As they crossed Main Street and passed the café, he spotted a small marquee over the service window noting the various ice cream flavors served there. Good to know. More than knowing where he could fulfill a promise, Tristan needed to find out more about Cari.

"Can I ask you something?" Tristan decided to dive right in as he walked alongside Mark after leaving the hardware store, hinges purchased and bagged.

Mark looked over, awaiting Tristan's question.

"Cari mentioned something as we traveled here, and I was just curious as to what you knew about it."

"What's that?" Mark's demeanor remained open and friendly.

"She said she got engaged at the top of the Eiffel Tower, yet I didn't notice her wearing a ring." Tristan let his voice trail off, and he looked down as he finished.

Mark's reply surprised him: he laughed. "Oh, she got engaged all right," he said with a huge grin. "Top of the Eiffel Tower. I was there. It was quite the romantic moment too." His laughter continued.

"So," Tristan responded quietly. "That's that then." He looked at Ethan, who shrugged. He obviously had no idea either.

Mark looked over at his two companions, still smiling brightly. "Oh, sorry. I guess I'd better explain, huh?"

The men continued to walk, with Mark waving to people on the street who, in turn, responded with either a "Hey, Mark!" or "How's it going, Coach?" Then he signaled for them to cross another side street toward Canyonville Elementary School and turned up its driveway. "Come here. I want to show you something."

He opened a gate leading to the back of the school. Around the corner of the one-story brick building was a recreation area. A variety of slides and swings and climbing apparatus were positioned between a few large shade trees. In the middle was a tall metal structure...that looked like a miniature Eiffel Tower.

"Cari and her dad used to stay with my family for two weeks every summer," Mark began as he sat down on one of the benches at the edge of the play area. Ethan followed and sat down, but Tristan was too nervous and remained standing, hands in his pockets, kicking the sand lightly with his foot. "One of those summers, Cari fell in looooovvve." Mark patted his hand over his heart mockingly. "She was fourteen, and my friend Zack was fifteen." He paused to chuckle again. "She had it bad for him that summer. She was getting kind of pretty at that point, so it wasn't surprising that Zack took a liking to her too. I kept an eye on them, of course, but we did lots of things together: Zack and Cari along with me and my girlfriend. Nothing happened other than handholding under my watch, although I suspect he might have gotten a kiss or two. But on the last night before Cari headed back with her dad to Washington, she and Zack climbed to the top of the Eiffel Tower here, and he told her he loved her."

Mark snickered and scrubbed his jaw with his palm. "Later, as she and I walked back to my parents' house, I noticed she was wearing this ring on her left hand. I asked her about it, and she got all embarrassed, started to cry a little. She said he'd asked her to marry him in ten years, and he gave her a ring to seal the deal. Had a real diamond chip in it too."

"So what happened after that?" Ethan asked.

"Time goes by, you know?" Mark said. "Cari and Zack stayed in touch over that next school year, but it was just, you know, school stuff. Uncle Ronnie never knew—he'd have never approved of Cari being *engaged!* By the following summer, Zack was sixteen and dating a high school girl. Cari was hurt, but she and I hung out and went on adventures and, soon enough, she was over him. They were never going to last anyway. She was way too smart for him and, frankly, way too pretty once she hit eighteen. He married his high school sweetheart, has two kids, and owns a chain of surf shops in California. His mom still lives here, so I see him once in a while."

The men all smiled at the sweetness of the story. Mark lifted his head to Tristan, putting his hand across his forehead to shade his eyes. "How about you and Cari?"

"Well," he stammered, "we've only just met. Neither of us knew my sister was hoping we'd pair up. And we've hardly gotten off to a normal start, have we? Within a day of meeting her, I've got her literally running for her life."

They laughed uncomfortably, but Mark's voice turned serious. "She likes you. I can tell. And you're smart, focused, just like her."

Tristan shifted his feet in the sand and looked toward the trees over his companions' heads, suddenly feeling like an embarrassed schoolboy. "I don't know…She's a lovely girl, but I'm only visiting for a short time. I certainly don't want to assume anything," he admitted shyly. "The fact that she hasn't slapped me for putting her in this situation might be a positive sign, though, eh?" He laughed and ran his hand across the razor stubble he'd not shaved.

"Nothing would please me more," Ethan said. "Because that would mean Gemma was right and can stop trying to push you two together!"

"Hey," Mark said, "I've got one more errand to run and then we can hit the high school. I've got a key to the gym and weight room. Let's go."

Their walk to a larger grocery store a few blocks north was filled with talk of American sports (Ethan and Mark mostly), world business news (Ethan and Tristan mostly), and what kind of flowers to get for the dinner table tonight. Mark had bombarded Ann with all of those flowers years ago and he reported that every Saturday he bought flowers for their evening meal. Cari had told Tristan he'd like Mark. She was absolutely right.

As they neared the B&B once again on the way back from the grocer's, which housed the town's only florist, the men passed the Canyonville Community Center, a large gray building with arched windows along the sides and a glass front entryway. Signs posted on a framed corkboard next to the front doors noted nights reserved for bingo, karaoke, youth events, town meetings, and themed dances.

Noticing Ethan and Tristan's hesitation and a peek in the glass front door, Mark spoke up. "This is my weekend job," he explained, stopping in front of the building. "This other guy and I share DJ responsibilities when they have events involving music. Jeez, my first experience with this place was playing a stalk of corn in a kindergarten play."

Ethan and Tristan began to laugh.

"What? I was the tallest kid. And I still remember my one line." He stood still, put his cupped hand by his ear and said, "I can EAR you!" He smirked. "It was stupid, but my parents took, like, a hundred pictures. Even my dad had *his* first school dance in this old place. And, honestly, I don't think they've changed a thing—including the horrible sound system—in all those years."

Tristan could see the bed and breakfast next door and back a half-block. The community center extended back so far that the two buildings shared the same alley-like road behind them. In the space beside the community center and in front of the inn was a shaded courtyard with a simple fountain and lots of tall, stately trees. The sound of squirrels scampering and jumping across the high canopy was soothing.

"That was my first job too," Mark said. "Being the DJ for the middle school dances when I was seventeen. It was great." Then he dropped his voice to nearly a whisper. "The sound booth has a great little place to make out, under the soundboard. I must have taken, oh, ten different girls there between high school and college—before I met Ann, of course!"

"So, you'd be kissing girls while people were dancing right nearby?" Tristan didn't quite know what to think.

"No, no. The sound equipment is on this huge table behind Plexiglas and paneling, and the DJ side has this curtain thing so there was total privacy." He snickered. "I tried to get Ann to come under there with me when we were dating, but when she saw how gross the carpet was, she wanted nothing to do with it."

Before moving on, Mark pulled on the double doors to be sure they were locked from the previous night's seniors' meeting. He had keys to the place as one of the building's caretakers now. He said he didn't mind the work, though it only paid a pittance; often Ann would walk over and he'd arrange for a series of slow songs to play so he could escape to the dance floor with her.

Tristan looked at the corkboard again to see that the next dance was a week away. The three men turned from the sidewalk and went down a dozen steps to the inn's courtyard. As they passed the fountain, Tristan decided that if they were still here then, and the danger was past them, maybe he'd ask Cari to dance.

Chapter 16

"Cari," Gemma began from the middle of the back seat, "what do you think about weekday weddings?"

They'd just gotten on the highway to Roseburg. Cari sat sort of sideways in the front passenger's seat so she could face both Ann and Gemma.

"Um," she hesitated. *What kind of question is that?* "I guess they're good, you know, if you're going to a justice of the peace or something. Why?"

"No reason." Cari caught Gemma's glance toward Ann in the rearview mirror. Ann smirked but didn't say a word. "So, what are we shopping for, Ann?" Gemma asked next.

Ann sighed. "Well, some groceries for sure. I wanted your input on dinner for the next few nights."

"Oh, we're really putting you out, aren't we," Cari said.

"No, no, quite the contrary!" Ann quickly replied. "I love to cook; you know that! Honestly, I'd like some ideas for something new or different. When it's just Mark and me, I tend to keep the creativity to a minimum, especially when he's coaching this or that at night. Maybe you two have some favorite dishes we could make for the guys?" She winked at Cari.

"Well, that'll be up to Gemma," Cari replied. "She knows their tastes more than I would."

Gemma leaned forward and patted Cari's shoulder. "I've got some ideas for Tristan, don't you worry."

"Gemma!" Cari said, exasperated.

"What?" She leaned back in her seat, feigning innocence.

"I thought we'd go to some fabric stores too, if you don't mind." Ann raised her eyebrows as she glanced over. "I still need to finish two rooms."

"Love it!" Gemma said. "And you made the drapes in all the rooms, didn't you, Ann."

"Oh, God, are they that bad?"

"No! Just the opposite. You can't get those designs and fabrics ready-made from a store. You've got an amazing eye." Gemma was quiet for a moment. "I'm picturing tapestries as an option for wall hangings too, especially in the room Cari and I are sharing. Am I close?"

Ann nodded. "Yes! Thank you! I was thinking a pair of tapestries would work there, but I don't know, I guess I just needed a second opinion." She slapped the steering wheel. "Tapestries it is! Oh! And there's a huge store that resells estate stuff. You up for starting there?"

Cari looked at the others to see smiles all around. "This sounds like fun," she said as she settled into her seat for the drive.

As Ben packed a few things, Jenny checked her BlackBerry—still no update on Saunders's whereabouts. She'd just have to keep trying as they drove. She couldn't see any logical place to the east or west of Portland for him to go, so he was either there or had traveled farther south. With the highway providing a direct route to California, this seemed his likely course.

Ben offered to drive, but his Camaro, pimped as it was, didn't look ready for a high-speed chase, regardless of whether they were the pursuers or the pursued. Instead, they loaded his bag into the trunk of her BMW, and she let him drive the first shift. After droning on for ten minutes about its "bad-ass engine," he finally settled down, and they were able to talk.

"I've never done this before." Jenny blinked at Ben shyly. "I mean, spending the night with a stranger and then just taking off for the hell of it. I'm usually much more reserved." This was going to work like a charm.

He took her hand and raised it to his lips, once again giving a gentle kiss. "I like both sides of you. You've got a definite wild side, but you're sensitive too."

Sensitive, my ass! If you only knew... "I don't know...you just..." She looked down. "I like you, Ben. I trust you."

Jenny was laying it on thick, and Ben was buying every bit.

He lowered their still-clasped hands to rest on his thigh. "I'm glad. I believe in taking care of a woman. My dad taught me right. You can trust me, Jenny. I'll take good care of you."

"Thanks," she whispered. Of course, if he didn't cooperate with what she had planned, it would be her taking care of him. She had a little concoction that would kill him before he knew he'd been poisoned.

"So...where do you want to go?" he asked, stroking the back of her hand with his thumb.

"Oh, let's just drive for a while. Once we get on I-5, we'll have options and can decide then." She hesitated and looked over to him. "Ever been to California?"

"You want to drive that far?"

She shrugged. If that's where Saunders had gone, then yes. "It was just a thought..."

Ben laughed. "What the hell! I'm game, I guess. Let's just drive as long as we want to, stop when we want to, and not plan a thing!"

She smiled lovingly at him. *Perfect.*

It was time to get down to business. They'd perused the massive warehouse of estate goods, and while Gemma was being good and not purchasing anything, she did like the pair of tapestries and the Persian rug Ann had found. With the SUV now loaded down in back, Ann had taken them to a small sandwich shop she loved.

"Did you know that Tristan has a PhD in the same area as you're studying, Cari?" Gemma asked as she forked a piece of fruit.

Cari seemed to choke for a second, took a drink of iced tea, and swallowed. "Uh. Yeah. Actually, he and I have talked a lot about my dissertation."

"Really..." she replied calmly. Her insides danced.

"He was really nice the other night," Cari continued. "He was probably exhausted and sore from his trip, and yet he was willing to help me come up with a new topic."

"Wait a minute," Ann interrupted. "New topic? Oh, God, Cari, you'd done so much work on that proposal!"

"Yeah, well, no means no." Cari sighed. "Besides, my heart wasn't in it anyway. But Tristan gave me some really interesting avenues to consider. And I would be working on it right now if it weren't for..."

"Well, I'm sure if Tristan said he'll help you, he will," Gemma offered. "He's had quite a lot of interesting adventures around Europe since joining Carson."

Quiet settled over the table. Gemma shivered, remembering what Tristan had endured at the hands of Aleynekov's men.

"How's his leg been?" she asked Cari.

"Getting better, I think. He's willing to give it some exercise, so that's a good sign. We went walking Thursday night."

Gemma exchanged a glance with Ann.

"So, have you two gotten to know each other, then?" Gemma asked. "He *is* a very eligible bachelor, you know. I think you two make a smart match."

"Gemma..." Cari sighed.

"What?" she asked. "I've known him all my life, and I've known you for the past three months. You're both intelligent, have similar interests, neither of you is dating anyone. Besides, I've seen how he looks at you."

"What?" Cari's face turned red.

Gemma put her hand over Cari's. "He likes you, silly girl. Can't you see that?"

"No," she protested. "He just has this insane guilt complex about Aleynekov and feels like he has to protect me."

"Well, true," Gemma conceded. "That would be Tristan's first reaction." She looked into Cari's eyes. "But I see more to it than that. He cares for your safety, yes, but I think it's because he's come to care for *you.*"

"Ann? Help?" Cari looked over at Ann.

"Sorry, Cari, I see it too," she said with a shrug. "I think you ought to see what could happen. You've been single for a few years now. Not saying that's a bad thing, I might add. You had a string of less-than-suitable dates for a while there. But I agree with Gemma. Tristan's the kind of guy you'd be perfect with."

Cari looked down at the uneaten crust of her sandwich, moving it around on her plate with a toothpick. "He lives in England! He's only visiting for a few weeks. Besides, I can't think of that right now."

"So when, Cari?" Ann asked. "Every time Mark and I ask if you're seeing someone, it's always some excuse or other to be alone. Yeah, he's from England, but don't just rule him out. I'll bet you've probably had some decent dating offers around Seattle and turned them down, am I right? Maybe even a professor or two at the university has had an eye on you."

"No."

Cari's answer seemed quick and pointed. Gemma raised her eyebrows, but Ann seemed to take no offense and continued.

"What about in your apartment complex? Anyone single there?"

"There's a sweet foreign guy," Cari offered, and she looked at Gemma with a smile. "But Rudy has big like for Mees Gemma," she added, laughing.

Gemma giggled too. Rudy was a sweet man but not Cari's type at all.

"All we're saying, Cari, is not to close the door on someone like Tristan," Ann reiterated. "At least for now, enjoy his company."

Gemma could see Cari considering their encouragement. The seed of interest had been planted anyway. She was pleased that Ann agreed with her too. Probably even Ethan and Mark believed a romance between Cari and Tristan was inevitable.

Josef was pleased when his American colleague picked up on the first ring. Good. "I will need to know whereabouts of Miss Lopez," he stated immediately.

Evgenia had been avoiding his calls and texts. There must be something wrong, and he did not have time for Tristan Saunders to be out from under his watchful eye.

"I don't keep up with my doctoral students' social lives, Aleynekov. Not my business."

"Ah, but it is your business now, my friend, because I say it is. You have access to personnel files, yes?"

"No. Why would I?"

"Because I need you to." Josef paused and then made sure the professor heard his calm exasperation over the phone. "Dr. Lassiter, you know how business works, yes? I expect you find information on Carolina Lopez, and I expect it before nine o'clock morning for you. I need to know where family live—all contact information she put on documents. I also need picture of woman. You understand, yes?"

"It's the weekend. How am I supposed to get into offices I don't have keys to?"

"You are smart man, Dr. Lassiter. I know you will do as I ask."

"Jeez. I'd be putting my ass on the line. I can get it for you Mond—"

"We are not negotiating, Dr. Lassiter. I have told you when you are to have this to me."

"Can I just ask how it is that a doctoral student in our program is suddenly a part of all of this? I know this woman…enough to know that she doesn't play games or get involved in things like this."

Interesting, Josef pondered. The American sounded frustrated. Perhaps he knew her better than he'd let on…or *wished* he knew her better. It didn't bode well for the professor, though, that he personally knew one of Aleynekov's newest targets.

"She is with Tristan Saunders, therefore she is involved. You find family information, Dr. Lassiter. I expect to hear from you soon. I won't ask twice."

Josef hung up before Lassiter could respond.

As they cruised the aisles of the grocery store, Gemma made dinner suggestions, and she and Ann discussed recipes for sauces and such. Cari's ability to make a killer mac and cheese from a box would add nothing constructive, so she kept quiet, nodding politely as the other two planned the next few nights' meals.

At one point, Cari told Gemma she'd be paying for the groceries and needed help distracting Ann when they got to the checkout. Gemma wanted to pitch in too, but Cari told her to wait; if they had to stay beyond Monday, they'd have to shop for more food anyway.

When they checked out, Ann protested, of course, but Cari reminded her it was either she pay for the food or they'd pay for their rooms. Ann began to argue but then she smiled, hugged Cari, said it still wasn't necessary, and finally let her pay.

On the way home, Caria had Gemma take the passenger seat and she sat in back, surrounded by grocery bags. The three had become fast friends over the course of the past few hours. Cari was especially pleased to have learned more about Gemma, and even more pleased that she and Ann got along so well.

"How did you like Ethan's car?" Gemma looked back toward Cari, all smiles and twinkling eyes.

"Wonderful. The Hummer is comfortable enough, but it's horrible on gas. Besides, it would have been, you know, pretty noticeable. Tristan did well, by the way, driving on the wrong side of the road." They all laughed at that.

"Ethan's still in shock that his boss allowed a client to give it to him."

Ann raised her eyebrows. "Ethan got a Lexus from a client? Was that in lieu of a bonus or something?"

"Yes," Gemma shifted so she could tell Cari the story as well. "Ethan's got a few international clients, and he makes sure their businesses are profitable. One of them is some Ukrainian man who runs a major company and lots of charitable foundations in his country. Just over a month ago, he had a fully loaded Lexus delivered to Ethan at work. His boss spoke to the Ukrainian and got talked into letting Ethan keep it." She giggled. "It's got everything!"

Suddenly, Cari got a sick feeling in her stomach. "Has anyone else in Ethan's office ever gotten anything like that? I mean, getting a bonus of sorts from the client instead of the company itself?"

"Not that I know of. But that's what was so wonderful. Ethan didn't feel he'd done anything overly extraordinary, and he'd really only been working with the client's company a short time, yet the man did this for him."

Cari's mind began to turn: a Ukrainian gave Tristan's brother-in-law a car "just because"? Suddenly Tristan's words came back to her: *Anyone can be bought, even me.*

Suddenly nauseated, Cari got out her phone and began to text Tristan. Gemma and Ann slipped into more conversation about dinner.

Does Aleynekov have any friends from Ukraine?

Cari prayed his response would be quick — and no. Two minutes passed and a text came back.

He has friends from all over, many from
former Communist countries. Why? Are you okay?

"Gemma? Do you happen to know the name of the client who gave Ethan the car?" Cari tried her best to act casual. Luckily, Gemma and Ann were discussing dessert and neither of them seemed to notice her nervousness.

"Um…It was one of those Ukrainian names that ends with 'shen-ko' or 'chenko.' I don't remember. His first name was Vasily, though. That's how Ethan always referred to him. Why?"

"Oh, just curious. I studied a little about Ukraine and was wondering, that's all." It wasn't a complete lie. Cari remembered that part of her world history class in college because the professor had lost family during the revolution and was quite a storyteller.

Ann and Gemma returned to their conversation, and Cari texted Tristan.

> We're all fine. Don't worry. We're heading back
> to Canyonville. Did you know a Ukrainian client
> named Vasily gave Ethan that Lexus? I just couldn't help
> but wonder if Aleynekov had anything to do with it.

You're just paranoid, Cari told herself. Her imagination had run wild. She was sure of it. She'd have to apologize for worrying Tristan.

> Ask Gemma if Vasily's last name is Shevchenko.

"Gemma? Sorry for interrupting. Was it perhaps Vasily Shevchenko?"

Gemma thought for a moment. "You know, I think it was." She put her index finger to her chin. "Yes, I'm sure of it. Wow. How did you know?"

Cari had to think quickly. "I had a class on international nonprofit agencies. I think I saw his name in one of the articles. Just a lucky guess."

Gemma seemed satisfied and immediately returned to her discussion with Ann as Cari began to type on her phone again. Cari threw out an occasional "Oh, that sounds delicious" when they asked for her opinion. Honestly, she had no idea what foods she was agreeing to eat.

> Yes. Gemma confirmed the name. Is he a good guy
> or a bad guy, comparatively speaking?

Tristan responded almost immediately.

> He's on the list of people the UN doesn't quite trust,
> but he's also one that Aleynekov's cheating. I'm not sure
> what to think. I'll talk to Ethan, find out what he knows.
> See you soon?

Cari felt her heart rate quicken and her face redden at his last words. She had to maintain her composure.

We're about 2 miles from the Canyonville exit.
Let the guys know we have groceries and stuff for the inn.
We'll need help unloading. See you in a few minutes.

Cari realized she'd actually missed him over the past few hours. Maybe she *should* at least see what could happen. They'd had some flirty moments—memories of the grocery store in Bainbridge Island came flooding back, and she smiled. Maybe…just maybe.

Chapter 17

After dinner, Gemma suggested they go for another walk to exercise Tristan's knee. Knowing there was an ice cream shop up the street only added to Tristan's wanting to go. And he was relieved when everyone agreed…at first.

As they cleaned up dishes, Ann and Gemma talked excitedly about the items Ann had purchased, and when they'd finished they skipped upstairs, apologizing for backing out. Ethan and Mark caught each other's eye and discussed going to see Mark's friend who could examine the GPS in Ethan's car.

It didn't seem to throw Cari that the others were obviously manipulating their evening. Neither did she seem bothered, and Tristan was very glad. Now that he knew Cari wasn't engaged, Tristan liked the idea of getting to know her. It didn't mean anything had to come of it; he simply liked her company.

Tristan smiled. As they went down the front steps of the inn and began their uphill walk toward Main Street, their conversation once again found an easy rhythm.

"So…" Tristan chuckled. "Hairy Cari?"

Cari smiled and lifted her chin high. "Yeah, Mark's always had some sort of nickname for me. When I was really little and still called by my full name, he'd come up with as many rhymes as he could. Until I was about ten years old, I was Carolina Serafina Magdalena Boo." She laughed quietly and Tristan grinned.

"Where'd the 'Boo' part come from?"

"Oh, I don't know, he was just being silly with me. I kind of liked it, though. It made me feel a special bond with him. No one else was allowed to call me that." She paused. "When I was in middle school, I informed him that I was now Cari. He initially balked, but then started calling me Hairy Cari. At first I didn't like it. As you can see, I've got a lot of hair," she noted, pointing at her head. "And it was pretty hard to control as a kid. But then he told me that boys like girls with long, curly hair. Thirteen-year-old girls definitely want to know what boys like, and from that point on, I liked my thick and wild hair, and I liked my nickname."

"And was Sparky Marky also a reference to—"

"His hair? Oh, definitely. He thought he was God's gift to high school girls with his hair full of gel. It looked like he'd been hit by lightning, and it actually hurt if you touched his head. I'm sure Ann's got some family photos we can sneak a look at."

"And they'd include you as well?"

"Oh, God. Yes. Okay. Scratch that idea."

"No," Tristan argued with a laugh. "I'd love to see Carolina Magdalena…I've forgotten the rest."

"Carolina Serafina Magdalena Boo is long gone, Tristan."

He smirked and looked away. He'd ask Ann about photo albums as soon as he had the chance.

They walked to Main Street and crossed over to Ken's Sidewalk Café. A few aged picnic tables gathered under an overhang next to the window for ordering ice cream, hot dogs, and a few other simple items. Two sets of parents chatted at one table while three young children squealed and ran around them, playing tag.

Tristan and Cari ordered their desserts, and Cari nodded to a door along the back wall of the overhang. Tristan followed her inside.

Soon they were sitting at a small table along the front window, Cari with her ice cream sundae and Tristan with a chocolate cone. He took a deep breath between nibbles, hoping she'd be all right with him asking some questions.

"Care to play another game with me?" He smiled.

"Okay. Shoot."

"If you could do anything and know you'd be good at it, what would it be?"

"What—you mean like an occupation or something?"

"Could be, or even a one-time experience that you'd be guaranteed to be successful at."

"Hmm…I like that. Might need to ask that of my students next semester." She tapped the end of her white plastic spoon against her chin. "I think…I'd want to be a linguist. You know, someone who works for, like, the UN or something and can translate peace talks and stuff. I think that would be cool. And on top of that, I'd understand foreigners' conversations, help root out terrorists!"

"A female version of Jason Bourne, eh? You sure you'd be up for all the danger and espionage?"

Cari's shoulders dropped, and Tristan immediately hated himself for bringing up danger. But then she surprised him.

"You're right. I'd be lousy at karate-chopping somebody or jumping from rooftop to rooftop. All right. I'm changing my answer," she offered brightly. "I'd want to write a bestselling novel."

"Really?" This was an intriguingly different answer. "Any particular genre?"

"Well, I've already told you that I'm a romantic, so I guess that's what I'd write."

"Have you ever written anything?"

"Nothing worth sharing." She played with her hair, spinning a ringlet slowly around her index finger. "That's been my problem: I don't ever feel anything's good enough." She glanced over to Tristan again. "How about you? What's your response?"

"Have the opportunity to play in the London Symphony like my father used to."

"What instrument?"

"He was an amazing violinist. The best I've ever heard. He toured the world."

"Wow. That's quite an occupation."

"And he was brilliant at it, too, until he suffered a stroke about four years ago. His right side retained permanent damage, and he just couldn't play anymore. Now he teaches music theory and tutors a little at the Royal Academy of Music. I know it breaks his heart, not being able to play for his own pleasure anymore."

Tristan paused, picturing his parents in their modest home outside of London. He followed Cari's gaze out the window toward the children and the picnic benches for a few moments. Just as he worried it was becoming too melancholy again, Cari became ready to resume their game.

"Next question. What's your biggest pet peeve?" she asked.

"You mean other than people who use abbreviations in their texts? Well, that's easy. People who talk loudly on their cell phones—or worse, when they've got an earphone attached and it looks like they're talking to themselves."

Cari nodded in agreement.

"I mean, it amazes me how oblivious people are in public. I was in a pub one night with some mates, and in the booth behind me, this elderly man was having a—well, let's just say it was a private conversation that included intimate information. And he wasn't being discreet. We lost our appetites pretty quickly and finally had to leave!"

"That is just wrong on so many levels," Cari said with a laugh. "Yuck!" Once she was composed again, she offered her response. "I have two, I guess." She hesitated as she attempted to put loosened curls behind her ears. "Missing socks…and, um, snobby people."

"Okay, the snobby people part I understand—and completely agree with. But missing socks?"

"Yeah. You know, when you do laundry and you know you had every sock accounted for when you started but, sure enough, one ends up missing when you pull them out of the dryer. I swear, I've spent a small fortune on replacement socks."

Tristan laughed. Her utter honesty and simplicity were so refreshing. "You're really serious, aren't you!"

"I'm telling you," she said firmly, "someday they're going to confirm that there really are sock elves, and some hidden mountain of single socks will be found in the Amazon jungle or something."

Tristan's heart lightened with every word Cari spoke, every gesture as she fussed with her hair, every smile and laugh. He could have leaned forward right there at the table and kissed her. They laughed a few moments more and then the question Tristan wanted to ask most suddenly returned to the forefront of his thoughts.

"So, when are you getting married?" He kept his tone casual and chose not to look at her as he awaited her response.

"Huh?"

141

Tristan couldn't hide his smile. "You told me yesterday that you got engaged at the top of the Eiffel Tower. I was wondering when the big event was going to be."

"Oh...that. Um..."

She stumbled for words, and Tristan decided to rescue her. "Don't worry. Mark told me about your summer romance and engagement over at the playground."

Cari blushed, seemingly surprised at the topic of conversation.

"He also told me how it happened many years ago and things never worked out. So...why the lie?"

"Well, it's not *really* a lie. I did get engaged at the top of the Eiffel Tower — that's what the school calls that particular piece of playground equipment, and I did have a diamond ring," she said proudly, looking down at her sundae. "Between flirtatious students and colleagues, and my run-ins with Dr. Lassiter, I needed people to believe I was in a serious relationship. I had a grand story about how he was always traveling. I put a picture of Mark and me in a frame, and he became my mysterious missing fiancé. Some people bought it..."

"Lassiter didn't believe you, though, did he," Tristan said solemnly.

"No. Although I doubt even meeting Mark, or anyone else I claimed to be dating, would have stopped him." She shook her head and stabbed her spoon deep into her ice cream. "I've got to find a way to finish my degree despite him."

"I've promised to help you, and I will."

"How? How do you think you can help?" Her voice was sarcastic, doubting, defeated.

"I don't know, but I'll find a way. I'm not without connections."

"How about you send your buddy Josef Aleynekov after him, eh?" She laughed sardonically, staring at the spoonful of fudge-covered ice cream in front of her mouth. "That would get him to back off!" Suddenly her tone changed, got quieter. "Speaking of which, what did you find out about Ethan's gift car and this Vasily Shevchenko character?"

"Nothing yet, but I've got a theory," he half-whispered, leaning in as she did the same. "It may be that Aleynekov recommended Ethan to Shevchenko, and then encouraged Shevchenko to give him the car."

"But why?"

"Remember how I said everyone can be bought? I've been worried ever since my colleague and I sent in that report absolving Aleynekov of any wrongdoing—worried that somehow he'd find a way to keep something over me that would tie me to him. My parents recently 'won' thirty thousand pounds in a contest they didn't remember entering. I had my suspicions, of course, so I investigated as much as possible, but I couldn't find anything that tied the money to Aleynekov or his colleagues, so I naïvely chalked it up to their forgetfulness. But now, with Ethan, I worry that that's what Aleynekov will use against me should I turn him in." Tristan ran his hand across his jaw and sat back in his chair. "He probably has a paper trail that links me to the money my parents received, Ethan's car, and God only knows what else—a paper trail that implicates me in illegal activities but has no link to him at all. I think I've unwittingly been bought by the Bulgarian mafia, and I have no recourse unless I can get someone like Vasily Shevchenko on my side."

"If this Shevchenko guy is being duped too, wouldn't he do what he could to undo whatever evidence Aleynekov may have, if you're right on your theory?"

"Possibly. I've never met the man, but I can't imagine he'd want to cross Aleynekov, even if they're good friends. And I certainly can't ask him to, especially if neither he nor I know who Aleynekov still has on his side. Shevchenko risks losing millions, along with putting his and his family's lives in jeopardy. Money laundering is a perfected business, Cari. It's much more prevalent than most people could begin to understand, and it's usually linked to really nefarious business like the trafficking of drugs or even humans. That's why I didn't want you calling the police. We have no idea who else is on Aleynekov's payroll."

"God, I can't even begin to imagine the kind of people who would choose to do things like that! Were there any Americans on that list?"

"A few. And you'd be surprised: most are names you'd recognize from major corporations and even some in your government."

"Dirty politicians don't surprise me but, wow, this is huge."

"Absolutely. And dangerous." Tristan hesitated. "I don't think you're out of danger, either. Now that your name is involved, I'm not sure what's going to happen. I've got to assume that Aleynekov will think I've told you things at this point, especially if he's discovered you and I are still traveling together. Even if I didn't tell you a thing, he'd still figure you know enough to be a threat."

"So this isn't going to end any time soon, is it?" Cari's voice was a whisper, her eyes full of concern.

"I don't think so." He reached for her hand as it rested on the table. "I'm so terribly sorry."

Cari shrugged and gave him a half-smile. "Hey, we'll work through it, right? We'll stay alert and watch our backs and hope for the best." She took her hand back and put it in her lap. "Are you sleeping okay?"

"Not much. Feeling a little stressed lately." Tristan smirked, nervously folding and unfolding the paper napkin in his hand, having finished his cone.

"That's what I thought." She suddenly sat up straight in her chair. "I want to show you something. You ready to walk a little? It's not far."

The couple got up, cleared their table, and began their walk back toward the Canyon Creek Bed and Breakfast.

"Wait a minute." Tristan turned toward Cari as they strolled back down the small hill. "If the engagement was a lie —" Cari raised her eyebrows. "Okay, an embellishment, then what about the other things you tell your students? Your uncle or somebody being in sports and your allergy to strawberries — are those *embellishments* as well?" He exaggerated dramatically, and she smiled crookedly.

"My uncle is an Olympic luger. That's the truth. As far as the strawberries, I just don't like the taste of them or the grainy feel of the seeds. Keeps people from expecting me to eat stuff like strawberry shortcake at work. Love the smell, though. It's strange."

"So this morning's breakfast...?"

"I kind of picked out the bits of strawberry and then tucked the stash under the last little bit of bread I didn't eat. When I was done, I made sure I cleaned my own plate before Ann could see."

"You're sneaky."

"Says the M&M Mystery Man! But you're right, I know. I'm bad." She held her hair back from her forehead and looked down. "But I didn't want Ann to feel bad, either."

"All right. Note to self: Do not buy Cari any food that has strawberries. Got it." Tristan pretended to check off a list in the air in front of him.

They walked behind the bed and breakfast and around the back of the community center. Cari reached into her hip pocket and pulled out a lanyard with what looked like a hotel cardkey attached. She swiped it across a lockbox located next to an unmarked door. There was a click, and she opened the door. "Mark's pass key," she said breezily as they entered.

As soon as they were inside, she flipped on one of the six or seven light switches, dimly illuminating a long stairway ahead of them and a room to their left.

"Okay." She turned to him and smiled. "You have to close your eyes and let me lead you to what I want to show you."

Cari took his hands and Tristan conceded, closing his eyes. She walked backward slowly as she inched them up what seemed to be a dozen steps and then along a hallway.

"You're going to take two more steps up, okay?"

He didn't peek; he chose to trust her. But he also assumed she was watching him like a hawk.

They went a few more steps, turned slightly to the left and then to the right. Then she moved beside him and pulled his hands outward to touch something at about hip-height. She pressed his fingers down, and he realized right away what she'd wanted to show him. Tristan opened his eyes to an acoustic guitar on a stand. He turned toward Cari, his mouth embarrassingly agape.

"I know the violin is your specialty, but you mentioned you play the guitar too. I thought you might like to play, to relieve some stress. You know, maybe it would help you sleep better." She shrugged shyly, but her smile was brighter than ever.

Tristan suddenly realized how much he'd missed playing. And she was right—it was a source of relaxation. "Whose is this? Are you sure it's okay for me to play it?" He gently touched the strings, hoping desperately that it was. He glanced around quickly and saw that they were on a stage.

"Yeah. It belongs to one of the guys Mark knows. They like to hang out here once in a while when the hall isn't being used. I asked Mark before dinner if Lou would be practicing tonight, and he didn't think so...so I figured I'd take the chance. I'm sure he'd be fine with it."

"Mark doesn't know you took his passkey?"

"I'll tell him later. He won't mind. I'm sure of it," she said with confidence. "Go ahead, try it out. I'm guessing it's in tune, but you'll know better than I will."

Tristan sighed heavily. So many burdens simply disappeared as he picked up the guitar and walked over to a bench on the back wall of the stage. He gestured for Cari to sit beside him, and she obliged, albeit hesitantly. He smiled, closed his eyes, and began to play.

I need to hear from you.
Where are Saunders and the woman?
I'll send others to find out if you do not respond.

Jenny sighed in exasperation. The Bulgarian texts were getting annoying—and so was her inability to find Tristan. He'd either figured out he was being followed, or the system had stopped working. Either way, Jenny was in the dark until that satellite started sending her signals again. *Damn it.* Maybe there were others already on the trail, and she hadn't been told. Aleynekov double-crossed people on a regular basis, why not her? He'd never respected any woman — never trusted any woman completely. No matter how often she did his bidding and regardless of how much she sacrificed, Jenny knew she'd never be anything to him but a lowly, dispensable female.

What if he sent someone with no track record — or worse, that crazy SOB Vlad — to usurp her authority and bungle the whole plan? She didn't want outside help. She had good reason for wanting to find and face Tristan Saunders on her own.

"Jenny? Honey?" Ben patted her arm gently. "It's getting close to dinner time. I don't know if a hotel room will be hard to get at this time of day. We may want to think about finding one soon."

She instantly turned her charm back on, begrudgingly, and smiled. "Sure, Ben. We're, what, about a half-hour outside of Salem? Want to stop there?"

Jenny considered her options. Maybe if they stopped for the night, she could do further investigations on her laptop. While it seemed likely Saunders was heading to California, she didn't want to travel too far south in case he'd stopped in Portland or turned and headed back toward Canada. She'd have to contact Bulgaria eventually, as well as tell Ben about their mutual boss. It was possible Josef had connections in Oregon and California at the DMV, and they could check for Stonecipher's Lexus from video feeds along the highways and any tollbooths they may have gone through. She'd be grasping at straws, but maybe at this point she did need some help.

Before long, they were checked in at the Phoenix Grand Hotel. It wasn't the best place she'd ever stayed in, but it would just have to do for the night. Ben's jaw hung open as he surveyed the surroundings.

Over a romantic candlelit dinner delivered by room service — evidently another new experience for Ben — Jenny broached the subject of their "coincidental" meeting that night at the bar.

"You know I'd been watching you, right?"

He smiled slyly. "I'd been watching you too. Hell, every guy in that bar was picturing you naked except for that guy you were with."

Jenny smirked. "Who? Nick? No, he's one guy who'd *never* think about me that way. But what I meant is that I was watching you at the shooting range and in the field. I'd been watching you for weeks before you ever knew it."

"Well, why did you join my competition, then? Once I saw how perfect a shot you were, I wanted to claim you." He reached across the table and placed his hand on hers.

"What? And abandon College Boy's pitiful squad of misfits?" she asked mischievously. "God knows they need someone who can complete a takedown in one shot."

"I was just glad you didn't hook up with Chameleon. I hate that guy." He spoke through gritted teeth.

Ben's emotion was exactly what she needed to get him to buy into her plan. "Why, Ben?" she asked quietly as she stroked the side of his hand. "You seem so kindhearted, but you looked ready to take his head off at the shooting range today."

Ben turned his head away as he spoke, his jaw still firm. "I met Lamb in September when he backed into my car at the university."

"I didn't know you're a student," she said, smiling encouragingly.

"I'm not. I used to work there as a groundskeeper." Ben stopped, rubbing his face roughly with his hand. "I had a damn good job there, and I worked hard. Then that idiot hits *my* car — nearly takes off the fender. I'm right there and see it happen, but he guns it out of the parking lot before I can say anything. When I go up to him about it the next day, expecting him to own up to his stupidity and pay for the damage, he's had Daddy Moneybags write me a check for twenty-five freakin' bucks. He said my car was a piece of shit and 'that should cover it.'" Ben spat those last few words. He pulled his hand away from Jenny's and leaned back in his chair before continuing. "Next morning, my boss calls me in and tells me I'm fired. No explanation. Nothing."

"Oh, Ben." Jenny's first thought, other than actually feeling bad for Ben, was to put in a call—see if she could order a little dark-alley head-beating on Kevin Lamb while they were out of town.

For now, though, it was time to turn on the charm again. Jenny stood and came around to sit on Ben's lap, wrapping one arm around his neck and caressing his face with the other. "I want you to know that you—" she kissed him quickly "—are so much better than that jerk. You—" she kissed him again "—are exactly the type of man who turns me on."

She was getting the reaction she wanted, so she slid off his lap, took his hands in hers, and led him to the bed. "You make love more passionately than I could ever imagine. Love me, Ben. Make love to me," she whispered as she peppered his neck with more kisses.

Jenny let go of worrying about tracking Tristan Saunders for the night. If Josef had someone else on his trail, so be it. Instead, she allowed the rest of the night to be pure bliss.

Carolina Lopez's contact info: Cell phone 206-555-0109. Ronaldo Lopez, father, Kirkland, WA. 425-555-0318. Mark Stoddard, other (not specified), 541-555-1969.

As Lassiter sent Aleynekov information he knew would not bode well for his doctoral student, he hoped to God it would at least get the Bulgarian off *his* back.

Lassiter hadn't been smart six years ago when he'd agreed to meet with the Eastern European businessmen. He'd done some research on the effects of ethnic fighting on the economies of many of the smaller, formerly Communist countries, and these men said they were interested in his findings and recommendations.

Soon Lassiter found himself the recipient of cash "gifts" as he, in turn, created accounts at various US banks for corporations he suspected didn't exist. He got to keep a significant portion for his troubles — and as far as the IRS was concerned, these were earnings for speaking engagements. Half-truths at best, but he *had* met with them to share his knowledge. How was that any different from giving guest lectures at universities or being the keynote speaker for a business convention?

Earning seven figures instead of his usual ten thousand dollars per engagement could have raised suspicions...but he'd deal with that if they ever found the additional accounts he'd opened at foreign banks to hold the excess. At least he knew he could retire without financial worry. Lassiter had helped them; they'd helped Lassiter. He'd thought that was the end of it.

Then, about six weeks ago, Aleynekov had contacted him for information about a local man named Ethan Stonecipher. When he provided the details he'd gathered, he was given directions to purchase a Lexus for him. Lassiter was sent false identification — he was to portray an American employee of Ukrainian diplomat Vasily Shevchenko during the transaction. Along with the false ID was an envelope with ninety thousand dollars in cash for the purchase. Ethan Stonecipher was the brother-in-law of Tristan Saunders, a man who had evidently crossed Aleynekov just enough to get on his bad side — something Lassiter knew now was a death sentence. This was a bribe, from what Lassiter could figure, and he simply did what he was asked and walked away. The less he knew, the better.

Tristan Saunders had been either very smart or very stupid for having somehow outwitted, and thus angered, Josef Aleynekov. The last thing Lassiter had expected was for the man to show up at the university — let alone know who he was. Now, with Cari Lopez involved somehow, he wished to God he hadn't called Aleynekov after his encounter with Saunders. He'd wanted to put Aleynekov in his past. But he also had a more immediate concern: he'd be up on ethics charges with the university if anyone found out he'd revealed a student's personal information. Lassiter's heart raced. What had he gotten himself into?

Chapter 18

Sunday morning in Canyonville began full of unseasonable sunshine. And no one was complaining, that was for sure. As they sat around the table eating a southern breakfast—biscuits and gravy, ham steak, grits (and not that lumpy instant stuff), and fried eggs—the four guests drilled Mark and Ann about what they could do around the B&B to help get it ready for *real* customers. They'd obviously robbed the Stoddards of a few days' work time, and they wanted to earn their keep.

By the end of the meal everyone had their tasks, and the day was spent blissfully gardening, fixing loose shutters, doing paint and caulk touch-ups in the kitchen and bathrooms, hanging more of the wall décor Ann had purchased, and taking numerous walks to the hardware store as they needed supplies or a break. Cari found it physically tiring but mentally very relaxing.

She had offered to work with Tristan on the shutters on the side of the house, and luckily, the others were busy elsewhere so they could talk in private.

"You look well-rested," she began as she handed him some nails.

"Best night's sleep in ages. God, it felt good." He hammered for a few moments, then stopped and looked down at Cari from halfway up the ladder. "You think we could go there again tonight? You were right, you know. Playing released a lot of stress."

"Yeah, sure!" Cari hoped she didn't sound as excited as she felt.

Last night had been magical, just talking to him and listening to him play. Once Tristan had taken hold of the guitar, his whole demeanor had changed. He played for nearly five minutes without stopping, mostly with his eyes closed. It was a haunting melody—she'd closed her own eyes as the melody journeyed through angst and sadness—but she'd really felt the mood of the music change as he'd progressed through the piece. Cari had asked the name of the composer when he finished.

"It's one of mine," was all he'd said.

"You play beautifully," she'd offered shyly.

After a moment he'd begun to play a song that created visions of soft white beaches and the ocean rhythmically reaching in and drawing back from the shore. This music wasn't at all moody or angry or bitter.

"That's so peaceful, what you're playing right now."

He'd glanced over at her with a smirk. "Uh-oh. Is it putting you to sleep?"

Cari smiled and watched Tristan's hands move nimbly across the guitar strings. "No. I mean it's very soothing."

"I'm just playing something for you. My fingers sometimes just do their own thing, and I let them. Do you like this, then?"

"Yeah. It's pretty. It's…calming, like being on a beach when no one else is around."

"I'll have to remember this tune, then. I'll call it 'Cari's Walk on the Beach.'"

Cari had liked the sound of that, and she went to sleep with the melody still in her head. He'd created a song just for her.

"There!" Tristan banged the hammer with gusto, bringing Cari back to the present.

As they moved on to secure the next set of window shutters, Cari bounded up the ladder before he could. "My turn!" she announced.

"So, you're good with tools, hmm?"

"My dad owns a hardware store. Do you think I ever had a choice?" she said before turning to the hammering. "He even taught me how to rewire the light switches in our kitchen one summer. My mom was worried I was going to electrocute myself, but I followed Dad's directions and did just fine. From then on, they both called me Miss Fix-it."

"You're full of surprises, Ms. Lopez, you know that?"

"So is that something I should share with my students next semester?" She giggled, but then something occurred to her. "Oh, shoot!"

Tristan looked up in alarm. "What? Are you all right?"

Cari quickly climbed down the ladder. "Shoot! Shoot! Shoot! I have classes tomorrow, and I'm not going to be there!"

"Sounds like a — " he started, and together they said " — research day!"

Cari was already hustling toward the house as she called back to Tristan. "Can you finish the last three windows? I need to email my students right now or I'll forget."

"Are you going to cancel Tuesday's classes as well?" Tristan asked hesitantly.

She stopped and turned around. She stared at him, as if that would help her decision. Then she scrunched up her nose and said, "I may have a better idea. I'll be back in a few!"

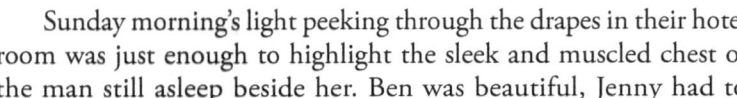

Sunday morning's light peeking through the drapes in their hotel room was just enough to highlight the sleek and muscled chest of the man still asleep beside her. Ben was beautiful, Jenny had to admit, but she wouldn't let his amazing abilities between the sheets distract her — for long. She had to find Tristan Saunders, and she had to find him soon.

On the plus side for this "relationship" she was developing with Ben, in addition to the amazing nighttime activities, she had him hooked. He had to care for her deeply if she was going to depend on him to complete one, maybe two, assassinations. Yeah, he was paid well, but she knew Josef would not have told Ben what the money was potentially buying: unquestioning loyalty and completion of assignments, no matter what they were. Putting that kind of stuff in a job description tends to scare off new guys. Up to now, Ben had likely been too awestruck to question why he was earning so much money for such mundane tasks: collecting and delivering packages and spying on a man he knew nothing about.

It was time for him to know more, time for him to become an official part of the "family" — or a decomposing body in a ravine along the highway. It would be his choice, of course, which way he wanted to play this new game. But there was no third option; there was no going back, no returning the money, no forgetting what he'd seen and heard. Kind of like marriage vows, really. "Till death do us part." Only in the Aleynekov family, death came immediately and often painfully to betrayers, no matter how loved they were or how loyal they'd been in the past. No forgiveness. Ever. Jenny sighed, then began to stir in their bed.

"Hey, Ben," she cooed in his ear as she snuggled up against his warm body. "It's morning. Want some breakfast?"

He turned slightly only to pull her on top of him, holding her tight. "Why don't we just stay here for a month or so? I could get used to waking up like this, you know." He began tracing circles across her back, his touch intoxicating. Before she could gather her thoughts, he was once again making love to her…

An hour later they'd showered, checked out of the hotel, and chosen a Starbucks for breakfast. Jenny had her laptop and hoped to finally have some information. She logged on to the tracking program, sipping her coffee anxiously. Then she saw it, a little dot on the map along I-5.

Canyonville, Oregon. *Gotcha.*

Tristan made quick work of the last shutters on the ground floor and headed to his room for a few moments. He'd gone long enough without checking his BlackBerry and knew he was living danger-ously, not knowing if Aleynekov had tracked the car to Canyonville. He had four new emails, none of them emergencies, and thankfully no new texts. Maybe they'd escaped Aleynekov after all…for the present anyway.

He heard a light tap on the door. "Tristan?" Cari called.

"Come on in," he called. "Got your class situation figured out?"

"Yeah. I decided not to cancel. I didn't want to raise unnecessary questions, you know? Instead I called my friend Jazmyn. She's another doc student who teaches the same course as me in a classroom in the evening. I explained it was a family emergency, so she was more than happy to combine our classes — for a few days or the whole week, if needed. So, I emailed my students and told them to go to one of her classes until further notice." She cast her eyes downward. "That should help until all of this is over."

Cari leaned against the doorframe of the bedroom. "Anything?" she asked, gesturing toward the BlackBerry in Tristan's hand.

When he told her he'd not received any new texts, her shoulders visibly relaxed and she sighed loudly. "That's good news...at least for now, right?"

"Yes, I believe we can consider that good news," he said. "But we both know it's not over."

Cari pursed her lips, crossed her arms, and nodded. "How soon can you try his office?"

"Sofia's ten hours ahead. I know he goes in early so I can call around seven thirty a.m. his time, nine thirty tonight for us. Nothing I can do until then, I'm afraid." He paused but quickly became uncomfortable at the silence. "Ready to tackle the second-floor shutters?" he asked, hoping she was as ready as he was to discuss something, anything other than Aleynekov.

Again she nodded, but this time with a small smile. They ambled down the stairs and back outside, this time to the scaffolding Mark had erected along the back of the house.

"You good with heights?"

"I think so." She shrugged, her hands in her back pockets as she looked up at the elaborate ladder-work in front of her.

"If you're not, you could help me from inside the various windows," Tristan offered.

Cari scrunched her nose again — Tristan thought she had no idea how lovely she looked when she did that — and tilted her head, squinting as she took another glance toward the second floor. "Well..."

Tristan waved her inside, and in the time it took him to climb halfway up the scaffold, he found her sitting on the sill of the open window.

"Romeo! Romeo! Wherefore art thou Romeo?" she called.

"I don't know about this Romeo fellow—" he winked as he reached her window "—but I'm making sure my knee cooperates properly so I don't damage it or any other part of myself further."

"Oh, Tristan! Do you want me to do the outside part?" she asked, suddenly serious. "I forgot about your knee. I'm sorry."

"No, Juliet, just be ready to call emergency services should I topple over the edge."

"Now you're scaring me. Are you sure you're okay out there?"

"I've done this kind of thing at my parents' home many times. I'm perfectly fine, knee included."

Although two of them gave him trouble, attached with ancient and rusted nails that were difficult to remove, Cari and Tristan were able to straighten and secure all of the second-floor shutters in just over two hours. And because the third-floor windows overlooked a balcony that spanned the back of the house, they went much more quickly.

The work crew of six completed all of their tasks by four in the afternoon. While the women showered, Ethan, Mark, and Tristan began to prepare steaks and roast corn-on-the-cob on the outdoor grill that Ethan had cleaned and repaired. They ate dinner on the front porch and enjoyed glasses of wine and beer, soothed by a cool breeze, the sound of crickets, and their own laughter as they shared stories until it was dark.

Jenny and Ben had only a few hours' drive to Canyonville. Tristan Saunders was still there; Jenny was sure of it. He wouldn't have given his BlackBerry to anyone else, nor would he have thrown it away—he *had* to keep it if he wanted to know Aleynekov's next move. Thank heavens a tracking chip had been installed there while Saunders lay comatose in a hospital bed back in Sofia.

When Jenny had called Aleynekov this morning, she'd reluctantly let him know that she'd located Saunders, and he in turn provided her with Lopez's cell phone number and other contact information. That was going to be very helpful, of course, but Jenny had a personal score to settle with Saunders and frankly wanted to see him again in person. He'd scorned her in Bulgaria, and she didn't forgive easily. If he was still with Carolina Lopez, Jenny would make both of them suffer. Tristan obviously had feelings for her—he'd taken off from his sister's apartment with this woman, caring enough to help her escape danger. Jenny knew he wouldn't tolerate any harm coming to her.

This was going to be fun.

Jenny's next step, however, had to be getting Ben onboard and on her side. She needed to know he'd do anything, sacrifice anything for her. It was time to let Ben in on the situation…with some lies thrown in to ensure his allegiance.

"I'm going to stop by the bank before we get back on the interstate," she said casually as they pulled out of the hotel parking lot. "I need to be sure you get paid."

Ben looked out the passenger window—Jenny had chosen to drive now—and at first it didn't seem that what she'd said had registered with him.

"Huh? Why would you need to pay me anything? I get my income kind of mysteriously back in Poulsbo." He snickered. "I didn't tell you, but I'm kind of a private investigator. Maybe even a little bit of a secret agent." Ben beamed with pride as he glanced over to her.

"I know."

The look on his face combined shock and disappointment. "You know? What do you mean you know?"

"I work for Josef Aleynekov too. I take care of the finances for us and a few others. I've been delivering those envelopes to you."

"What the hell?"

Ben was bordering on anger, and Jenny had to defuse the situation quickly. "Honey, don't be mad at me for not telling you." She brushed her hand along his thigh. "You're right. We *are* sort of secret agents, even to each other."

"Start talking, Jenny." His lips pursed and his jaw clenched.

"Josef does business internationally, and sometimes he needs people like us to make sure his investments—and the people he's investing in—are taken care of properly. This Tristan Saunders you've been watching?" She turned to look at him quickly before returning her eyes to the road. "Ben, Tristan Saunders is a thief and a cold-blooded killer. He's stolen over fifty million dollars, and Josef's pissed as hell about it. He wants his money back, and he hired both of us to track Saunders when he came to the US to his sister's place. Josef needs local people with a sharp eye and keen senses to watch this jerk."

Jenny glanced over at Ben again, and it seemed he was starting to relax his shoulders. His gaze remained intent on the highway in front of them, but she thought she detected a bit of a proud smile.

"So, how long have you worked for Josef?" he asked.

"A few years," she said. "When Josef discovered Saunders had stolen all that money, he found out where the guy had family and set up people like me to watch them. A few are in England, watching his parents' house, and I was sent here because his sister, Gemma Stonecipher, lives in that apartment you were watching on Bainbridge Island. When Saunders bought a plane ticket to Washington, Josef had me hire you to help keep an eye on him, see if we could somehow get that money back."

"But why me?"

"I watched you. I watched how you planned things out, how you didn't overreact but instead acted quickly and decisively in the field."

"So…what? Is this guy now a target?" he asked sarcastically.

"I've observed your skills, and I've been impressed." Jenny offered him a smile, and he seemed to be forgiving her. "I never imagined, though, that I'd get to experience your *other* very impressive skills."

That brought back the sexy side of Ben that Jenny was counting on. "You like my skills, huh?"

"Oh, like you have to ask?" She gave him a coy look.

"So this trip we're on here, this is job-related, then? I'm on the clock?"

"Oh yeah, most definitely. I'm sorry I had to lie about that. I didn't know where Saunders had gone yesterday, just that he'd somehow escaped our watch, and we needed to find him quickly. I wasn't sure you'd want to do this. And Josef, I'm sure, hadn't mentioned that there might be instantaneous travel involved."

"Well," Ben said with a sly grin, "instantaneous travel with you has been fantastic."

"I honestly don't do this, you know, jumping into bed with colleagues or charging out of town on a whim!" Jenny was being truthful here. She didn't sleep with other assassins—targets, yes, assassins, no. It was too easy to be betrayed in the name of the almighty payoff. Ben was still pretty clueless about the stakes involved here, though, and he was hotter than any guy she'd been with in a long time. He'd proven to be worth the indiscretion—just as long as Josef didn't find out. Jenny didn't need Josef proselytizing about morals to her.

"So, where are we going and what do we do when we get there?"

Jenny thought carefully before answering. She wasn't sure of the "what" yet, except that she'd want to watch Saunders and that woman for a day or so to get a feel for whether they'd let their guard down. She'd gotten Josef to agree not to contact Saunders for a little while longer, so as not to send him on the run again, and she felt certain he wasn't going to send anyone else to Canyonville. He said he trusted that she and Ben could handle things and had to know that the more people following Saunders in such a small town, the more likely the Brit would figure it out and take off. Yes, just laying low was a good idea. Jenny needed to learn about the town, about the people Saunders and

Lopez knew and whether they'd be trouble or not, as well as determine where her "meeting" with Saunders could take place.

She told Ben their destination and that for the time being, they'd be back on surveillance until they knew more. He nodded excitedly—exactly what she needed him to do.

"Gimme background, Jenny." His eyes on her were focused, intense. "What else do I need to know about this Saunders creep? You say he's murdered someone too? Shit, you wouldn't know it to look at him. He looks all high-end, you know? Wealthy, classy."

"That's exactly how he's gotten away with all that he has. Do you even know who Josef Aleynekov is? He's the Bulgarian Minister of Finance. He's a big deal, and then this British hotshot developer, Tristan Saunders, enters the scene and pretty soon lots of money is unaccounted for, and one of Josef's most trusted employees turns up dismembered in a sewer pipe. Right around the same time, Saunders suddenly leaves Bulgaria and turns up in the US. Do you see why Josef wants this guy followed and why we have to be as covert and consistent in watching him as possible? Saunders is dangerous, Ben. And now he's got this Carolina Lopez with him too. I don't know her deal, but I'm not trusting her one bit. She may be his accomplice or even a killer herself, I just don't know."

Jenny hesitated so her story could sink in. This was working perfectly: The worse she could make Saunders seem, the more likely Ben would shoot to kill if, or when, she needed him to. And now for the final touch: "I know I'm dragging you into something that maybe you don't feel comfortable with," Jenny said apologetically. "I mean, I know you had no idea you were being asked to follow a criminal." She hesitated for a moment. "Look, I'll stop by the bank right now and get you cash for the work you've done, bring you back to Salem to rent a car—on me, of course—and you can go back to Poulsbo and wash away any involvement in this. Just say the word, and I'll let Josef know you want to quit."

"But that would mean you'd be following this guy on your own," Ben said after a moment. "What if he's as dangerous as you say? That Lopez chick too. You'd be up against the both of them, right?"

"Yeah..." Jenny said with enough worry to sound convincing. "But I'd be okay, Ben. I know how to take care of myself. Josef's never given me such an important assignment, and I promised him I'd follow through, no matter what."

"No." His back straightened. "I can't put you in that kind of situation," he said resolutely. "I won't do that to you. I'm a lot stronger than you, and I'll take that asshole down if he even comes near you."

"Really, Ben, I—I can keep myself safe."

"I'm staying with you." He spoke now through gritted teeth, his fists on his lap. "We'll get this dirt bag, and we'll get Josef's money back. And if Saunders or that bitch he's with gets hurt in the process, well, so be it. That's just what happens to cheaters and murderers."

Jenny smiled. *Welcome to the family, Ben.*

No one asked any questions when, after getting the porch cleaned up and the dishes washed, Tristan and Cari went for a walk. Once again, Cari took Mark's passkey without saying anything. She didn't want him spying on her like the protective cousin he could be.

The moon was full, and as the two entered the back door of the community center, it was easy to see how beautiful the huge dance hall was, awash in the light from the arched windows. Just as the night before, Cari turned on only the dim track lighting above the bench. It created delicate shadows around them as Tristan pulled the guitar onto his lap and began to play.

"So…shall I create something new or do you want me to play 'Cari's Walk on the Beach'?" he asked, his fingers positioned over the frets.

"I don't know. How many songs have you written?"

He plucked a few notes as he tilted his head in thought. "Let's see…maybe about a hundred? But I can't say for sure. I've only written down those that truly spoke to me."

"A hundred? How is it you became an accounting expert when you could have easily been a musician?"

Tristan glanced at her sideways, looking a little embarrassed. "This is just a hobby, really."

"But you're really good!"

"Well, despite my father's international success, my loving parents didn't recommend such a life for Gemma or me. Instead, they made sure we were exposed to many career options." He grinned. "Besides, I *do* enjoy the financial world. I find it challenging and intriguing. This is my escape from that world when I need it."

"How wonderful to be able to play like that, though." Cari was in awe of his talent and his humility toward it. "I wish I could—"

Suddenly there was knocking at the door they'd come through. Cari's first instinct said it was Mark, coming to scold her and get his passkey back, but then the voice left her frozen.

"Hey, asshole!" the voice called through the door. "We saw you go in there. Think you can hide from us? Come on! Let us in, huh? We just wanna talk to you."

A second voice joined in above the rough banging on the door. "You're not getting out of there. We'll catch you! And don't worry, if you'll just let us in, we won't *hurt* your girlfriend..."

"Shut up. We'll do what we want to," the other voice said in a loud whisper.

Oh, God, they've found us!

Tristan immediately put his finger to his lips as he looked at Cari—of course she'd stay quiet! Then he scanned the room quickly and whispered, "Is there any other way out?"

Cari felt panicked but knew she had to keep her focus. "The front door has a double lock with an actual key." She thought again; the other way out was a back door on the opposite side of the stage, but it opened to the same alleyway as the door they'd used. They'd surely be seen. She looked back at Tristan and shrugged, having no idea what they should do.

They heard the thumping of people running through the bushes between the community center and the grocery store. Cari now wondered exactly how many people there were outside.

"Quick!" Tristan said. He silently placed the guitar on its stand and pulled Cari away from the bench, out the side entrance to the stage, and toward the sound booth that spanned a portion of the north wall of the building.

They crouched as they darted from the short hallway through the half-door that led into the long, narrow sound booth. "Under there," he whispered as he pointed to the table that held the electronic equipment, covered with hundreds of levers and buttons for the sound system.

Cari crawled over and got behind the thin cloth drape that covered the table. Tristan eased the door shut and joined her. He maneuvered himself to have his back against the paneled "wall" that separated the booth from the dance floor; Cari lay flat on her back, dragging her focus from Tristan's wide eyes to the curtain that hid them.

He shifted, pulling his cell phone from his pocket. He pressed the "off" button and raised his eyebrows at Cari. She felt her back pocket and realized she'd left her phone in her room. She shook her head, and he looked relieved.

Sure enough, a minute later, they heard glass break and the scuffle of bodies climbing through a window on the other side of the dance floor.

"We know you're in here!" one of the voices called.

Try as she might to be still, Cari knew she was visibly shaking. "Come here," Tristan whispered and gestured for her to turn her back to him. He put his arm around her waist. "I'll keep you safe. It's me they want more than you. Don't worry."

Despite his comforting arm, Cari couldn't get her body to relax. Nor could she stop the tears that silently escaped. "Don't leave me, Tristan. Just don't leave me."

"Shh—" he leaned in to her ear "—I'm not going anywhere. They won't find us. All right? Keep thinking that: they won't find us."

"Check the front door! Maybe they got out. Man, I've got such an adrenaline rush," the first voice said huskily.

"Just be quiet and keep looking."

Tristan continued to hold Cari, and she put her arm and hand over his, pushing herself closer to his chest. The two people searching the building moved nearly silently, and she gasped to hear the door to the sound booth open. Tristan tightened his grip around her waist. The moonlight illuminated their view, and they watched as a pair of large boots made their way slowly forward, stopping directly in front of Cari's face, a mere ten inches from her. She prayed the curtain was dark enough to conceal their tense bodies behind it.

"Well, well, well, what have we got here!" the voice boomed overhead. "Do you have any idea what a piece of shit you are? Total. Piece. Of. Shit." He laughed and then snarled his next words: "Time to die."

There was the distinct sound of cocking a gun. He laughed once more and fired.

Chapter 19

As soon as Tristan realized the person standing over them had a gun, he put his hand over Cari's mouth, afraid she'd scream. She must have had the same thought because rather than fight Tristan off, she added her own hand, holding his across her face.

When the gun fired twice, Cari slumped to stillness, her hand falling down and forward, almost through the curtain to their intruder's feet.

She's been shot. God, no! Please, God, no!

Tristan felt across the top of her head and was relieved not to feel the wetness of blood. He checked her pulse and realized she'd simply fainted. He gently pulled her hand back toward them so it wouldn't be seen and put his arm around her waist, holding her close.

"What the hell are you doing, you idiot!" the other voice called. "People can hear that! Shit! You're a moron!"

"Have you seen this stuff?" the voice over them retorted. "This piece of shit equipment has been here forever. I just put it out of its misery. Now the freakin' people who run this place will have to buy something new."

"Great, shithead. You killed the soundboard. Now let's get the hell out of here before someone calls the police!"

"Hey, they've got insurance. They'll get new stuff for free," the voice nearest them justified as he stomped away.

Hasty footsteps down the back stairs and a slamming door reassured Tristan that the intruders were gone. No sirens sounded in the distance; it appeared no one outside the building was aware of the breakin. He shifted back from Cari as she lay still. He needed a moment to process what had just happened.

Those hadn't been Aleynekov's people, Tristan was sure. He and Cari had just been in the wrong place at the wrong time. They'd certainly not had good intentions, though, so he was even more relieved they'd been able to stay hidden.

For now, Cari and Tristan were still safe — from Aleynekov and from the two who'd broken into the building. He looked above his head and found, as Mark had described, an open box of T-shirts. He grabbed a few, wadded them into a makeshift pillow, bent his arm up under his head to hold them in place, and breathed deeply to encourage his heart to resume a normal beat. He pulled out another bundle of shirts and put it under Cari's head.

He was pulling her — the man with the boots was pulling her from under the table. She screamed for Tristan, but he'd been hit. The monster who'd shot Tristan now held Cari tightly, despite her attempts to fight.

"Josef Aleynekov will be pleased we've found you, Ms. Lopez," the man whispered, his voice dripping with evil. "Maybe Dr. Saunders will give us what we want if we show him what we'll do to *you*. I like *doing things* to women."

Tristan appeared in front of Cari, holding a bloody arm. The man pulled her away as Tristan tried to reach for her. "Tristan!" she screamed without any volume. "Tristan, help me!" She moved rapidly through a tunnel, farther, farther away from him…

Cari came to with a start, her heart pounding. Beyond the curtain in front of her, it was quiet: no more threatening voices, no more shooting. But Tristan — he'd had his arm around her. Had he left her? Had he been taken? Was she alone?

She rolled onto her back, shifting carefully in the confined space, and turned her gaze to find Tristan. He'd kept his promise. He'd kept her safe. She turned her body further and lay on her left side, facing him. He gave her a small smile.

"What happened?" she whispered.

"You fainted. You've been out for about five minutes or so."

"But…what about…?" She hesitated. "Are we safe?"

"For now, yes. It wasn't Aleynekov's people, just teenagers out to cause trouble, I'm guessing."

"But one of them shot at us." Cari couldn't stop her tears. "I thought they saw us. I figured…that was it, you know? And then I had a dream that you'd been shot and—"

Tristan placed his hand on her cheek for a moment, quieting her. "We're all right. I promise."

She shivered uncontrollably—even her teeth chattered a little. She had to calm herself mentally if she wanted her body to relax. "I thought we were going to die," she whispered.

"God, I'm so sorry to have put you in this situation." Tristan shut his eyes and clenched his teeth. "I hate that my actions have endangered you. I hate—"

"*You* didn't do anything wrong."

"I crossed a bloody mafia boss!" he said as he opened his eyes again.

"You didn't know that—"

"I had that incriminating account information sent to the States *after* I woke up in hospital. I just had to be self-righteous and try to get that bastard. If I'd simply kept my damned mouth shut, none of this—"

"Stop, Tristan. You did nothing wrong. You didn't steal money from the Bulgarian government or its people. Aleynekov did."

"I knew he was dangerous. I was too selfish to consider how my actions might affect my family…and now you."

Cari put her fingertips on his mouth before he could say another word. "You did the right thing. And tonight, you kept your promise to me." Tears escaped again as the shock came back to her. "You kept me safe."

"God, Cari, I—"

"You kept me safe," she repeated. Suddenly she felt overcome with a need to be closer to him. Her eyes focused on her fingers as they traced the outline of his mouth, and without thinking or hesitating, she leaned forward and kissed him.

He didn't seem offended by her actions. She pulled back and looked in his eyes again. He smiled, then moved his hand to her waist and kissed her back.

"And you've kept me sane through all of this," he replied. He smirked as they looked at each other. "You know, I've wanted to do that since we went for that first walk," he said. When Cari grinned, he snaked his hand around to her lower back and returned his lips to hers.

Soon he rolled her onto her back and hovered over her, never breaking their kiss. Her hands wound around to the back of his neck, her fingers laced into his hair. As things intensified, she positioned her arm to move around his shoulder, lowering her hand to his upper back—and froze.

Cari pulled away and looked at her palm; it was smeared with blood.

"Oh, my God, Tristan, you've been shot!"

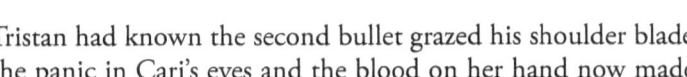

Tristan had known the second bullet grazed his shoulder blade, but the panic in Cari's eyes and the blood on her hand now made him realize that his back hurt like hell. He'd ignored his injury, too concerned about Cari and the situation to react—or even really feel it.

"We've got to get you to a hospital!" Cari cried, her voice back to just above a whisper, and her eyes brimming with tears. "God, Tristan, you're bleeding so much."

"I'm fine. It's just a surface wound." Tristan's tolerance for pain had increased tremendously while in Bulgaria...He took her hand and pressed it against the front of his shirt, attempting to wipe the blood away.

"Is it safe for us to go back to the inn? We've got to get a doctor to look at that."

"We can't, Cari. People at the hospital will see that it's a bullet wound, and that'll mean we have to reveal our names to authorities. It's just something we can't risk."

"Then Mark—he's got first aid training because he coaches," Cari immediately responded. "He can help." Cari turned over and began to crawl out from under the table.

Tristan stopped her before she stood up, though. He wanted to be sure they weren't going to be ambushed. It had been quiet since the intruders had run out the back door, and Tristan took a moment to scan the dance floor before he allowed Cari out from under the table. Before leaving the sound booth, they looked at the now-destroyed equipment. Whoever fired those shots had been using a very powerful gun.

Tristan could tell as they walked out the rear of the building and around to the inn that the back of his shirt was soaked in blood. He didn't tell Cari, but as he'd moved from under the table, he'd noted where the bullets had hit. The one that grazed him was driven into the wall behind where he'd been lying. The other had been embedded in the floor just inches from where Cari's head had been. He cringed again just thinking about it.

Cari put her arm around his waist, and he draped his around her shoulder for support—and to have her close to him. As they approached the inn, they found the others still enjoying quiet chatter, drinks in hand, and likely refilled many times during their absence.

"Ho ho! Would you look at this!" Ethan was the first to notice them as they approached, arm in arm. "Sure enough, baby, you were right," he added as he glanced over at Gemma.

Cari didn't smile, though. "Mark, we need your help. Tristan's been shot."

The immediate scraping of deck chairs against the wooden porch was deafening as they all scrambled down the front steps.

"Jesus, Tristan!" Mark made it to them first. "What happened?"

Ethan came next with his arm wrapped around Gemma. She simply stood, her hands covering her mouth, her eyes filled with tears. Ann darted into the house, likely going for the medicine kit.

Mark supported Tristan's other side, and he and Cari helped him up the steps and into the B&B. Tristan told them repeatedly that he was fine, but they didn't seem to be listening as they guided him to a chair at the table in the kitchen. Ann was already opening a first aid kit and pulling out various supplies.

"We need to cut your shirt off, okay?" she said from behind him, not waiting for an answer as she began to cut away the material. "Cari, please get me some gloves and give Mark a pair too. Then open up the package of gauze and the antiseptic ointment."

Mark and Ann made an efficient team, and Tristan's upper back was soon cleaned and bandaged. Tristan had nodded for Cari to pull up a chair beside him while they worked, and she grasped his hand. Despite the tears brimming in her eyes, she smiled warmly at him. Ethan gathered the blood-soaked shirt and used bandaging to throw away, while Gemma watched every move, her hands still over her mouth.

"You shouldn't need stitches, but don't think you're getting away without a nasty four-inch scar from that, Tristan," Mark concluded as he packed up the medicine kit. "What the hell happened? Are you okay, Cari?"

A short time later the six gathered in the living room to discuss what had transpired at the community center. As soon as Tristan recounted the conversation he'd heard between the two intruders, Ann looked over at Mark knowingly. She volunteered a lot at the high school and knew many of the students, especially the troublemakers.

"Tim Gosten and Davey Malone," they said together.

"Tim's dad's a retired police officer with a massive gun collection, a passion for hunting, and absolutely no idea what a screw-up his kid is," Mark explained. "Davey dropped out of school a year ago and already has a rap sheet for petty theft, vandalism, and the like. You say they thought you were someone they knew?"

"That was our impression," Tristan said as Cari nodded.

"Maybe Matt Kennedy?" Ann asked her husband. "Matt's build and hair color are similar to Tristan's, and the three of them used to be inseparable. I'd see them around the school all the time."

"Yeah, and Matt's been trying to go his own way since there's been talk of a baseball scholarship. That would make sense. I've seen him around after school talking to any number of girls with hair similar to Cari's. Tim and Davey would be out to give him some trouble since he dumped them a few months ago."

"Will you have to file a police report that includes us?" Cari nearly whispered. Ann noticed her lean slightly closer to Tristan on the sofa as she spoke. Tristan took her hands in his once again.

Mark put his hand to his chin, rubbing it thoughtfully. "I don't think so. Davey—assuming it was him—broke in and shot up the soundboard. He wasn't aiming for you two, thank God. Although, Christ, he's damn lucky he didn't leave a bullet in either of you, or I'd be the first to have him brought up on charges that would land his ass in jail. No," he continued, "I can simply discover the break in tomorrow and have the police do their investigation. They'll probably be able to trace the bullets back to Arthur Gosten's gun, and Davey's such an idiot, he'll likely brag about the whole thing and someone will turn him in."

Ann watched Cari's shoulders relax as she looked over at Tristan.

"I can't believe we didn't hear anything, though," Gemma said. "Gunfire? How'd we miss that?"

"The position of the two buildings would be just right to muffle the sound enough," Ethan reassured her. "I thought I heard a car backfire a while ago; that was probably when the shooting happened. Small town—I wouldn't have thought it was a gun going off."

"Well," Tristan said with a sigh, "I think I've had quite enough excitement for tonight. I hope you don't mind..." He winced as he shifted to standing. Cari stood as well.

"I'm going to head upstairs too." She shrugged. "I'm going to try to get my nerves to settle down, you know?"

Mark ambled over and pulled her into a bear hug, kissing the top of her head. "I hope you get some good sleep, baby. You come get me if you need anything, okay?"

"I will," Cari whispered. "Thanks." She waved to the rest of them and turned toward the stairs, with Tristan right behind her.

Once they were out of sight, Gemma smiled and let out a small sigh. "Well, at least now they've kissed!"

"What? How do you know that?" Mark asked skeptically.

"I just know," she replied.

Ann nodded in agreement. She could tell, too.

Cari stopped outside her room, just around the corner from the top of the stairs, and turned toward Tristan. He immediately leaned forward and kissed her. She wrapped her arms around his neck, and he pulled her into a warm embrace. Cari was careful not to touch the bandages on Tristan's back, but he didn't seem to be thinking much about his wounds at the moment.

She let the kiss deepen, and, wow, could this guy make her legs turn to Jell-O! As she stopped momentarily to catch her breath, he lowered his forehead to touch hers. God, her heart was about to pound out of her chest. It felt so good to have him holding her, kissing her, loving her.

*Wait a minute. Loving me? No...*It was just the night's excitement. Right?

Suddenly he pulled away to the opposite wall, hands by his side, a smirk on his face.

Cari gave him a quizzical look, and then heard Gemma's singsong voice as she ascended the stairs. "I'm just coming up to my room for a moment...not wanting to surprise anyone...I'll be going back downstairs quick as a wink," she announced to no one in particular.

Cari could feel Tristan's eyes on her; all she could do was look down, her blushing cheeks certainly giving her away even in the dim light of the wall sconces.

"Oh, hello!" Gemma said in mock surprise as she appeared at the top of the stairs. "Don't mind me," she said as she disappeared through the doorway of the bedroom. A few moments later, she returned, three-ring binder in hand. "All right. Good night, you two!" she called as she bounced back down the stairs.

"Well..." Cari hesitated once they were alone again. "I guess, um, we should probably go to bed now, huh?" As soon as the words were out of her mouth, she realized her faux pas.

So did Tristan. He raised one eyebrow and grinned, while trying not to actually smile or laugh.

"What I mean is—" she stumbled "—um, we should, you know, get into bed. Shoot! I mean in our own rooms. Separately. Jeez, I'm embarrassing myself royally here. God, make me shut up, will you?"

In one step he was back in front of her, cupping her chin with one hand and maneuvering the other around her back. "If I must," he said with a wickedly sexy smile.

This time his kiss was gentle, lingering. Cari laid her hands on his chest—so warm and strong—and once again let things intensify slowly. He moved even closer, and she could feel his racing heart through his shirt. What if this was something more than a post-traumatic make-out session?

Again, Cari scolded herself for irrational thinking. She needed to stop over-analyzing the situation and enjoy these amazing lips while she could.

"I hope you won't mind if I want to kiss you some more tomorrow," Tristan finally said softly, his hand caressing her face.

"I hope you won't mind if I sometimes kiss you first."

"That would be lovely," he whispered as he placed one more kiss on her forehead. He slowly backed away and gave her a sheepish grin. "Good night, Cari." He turned toward the stairway and headed up to his room.

Chapter 20

Josef Aleynekov sipped his vodka and continued to stare at the photo that had been scanned and emailed to him. Carolina Marisol Lopez's brown eyes and loose curls looked familiar. Was it a Spanish actress she resembled? He thought back through movies he'd seen with Latinas as main characters. *And those freckles.* He'd either seen her before or someone who looked hauntingly like her.

Something to do with an outdoor café? He considered the possibility...but where? Portugal? Italy?

A knock at his door distracted him, and he let his thoughts on the subject go. Where he'd seen her would come to him eventually. He stood, stretched his legs, and called to his guest to enter.

"*Ah, Alexei. Please come in, young man,*" Josef said in Bulgarian with a smile, his rich voice booming. "*I want to know how things went today.*"

"*Good, sir. I brought photographs, as you requested.*" Alexei nodded respectfully as he entered. He reached into his satchel, pulled out a handful of black-and-white pictures, and passed them to Josef.

The older man gestured to a stuffed chair as he settled on the sofa. Alexei sat on the edge of his seat, and Josef noted a nervous look in his eyes.

"*You've done well. Your targets didn't stand a chance, did they!*" Josef laughed.

Alexei responded with a slight snicker. *"No, sir. They never saw it coming."*

"And from what distance?"

"Twenty meters, perhaps?"

"I'm impressed. I'm sure Evgenia will be very pleased when I tell her."

Cari wasn't sure what to expect when it came to seeing Tristan in the morning. But when she walked out of her room about ten minutes after Gemma, Tristan was there. She couldn't determine if he'd been waiting for her or if their timing had been coincidental. But he approached her shyly, apparently also unsure about the night before.

"Good morning." He ambled over from the stairs, hands in his pockets.

"Hey. Sleep well?" Cari couldn't hold back her very seventh-grade-girl-with-a-crush grin, with a free blush thrown in for good measure, of course.

"On my side—not my usual—but, yes, I did sleep well."

His back! Cari had been so nervous about seeing him after their kiss that she'd temporarily forgotten the huge gash across his back. "Do you need, um, any pain medicine or anything?" God, she felt like a goof.

Tristan smiled crookedly, stepping closer, removing his hands from his pockets, and reaching for her waist. "I know it's corny, but maybe a kiss would make it better?"

Cari tried to hold back a smirk and failed miserably. "Well, I could maybe assist you with that…if you think it'll help. Unless you wanted someone else?" She raised her eyebrows quizzically.

"No. You. Definitely you."

There was no building up to it this time. His arms were around her, his mouth on hers in a flash, and—geez Louise—Cari was getting a kiss like she'd *never* had in her life. She responded in kind, lacing her fingers into his hair and pressing herself against him.

They parted after a minute. "Wow" was all Cari could come up with. Tristan simply responded with a smile.

"This is starting out to be a *very* good morning," he whispered. "I'm feeling better already."

"Well, that pain is likely to endure." Cari sighed. "I guess I'll have to be constantly available in case you need more pain relief."

Suddenly he winced in agony, arching his back. "Oh, the pain is excruciating!" he groaned.

"God, what is it? What happened? What can I do?" Cari felt rising panic.

But then he looked down at her with a twinkle in his eye, just as suddenly *not* in any apparent discomfort.

"You're pathetic," she said with a smirk, realizing she'd been duped. But she didn't hesitate to get back to kissing him before they finally headed down to the kitchen for breakfast.

Ethan couldn't help but roll his eyes as Cari and Tristan practically floated down the stairs together for breakfast. This morning the spread included blueberry muffins, fresh grapefruit halves, and plenty of coffee—and Cari and Tristan sat rather close together. It wouldn't have surprised Ethan to find them holding hands under the table when they could. Young love…or infatuation anyway. Reminded him of how taken he'd been with Gemma when he'd met her and how he'd wanted to be close to her every second of the day once they'd shared their first kiss. Yep. Gemma was right. Cari and Tristan had most definitely done some making out, probably even before she'd caught them blushing upstairs last night.

It was Monday morning. Mark had taken off before the rest of them even came downstairs. He had some work to do and a Tuesday basketball game to prepare for. He'd asked Ethan and Gemma if they'd like to come see his team…provided they were still in town, of course. Both Mark and Ann had let everyone know they were welcome to stay as long as they wanted. And somehow the reason for their visit had been almost forgotten as they'd all gotten to know each other. But Ethan knew, as did Tristan, that they were still likely in danger, and Ethan was getting worried that his brother-in-law had not heard from the Bulgarian lately. Sometimes no news was *not* good news.

Ethan had called in to work and let his boss know he was taking an additional week off, but would check in regularly. Gemma had also called Betsy, her assistant at the boutique on Bainbridge Island, to tell her they were extending their vacation. Ethan wanted to be available to Tristan and Cari, and keep Gemma safe, whether they stayed in Canyonville or suddenly had to be on the run.

For now, he wanted to keep things positive, especially as he looked at the two lovebirds across the table. "Hey, Tristan, Mark's team is playing a home game tomorrow night. How about we all go and watch?"

Tristan—like Gemma and probably the majority of Brits—wasn't big on basketball, but when Cari perked up at Ethan's suggestion, he automatically agreed as well. *Sucker*, Ethan thought with a smirk. *Just like any guy when he's found the right woman.*

Once the dishes were cleared and all had showered and changed, Ethan pulled Tristan outside to the porch while the women chatted inside.

"You doing okay, pal? Your back, I mean?" he asked as they settled into wooden deck chairs.

"Showering was interesting, trying to keep the bandages dry, but other than that, I'll be fine." Tristan winked in an I'm-in-pain-but-we're-not-going-to-talk-about-it way, so Ethan didn't ask anything further.

He sighed before forging ahead. "The friend of Mark's that checked the GPS said it's fine. If there's a tracker on that car, it's not in the GPS. The guy assured me of that."

"Well, I've received no new texts, nor has Aleynekov returned the call I made late last night. I'm hoping that perhaps the person who'd seen us at your apartment only followed us to the highway, noted us heading south, and Aleynekov based his text on that." He pushed his hand through his hair and looked out over the front yard, seeming to study the huge trees and fountain in the center. "He either knows where we are and is lying low, or we've escaped him." He paused, meeting Ethan's eyes. "For now."

"How's Cari with all of this?" Ethan wasn't intending to pry, but it seemed a fair question since she was on the run too.

Tristan leaned back gingerly in the deck chair and sipped his coffee. "I told her I think we need to stay here a few more days. I just don't feel comfortable letting her go home yet. We talked about it, and she's okay. She's willing to take it all day by day, just like me. God, Ethan, she could so easily hate me for what I've brought her into, but..." He looked down and laughed lightly. "She doesn't. She doesn't hate me."

"So?" Okay, maybe Ethan would pry a little. Gemma would give him hell if he didn't have *something* to report.

"So…I like her. My crazy romantic sister found me someone I can truly relate to." Tristan's face lit up. "I like her, and for a reason I can't figure out, she seems to like me too."

Ethan controlled his impulse to slap the Brit on the back, knowing the pain it would inflict. "Then go for it, Tristan. She's a nice girl, smart as a whip, and easy on the eyes, you know?"

"I've known her for all of four days, Ethan. I live and work in Europe. I've got known killers out to get me, for Christ's sake! The situation just doesn't lend itself to building any sort of relationship." His face became pensive again as he paused. "God, what a mess."

Ethan could see the frustration as Tristan tensed his jaw. He had it bad for this girl. "Yeah. I had similar thoughts as I toured museum after museum in Spain with this amazing British girl. I was from the States, had job prospects lined up, my future really mapped out, and I certainly didn't have room for some inconvenient cross-Atlantic romance." Ethan smirked, catching Tristan's eye, and left it at that.

The men sat in silence for a minute or two, sipping their coffee and reveling in the early morning air, before Ethan broached another important subject.

"I've left a message for Vasily Shevchenko," he said. Tristan suddenly turned to face him. "I think you need to fill me in as much as possible about what happened in Bulgaria and where Vasily fits in to this puzzle. You need to tell me what I should and shouldn't reveal about where you are and what you know." Ethan paused. "And I'm wondering if it might help for you to talk to him. *If* he calls me back, of course. Although if he's after you too, I may have just increased the odds they'll find you…"

"Don't worry, Ethan. I don't know Vasily Shevchenko, other than having seen his name on various falsified bank loans and money transfers. I doubt he knows me or is one of the people after me," Tristan said. "He's in deep, but I'm not sure why. I don't know how he fits into Aleynekov's inner circle, but I'm guessing he'd be pissed as hell to know he's been cheated."

"Tell me about the money laundering," Ethan asked, leaning forward and resting his forearms on his knees. "Tell me what caused you to be nearly beaten to death and has you and Cari running for your lives."

Tristan inhaled deeply, letting his breath out between pursed lips. "When the Eastern Bloc governments started to fall back in nineteen eighty-nine, so many countries were left in utter economic chaos. Various entities quickly found ways to take control of anything that could earn them money. Dealing in stolen cars, oil and other natural resources, narcotics, and even the harvesting of beluga caviar became quick routes to extreme wealth. To be fair, some of these so-called businessmen actually wanted to improve the lives of the people in their countries after decades of Communist rule. These rising stars of capitalism lined their pockets first, to be sure, but in some cases, their intent to change lives for the better was real.

"In countries like Bulgaria and Ukraine, where Shevchenko is from, new forms of dictatorship gained control within legally elected governments. People like Aleynekov and Shevchenko were savvy enough, or connected enough, to make inroads to the money. The International Monetary Fund, along with countries like the United States and Britain, literally threw billions of dollars at these fledgling democracies in their excitement to see the end of Communism in Europe. There was barely any oversight, though—little accountability as to what the money was being used for and where it was being spent. The mafia, already experts at money laundering and other lucrative schemes, was quick to set up dummy corporations and business and economic development plans they only followed through with until outsiders stopped watching. They easily swayed wealthy countries to donate 'in the name of democracy.' Meanwhile, they were laughing all the way to the banks, which they now controlled as well.

"These new leaders were smart enough to ensure that portions of their spending actually resulted in tangible improvements so that when the UN, the IMF, or donor countries requested updates, they could show progress. At the same time, though, a lot of illegal activities were reported and the corruption was being discovered. The UN and powerhouse countries soon decided to cut off trade as a form of punishment and a way to stop the crime, not knowing that those sanctions only fueled the mafia's business.

"That's been the situation since the early nineties. The mafia's got a lot of influence in government and business. In some cases, they're directly involved in setting legal policies and deciding how money is distributed. Yes, they *have* made improvements in the various countries' infrastructures, but billions of dollars have just disappeared. High unemployment rates strangle the economies of these young democracies, so the lure of earning money illegally, with little chance of getting caught, is understandable. Everyone can be bought for the right price.

"Over the years, Josef Aleynekov has risen through the political ranks to his current position as Minister of Finance, a position he's held for the past seven years. This role gave him final say on where every bit of money went, and he's been exceptionally savvy. About six months ago one of his employees, Karl Tresk, discovered some discrepancies in the numbers, as well as a duplicate set of financial records with different recipients. He contacted the UN, seeking help and protection. The UN asked Carson World Financial to investigate since we've done similar investigations in other countries.

"The UN wasn't able to protect Tresk, though," Tristan said, his eyes suddenly lost in the memory. "He left work one night and never made it home. A week later, his wife found his wallet and severed foot in a box on their doorstep. She knew it had to be the mafia, and she begged the UN not to pursue justice, fearing her children would be targeted next. Since she'd known nothing about the money laundering and was certainly not going to talk to anyone, the mafia has left her alone. They're probably still watching her, though, and I'm sure she knows it.

"Our investigation, however, was just beginning. CWF hired an accountant in Sofia to work with us—help us with translations mostly. He spoke English, Russian, Bulgarian, and three other Eastern European languages, including Ukrainian, and could translate all the correspondence we'd gathered between various people and countries involved. We checked the guy out to be sure he could be trusted, and soon a small team of us moved to Sofia to investigate locally. The Bulgarian accountant, Nikos Dobreyev, and I worked side by side, gathering facts and papers. He was invaluable.

"Nikos was supposed to come over to my flat the night I was attacked, but he called to say he was going to be late. Thank heavens he didn't arrive with me, or he might have been caught in that stairwell too.

"When I woke up in hospital over a week later, nurses told me he'd been the one to find me and that he'd been by my side the entire time. He was a good friend to me, so worried. He was the one corresponding with you and Gemma and my parents. I asked him to lie, and he agreed that it was too dangerous for either of us to reveal what had really happened. Once I was up to it, the two of us worked on writing the CWF report. We discussed Tresk's likely death and agreed that, for the safety of our families, we'd have to fully exonerate Josef Aleynekov of any wrongdoing.

"Jeez..." was all Ethan could muster.

"Ethan, I've tried to live my life as an honest man. I hated writing that report — knowing it was full of lies, knowing I was not only allowing this man to continue to steal, but raising his status in the world's view. Because a respected company like CWF basically found him not guilty, he was trusted even more." Tristan shook his head. "I'll never forget the smug look on that bastard's face when I delivered the bogus report."

Tristan leaned back and ran his hands along the arms of the chair. "But he didn't know until a month later that I'd made copies of all kinds of papers, the proof that he's been fooling dozens of his mafia colleagues around Europe. As soon as I awakened in hospital, I asked Nikos to get the sealed envelope from my office — I told him it was my will, in case I took a turn for the worse. He didn't question my request and sent the package to the US. It wasn't until I knew he'd mailed it that I told him what was really inside. Then I asked him to inform Aleynekov what I'd done. That's why Aleynekov hasn't killed me. He knows the value of those documents, but not where I've hidden them. Of course, you know where they are."

Ethan smiled. "I guess now I understand the message you sent along with it. I followed your instructions precisely. It's still sealed and well hidden, as requested. Don't worry, Tristan, it's safe."

Chapter 21

After breakfast, Cari left Ann and Gemma talking interior design, as usual, and went back upstairs to change her shoes and check for phone messages. She plopped down on her bed, legs criss-crossed, and turned on her phone. An immediate chime indicated she'd missed a call.

"Hi, baby girl." She smiled upon hearing her father's recorded voice. *"I figure you must be sleeping in or showering—or maybe you've already headed out the door. I left a message on your home phone too so you'd know my buddy and I are extending our stay at the cabin. We just came into town real quick to get some more supplies, and I wanted to catch you before I'm back out in the wilderness. We're having a great time—two old coots hiking and campin' out like we were kids. I should be home by Friday or Saturday. Gus and Julie said they've got everything under control at the store, so I'm going to enjoy myself. Miss you tons, honey. I'll call again if we come back into town. Love you."*

Cari tried right away to call the number registered in her phone but got the voicemail of someone named Gary. Again, she chose not to leave a message, just in case someone had a way of finding out. Her father seemed safe, though, out in the middle of nowhere—even Cari didn't know where he was. She hoped he'd not been too specific with anyone else he'd talked to either. She still worried about him, but was glad he was with a friend and having a good time.

She deleted the message and clicked over to texting.

Hey, Jaz. Looks like I need to stay with my cousin
for the remainder of the week. Are you okay
taking my students again? Good thing
we have Spring Break next week, huh?
I owe you big time.
Name your price and I'll pay it!

Cari and Jazmyn had combined their classes twice the previous semester, and it had worked fine. The two had similar teaching styles, and they'd created the curriculum together, so Cari had no worries about her lessons going astray. A minute later, Jazmyn responded.

No prob, Cari. Glad 2 help.
FYI there was a suicide @ your apt complex.
Lots of excitement & drama! Lots of police 2.
Some single guy, no fam. Sad.

Cari sat back against the pillows on her bed, selfishly thankful she hadn't been around for the chaos of a police investigation at Cedar View Apartments. She couldn't help but wonder if it was someone she'd seen around, though — maybe even someone she'd met. She made a mental note to go online later and check the local news to find out.

Ethan knocked gently on Tristan's door. After their morning talk on the porch, the two men had returned to their rooms to change. In passing, Gemma had reported her plans for the day to be working with Ann and Cari on more "finishing touches" to the inn.

"C'mon in," Tristan called.

"Hey. Got a sec?"

"Uh-oh. I don't like that look on your face. What's up, Ethan?"

Ethan settled on the edge of the king-size bed while Tristan sifted through the shirts he'd hung in the small armoire. He selected a loose button-down to accommodate the bandages Ann had said she'd replace later this morning.

Taking in a deep breath, Ethan delivered his news. "Vasily returned my call. We talked for only a few minutes, but he's currently in Vancouver. He's agreed to meet me for dinner tomorrow night. I've already gone online to book the flight."

Tristan stopped buttoning his shirt.

"I'm going to bring Gemma with me."

"Ethan, how can you be sure it's safe? What if——"

"I can't leave her, Tristan. I can't leave her *here* especially. Aleynekov knows who she is. Hell, Vasily knows who she is! You've got enough to deal with protecting Cari, and possibly Mark and Ann. I can check Gemma into a hotel there under a different name and pay cash. Then I'll meet with Vasily. That way if something happens to me, Gemma will be able to contact you and still remain safe."

Tristan began to pace. "Christ, Ethan…"

"I don't think anything bad will happen, honestly. You know I'm a pretty good judge of character, and in the short time I've known Vasily Shevchenko, I've found him to be just an aging man who cares about his family. I think down deep he's a good man. Whether I'm right or wrong, we've got to do something to stop Aleynekov from continuing to threaten you, Gemma, your parents, or anyone else. He's not going to stop unless we can find what threatens *him*."

"Are you sure?" Tristan was clearly conflicted. "What if I go with you?"

"No, Tristan. We can't leave Gemma and Cari alone, and we certainly can't bring them both with us, especially since Aleynekov may be tracking you somehow. I'm hoping he still doesn't know where you are. Much as I dread you getting any more texts from him, the silence is worse." Ethan stood. "I need to find out what Vasily knows about you, I need to find out if he realizes he's being cheated, and I've got to do this without exposing where you are. You're going to just have to trust me, Tristan."

Tristan dropped to the edge of the sofa in the corner, his head in his hands. "Christ…Four months ago I was just an accountant, doing my job. Now I'm a wanted man, endangering the lives of the people I care most about. I hate this, Ethan."

Ethan walked over and gently put his palm on Tristan's shoulder. "We'll end this, Tristan. Somehow we'll end this."

Ethan went downstairs to present his and Gemma's new plans and get an overnight bag packed.

Cari wished she could have stayed as composed as Ann as they hugged Ethan and Gemma goodbye. It was mid-morning, but the couple had a four-hour drive to reach Portland for their afternoon flight. Tristan came to stand by Cari's side as she wiped tears away. She'd watched him hold his sister tightly before letting her get into the car. He was scared, just like the rest of them. Cari linked her arm through Tristan's as Ethan's Lexus pulled out of the parking lot. Ann gave her a knowing glance as she went back up the porch steps and allowed them some privacy. Everyone now dealt with a new situation: the six of them no longer physically together.

Tristan and Cari began to walk down the road, away from Main Street. They meandered beyond the back of the inn toward the small creek that ran perpendicular to the road. As they crossed the simple bridge over Canyon Creek, Cari stopped to look at the clear water rushing over the gray stones of various sizes, all smooth from years of being endlessly washed. The trees on either side of the creek formed a canopy of branches that waited for the spring leaves to return. The sky was the lightest blue with only one or two clouds. Though they weren't far from the main road, nature's sounds were all Cari could hear, and it was soothing.

"Let's walk a little farther. I want to show you something," Cari said as she slipped her hand into Tristan's. He clasped her fingers, gently rubbing the side of her thumb with his.

The road curved and narrowed, and after passing a few ancient wood-frame homes taken over by weeds, vines, and time, the pavement came to an end.

"Follow me." She led him through leaf-bare trees and over fallen logs until they came to a small clearing with a few wildflowers that moved with the breeze. The creek, which wound around, was visible again, its water deeper here. They stepped carefully down a slope toward the water's edge, where a wide, flat patch of moss covered the ground.

"This is beautiful," Tristan said reverently.

"It's my haven."

"Your haven?"

"Well, I like to think of it that way. My parents and I were visiting Mark and his family when they told me they were splitting up. I was eight years old, and I just took off, you know? I was angry, hurt,

182

scared—I didn't know what to do. Mark found me and took me here, and we just sat for hours while I cried. Mark told me this could be my safe haven whenever I needed time to think or dream or whatever."

"He's a good man."

"I told you you'd like him." Cari smiled at Tristan.

"I can see why you like coming here. It's quite peaceful, isn't it."

"It's perfect, really." She pointed to a set of stones that gradually descended to the water. "Over there is the best hiding place. Just where those stones end, the tree above is, like, a hundred years old, and the root system underground created this sort of cage. As the creek has widened through the years, erosion exposed the roots. Mark and I cut some of them so we could climb inside. It's nice to sit in there when it rains."

"This whole area is lovely. I especially like it right here," Tristan said, looking sideways at Cari. "I can see why you call it your haven."

"Well…" She paused. "This is also where I had my first kiss." She immediately felt a blush warm her face.

"With that cad who proposed and then went off and married someone else?"

Tristan's disdain and the ensuing laughter was just what she needed right now. Cari smiled. "Yep. The very cad."

She sat cross-legged on the moss, and Tristan carefully lowered himself beside her. He then stretched out onto his side, facing her, his head propped up with his hand.

"So how was it? That first kiss, I mean."

"Amazing…" Cari said dreamily as she played with a few strands of long yellow grass that edged the moss.

Tristan's eyebrows rose.

"Amazing in how awful we both were," she added with a laugh. "He'd only kissed one other girl but, God, he thought he was all that. Tried French kissing me right off the bat, and I had no idea why he was trying to get his tongue in my mouth. I kept backing up until he finally had to tell me what he was doing."

Tristan was laughing now.

"Yeah. Disastrous. But then I let him try again, once I was over my thorough embarrassment, and we did okay. He was slobbery, though. I couldn't help but think later that I felt like I'd been licked by a golden retriever. But…still, it was my first kiss, and I'll always remember it."

"Ever kiss anyone else out here?"

"No, just him."

"Mind if I replace those horrific memories with some new ones? I promise not to slobber."

Cari shifted to face Tristan, her position mirroring his.

He caressed her face. "I still think he was a cad for leaving you like that. He has no idea what he gave up."

"Yeah, an anal retentive bookworm who can't cook to save her life."

"Oh, no, no, no," Tristan said softly as he kissed her lightly on the lips. "I see so much more. You're beautiful…" He kissed her again. "Highly intelligent and driven…" Another kiss. "Funny…" Another kiss. "Kind-hearted…" Another kiss. "And did I mention how amazing you kiss?"

"Oh, really?" was all Cari could get out before he rolled her onto her back, deepening their kiss. This would definitely replace any and all old memories of time spent in the haven.

They kissed for a while, adding whimsical comments when they seemed appropriate, and eventually Tristan returned to his side-lying position while Cari stayed flat on her back, looking up through the bare branches into the cloudless sky.

In their silence, reality hit her: she was falling for him. She knew it was stupid, but she couldn't help it.

Tristan looked at Cari and realized something was happening between them. He could reason that they simply hadn't known one another long enough for such feelings to surface, but his heart wasn't buying it. It'd been a mere four days, but they'd been nearly insepa-rable—sharing fears, views on a variety of subjects, childhood stories, and their hopes and ambitions. They'd crammed three months of date-night conversations into little more than a weekend.

It only took a moment for him to know he was falling in love with her.

But as soon as Tristan admitted that, reality came rushing to the surface. Cari's life, family, and work were here on the far west coast of the United States, and his were thousands of miles away in England, a place he'd be returning to in a few short weeks.

Suddenly the thought of London held no appeal at all.

He wondered whether Cari might be starting to feel the same about him, and if she might be willing to consider a long-distance relationship, just to see what might come of it. Just like he'd felt in grade school, fearful of asking a girl to dance, Tristan had no idea what to say. Surprisingly, Cari took the lead.

"I wish you didn't have to go back to London," she said. Her voice was but a whisper, and she didn't look at him when she spoke, but it was out there now.

"I don't think I want to go back."

That was all they needed to say. This moment was enough for now. She reached for him, pulling him toward her, but her purpose was not to kiss. Tristan rested his head between her jaw and shoulder and laid his arm across her stomach.

"Gemma and Ethan are going to be okay, Tristan. They are. I just know it. He's smart, and he won't let anything happen to her."

"How'd you know what I was thinking?"

"It's what I'm thinking about too."

Tristan wrapped his arm around Caria little tighter and sighed. Her fingers traced light circles on his arm and shoulder, and he let himself be soothed by the gentle breeze and spring sunshine of Cari's haven.

As Jenny and Ben drove down Main Street in this spit of a town called Canyonville, she couldn't help but think of Bulgaria. Outside Sofia there were plenty of villages like this dotting the rough countryside. Canyonville was obviously a number of steps up economically—with technology, infrastructure, and modern conveniences readily available—but she still missed the big city. When this assignment was over, she'd do what she could sneak away with Alexei. She hadn't seen him in nearly a year and deserved time alone with him. The farther they could get from Josef's influence and power, the better. For that to happen, Tristan Saunders needed to be dead and those papers he had back in Josef's hands as soon as possible.

She allowed herself a moment to remember Alexei. His piercing green eyes, tousled sand-colored hair, and obvious love for her made her smile. As always, her heart began to pound—missing him did that to her. But she knew what she'd face if she returned to Sofia; she couldn't go back, not until she could gain control of the situation there. She sighed. *I did not bring this fate upon myself. And if killing is what will bring Alexei back, then I will kill. And I'll kill again and again and again, until we're together.* Jenny clenched her jaw, more determined than ever.

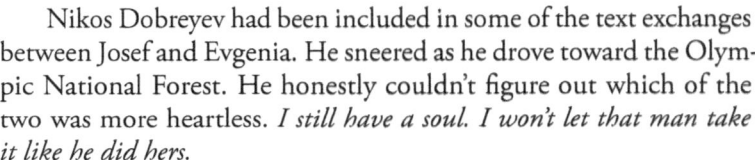

Nikos Dobreyev had been included in some of the text exchanges between Josef and Evgenia. He sneered as he drove toward the Olympic National Forest. He honestly couldn't figure out which of the two was more heartless. *I still have a soul. I won't let that man take it like he did hers.*

He hated his father; he hated being the son of someone so powerful and so evil. There was no leaving this family's "business," and he cursed the life he was forced to lead. Even with a different last name—his father's idea so Nikos could work in the public eye without being associated with the Aleynekov family—he still felt trapped. He'd tried to convince his father to let him be. He knew the rules: he was sworn to secrecy and there would be consequences for breeching any confidences. Meeting Mila Yankova at university had provided the only light in his world. She'd known marrying him would be a life sentence for her too, but she'd married him anyway.

It would've been their second anniversary this summer, but the pressure of a mafia family had proved too much for Mila. Nikos was gone for weeks—even months—at a time, sent on assignments his father claimed were necessary. Mila was left in Sofia, not allowed to work—Josef's decision—and followed everywhere she went. Nikos had seen how this life was slowly draining her, destroying her, and he'd asked his father not to send him away so often or for so long. Josef would only smile and say the family needed everyone to do their part.

Fourteen months after Nikos and Mila's wedding, he came home to find her lifeless body in bed, an empty prescription bottle and a note in her hand. He'd read it so many times that night, he'd nearly memorized it.

My dearest Nikos,

I'm so sorry to do this to you. I know you've tried to make our marriage a happy one, and I love you for that. Everything else, though...it's too much. I didn't know how else to get out and couldn't risk you getting hurt. I need you to do one last thing for me, my love. Please convince others that this was an accidental overdose and not a suicide. My family would never understand, and yours might make things difficult for you or my family if they knew.

I have left a card for you on the table, welcoming you home, telling you I haven't been feeling well and to wake me so we can have dinner. Burn this letter so only you will know the truth.

I wish things could have been different. I wish we could have raised a family and grown old together. This was not an easy decision, leaving you. I believe I'll see you again someday, though. Please, Nikos, my only love, live a good life. I'll be watching over you.

My love to you forever,

Mila

He knew she was dead, but still he'd tried for nearly an hour to breathe life back into her. After another hour of lying beside her and holding her in his arms, he took the letter into the bathroom and held it over the toilet, ready to burn it, but he couldn't do it. He couldn't destroy this love letter from his wife. Instead, he folded it and tucked it deep into the lining of his wallet. Finally, when he couldn't postpone any longer, he called his father.

Josef's reaction surprised Nikos: the man was furious. He disowned Mila post mortem and told Nikos that her grave would not be within the Aleynekov family's compound. Despite the card Mila had written, Josef bluntly asked his son if his wife had killed herself.

"Your woman was weak, Nikos. I never should have allowed someone so inferior to marry into this family. She was a dirty little stain," he said with a sneer. "I wash her from my memory. Bury her and be done with it."

Josef had forced Nikos to refuse the coroner's request to perform an autopsy, saying the sooner she was out of the Aleynekovs' lives, the better. Given Josef's position in the Bulgarian government, he was able to quash notices in the paper about Mila's passing and circumvent the routine police protocols for accidental deaths like this. A mere two days after Nikos had found his wife's body, he stood alone, throwing flowers onto her casket as two gravediggers lowered it into the ground.

Nikos's personality had changed the day he buried his precious Mila. People around him noticed it immediately, and now they feared him. They saw his dead eyes and knew he was in mourning — but he was also the next generation in the Aleynekov dynasty, not to be crossed. Unbeknownst to others, however, Nikos had a plan for his future. One that did not include his father.

He was nearing his destination now; the sign for Hoodsport and the Staircase Trails on the eastern border of the Olympic National Forest brought him back to the present. Evgenia and Josef's text exchanges had indicated that Carolina Lopez's father lived and worked in Kirkland, Washington, northeast of Seattle. The man owned the town's lone hardware store, and Nikos stopped in to purchase a ratchet set he didn't need. Through casual conversation, he found out Ronaldo Lopez was hiking for a week.

Nikos had gotten a map, stopped next door at a small sandwich shop, and then headed south on the 405. When he arrived two hours later at the campground where Lopez had rented a cabin, the jovial groundskeeper said most of the guys had gone up to a local hangout in nearby Lilliwaup. Nikos thanked the man and soon arrived at Fred and Shorty's Tavern, where he promptly bought himself a beer.

Canyonville had few options for accommodations. Jenny had been roughing it in Salem in what Ben considered a high-end place, and she wasn't about to stay at the Best Western or Valley View Inn.

So they doubled back to the Seven Feathers Casino they'd passed as they arrived. It wasn't the Ritz-Carleton, but it would do. Besides, it would be full of people around the clock, so it would be easier for them to blend in.

Ben examined their hotel room like a child on a sugar high, opening and closing every door, drawer, and cabinet. Then he began to leaf through the hotel's coffee table notebook of amenities, reporting to Jenny what the place had to offer. "You mind if I go check out the casino? You wanna come?"

Jenny was already seated at the small desk, trying to get her computer connected to the internet. "What? Oh, no. You go ahead. I'll stay here for a bit." As he walked toward the door, Jenny called out to him. "Cash only. We have to be nobodies while we're here. And don't do anything that will bring attention to yourself, okay?"

He gave a thumbs-up and lumbered out the door. Once he was gone, she did a search for "Mark Stoddard" in Canyonville and got a few hits, most being quotes in the sports section of the local newspaper about high school athletics. She still didn't know his connection to Carolina Lopez—other than being her emergency contact where she worked.

Among the newspaper articles she'd perused online, she'd found one about the renovation of an old inn by Mark and Ann Stoddard. An address was included, which Jenny wrote down. If this place was in business, perhaps that's where Saunders and Lopez were hiding out.

Jenny opened her travel bag and pulled out her brunette wig, setting it by a change of clothes. The last thing she needed was to run into Tristan Saunders. The hotel had security cameras everywhere, able to track her movements quite easily, so a disguise was definitely needed. After a quick shower and the addition of brown contact lenses, she texted Ben to let him know she was going to run some errands.

Ethan had held Gemma's hand nearly the entire drive to Portland, and again once they boarded the plane for their early afternoon flight to Vancouver. They often traveled like this, but today...today he felt desperate to hold her as much as he could, even if it was just her hand.

It was strange: he'd never gotten a bad feeling about Vasily Shevchenko before. The Ukrainian had allowed Ethan access to much of his business files, including portions of his finances that would help Ethan in his consulting work, and the man had always impressed him as a loving grandfather-type. He had an endless array of photos of his three grandchildren in his Seattle office, a beautiful painting of him with his wife, Nadia, and a family portrait with his daughter and son-in-law. It was his daughter's home in Vancouver he was visiting when Ethan had called, and his voice indicated genuine concern at the younger man's request. Shevchenko gave Ethan the address of the small Vancouver apartment where he and his wife lived.

Either Vasily Shevchenko was very good at conning Ethan or he was honestly ignorant of Aleynekov's financial endeavors and what the Bulgarian was doing with regard to Tristan and Cari. It was time to find out.

With the place to herself, Ann began to distract her errant thoughts with a pot roast. It was a little past two, and Mark would probably stay after school to prepare for the following night's game. Whether he was able to slip home for a quick dinner or she had to bring it to him in a Thermos, this way he'd have a good, hearty meal before the team's practice. He was an enthusiastic coach, to say the least, always willing to put in late hours to help "his boys."

Once the meat was simmering and the aroma had begun to waft through the downstairs, Ann set the timer for two hours. Then she'd need to chop the carrots and potatoes to add to the pot. Some bags of mulch by the side of the house needed to be dispersed around the newly planted flower beds, so she grabbed her gardening gloves and headed outside.

A little after three, a BMW pulled into the side driveway and a young woman in slim-fitting jeans and lavender silk shirt got out. Ann stood, brushed the mulch from her gloves, and headed over.

"Hi," the woman said cheerfully, offering her hand. "I was just driving by and—wow! Is it open for business?" She stood back and took in the expanse of the inn, cupping her hand over her eyes as she looked up toward the third-floor dormer windows.

A potential guest! Ann's heart leapt. "No, not for another few weeks. We're almost ready, though. Once we get the scaffolding down from the back of the house and do some last-minute primping, I think we'll be ready to host our first guests. You're welcome to take a peek at the first floor, though, if you want."

The woman smiled and nodded, and they walked slowly toward the front porch. "I couldn't convince you to provide a place for me and my husband for a few days, could I?" she asked with a sideways glance.

Ann grinned. "No, sorry. I've actually got family in from out of town right now, so even if we were open, I wouldn't have any room."

The woman nodded. "Nothing like having family be your guinea pigs, eh?" she said with a laugh.

"Exactly! But it's been really nice. I've gotten a chance to try out some breakfast recipes and, well, so far so good! Come on inside. I can at least provide you a brochure."

Ann held the door as her visitor entered the foyer. The woman didn't stop there.

"Wow," she said from the living room. "This place is gorgeous. I'm definitely telling my husband about it!"

"Are you from around here?" Ann asked as the woman continued her slow stroll around the room, gently touching the tables, frames, and lamps.

"Just up in Eugene but, you know, it just doesn't have the quaint feeling that Canyonville does. It's nice to get away sometimes. I'm just on my way back from visiting my mom in Medford, and I've been meaning to take the side trip to check out this little town. It really is quite sweet!"

"Sometimes it's a little too small," said Ann. "But my husband and I like it here."

"Does he run the inn with you?"

"No, he's a guidance counselor at the high school, as well as the coach of nearly every sport they have. He's been a great help, though, and he'll always be around on the weekends when we'd be likely to have the most guests."

"Well, I think this place is just darling. You've done a wonderful job decorating," she said as they walked back toward the front door. "You said you have a brochure?"

"Oh, yes!" Ann picked up a freshly printed pamphlet from a marble-topped antique table in the entryway.

"Can I take one for my mom too?"

"Certainly. You're my first unofficial advertisement! Take more if you want."

"No, I'm sure word of mouth is going to bring you plenty of business. Sounds like you've got everything just about ready, and I'll be showing this to my husband tonight." She smiled. "We've got an anniversary coming up in June."

Ann returned her warm smile. "Well, thank you for stopping by. I'm the owner, Ann Stoddard. My contact information is on the back of the brochure. We've got a website too," she added, pointing to the folded paper in her guest's hands. She extended her hand once again and the woman immediately reached out to shake it.

"Nice to meet you, Ann. Thank you for taking the time to share so much about the place. I appreciate it more than I can say."

Ann smiled again.

"Oh, and so you'll know it's me when I book a room, my name is Jenny Allen."

Chapter 22

Josef was beginning to find this whole situation tiresome. He needed the information Tristan Saunders had, and he did not want to deal with those whose loyalty seemed questionable any longer. One of his colleagues, shall we say, had definitely outlived his usefulness; it was time to take care of him. Josef opened his cell phone and began to type to Evgenia in Bulgarian.

**Please have someone check on my aging American friend.
I fear he is not happy anymore.**

He followed that message with a cryptic synopsis of how he'd procured Carolina Lopez's contact information. Evgenia would understand. He could count on her to assign the right person to this task, someone who could guarantee it would be completed soon and without any way to trace it to the Aleynekov family. Once sent, he deleted the message and mentally crossed this loose end off his list.

Ah. Dear Jonathan. Jenny had found him to be a lousy lover who never showed true loyalty to the Aleynekov family. Sleeping with him had been a chore. The arrogant jerk! Honestly thinking he'd bagged a woman half his age because he was attractive or sexy...Not even close! She'd nearly vomited afterward. Jenny had done a lot of horrible things for Aleynekov, but this had been the worst.

Having the professor break into personnel files for Lopez's contact information had been a huge help, but Dr. Lassiter had no idea they had also set him up. Jenny's colleague Grigor was exceptionally gifted in technology (among other things, she remembered with a smile), and they were now in possession of the university's security tapes, which clearly showed the revered Dr. Jonathan Lassiter breaking and entering the university's administrative offices. Now it was time to tie up loose ends. Jenny began typing a quick text to Grigor.

> Send the video to our esteemed friend, as well as
> the university's president and board of trustees.
> Meet our friend at home and help him realize his only option.

Just like that stupid maintenance man, Rudy, Lassiter would be found with a suicide note in his own handwriting and his body stiff as a board. This time, hanging made the most sense, Jenny figured. No noise to alert neighbors like a gun to the head would invite. Besides, Lassiter liked being seen as over-the-top; leaving this world via noose would make sure people read about him even after he died. The police would, of course, find his computer opened to the incriminating email. Poor Jonathan.

Good riddance.

Before sending the text, Jenny thought for a moment. She added one other minor task for Grigor, and just as she hit send, Ben returned to the hotel room.

"Baby, baby, baby! Look at what papa brought home!" He flopped on the bed and spread out a wad of hundred-dollar bills. "Three grand, honey. Three grand! I'm taking you out tonight, and I want to buy you the sexiest dress so I can show you off."

"Please tell me you were discreet down there, Ben," Jenny said, feeling a little peeved. Three thousand dollars wasn't a huge win, but it was big enough to catch security's attention in a small casino like this. They'd have to be sure Ben appeared as just some lucky tourist who'd turn around and lose half his take on the next round.

"Chill, Jenny," he said with a grin. "I was very cool down there, I promise." He swiped up the loose bills and stuffed them back in an envelope. "So, where were you?"

"I was working," Jenny said with confidence. "I found out where Saunders and Lopez are staying and got to meet Mark Stoddard's wife, Ann. They're less than two miles from here."

"Wait a minute. You *went* there? Without me? What the hell were you thinking? You could have been seen! You could have been hurt!"

Jenny began to quietly lose her temper. She would not be scolded by this underling. She needed to put his disrespectful ass in its place right now. "First of all, don't you ever speak to me like that again." The look on Ben's face told her he knew she was serious. "Second, we're here on business—remember that. My only purpose for being in this shithole is to find Saunders. And give me some goddamn credit, will you? I checked my BlackBerry right up until I got out of my car at the Stoddards' place to be sure Saunders wasn't there. I told that woman I was a tourist, and she believed every word. She even confirmed that family was staying there right now. I think what we'll earn from finding Josef's fifty-two million will be a whole lot more than the three grand you just won."

Jenny paused to watch him; he was clearly embarrassed and humbled after challenging her. "Now, here's the plan: tonight we lay low. I'll see what else I can find out about the Stoddards and whether we need to be on the lookout for anything. Josef hasn't contacted Saunders in a few days, so it's likely he and Lopez are starting to relax. It's good to make them think we've stopped trailing them; they'll be less on guard, less likely to take off, and easier for us to watch. To-morrow night, though, it'll be all you, darlin'. You and a basketball game. You do this right, and I'll buy myself the sexiest dress you can imagine and let you peel it off me when we're done here." She was still pissed as hell at Ben, but she knew she'd be in bed with him again... *if* he did what he was told.

A hornet buzzing near Cari's ear stirred her, and she realized she—and Tristan—had fallen asleep. She flicked it away with her hand, thus jarring Tristan, whose head still lay on her shoulder. He squeezed her tight for a moment before pulling himself up to sitting.

"I've now slept with you three times and always been the perfect gentleman," he said with a wink. He gently brushed her hair back from her forehead, pulling away a few pieces of yellowed grass that had gotten caught in her curls.

"Three times?" Cari smirked.

"Gemma and Ethan's flat that first night you were locked out," he said as he began to count on his fingers, "under the table when we were shot at—well, technically you fainted, but still—and just now."

Cari smiled. "I guess you're right. Wow. Imagine the gossip if that news got out."

"What? About us sleeping together or me being a perfect gentleman?" Tristan asked with raised eyebrows.

"I don't know. Which would bother you more?"

Tristan moved closer to Cari and kissed her sweetly. "I would never want to sully your reputation, so I'd far rather be talked about as a perfect gentleman, thank you. I've never found that to be an insult and, frankly, I'm quite proud of myself."

"I'm sure Mark would agree," Cari added with a snicker. "I'm all grown up, but that doesn't mean he wouldn't try to defend my honor."

"I'll promise to behave myself especially around your cousin, then."

"And when he's not around?"

"Hmm…" Tristan eyed Cari seductively. "Sorry, but I may slip up a bit. I hope you don't mind."

"As long as the slipping up results in you kissing me, I won't mind at all."

Tristan kissed her again quickly. "All right, future Dr. Lopez, we need to get some work done."

"Work?" Cari suddenly felt confused.

"Didn't I promise I'd help you with your dissertation topic?" he asked as he stood and offered her his hand. "You've got a deadline coming up, and I refuse to be the reason you don't meet it."

"Tristan…" Cari began to whine.

"Hush, now. Ann provided me with her library card and directions to said place. Let's get at least an hour of work in this afternoon, shall we?"

Before she could protest further, Tristan leaned forward, kissed Cari's forehead, and grabbed her hand, pulling her gently up the grassy hill and back toward the road that would lead them to Main Street.

Grigor Matveyev gazed into his own eyes as he brushed his hair away from his face. The man staring back was equal parts fearsome and captivating. Men knew not to cross him, and women smiled and bought him drinks whenever he went out, hoping it would result in a romp in the sack later. He usually obliged.

He'd received another assignment from Josef via Evgenia, and his thoughts drifted back to the times he'd been with the minx. He'd been her first lover when they were teens, and she was wild even then. She was the feminine version of him, and in some ways that was a good thing: hot times with no strings attached and no expectations.

He'd been lucky, really, to have worked his way up through Aleynekov's dynasty enough to be included on private matters and important business. Pretty good for a Romanian orphan who'd been charming his way from place to place since age ten. After five years, he'd finally landed on the streets of Sofia, Bulgaria. He'd been born Grigor Nikolai Mateyescu, but he'd changed his name once he left Romania. He'd severed all ties to his homeland, a place that only brought him anger and pain.

For the first few years in Bulgaria, he'd pretended to be mute. He hadn't known the language, but he'd looked the right way to fit into street society. Because he never spoke, no one guessed he was a foreigner — someone from a place even more dangerous and corrupt than Bulgaria. He'd gotten money from begging and petty theft at first. His good looks, however, became a profitable asset as he discovered the lonely wives of wealthy men were willing to pay for a night's comfort in the arms of a silent, virile young man.

One of those women, Irena Aleynekova, saw potential in Grigor, and she convinced her husband to hire him as her personal body-guard. Whether Josef ever suspected his wife's brief infidelity or not, he never revealed it to Grigor; instead, he took him under his wing at age eighteen and began to help him. Josef allowed Grigor to live in the gatehouse so he'd be readily available any time Irena wanted to travel about Sofia. He'd also paid for him to attend university, insisting that he study technology and mechanical engineering, and learn to speak English. Over the next ten years, Grigor came to feel like a member of the family, and he was given all the same privileges as Josef's son, Nikos.

Thus, Grigor the Romanian orphan had become a member of Bulgaria's most powerful family. He knew as long as he did what Josef asked, he'd continue to live among high society, never having to worry about his next meal ever again. He'd long ago given up any semblance of morals or ethics. He had a heart; he just chose not to share it with anyone. His childhood had been brutally unfair, but he'd worked his ass off to get where he was now. That's all that mattered. He'd followed every bit of advice his mentor had given him. His English, although spoken with an Eastern European accent, was excellent. Actually, it was quite the turn-on for the American women he'd met since moving to Washington for his current assignment. His life was just about perfect.

Well, perfect for a mafia assassin, anyway.

He pulled the comb through his hair one last time and winked at his reflection. It was time to go to work.

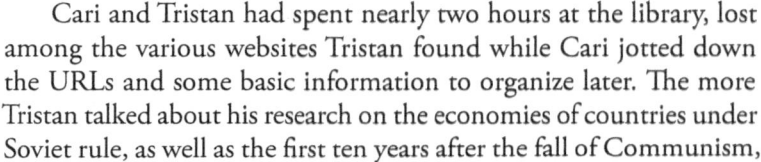

Cari and Tristan had spent nearly two hours at the library, lost among the various websites Tristan found while Cari jotted down the URLs and some basic information to organize later. The more Tristan talked about his research on the economies of countries under Soviet rule, as well as the first ten years after the fall of Communism, the more fascinated Cari became with finding ways to expand on what he'd studied. Of course, there was the chance she'd have to cite Jonathan Lassiter's work, and that made her cringe. The last thing she wanted was to boost that man's ego any larger than it already was.

Their conversation had also drifted to Tristan's most recent work in Bulgaria. He explained further about how the mafia had been strong under Communist rule but began to truly thrive on its own once money was free-flowing from Western nations. It was evidently quite easy to hide money here and there through what looked like legitimate business and trade. Cari began to wonder...Might money laundering in former Soviet countries be what she wanted to study for her dissertation? The bigger concern would be whether she'd be endangering her life if she took on such a topic. She decided not to ask Tristan until she was able to do a little Web searching on her own first, something she'd try to do when they returned to the library tomorrow.

Jonathan Lassiter hadn't slept well Sunday night, and he'd spent all day Monday looking over his shoulder, jumping at the slightest comment or greeting from colleagues as he crossed the campus to return to his office after the faculty meeting. He'd avoided the administration building. Any mail for him could wait another day or two.

What would Aleynekov tell him to do next? Commit murder? He'd already laundered money—his own and that of people associated with the Bulgarian Minister of Finance—so he knew he'd face prison time if caught. He became so concerned, he went to a cyber café and logged on with his alias so he could be sure his accounts were safe. He was a weak man; he knew that. He'd been lured by money and had made decisions he knew were irreversible. He belonged to Aleynekov, of that he was now sure. That money was his only safeguard. His heart raced as he realized what he needed to do: escape.

When he got home from the café, he lay awake, wondering where he'd want to live and decided Australia would be ideal. That made him smile for the first time in days. He'd have to book his flights under his alias—a name he'd never shared with Aleynekov—and, of course, he'd have to book multiple flights to various places, in case the Bulgarian should catch on to what he was doing. He'd seen enough movies to know that the greater the number of stops, the less likely Aleynekov or his associates would be able to accurately track him. Early retirement with enough money to live two more lifetimes sounded good to him. He'd begin booking flights the next day back at the cyber café.

Chapter 23

Ethan and Gemma had stopped for the night at a seedy hotel just outside Vancouver: the kind that had a wink-and-a-smile check-in policy, frequent use of assumed names, and payment only accepted in cash. Once Ethan had ferried their baggage into the room — which was surprisingly and thankfully odor- and insect-free, they settled in to discuss a contingency plan, should he fail to return or call Gemma by ten o'clock the following evening.

He planned do some investigative work in the morning and then go to Shevchenko's apartment. He wanted to arrive early enough to watch the place for a few hours, make sure he wasn't going to be ambushed. If he saw anything suspicious, he'd promised Gemma he'd call off the meeting and talk to Shevchenko only by phone.

Gemma finally fell asleep in Ethan's arms around two in the morning. At eight o'clock on Tuesday, they grabbed a bite of breakfast at a local diner. By nine, Ethan was ready to head out. He gave Gemma enough cash to grab a cab out of there, should she need to. But, God willing, that wouldn't be necessary. With a passionate kiss and long embrace, Ethan promised her he'd return soon.

After breakfast Tuesday morning, Ann shooed Cari and Tristan from the inn. "You two were nonstop at dinner last night about the articles you found. Go. Get back to that library. If I hear another word about accounting or international economics, I'm going to start singing—loudly. And believe me, you don't want that. Now, get out of here," she said with a smile.

Cari and Tristan grabbed their laptops and notebooks, and Cari thanked Ann for another wonderful breakfast—quiche Lorraine today, with fresh cantaloupe on the side—before they headed up the hill to the Canyonville Public Library. They quickly got to work, and Cari covertly saved articles and websites she'd want to investigate again if Tristan felt the money laundering angle was a good one to pursue.

At noon, they walked down to the Canyon Café, and they promised to not talk about the dissertation until they returned to the library.

"So…" Cari ventured, looking shyly at Tristan. "You know about my engagement and first romance. Care to share some of your escapades?"

Tristan coughed, brought his napkin to his mouth, and let out a laugh. "Escapades? I don't think anything from my past would even remotely qualify as an escapade."

"Okay." Cari decided to be brave. "I am curious, though…Are you dating anyone? I mean, is there some leggy blonde waiting for you back in London?"

Tristan's face reddened as he shifted in his seat, and Cari almost regretted her question.

"No," Tristan replied softly as he looked out the window. "My last date was, oh, six months ago, maybe? It was the last time I went out with a woman I'd been dating for nearly a year." He stopped and looked down at his plate. "Melanie. She was a colleague with CWF, but when I got injured, she wanted nothing more to do with me."

"God, but you got attacked because—"

"My boss in London chose not to reveal what happened to me. He worried that if anyone knew what was going on in Bulgaria, they'd be in danger too. So only those of us on that assignment knew the truth. The London staff was told I'd been in a car accident."

"So your girlfriend left you because she thought you were in a car accident?"

"I don't know. She simply refused to take my calls or return any messages I left her. One of my mates told me she moved out of our flat pretty quickly as well."

"I'm so sorry, Tristan."

"God, don't be. Mel and I had barely talked to each other once I'd been assigned to the investigation in Sofia. Absence did not make either of our hearts grow fonder. She wasn't right for me, and I knew that. It was just nice to have someone to come home to."

"And how long were you in Bulgaria?"

"A total of five months. The last three were spent in a hospital bed."

Cari sat up a little and decided to change the topic. "Okay. So Melanie was your most recent girlfriend. Who else has fallen for those eyes of yours?"

"You mean other than you?" Tristan shot back with a smile.

It was Cari's turn to blush. "Yeah. Other than me."

"Wanda Fitz-Cleffington."

Cari covered her mouth as she laughed. "Wanda Fitz-Cleffington? All right. Tell me about Wanda Fitz-Cleffington."

"Oh, she was a much older woman, easily twenty years my senior."

"Really!" Cari's eyebrows raised in interest. "A cougar, huh?"

"She was the school's violin teacher during my teen years. She was a divorcée who wore low-cut blouses and tight skirts, and she flirted with me to the point of embarrassment. She'd always say, 'Oh, your eyes are just gorgeous.'" Tristan offered in a high, breathy voice.

"Well, she's right, you know."

"So everyone tells me." Tristan sighed. "It'd be different if I were complimented for something I had control over. Then I could say thank you. But my eyes are just…my eyes. Gemma's aren't much darker."

"Hers are a true sky blue, but yours are more like a wolf's. They really are very pretty."

Tristan squirmed in his seat again and ate another French fry, his eyes focused downward.

"Okay. I won't compliment you directly. Give me your parents' phone number, and I'll call them and tell them it's a good thing they got together so they could have you with those beautiful eyes."

That got a laugh out of Tristan, and he looked up. "I'm sure they'd be thrilled to have some American woman call them randomly to thank them for giving birth to me." He paused. "Are we done with lunch and talking about my irises? Or are you trying to avoid getting back to your dissertation?"

"Guilty as charged." Cari grabbed her purse, threw a few dollars on the table, and stood. "I've got this one," she said as she went to the front counter to pay before Tristan could protest.

They left the Canyon Café at nearly one o'clock and vowed to get in at least two more hours of library research before calling it quits. They needed to be back at the inn early enough to walk over to the high school with Ann and wish Mark good luck before tonight's game.

Ben had spent the afternoon strolling the few streets of Canyonville, stopping in local shops and grabbing lunch at Ken's while he kept a distant eye on his targets. As he tossed the waxed tissue liner from his burger basket into the trash can, he felt his phone vibrate. There were two new text messages.

Hey thot you'd want 2 see pics of ur niece. Chloe luvs the stuffed panda u got her. Its ears have withered a bit – she likes 2 suck on them when she's sleeping in her new big-girl bed. Visit soon. XOXO Talia

Ben smiled as he scrolled through the three pictures his sister, Talia, had sent. They didn't live far from him, but it had been a while since he'd visited her and her family. Once this gig was over and Saunders got his due, Ben would make a point of going to see little Chloe. Maybe he'd find another stuffed animal she might like.

When Ben opened the second text, he sneered. What did that asshole Chameleon want this time?

That chik ur with may b hot shit but the cops r looking 4 her. Im only telling u cuz we gotta take care of our own, kwim?

Ben scrolled down, clicked on the link Lamb had included, and soon saw the front page of the *Seattle Times'* Local section. To the left of the article was a grainy photo of a thin blonde in a floral dress. Ben recognized the background: Cedar View Apartments. He perused the article about a maintenance man who had been found dead in his apartment. A suicide, it said, but the police were investigating the circumstances. Interviews with neighbors noted that the man, Varuud "Rudy" Zakharov, had always seemed upbeat and mentioned to one person his enthusiasm about a date he had that night. Three witnesses described a pretty blonde woman with him on the night in question. She was not identified, and police provided the picture from one of the complex's security cameras, hoping someone might know how to reach her for questioning.

Ben studied the photo as best he could, given it was on his cell phone. Yeah, it looked a little like Jenny, but that was the night she was with *him*. He was most definitely her alibi, as they'd gone straight from Zimm's to his apartment and spent the rest of the night in his bed. They hadn't been apart since. That idiot Chameleon was wrong; the picture could be anyone. He closed the link and pocketed his phone. He couldn't think any further about that right now; it was time to follow his targets again as they headed back to the library.

As Cari and Tristan descended the stairs to the foyer of the inn at six o'clock, Ann came around the corner from the kitchen. "Ready to head over?" she asked.

When they arrived after the short, one-block walk to the gymnasium, there was still a little time before the game, so Ann led them around to the coaches' offices to say hello. After greetings, Mark thanked Ann for the reheated pot roast she'd brought over earlier. They were playing Days Creek High School, a school of similar size that was located a few miles away and was Canyon Creek's fiercest competition. Tonight's game was the first of the post-season district tournament, and Cari knew it was an important one for Mark's team to win. She could see the focus in her cousin's eyes, and she pulled Tristan from his office as soon as they'd said hello and good luck. Ann lingered a moment to get the score sheets she'd be filling out during the game, and Cari led Tristan around to the front entrance of the gym where she purchased two tickets.

She knew Mark would have insisted they enter without paying, but she figured every dollar helped the athletic program. It was money well spent. They passed the concession stand and walked into an already half-full gym. With their long rivalry and close proximity, the two high schools' games always filled the stands with rowdy fans. Cari held tight to Tristan's hand so they wouldn't get separated and smiled. He was in for an interesting experience.

Cari surveyed the scene and figured where Mark and Ann would be sitting. She selected seats a few rows up and a little to the right of center court, just behind where they'd be.

"You realize I do understand basketball, don't you?" Tristan asked.

"Well," Cari sputtered, "I guess I do now. But you're in for a real treat 'cause with teams this good, this place is going to get a little wild." She glanced over at the doors, and sure enough, two police officers were situated at the end of the bleachers on the other side of the gym. She pointed them out to Tristan. Cari also looked around behind her, wondering if the two men who'd broken into the community center were there. She shivered and moved a little closer to Tristan, not saying a word.

Grigor had watched his target for the past two days, ever since Evgenia had given him the assignment. He contemplated his instructions and wondered if he could get a little creative without backlash from higher up. The job would still get accomplished, but after following this arrogant jerk for the last forty-eight hours, Grigor felt compelled to add a little extra punch, as it were, because the guy was just that obnoxious.

Hey, wasn't it "easier to get forgiveness than permission"? Yeah, he'd be forgiven—if he was ever even questioned. Grigor checked the gear he'd need and started toward the address he'd written down, near St. Eustachius University.

Ethan easily found Vasily Shevchenko's apartment. His heart rate quickened as he parked the rental car. He texted Gemma quickly to let her know he'd arrived and would contact her as soon as he left. With a deep breath, he opened the car door and stepped out into the cool Vancouver air.

Before Ethan could ring the bell, Vasily was at the door, opening it wide for his guest to enter. "My friend, my friend, I am happy to be seeing you!" The Ukrainian's baritone voice was hearty and warm, his laugh deep and genuine.

Vasily Shevchenko was in his mid-sixties, Ethan guessed. The man's thinning white hair—slicked back neatly—and laugh lines around his dark blue eyes showed his age, but his trim build and strong shoulders indicated someone who exercised regularly. And this man was flat smart; Ethan had determined that within minutes of meeting him three months ago.

"Come in, my friend Etan," Vasily continued. "Nadia, come to meets my wonderful friend."

A bit of Russian conversation passed between Vasily and the sophisticated woman who entered the living area carrying a tray with fruit and two cups of tea. Nadia placed the tray on the coffee table and extended her graceful hand. "I em heppy to meeting jou, Etan. I em soory my Englis no is bery goot to saying." She smiled, embarrassed, as Ethan held her hand.

"The pleasure is mine, Mrs. Shevchenko. And, please! Your English is wonderful. I can't speak a single word of any language other than English, so I am very impressed." He spoke slowly as he watched her trying to understand what he was saying.

"My Nadia can speak five languages," Vasily boasted as he put a loving arm around his wife. "In Ukraine, she work for journal. She was editor—I have good word, da?"

Ethan nodded.

"Nadia made journal for Ukraine, Croatia, Czechoslovakia, Soviet Union, and Bulgaria. Government journal for peoples to read about great Communism." Vasily shrugged. "When there is beings no more Communism, there is beings no more journal. But my Nadia is smartest woman. I am lucky man to having such smart woman I loves." He pulled his wife closer and kissed her temple.

Ethan smiled. Vasily's love for Nadia seemed just like his love for Gemma. After a moment, Nadia bowed politely to Ethan, spoke to Vasily in Russian again, and went into another room.

"Now, my friend Etan, tell me whys you traveling to see me? Is something I am doings wrong?"

Ethan sighed, picked up his teacup for a quick sip, and leaned back into his plush floral chair. "I need you to explain a few things to me," Ethan began. "I don't want to seem ungrateful, but I need to know why you gave me that car."

Vasily's eyebrows furrowed. "Is not good car?"

"No, no, it's an amazing car. But I need to know if you..." Ethan paused, trying to find the right words. He had to know the truth, even if it meant endangering himself. "I need to know if you giving me that car has anything to do with a man named Josef Aleynekov."

Ben Pritchard went over his instructions, if that's what they were, with Jenny before leaving the hotel room. She said while he was at the game she'd be doing more investigating on Mark and Ann Stoddard, as well as finding out if there was anything new from Josef regarding Saunders and Lopez. Ben left for downtown Canyonville a few minutes after seven.

Parking was at a premium; all the small streets within four blocks of the high school were lined with cars and trucks, and even a few school buses. The fans' excitement inside the gym was audible when he finally found a spot over on Huffman Street, in the parking lot of a manufacturing plant. The weather was pleasant and cool, and the five-minute walk was refreshing.

Jenny had shown him the photo Josef had sent, so Ben knew what Carolina Lopez looked like; he'd only seen her from a distance that first night Saunders arrived in the US. Lopez was pretty. And, jeez, she looked familiar to him now that he had a close-up of her face. Her smile was wide, her eyes a mix of green and brown, and her face surrounded by a mass of reddish-brown curls. He could see her Latina heritage in her skin tone and wondered if she was bilingual. That would be handy if she were an international assassin as Jenny claimed she was.

But this woman didn't look dangerous. Ben furrowed his eyebrows as he stared at her picture once more before turning onto Third Street. He tried in vain to figure out where he'd seen her before. They lived less than a half-hour apart, so it was possible she'd crossed his path at some point. Maybe her striking features had just left a subconscious impression on him.

Ben paid his admission and tentatively walked into the raucous gym. A quick glance at the scoreboard showed Days Creek ahead by a few points five minutes into the game. He stood just inside the doorway on the home team's side and began to scan the crowd. Hundreds of people dressed in school colors and waving giant foam No. 1 hands or banners slowed the process. He glanced over at the Days Creek side and found an open spot at the end of the bleachers—right near two police officers standing guard. He went back out the same doorway, past the concession stand, and in through the other door by the officers, quickly settling in three rows up.

The game moved quickly, and the teams were evidently well-matched. They traded possession repeatedly. In the few minutes since

Ben had arrived, Canyon Creek had pulled ahead by two, and it was still the first quarter. He liked basketball—he'd liked to scrimmage with friends in high school—so it was easy to get into the spirit of things. He began to root for Days Creek with the people surrounding him.

At the end of the first quarter, he'd still not spotted Lopez or Saunders. The couple sitting in front of him cheered for what Ben assumed was their son, and he leaned forward and asked about him.

"Number twelve? Yeah, that's our son, Danny. He's good, isn't he!" the boy's mother said proudly. "He's only a junior but scouts from UCLA and Texas Tech have been up to watch him already."

Ben congratulated them and looked at the simple program he'd been handed when he purchased his ticket. Number twelve...Dan Morrisette, junior, six-foot-five, pretty decent stats. As the second quarter began, so did Ben's focus on the game—and on finding Saunders and Lopez.

Just when he was all but convinced the two hadn't come to the game, one of the Canyon Creek players scored a three-pointer and the crowd on the other side erupted with screams. Ben scanned the program again. Walker Jamison, senior, six-foot-nine, had hit that baby from half-court. Ben was impressed. As the crowd settled into their seats again, a shock of reddish-brown curls caught Ben's attention. And next to that head of hair was most definitely Tristan Saunders.

Ben smirked with satisfaction. They didn't look like the types who would have tortured and murdered a man. Of course there were people in this world who were so evil that such actions could be forgotten easily, no more than tasks to check off a list of things to do. Maybe Saunders and Lopez were like that.

They certainly weren't aware they were being watched, that was for sure. They followed the game intensely, Lopez leaning in to Saunders while pointing to the court every once in a while. Then Ben watched Lopez put her hand on Saunders's leg and leave it there. Yep, they were a couple—a real Bonnie and Clyde living normal lives when they weren't stealing millions and killing people who got in their way. Ben sneered. No wonder Aleynekov wanted them tracked down; they obviously showed no remorse for their actions. He got out his cell and texted Jenny.

watching them @ game. get back 2 u l8r

Ben thought about Jenny. Man, she was hot. She could hit a target like nobody's business, she had a body that drove him wild, and she was very smart. He was lucky to have found her. Feeling good, his targets acquired and completely absorbed in the action, Ben relaxed and let himself enjoy the game as well. It was a few minutes to halftime, and the lead kept changing. This was a nail-biter, and that couple's son, Danny, made basket after basket. The next time he swished the ball through the net, Ben stood to cheer with the crowd around him.

Cari was thrilled at how Tristan cheered and clapped along with the rest of the crowd. Once in a while she'd explain something she'd learned about Mark's strategy or the sport in general. She was having a wonderful time, and given Tristan's constant smile, she could tell he was too.

A few minutes before halftime, Tristan suddenly pulled out his cell. He checked the screen and turned to show Cari.

Update from Shevchenko. Care to give me a call?

Cari met Tristan's eyes and knew the worry on her face matched his.

"Let's stay positive and assume this is good news, okay?" Tristan said into her ear so she could hear him above the din. "You stay here with Ann and Mark. Don't leave this building, do you hear me?" His gaze was intense. "I'm going back to the inn to give Ethan a call."

When she began to protest, Tristan quickly added, "I'll be fine. I'll text you to let you know I'm inside with doors locked, all right?"

She did her best to smile, despite her lingering worry. Tristan kissed her forehead and tapped Ann's shoulder to get her key. Then he navigated his way down the bleachers and out of the gym. Just before the buzzer for halftime, Cari received a text — in full sentences, of course — indicating Tristan's safe arrival at the inn. She smiled at her phone and tucked it back in her pocket.

The fifteen-minute break in the game would be just long enough for Cari to walk around a little. These bleachers were typical: hard and uncomfortable. She spoke to Ann, who was focused on totaling the team's first-half statistics, and strolled out to the lobby.

Ben had noticed Saunders leave a few minutes earlier and thought about following him. Lopez had stayed, though, and he couldn't watch both of them. Without informing Jenny, he opted to stay in the gym, keeping an eye on the game—and Lopez. But when Lopez left the gym a few minutes later, Ben knew he had to follow.

He was ready to make a quick exit but spotted his target in the lobby, standing in line at the concession stand. Lopez spoke to no one, evidently looking over the menu options on a display over the serving windows. *Perfect,* Ben thought as he concocted a plan different than Jenny's. He'd take this opportunity to find out what he could about this woman without her suspecting a thing.

Casually, he got in line behind her and looked over the menu as well. Saunders had not yet returned, so he'd try to engage her in conversation. Couldn't hurt, he figured. He approached women in bars all the time. Lopez was the type he'd go for, so he'd just treat this as another pick-up scenario.

"Are the soft pretzels fresh, do you think?" he asked softly so as not to startle her. She jumped anyway, turned to face him, and blushed. *A cold-blooded killer who gets embarrassed easily? That's a surprise.*

"Excuse me?"

"I'm sorry. I haven't been to this gym in a few years," Ben said. "I was wondering if they've improved on the quality of their pretzels."

"Oh, um, I don't know," she answered. "I've never had the food here."

"Ah," Ben laughed lightly. "Then it may be better to pass on that. Popcorn can't be too risky a bet, though, do you think? It's popping right now, so we at least know it's fresh."

Lopez turned toward the popcorn machine, which steadily pumped out puffs of yellow and white. "Yeah, I guess." She faced forward again as the customers in front of her moved closer to the counter. She seemed done with the conversation, but Ben hadn't even gotten started.

"Close game, huh? That three-pointer from Jamison was impressive. Looks like that's what Canyonville needed to get back into the game. Are you cheering for them or Days Creek?"

Lopez reluctantly positioned herself sideways. She was polite enough not to ignore Ben's questions, something he would take advantage of as long as they were waiting in line.

"Canyonville. My cousin is the coach."

Ben took mental note of that fact, now understanding the link between her and Mark Stoddard. "I'm on the Days Creek side. Did you see number twelve? Danny Morrisette? He's my nephew." Ben was quick with the lies, and now particularly glad he'd spoken with the couple in front of him. When they returned to the game, Ben's seat behind Morrisette's parents would make his story believable should Lopez see him across the basketball court.

"Yeah," Lopez offered. "He's a good player."

"So…" Ben decided it was time to segue. "You're from Canyon Creek, then?"

Lopez suddenly eyed him suspiciously and seemed hesitant to respond. Ben would have to tread lightly.

"No. Just in town for a few days."

"I'll bet your cousin likes that you're here, though, yeah?"

Lopez smiled, which surprised Ben again. "He does. I've promised for a while to come see his team, and since this is one of the big games of the season, I wanted to be here for him."

"He seems like a good coach. You can tell his players respect him." Ben let that statement sit, and Lopez turned again toward the counter. She was next in line after two teen girls who were busy commenting on the players they thought were cute. Ben would wait until they both got their orders and hope to continue the conversation, at that point adopting a new, and reasonable, approach: a guy interested in a pretty girl. He glanced over at the exit doors, hoping Saunders wouldn't return until after the third quarter began.

"So, you're in town for a few days?" he asked smoothly once they'd each gotten a soda and small popcorn. He'd followed her to an open spot in the lobby, away from the pathway to the restrooms, where there was a ledge along the wall for their drink cups.

"Um, yeah. I'll probably be heading home in a day or two." She looked toward the exit doors repeatedly, rarely making eye contact with Ben as they talked.

"Hey, uh, the players are starting to warm up in there. You interested in grabbing a cup of coffee or something after the game tonight?"

Lopez blushed and glanced at the door again. Ben knew she'd say no but couldn't stop himself from asking anyway. Watching her, he couldn't believe she'd not only killed someone but dismembered him too. She just didn't seem the type—at all. He wondered if Jenny had the wrong girl; maybe Saunders had been with someone else in Bulgaria and this woman was someone new in his life who had no clue about his past. The more he considered this, the more he wanted to somehow warn her about the creep she'd been traveling with.

Sure enough, Lopez declined his offer. "Oh, gee, thanks, but no. I'm sort of with someone," she said shyly, crinkling her nose. "I, um, better get back in there before my cousin wonders where I've wandered off to, you know?"

"Yeah. Well," Ben replied as he extended his hand, "it was nice talking to you. I'm Ben, by the way."

"Hi. I'm Cari. Tell your nephew he's a great player."

Ben almost stumbled over that, momentarily forgetting his earlier lie. "Oh, yeah. I will. Good luck. I think your cousin's team might just beat us tonight," he said with a wink. "But I'll still be cheering for Days Creek."

Carolina Lopez smiled before turning back to the gym. As Ben walked toward the visitor's side entrance, he considered what he'd learned: Carolina Lopez went by the name Cari, the man who owned the home where she and Saunders were staying was her cousin, and she and Saunders were officially a couple. He smiled. Jenny would be pleased.

Nikos didn't like his current assignment. So far it had proven to be a dead end. Watching Ronaldo Lopez swap stories over beer with his friend was a waste of time, and yet he knew if he didn't do it, Josef would have some bitter consequence ready. Evgenia had indicated she was tracking Saunders and the woman south of Portland. Josef didn't confirm or deny whether she'd found them, thus "justifying" Nikos's need to track his own target in case Evgenia was wrong.

Fred and Shorty's sported two televisions hoisted up on tilted shelves at each end of the bar and a pool table in the back. A jukebox by the door played a Willie Nelson tune, and a few couples danced slowly nearby. The booths all had at least one or two people in them. Most of the bar's inhabitants were men, and the women there were either obviously with a date or eager to find someone new to brighten their lives. Lopez was sitting on a barstool near the second television, talking to a man about his same age. Nikos had planted himself on an empty stool at the end of the L-shaped counter.

For the first few minutes, Nikos peeled at his bottle's label between sips of beer. No one paid any attention to him, and he was glad to blend in. He glanced over at Lopez whenever the two men's laughter got loud, but his main focus was to once again drown his sorrows at losing Mila. Nikos's position at the bar provided not only a perfect view of the door and the man he was watching, but he was close enough to hear much of his target's conversation.

"…seems to like her new apartment over on the island. That other place was really more for college students, and she didn't need to be running into them every time she went to the mailbox, you know?"

"Sure wish my son could find something better. He refuses to take handouts from Bonnie and me, but the poor kid is stubborn to the point he's only hurting himself. I even offered to write up loan papers, charge him interest and everything, so he could start taking classes this spring."

"At SEU?"

"Yeah. But, man, I musta said the wrong thing 'cause he just stormed out of the house." The man's friend sighed. "He's turning out to be hard-headed just like me—proud to the point of stupidity." He took a long drink from the bottle of beer in front of him.

"Is he working?"

"Aw, I don't know. He says he doesn't need money 'cause he got himself some new job, but he won't tell me a thing about it."

"He's a good kid, Gary. He'll figure things out." The man gave his friend a sideways smile. "Maybe we ought to get our kids to meet, eh? My daughter's not much older than he is, and she's single."

The friend laughed. "Ron, there's no way in hell I'm gonna corrupt your daughter with my son. He needs to figure himself out before he starts committing himself to any sort of relationship." He suddenly looked at his watch. "Hey, if we're going to be up at dawn, I gotta get back to the cabin. I need my beauty sleep."

"Gar, I don't think one night's sleep is gonna improve that mug of yours." Lopez laughed as he clapped his friend on the shoulder. "But I guess you're right. Let's settle up and head back to camp."

The two men laid out some bills, slapped the countertop, waved to the bartender, and meandered out the door. Nikos nestled his beer between his palms and casually glanced at the tennis match on the television at the other end of the bar. He waited another twenty minutes and then walked out to his car, thankful he'd been able to rent the last available cabin at the campground where his target was staying. His duffle bag on the passenger seat, Nikos made the short drive along the rutted road to the secluded campsite.

Chapter 24

Tristan opened his cell and punched in his brother-in-law's number, not sure what sort of news he'd hear. Ethan didn't waste any time, first telling him he was back in his car and returning to the hotel where Gemma was waiting. Tristan sighed. Knowing Ethan was all right was a positive, even if nothing else he said was good.

The information gathered from the meeting had actually been more than either Ethan or Tristan expected. First and foremost, Shevchenko had confirmed that Josef Aleynekov had encouraged him to hire Ethan specifically. A month later, Aleynekov checked up on the situation, and Shevchenko had had nothing but compliments about Ethan's knowledge and business savvy.

Then Aleynekov told Shevchenko he wanted to give Ethan a gift for services he'd provided to the Bulgarian government, and that he hoped the two of them could provide special compensation together. Shevchenko was told not to worry; Aleynekov would wire the money to an American colleague and have the car paid for in full—but it would have to appear to come only from Shevchenko. Shevchenko said Aleynekov's actions hadn't surprised him; Josef had regularly given extravagant gifts to foreign businessmen in this manner. As a public figure, Aleynekov was severely limited in the types and value of gifts he could accept or present. Shevchenko explained that over the past ten years he'd become accustomed to Aleynekov finding creative ways to reward good work.

Ethan said that the Ukrainian was genuinely surprised that this was being viewed as improper, as Josef always seemed to give from his heart. Shevchenko apologized profusely for Ethan's discomfort at receiving the car so covertly—and possibly illegally. When Shevchenko began to contact Aleynekov right there, with Ethan still sitting in his living room, Ethan said he'd stopped him and cautiously provided more information about the situation.

"I was careful what I revealed, Tristan, but I'm convinced Vasily Shevchenko has no idea that money he's received or passed on was part of a worldwide money-laundering scheme. He simply chalked it up to Aleynekov being a savvy private investor who desperately wanted to give what he considered due compensation to people who did good work."

"And so…to what extent does he know about Aleynekov's dubious other life and mafia connections?" Tristan asked.

"Enough. I didn't have to actually say it; he's a smart man."

"And?" Tristan was still not sure what was gained.

"Shevchenko doesn't care about the money. His main focus is keeping his family safe. He said he's going to make some phone calls and get back to me. I get the feeling he's got some connections of his own that might be able to help."

"Does he know anything about me?"

"No. He's not regularly in contact with Aleynekov. They became acquaintances back when the Soviet Union broke apart. They'd worked on numerous business ventures, but Vasily swears everything *he* did was legit; he assumed Josef was legit too, especially as he watched him climb the ranks in the Bulgarian government. The last time they talked was when they arranged for my car to be purchased."

"Vasily Shevchenko was the recipient of a lot of money, Ethan. I saw his name numerous times on the evidence I gathered in Sofia. That's hard to ignore."

"I'm not saying Vasily wasn't savvy with his business deals, and maybe some of his deals with Aleynekov were shady and he came out of them with big profits. But I watched the man's face, Tristan. Maybe he ignored the possible mafia connections, but I doubt he knew how intricately Aleynekov was involved."

Tristan was quiet for a moment. He got up from the sofa in his room and looked out the window. The moon was low in the sky, and a few clouds had appeared over the eastern tree line. He could see the gentle flow of Canyon Creek and smiled as he remembered the afternoon he'd spent with Cari. "When do you expect to hear from him?"

"I don't know. He made it seem like the less I know, the better. Now that he's aware of what Aleynekov's been doing, he may take it upon himself to contact others he knows have done business with him. I get a feeling that if Shevchenko really thought about it, he could identify a few mob guys, or he could find out who they are pretty easily. Let's hope they decide to take care of their own and leave you out of it."

"Does he know I have a list of names that covers six European countries, a few South American governments, and the US? I can't imagine anyone on that list would want those names revealed. What's to stop one of them from picking up where Aleynekov left off if he gets killed? And what if—"

"Tristan." Ethan's voice was calm but direct. "Right now there's no need to give yourself an ulcer over this. Shevchenko is not an enemy. I believe he'll try to help if he can. There's nothing else either of us can do tonight." He paused and then spoke more quietly. "Anything new on the BlackBerry?"

"No. And I'm with you at this point; no news is more frightening than hearing from him."

"And you never got a call back from his office?" Ethan asked, seeming to hesitate.

Tristan sighed heavily. "No. I left a detailed message. I told him Cari has nothing to do with this. The last message from him came when we were on our way here Friday night. I'd rather hoped he'd given up, but I know I'm a fool to think that. Not with what's at stake for him."

"Where's Cari right now? Is she with you?"

"No. She's at the gym with Mark and Ann. I came back to the inn so I could talk to you privately. I'll head back over there in a few minutes."

"I'm almost at the hotel. It's been a bit stormy up this way, so I'm glad we're not flying out again until tomorrow. We should be back in Canyonville before dinner tomorrow night."

"All right, Ethan," Tristan said. "Thank you for doing this."

"Sure thing. I'm glad it went well. I'll see you tomorrow. Get yourself some sleep tonight, will you? You're already pale enough; you don't need dark circles under your eyes too."

Tristan laughed. "Give my sister a hug for me. Goodnight."

After he hung up the phone, Tristan went into the bathroom and splashed some cool water on his face. He looked at his reflection and knew Ethan was right: a decent night's sleep would do him a world of good. He texted Cari and began his walk back over to the gym.

Ethan Stonecipher had driven away, but Vasily Shevchenko was still in the parking lot—twenty minutes and three cigarettes later. As he crushed the last butt under the sole of his Italian leather shoe, he made a decision. He turned toward the entryway, went back inside his apartment, and slumped in his favorite chair.

"*What's wrong?*" Nadia asked in Russian. Vasily knew she could see both anger and concern in his eyes. She came over and caressed his hair.

Vasily immediately softened his expression; no need to worry her. This new situation could be taken care of with one phone call. "*It's fine.*" He pulled her hand to his mouth and kissed it gently. Then he gave her a quick wave, his signal that he wanted to be alone. She kissed the top of his head and said goodnight.

Vasily let another half hour pass before he made the phone call he knew would help him choose the right path. A voice answered on the second ring, and the conversation proceeded in Russian.

"*Did you know about Josef's actions?*"

There was hesitation on the other end, but finally, "*Da.*"

"*Do you know who Tristan Saunders is?*"

"*Da.*"

"*Did you know he has information that could ruin me and a lot of other people? Do Sergei, Ivan, or Georgiy know too?*"

Another hesitation. "*Nyet. Only Josef, and now you. But Josef is handling this. Saunders will be killed as soon as those papers are secured.*"

"*How long have you known all of this? Why didn't you tell me?*" Vasily was pained to discover he'd been lied to, evidently for some time.

"I'm sorry. You know my hands were tied as well."

"Well, untie your damn hands and fix this. You know what I want done. I don't care if it's you or someone else who does it, but I expect to hear news of that man's dead body before the week is out." He paused for a moment, considering how his world was about to come crumbling down, and seethed, *"Finish this!"*

Chapter 25

Cari spotted Tristan on the sidewalk in front of the gym's entrance and worked her way through the chanting, cheering crowd around her. Mark and Ann soon joined them, and the four returned to the inn on a natural high. Mark recounted how their team had won by two points in the last few seconds of the game, advancing them to the district championship finals. He pumped the air every time he remembered a great play, and Ann would throw Cari a grin and roll her eyes. Cari smiled, though. She was proud of her cousin and pleased she'd had a chance to see him and his team in action.

Back at the inn, the ecstatic coach had to give Tristan a blow-by-blow of some of the key plays he'd missed during the second half, and Tristan listened politely, with Cari curled up by his side on the sofa. Once Mark calmed down, Tristan was able to share his conversation with Ethan. While Tristan admitted he still had reservations, Cari breathed a sigh of relief—at least for the night—as he spoke. Maybe tonight they could get a peaceful night's sleep. She knew her own body was feeling the stress and lack of rest; Cari was craving at least a good five or six hours uninterrupted. It was barely ten thirty when they all decided to call it a night.

Just like the night before, Cari tossed and turned for the first hour or so. Even though she lived, and slept, alone on a regular basis, she had trouble settling down knowing she was not only by herself in her bedroom, she was the only one sleeping on the second floor. She closed her eyes again, rolled over, and tried to fall asleep.

The low rumble of thunder awakened her, and when she glanced at the digital alarm clock next to her bed, it was a little past two in the morning. She'd evidently gotten a few hours of sleep. She turned to face the wide window across the room. Sometimes storms could be calming, and she liked watching the flashes of light and counting the seconds until she heard the thunder. Sure enough, this process began soothing her back to sleep. She closed her eyes and began to drift off.

When Cari's eyes shot open again, it wasn't because of the thunder. She'd distinctly heard a noise outside her window. The sheers that covered the window distorted the shadows of the branches as they swayed with the storm's wind. *Must be part of the tree scratching against the inn,* she told herself.

She relaxed, occasionally opening her eyes when gusts of wind spattered rain against the window more harshly. She liked listening to the storm and smiled contentedly. Then a new sound came from outside, and she opened her eyes. This time she saw the shadow of a person—a man—standing on the scaffolding, his hands cupped around his face as he tried to peer in the window.

If Cari's heart could have beat any stronger, it would have burst out of her chest. She stayed completely still as she watched the figure move to various parts of the window, trying to get a better view into her room. She knew he couldn't see enough through the sheers to tell she was watching him, but she couldn't be sure he wouldn't spot movement if she tried to sneak out of the room. A slow glance toward the nightstand revealed no cell phone; she'd left it attached to its charger on the bathroom sink.

She was trapped.

Cari considered screaming but worried that would alert the person that the room was inhabited. But if she stayed still and quiet, he might assume it was empty and therefore a safe place to break in. As the man moved out of view, probably to check the room next door, Cari decided to make her move. She slid to the floor, turned the pillow parallel to the length of the bed, and pulled the covers up to make it look like a person asleep. Then, on hands and knees, she opened the door to the hallway as minimally as she could and slipped out, shutting it noiselessly behind her.

Tristan barely heard the rat-a-tat knocking at his door. He'd been lying awake, listening to the storm outside and thinking about what Ethan had said about Vasily Shevchenko. If Ethan trusted the Ukrainian, that was good enough for him.

A second set of knocks sounded more desperate, and Tristan threw off the covers and hastened to the door.

"Cari?" She held her arms to her chest, shaking. The dim light from the hallway sconce showed her eyes were wide and brimming with tears. "My God, what's wrong?"

At first she didn't move. Then, in just a whisper, she spoke. "I—I think—I think there was someone...someone on the scaffolding... outside my window."

Tristan immediately pulled her into the room and into his arms, closing and locking the door behind her. They didn't move for nearly a minute; Cari trembled as though in shock, and Tristan didn't want to risk moving even a little until he felt she'd be willing and able to come farther into the room.

As her shaking settled, Tristan tried to release her, but she held fast. "Don't let go. I just...God, just don't let go of me." She continued to clutch his T-shirt in her hands.

Tristan tried to draw away from her to look out the window. "Let me—"

"No! Please, no. Don't go near the window," she begged in a whispered cry.

"Cari. There's no scaffolding up here. We're safe."

He walked her over to the end of the bed and then advanced cautiously toward the window. Because the room was dark, he could see the alleyway below as well as the creek, both brightly lit by street lamps. He thought he saw a glimpse of something rounding the corner of a building a block south—either an animal scurrying in the rain or the lurker stealing away from the inn. He scanned the street and alleyway once more.

"I think whoever it was is gone," Tristan said as he closed the heavy drapes securely and turned on the small lamp beside the sofa. He returned to Cari's side and put his arms around her.

"Do you think...?" Cari began to ask.

Tristan knew her question. "I don't know. It seems unlikely that we'd be the victims of happenstance twice, but I've not received anything from Aleynekov either."

"I want this to end," she whispered as she drooped in his arms.

Tristan pulled her closer, rocking her gently. "I know, Cari. So do I."

They stayed in their embrace a little longer, remaining silent. Occasional shivers ran through Cari's body. Eventually she sighed and looked up at him. "And we can't call the police about this, either…"

"We have nothing to tell. With the rain, any traces in the dirt of whoever was on the scaffolding would be washed away already. Same with fingerprints, I'm afraid." He kissed her hair, and she wrapped her arms around him, laying her head against his shoulder. "I'll talk to Mark first thing in the morning about getting that scaffolding removed."

"But he needs it there until he can install a proper fire escape."

"Then we'll have to do something else to be sure there's no repeat of what just happened." He cupped her chin, raising her face to his. "You're staying with me until Ethan and Gemma return, though."

That brought a half-hearted smile to Cari's face. "Thanks," she said with a sigh. "I was hoping you'd say that. I didn't want to go back to being the only one on the second floor, even if it's unlikely that guy would return."

"Are you sure it was a man? Did you get a look at him at all?"

"He had broad shoulders and seemed tall; he didn't have a woman's stature. I think he was wearing a hoodie, and all I could really see was his outline. He wasn't too big around—thin from what I could tell."

Tristan pulled her closer again. "I'm so sorry for endangering you like this."

Cari smiled weakly. "Well, it could have been another bizarre coincidence. The inn's about to open, so people in town have probably seen the place getting new furniture and TVs and stuff. Someone watching over the past few weeks would know it's not open for business yet, but the upstairs rooms would possibly have things worth stealing. A stormy night like this, Mark and Ann wouldn't necessarily hear if there were thieves on the second floor."

"Maybe. Actually, let's hope that's the case. Petty thieves would be preferable to Josef Aleynekov." Tristan felt Cari stiffen. "God, I'm sorry. That was insensitive. Anyone lurking outside your window would be horrible. Do you think you'll be able to sleep at all?"

"Doubtful," she said but stifled a yawn. "I'm tired, but I'm afraid to close my eyes. God…" Cari wiped away fresh tears. "I was so scared, Tristan. I've never been more scared in my life."

"Even after being shot at only two nights ago?" he asked with a gentle laugh.

"I had you with me when that happened," she said softly. "Tonight I was alone."

"You won't be anymore." Tristan stood and moved to the side of the bed. "You need to get some rest. Climb in."

Cari got into the bed where Tristan had been sleeping, slid her feet under the covers, and laid her head back on the pillow. A distressed look crossed Cari's face as she watched Tristan reach for the other pillow and the blanket draped along the bottom of the bed, then turn toward the sofa. "Am I being too imposing to ask that you stay with me for a little while? Maybe until I fall asleep?"

"Ms. Lopez, you're not going to try to take advantage of me, now, are you?" Tristan said coyly.

Cari blushed but gave him a sad look. "I just need to know you're right here. Even across the room seems too far away right now."

Tristan tossed the blanket onto the sofa and came to the other side of the king-size bed. Soon he was under the covers and inviting her to lie against his chest.

"This time we can actually say we've gone to bed together," he joked. He felt Cari inhale deeply and let out a sigh.

"Thank you. You've rescued me again."

He kissed her temple and snuggled her close, playing with random ringlets of her hair until she was finally asleep. He held her a little longer and then moved to the sofa where he watched her sleeping peacefully for the rest of the night.

Mark hesitated before knocking on Tristan's door, but it was nearly daylight and a he'd found Cari's bedroom door ajar and her bed stuffed with a pillow. He'd decided in that moment not to pass judgment on her; she was a grown woman. If she wanted to sleep with a man she barely knew, that was her business. He wasn't happy about it, but he'd hold his tongue.

As Tristan opened the door, Mark knew his face was a mix of anger and fear. He quickly reminded himself that Cari being with Tristan would be preferred to her *not* being with him. If that was the case, they had a much bigger issue to deal with. "Cari's not in her room. Is she in here?"

"Yes," Tristan responded quietly as he rubbed the back of his neck, obviously freshly wakened. "But let's stay quiet; she's still asleep."

Mark sighed. Damn it, he couldn't help but be protective. He hesitated and gave Tristan a disapproving look before turning to go back downstairs. "Okay. Thanks."

"No, don't leave," Tristan said. "Let me get a sweatshirt on. Something happened last night that I need to talk to you about."

Mark hesitated at the door. He didn't want to see Cari in a compromising situation.

Tristan gave his host an odd look. "We didn't sleep together. Cari slept in the bed. I was over on the sofa."

Mark felt relief at the sight of a blanket and pillow on the sofa. Then he looked over at his sleeping cousin. Both of her arms were above the covers, one thrown over her head and the other resting on another pillow; her pajamas were obviously on.

"Let's talk outside," Tristan said as he pulled the additional shirt over his head. Once they were in the hallway, Tristan continued. "Actually, let's go down to Cari's room. I want to investigate things."

Mark furrowed his brow. "Investigate?"

As they went downstairs to the second floor, Tristan turned back toward Mark. "Someone was on the scaffolding outside Cari's room at about two o'clock this morning."

Mark stopped mid-step. "What the—"

"That's why Cari slept in my bed last night. She couldn't stop shaking for nearly a half hour after she came up to my room."

"Why didn't she come down—"

"Don't take it personally, Mark. I just think the last thing Cari wanted was to be closer to the ground where an intruder would have even easier access."

Mark realized that what Tristan said made sense. "So what did she see? How did she know there was someone out here?" They were now in Cari's room, assessing the window's lock and frame. Everything was intact. "God, poor Cari. She must have been scared to death."

"She was, and rightfully so." Tristan gestured for Mark to follow him through the bathroom to the adjoining bedroom. Again they checked the window and found nothing amiss. "What can we do about this scaffolding? Can it be removed?"

"I'll call the contractor who's supposed to be installing the fire escape, see if he can get things moving a little faster. The inn's not open yet, so legally I think we'd be fine to remove it. I can get a couple of guys from town to do it."

"Will a fire escape be any safer from intruders, though?"

"Yeah, yeah. It's one of those that the ladder stays stored on the second floor and drops down when needed. It's not completely fool-proof, but it's a hell of a lot better than what we've got right now."

"As soon as you know it's all right to dismantle the scaffolding, let me know. I'll do it myself if I have to."

"You think whoever Cari saw last night is one of the people you're worried about? Do you think they might have tracked you here?"

Tristan pursed his lips. "I honestly don't know, Mark."

Silence blanketed the room for a moment.

"I'll call about the fire escape first thing." Mark sighed. "Thanks, Tristan." Tristan nodded with a grin. "Can we go back upstairs? I want to check on Cari."

They stepped silently back into Tristan's room and watched Cari. She was still peacefully asleep, lying on her side now, clutching the pillow. Near the bottom of the bed, a rhythmic lifting and resting of the covers indicated that, once again, Cari's left foot was moving.

"Does she always do that?" Tristan whispered to Mark, pointing to the shifting covers.

Mark stifled a laugh. "Yeah. Seems to be a family trait. My mom says I used to do the same thing when I was a kid." Mark checked his watch. "Hey, I've got to get ready for work. I'll call some guys about the scaffolding." He extended his hand to Tristan. "Thanks, man, for taking care of Cari. I appreciate that more than I can say."

After shaking Tristan's hand, Mark went back downstairs to start his day.

Chapter 26

It was now Wednesday, and their imposition on Mark and Ann was bothering Cari. Although the Stoddards had invited them to stay until at least the weekend, Cari knew finances had to be tight, especially preparing three meals a day for additional people. However, after last night's scare, she didn't relish the idea of returning to her empty apartment, even with Ethan, Gemma, and Tristan next door.

For now, the best she could do was to offer to get groceries for the inn. With additional prodding from Tristan, she was able to get Ann to concede and come up with a list of items she and Tristan could buy at the market on Main Street. A bigger shopping trip to Roseburg would be needed, but Tristan insisted that until Ethan and Gemma returned, no one be left alone for too long.

With list in hand and their stomachs full (of cranberry nut muffins Ann had made at the crack of dawn), Cari and Tristan walked the short distance to Ray's Grocery Store. Cari groaned when he reminded her they needed to put in more library time to begin isolating dissertation topics.

They cruised the aisles together until Tristan mentioned wanting to treat Ann to some fresh flowers. He left the list with Cari and went to the smaller store attached to Ray's. As Cari perused the bread options, she was startled by the sound of a single cough. She turned to see a somewhat familiar face smiling at her.

"I thought that was you," the man said. "I'm sorry if I scared you. I wasn't sure if there were possibly two women in Canyonville with such beautiful hair, and I didn't want to say anything until I knew it was you."

"Um, hi." Cari was certainly surprised to see the man she'd talked to the night before, and she wished Tristan wasn't in the other store. Despite what she'd told him, this man—Ben, was it?—apparently planned to continue his flirting today.

"Your cousin pulled off an amazing win last night," he continued with a genuine smile. "He's a really good coach."

With Ben gliding into easy conversation, Cari relaxed a bit. She wasn't interested in him, of course, so she'd just keep her responses short as she awaited Tristan's return. "Yeah. He was pretty pleased. Days Creek played really well, though. A few bad shots on our part would have reversed the score."

Cari was startled again as Tristan approached her from behind, arriving silently. "Hi," he said as he glared at the man.

"Oh, Tristan, this is Ben. We talked a little last night during halftime. His cousin was on the other team."

"Nephew."

"Oops. Sorry. Nephew."

"I was just telling Ms. Lopez how impressed I was by her cousin's coaching skills."

Tristan nodded curtly and Cari could feel him remaining close behind her. He did not offer to shake Ben's hand, and the sudden silence between them was uncomfortable.

"It was nice to see you again, Ben," Cari said politely. "We've got to get a few things and get back to, um, back home. Take care." She smiled, waved, and turned toward Tristan, hoping they'd soon be somewhere, anywhere else in the store.

"Yeah," Ben called. "You too."

When Cari chanced a glance down the long aisle a minute later, Ben was gone. Thoughts that he'd followed her into the store gnawed at her. She surmised that if Tristan hadn't appeared behind her, Ben would have once again asked her out. Before all of this Bulgarian mafia mess, she would have seen such a gesture as complimentary—invigorating, even. Ben was about her age and certainly nice looking and friendly. But she was on the run from unknown people, and last night someone had been trying to peer into her room in the middle of a rainstorm. She wasn't about to let her guard down one bit.

"Where were you?" Jenny's question was abrupt as Ben returned to the hotel room. "I don't want you wandering off without me knowing what you're doing."

"Relax, babe," Ben said as he plopped onto the bed and stretched out. "I was doing a little research."

"Shit, Ben. Don't be going all rogue on me. You have no idea what you're dealing with. These two are killers who won't hesitate to take you down if they suspect anything."

"I got to meet the notorious Tristan Saunders a few minutes ago." Ben's smile was as wide as a Cheshire cat's.

Jenny's head whipped around from where she was working on her laptop at the small desk. "What?"

"Yeah. I can see what you mean. The guy's coldblooded. I kept my cool but, man, it wouldn't surprise me if he had a gun under his belt with a silencer attached."

"Was Lopez with him?"

"Yep. They were looking like the happy couple, grocery shopping at that store near the high school. I was talking to Lopez, and Saunders walks up—get this, he's got a bouquet of flowers in his hand. He still looked like a killer, though. I can just imagine how he bumped off that guy Josef knew and then went about his business like he'd done nothing wrong."

"Shit. This isn't good, Ben. I didn't want them seeing your face, let alone knowing your name. Please tell me they don't know that."

"Just my first name. Hell, don't get mad at me over that. If I hadn't introduced myself at the game last night, neither of us would have known that 'Carolina' Lopez goes by Cari."

"Shut up for a minute, will you? Let me think."

Ben waved Jenny off. "I'll go wander the casino for a bit and bring you back a coffee. You look like you need it." Before she could respond, he let the door slam behind him and headed for the elevator.

Ben didn't like being treated like an idiot. Nothing he'd done over the past two days had jeopardized what they were doing. He'd learned a little about Cari Lopez—and her relationship to Saunders—and he'd confirmed that she, or someone, was sleeping on the second floor of the inn. Knowing where they were staying and some of their daily habits was helpful, not stupid. Now that he'd been face to face with both of them, though, he realized he'd have to be stealthier as he watched their movements around town. He wondered if they'd be going to the library again today, and why.

Ben drove back into town and went into the Canyonville Market a few blocks north of Ray's. As he entered, he noted two high ledges along the left side of the store. He wouldn't have wanted to encounter any of the animals now displayed in prowling positions. The taxidermist had done a fine job. Ben strolled the aisles, stopping to consider a few things he might need, but then found what he'd come for. Jenny might think she was the only one with good ideas, but Ben had a few of his own. He counted out one hundred sixty dollars in cash for the clerk, received his change, and put the three items and a package of batteries into his backpack.

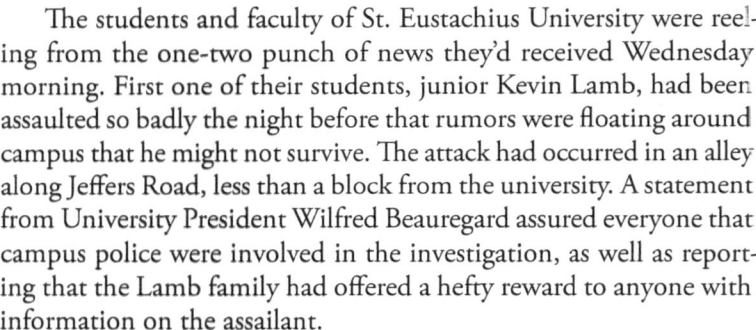

The students and faculty of St. Eustachius University were reeling from the one-two punch of news they'd received Wednesday morning. First one of their students, junior Kevin Lamb, had been assaulted so badly the night before that rumors were floating around campus that he might not survive. The attack had occurred in an alley along Jeffers Road, less than a block from the university. A statement from University President Wilfred Beauregard assured everyone that campus police were involved in the investigation, as well as reporting that the Lamb family had offered a hefty reward to anyone with information on the assailant.

People were still speculating on what had happened to Lamb as additional shocking news began to ripple across the campus. When Dr. Jonathan Lassiter hadn't shown up on Tuesday, most people figured he wasn't feeling well and had forgotten to cancel classes. No big deal. Students weren't going to complain about missing one of his long-winded lectures. But unanswered calls to his home and an anonymous email with video that had been received by a number of board members and President Beauregard resulted in Dr. Swanson being sent to Lassiter's home to check on him.

When Henrik Swanson had gained entrance to Lassiter's Tudor-style home via a key left under a potted plant, he'd nearly fainted upon finding his colleague hanging from one of the beams in the garage. With a shaky hand, he'd called the police and waited numbly on the front steps until they arrived. He was with one of the officers when a suicide note was found next to Lassiter's laptop, which had been left open to a video that had evidently been playing repeatedly since the man clicked on it the day before.

Swanson couldn't help but watch the laptop's screen, stunned by what he saw. The university's security camera video feeds were grainy, but there was no doubt the person shown breaking in and lurking around the personnel office's file room was Dr. Lassiter. With the officer's permission, Swanson clicked out of the video with a tissue-covered finger. The screen now showed an email sent to Lassiter:

> Dear Dr. Lassiter,
>
> Surely you must have realized the university has security cameras. What was so vital to you that you felt the need to break in?
>
> In the interest of the safety of all associated with St. Eustachius University, I have forwarded this video (see attached) to President Beauregard and seven board members. As esteemed as you are, I'm afraid breaking and entering and possible theft of personnel files is something I simply can't tolerate.
>
> I hope you have a good lawyer.

Swanson read the email again, hoping to ascertain who might have sent it—a vindictive colleague? An irate student? The return address was also Lassiter's. Computer hackers, no doubt. The professor sighed heavily. It didn't matter now; the video was real. It seemed Lassiter had understood the seriousness of his actions and the likely consequences, most importantly that his reputation had been destroyed. Swanson thought about his colleague's response and wasn't sure his wouldn't have been the same. He said a silent prayer for his friend and went home.

Jazmyn couldn't help but feel relief at the news that the re-vered—and lecherous—Dr. Lassiter was dead. She'd never revealed to anyone, not even Cari, how the professor had been manipulating her ability to progress through the program. She felt isolated; her committee members, Lassiter, Swanson, Dr. Earl Dukes, and Dr. Franklin Ujamwe, were colleagues as well as good friends. With nothing to back up her claims of sexual harassment, she was hesitant to report Lassiter's inappropriate, and often vulgar, comments.

One night a few months back, she'd shown up for a meeting with her committee in his office. When Lassiter closed his door, with a half-hearted apology for his colleagues who were unable to attend, she'd realized they'd be alone in his office. At that point, he'd told her point-blank what would be required if she expected a favorable review of her research.

She'd slapped his hand off her thigh and bolted from his office before he could do more. As soon as she'd gotten home, she'd dropped on her bed and cried.

Ronaldo and Gary got an early start. Luckily, Nikos was already having breakfast at the small diner in the campsite's main building. As the two men came in to fill their Thermoses and purchase some bottles of water, he studied them: they were in their fifties but in great shape and jovial moods. They'd talked the night before about their grown children with pride. Nikos scoffed. He and his father had always had a business, rather than familial, relationship. He couldn't imagine Josef ever wanting anything more than that.

He wouldn't be judgmental, though. Maybe Lopez's daughter was socially inept. His friend's son hadn't sounded like much to brag about, and Nikos decided that despite his father's lack of encouragement or interest, he'd turned out okay. He knew he had the intelligence to be a successful accountant; he'd proven as much as he worked for a few months as CWF's Bulgarian consultant. He and Saunders had actually gotten along pretty well. He'd had to shut off his conscience when he and Vlad, one of his father's musclemen, had attacked the Brit in the stairwell of his apartment.

Nikos had known better than Vlad how far to go in the beating, and he'd had to stop his colleague from bashing Saunders too many times in the head. They just had to be sure they weren't recognized and their message was clearly received. When Saunders awoke a week later in Sofia's Tokuda Hospital, Nikos had been there out of necessity—his father had insisted the man be watched to make sure he couldn't identify his attackers and to record any critical information he might reveal while in a half-conscious state. Josef had needed to know the extent to which Tristan Saunders was a threat to him and the underground empire he'd built over the past twenty years.

Nikos soon learned that Saunders had made copies of incriminating documents before he'd gone home that night and was using that to keep Josef away from him and his family. What neither Saunders nor Josef knew, though, was the existence of another set of copies. Saunders had lied about what was in the sealed envelope he'd asked Nikos to mail for him, and it was good fortune—or wise intuition—that he'd looked inside the package. Nikos now possessed his own copy of the incriminating documents as well. If they were leverage for Saunders, perhaps they'd prove useful to him sometime too.

As Lopez and his friend headed out for a day of hiking, Nikos remained seated. Once the waiter went to the back room and left the lobby temporarily empty, he went to the computer on the registration desk and accessed the guest list. Ronaldo Lopez was sharing Cabin Four with a man named Gary Pritchard.

Pritchard…Jeez, where had he heard that name before? Nikos headed back to his cabin to do a little research.

Chapter 27

"You look good as a brunette," Ben said. He cocked his head, studying Jenny as she adjusted her wig.

Jenny just scoffed.

"What's on the agenda? Saunders and Lopez are hiding out at that library again — not much going on there. And I saw the inn's owner leave too. She headed north on the interstate beyond the casino."

"Josef's getting tired of this. If the inn is empty, we need to go in and look through their things. Saunders has to have information that will lead us to the money he stole."

Ben smiled deviously. "Shall we leave some sign for them? Let them know we've tracked them here?"

Jenny glared at Ben. "We leave any evidence that we're here, we risk them taking off again. The longer we keep quiet, the more they'll let their guard down." She went back to applying her makeup as she continued. "I've been thinking about how we can end this, so today's agenda — outside of checking the inn while it's empty — is to get to know this little hellhole better. My goal is to get that money back and be done with Saunders by Friday."

Jenny snapped her compact closed and grabbed her purse. Ben followed her out the door a few minutes before noon.

Cari searched the library until she found what she needed. She approached the office of Librarian Judy Jones, according to the nameplate on the wall, located next to the checkout desk. She knocked on the doorframe, and a slender woman looked up from her computer. "Excuse me. Does the library have access to back issues of *Intercontinental Financial News?*" Cari asked.

Ms. Jones smiled sweetly. "It's on microfiche, if that'll work for you." She stood and waved for Cari to follow her to a small but brightly lit room to the left of the building's entrance. "I wish we could afford to have everything available electronically, but..." She sighed and then gave Cari a wink. "We do with what we can, given our limited resources."

Cari followed the librarian to the row of file cabinets and watched her locate the *IFN* files dating back to 1978. "You may also want to look at *World Chronicle of Economic Conditions* if you're tracking international trends. It's not as well-circulated as *IFN* but it might provide some additional information."

While Tristan sat in the main area of the library, perusing various newspapers online on his laptop, Cari set herself up at the antique microfiche machine to explore research on money laundering in post-Communist countries.

Although he knew it was evening in Bulgaria, Nikos dialed his father's number at the office. The man rarely left the government building before ten at night, always wanting to be the last to leave. Josef answered on the second ring.

"*I've found out something that might interest you,*" Nikos said in Bulgarian. The young man knew that news like this would raise his status in the organization as well as within the family. As much as he would have chosen a different career path than being the son and heir of an Eastern European mafia family, he knew his political—and physical—survival was dependent on keeping Josef Aleynekov happy.

Nikos shared the information he had found linking Ronaldo Lopez's friend Gary Pritchard to Aleynekov's newest hit man, Ben—the man hired to hunt down Lopez's daughter. The term "small world" was an understatement. This, both father and son realized, could play very well in getting Saunders to surrender the list of names and account numbers he'd stolen three months earlier.

Nikos knew Tristan Saunders well enough to feel sure that he'd not sacrifice the woman he was traveling with for self-preservation.

And if Ben Pritchard got cold feet about completing his assignment, they now had a way to force him to follow through. Saunders was going to be a dead man either way, something that Nikos had come to accept as the likely, and unfortunate, denouement. Now, having both Ben Pritchard's and Carolina Lopez's parents as very valuable negotiation tools — and at the same remote location — was simply an unexpected bonus.

Tristan and Cari were ready for a lunch break at one. They traveled the short distance to Ken's, bought sandwiches to go, and walked across the street to the small park next to a quaint covered bridge.

"How's the research going? Any closer to a topic?" Tristan asked tentatively.

Cari smiled. He'd been sweet not to pressure her, while at the same time keeping his word to push her to the library. She took a bite of her sandwich before responding and kept her eyes focused on the food on her lap. "I was thinking about doing a chronology of money laundering over the last twenty-five years, covering a time frame that starts just before the fall of Communism." She waited another moment and looked up. "What do you think?"

Tristan looked toward the trees as he sighed heavily and rubbed the back of his neck, saying nothing.

"I mean, it's a relevant topic, right? And surely it's not one that's been overdone." She paused, studying Tristan's face for a clue as to what he was thinking. "I've been finding some good stuff in a number of respectable journals."

Finally, Tristan met her gaze. "Cari, do you not feel you're endangered enough? Do you want to sign your own death warrant?"

He wasn't angry, exactly, but his face was stone serious.

"These people are ruthless and value their privacy," he continued. "They don't like people snooping around in their business, nor do they — "

"But I wouldn't have to name names," Cari interjected. "I'm looking at simply compiling accounting and economic data that's already been published by the IMF and UN, along with newspaper reports of court cases involving presumed mafia. I can generalize my results. It's not that unrealistic, you know. There are dozens of countries,

Communist and democratic, that have knowingly participated in activities associa—"

"God, Cari, you don't get it, do you?" Now Tristan was angry. He stood and began to walk away before turning back to her. "They will kill you. As sure as the ground you're sitting on, they will find you, and *they will kill you*." He was twenty feet away before Cari could even think to respond. She watched as he slumped against the trunk of a tree, glanced over at her briefly, and looked away.

The knock on Grigor's apartment door took him by surprise, and he grabbed his Glock off the bedside table. He peered through the peephole, immediately engaged the gun's lock, and tucked it in his waistband at the small of his back before he opened the door.

"What the hell are you doing here?"

Vlad Korsik didn't wait to be invited inside and pushed his way past his colleague. "*Nice to see you too*," the lanky assassin responded in Bulgarian. He plopped down on the living room sofa, spread his arms across the back cushions, and smiled. "*Josef wants things done right, so he sent me, of course.*"

"You're in the United States, for God's sake," said Grigor. "Speak English if you don't want to draw attention to yourself."

"Ah, good idea. I hear American womans like foreign accents, *da*? I think we go outside tonight and, how you say, take a good time, *da*?"

"God, maybe you're better off sticking with Bulgarian. It's 'go *out*' not 'go outside' and '*have* a good time.'"

"*Da*, you know lots of womans. You make datings for us."

"No, Vlad. I work alone, and that includes when meeting women."

Vlad made a chiding sound as he stood and meandered to the apartment's kitchen.

Grigor ignored him and squared his shoulders. "So, what do you mean about Josef sending you here. What's going on that he's not told me?"

After popping the cap off a beer and letting the small metal disk fall to the floor, Vlad returned to the sofa and took a quick swallow. "Pah! American beer is like piss!" That didn't stop him, though, from taking a longer drink before continuing. "Josef says Evgenia takes too long. He talks me to come to kill Saunders. He talks dat Saunders lies; dat Saunders no haves papers."

"Wait a minute. Why now? Why is Josef questioning this?" Grigor sat in the easy chair across from Vlad and leaned forward. "Why the hell have we been waiting if Saunders has been lying this whole time?"

"Eh. I no asks questions. Josef says 'Kill Saunders.' Dat whats I am doings."

"I want to talk to Evgenia and Nikos—"

"You doos what you doos. I am heres to get you talks to me where Saunders is."

"What? Josef hired you to do this alone?"

"Eh. Maybe you's not only one works alone, *da?*" Vlad replied coolly. "Why? You wants to come too?"

"Hell, yes!" Grigor stood. "I can't trust that you won't shoot the wrong person."

Vlad laughed and shrugged. "What you means? It was Nikos and me who putting Saunders in hospital. I am knows what he is looking like."

"What about that woman he's with — Lopez?"

"*Da.* Josef says okay if she gets kill too." Vlad took another swig of his beer and raised the bottle toward Grigor. "Maybe I gets more for dats too, eh?"

Tristan's sullen expression didn't fade as they picked up their trash and returned to the library. Cari was thankful she still had some microfiche to look over; that would keep her mind occupied while Tristan went back to reading in the main room.

She was surprised when her cell phone buzzed, indicating a text message. Her spirits lifted. Perhaps Tristan had decided to let their disagreement lie for now. She opened the message and furrowed her brow. It was a single letter:

I

A quick look at the number the message had come from puzzled her as well. It was unfamiliar, although the area code was Seattle's. Perhaps one of her students had started to text her and changed his mind? She put her phone down, figuring if it was important they'd try again, but even after Cari had finished perusing the articles she'd selected and made about forty pages of copies, no more texts had come.

The walk back to the inn at four thirty was awkward at first. Neither Cari nor Tristan seemed ready to speak. When they walked up the front steps, though, Tristan gently caught Cari's elbow. "Mind if we sit a moment before going inside?"

They selected two of the deck chairs, and Cari leaned forward, her hands clasped in her lap.

"Remember that whistle blower I told you about? Karl Tresk?" Tristan began. "He was the reason my company — the reason I — was sent to Sofia."

Cari nodded, and Tristan continued, finally telling her of the horrific delivery Tresk's wife had received that gave little doubt the man had been murdered.

Then he paused, taking a deep breath. "I know in my heart that Josef Aleynekov had him killed. He and people he works with." Tristan reached forward and rested his hand on Cari's. "You've got to understand that they don't care who they hurt. They will protect themselves at all costs and stop people from identifying them or bringing suspicion upon them. You *know* what they did to me. I live in fear every day that I'm going to get a phone call from London saying my parents have been murdered. And I can't tell them a thing. I can't tell them they're in danger. Gemma and Ethan didn't know any of this before last Friday. I've tried to protect them. I'm trying to protect you. I don't know how else to — "

"I won't do this topic, okay?" Cari smiled softly as she moved one of her hands on top of his. "But that means I still need to find something to study."

Tristan's shoulders relaxed. "I've made two promises to you: to keep you safe and help you with your dissertation. I have no intention of backing out of either one." He raised her hand to his lips and kissed it. "Thank you for understanding."

"Let's head inside, hmm? I think your sister and Ethan are back."

It was good to have the group together again. Ann smiled broadly as she looked around the living room where they'd gathered once again after dinner. Ethan and Gemma were visibly more relaxed than they'd been a few days ago, and Gemma seemed to have a permanent smile on her face as she watched her brother sitting next to Cari. Tristan was the only one still clenching his jaw occasionally. Aleynekov couldn't have completely disappeared, so Tristan and Cari—and perhaps the others—were still in danger.

"Vasily will protect himself first," Ethan explained. "He's out of the business, but he knows one is never *truly* free from the mafia stranglehold. I could only tell him bits and pieces, of course, based on what you've told me, Tristan." He stood, approached the bookcase to the left of the fireplace, and reached behind a tall stack of books. "But now," he continued as he noiselessly pulled out a manila envelope, "I think I'm ready to know more."

Tristan's eyes widened at the sight of the stamp-covered envelope. The others looked on with curiosity.

"Gemma and I took a flight in to Seattle and stopped on the island."

"He hadn't told me a thing," she said.

"And that was to protect you," Ethan added, kissing his wife on the temple. "Tristan chose not to tell me anything either." Ethan looked at his brother-in-law. "Care to share with the rest of the class?"

Tristan looked pained. "As much as Aleynekov doesn't deserve it, I promised him I wouldn't." He shook his head gently. "No, it's my only bargaining chip should he find me and doubt I've kept my word."

The room fell silent, and then Mark spoke. "What next, then?"

Tristan's face grew even more sullen as Ethan returned the envelope to its hiding place. "I think I should leave here on my own and try to contact him."

Cari gasped—he'd evidently not discussed this with her. Ann suddenly felt a bit uneasy about the envelope hidden in her house.

"If we're right that he's not found us here, then the rest of you are safe," Tristan continued. "Gemma and Ethan, I'll leave it up to you whether you stay longer or head back home. Cari, you sh—"

"You can't go! He'll kill you. You told me that yourself."

"I can't continue to endanger all of you. It's that damned envelope he wants. Maybe if he sees I never opened it he'll be willing to leave me alone, trust that I'll keep my word. He knows I won't betray him. He knows I won't risk your lives or my parents' lives."

Ann looked around at her distraught guests. Cari's eyes brimmed with tears, as did Gemma's.

"But he'll own you, Tristan," Cari said. "You'll never be free from him."

"I'm not free from him as it is, and neither are you. I'm living in fear, constantly worried one of you is going to be kidnapped or killed…I can't keep doing this to all of you. I just can't."

With that, Tristan got up and walked outside. After a few minutes, Cari decided to join him, and she settled into the chair next to his. They were silent in the darkness. Streetlights from the main road cast the only shadowy light across the courtyard.

"Where will you go?" she finally said.

"I don't know. Christ, I don't even have a car or a license. I may just have Ethan take me to Portland and I'll fly back to England, hide out there for a while until I can figure out how to end this. Maybe I'll go back to Sofia, show up at Aleynekov's office and face him directly. Running's not doing any of us any good."

Cari looked down at her hands, not wanting Tristan to see the tears in her eyes.

"Can I ask a favor, though, before I go?" he asked.

She swiped a palm across her cheeks. "Sure. Anything."

Tristan stifled a short laugh and gave her a half-hearted smile. "Can I at least take you out on a real date? I don't know the next time I might—"

"Yes, I'd like that a lot. And let's not talk about anything beyond that." Her face lit up as she looked in his eyes and rested her hands on his. "Where shall we go?"

Plans were made for dinner and perhaps some mindless slot machines at the casino. After another few minutes, they went back inside the inn, locked the front door, and climbed the stairs to their rooms for the night.

As Cari crawled into bed fifteen minutes later, her cell phone buzzed from the night stand. She glanced over at a sleeping Gemma, nestled herself further under her covers, and opened the text, encouraged that Tristan wanted to chat with her from upstairs. She'd been thinking about doing the same...Once again, though, the message was a single letter:

C

Cari again checked the number. Same Seattle area code but from a different phone, also unfamiliar to her. Now she began to feel uncomfortable, and her heartbeat increased with her growing anxiety. Without deleting the message, she closed her phone and slipped out of bed quickly to check that the windows were locked. As she crawled back under her covers, she decided to show Tristan the mysterious messages first thing in the morning.

Jenny's smile grew wide as she took out her ear bud and shut down her computer, pleased at the sound quality of the bugs she'd planted at the Canyon Creek Bed and Breakfast. She had a good grasp on what Tristan Saunders would be doing over the next few days and now had some quick plans to make. With Ben asleep, she silently left the hotel room, her thoughts running wild.

When she returned just after midnight, she realized this new set of events meant her time with Ben would likely be coming to an end. She slipped into bed beside him and kissed his chin, awakening him. "Do what you do so well," she cooed.

Ben willingly complied.

Chapter 28

W hen the hardware store opened Thursday morning, Cari and Tristan were there to buy motion-sensor lights to illuminate the back of the inn. The group decided that Tristan and Cari would work on that while Ethan and Gemma went with Ann on another trip to Roseburg for more groceries.

As soon as the others departed, Cari took out her cell phone and showed Tristan the strange messages she'd received.

"Why didn't you show me the first text when you received it?" Tristan sounded perturbed.

"I didn't think anything of it. I figured it was like a wrong number, only in text format. My students have my cell number; it could have been one of them," Cari said. "God, it could have been my dad borrowing his friend's phone," she suddenly realized. "He doesn't have a cell and certainly doesn't know how to text someone."

"Did you try calling either number? See if the voicemail gives any indication as to who sent them?"

Cari dropped her gaze to her lap. "After this second one, I was too afraid. I didn't even want to text back for fear it would reveal who I am."

Tristan reached for her phone. "We can't keep letting our fears control us. Like you said, maybe it was your father." He tried each number but an electronic voice answered both times, simply repeating the number. "Let me know if you get any more of these, and we can try to call the number or text back right away. For now, let's assume it was just someone's error." He smiled encouragingly at Cari, but she could see the concern in his eyes didn't fade.

Just before noon, the new motion lights were installed. After eating the last of the leftover pot roast, Cari and Tristan headed to the library. Although she'd conceded to change topics, Cari remained curious about the impact of money laundering and other illegal activities on the developing democratic nations of Eastern Europe. She'd hang on to the articles and websites she'd gathered, just in case.

Ben and Jenny spent the morning busily coordinating the plans she'd devised the night before. Jenny was relieved that Ben still didn't seem to have guessed her ultimate plans for Saunders and Lopez—or for himself—and she'd prepared responses to things she figured he'd ask eventually. When he questioned her plan to separate Saunders and Lopez, she convinced Ben she'd received new information that Lopez was a pawn, maybe even a hostage, and that if Ben followed the plan, he might actually be rescuing her from Saunders, the cold-blooded killer.

"She did seem nervous both times I talked with her. When Saunders came up behind her in the grocery store, her face went all white. God, I'm an idiot. I should have seen the signs. I could have helped her get away from that bastard!"

"And that's what your job will be tonight. Be aware, though, she may be brainwashed by this guy. You know, sometimes hostages start to sympathize with their captors. Maybe he's got her believing them being on the run is to keep her safe from unknown bad guys. If he's got her truly scared for her life, she's probably come to depend totally on him. *That's* how evil this guy is, Ben. He's using her and will throw her away as soon as he can. We have to separate them so we can get to *him* and find out where Josef's money is. After that, we'll call the police and have them take over. Saunders has to pay for the crimes he's committed."

Now that Ben was convinced, he listened to Jenny's plan, seemingly in awe and willing to be complicit in everything. She caught him smiling more than once at the idea that they were about to complete this assignment and reap a hearty reward from Josef.

Ben took off in the car to complete his tasks around town while Jenny stayed at Seven Feathers. She positioned herself in the lobby with her laptop where she was able to listen in on conversations at the bed and breakfast while observing the staff at the casino. She had to be sure things went smoothly later. If all went well, she'd soon be providing Josef with news he'd waited months for. All she wanted in return was time away with Alexei. Certainly Josef could grant her that.

Tentative plans were made: Ethan would drive Tristan to Portland in the morning. Tristan would purchase tickets at the airport so as to keep his flight information out of cyberspace and maximize his lead time against anyone tracking him. He'd return to London on the first available plane, get himself a new phone upon arrival, and keep Ethan informed as he proceeded from there. He'd contact Josef only after he knew Gemma, Cari, and the others were safe.

At half past five, Tristan and Cari sat in an overstuffed booth at Serafino's Italian Restaurant. As they perused menus, Tristan commented on the similarity to Cari's childhood nickname. "Is Serafina really your middle name?"

"No. It's Marisol. I'm named after my mother." She shrugged as she spoke.

"You haven't mentioned her much. I mean, that's all right...I was just curious as to what happened after your parents' divorce."

Cari straightened her shoulders. "My mom was killed in an explosion in Italy. She was on her honeymoon with her new husband."

"Oh, my God." Tristan sat back, stunned. "God, I'm so sorry. I had no idea..."

"No, it's okay," she offered. "It was nearly five years ago. She and Sergio were at a café in Brindisi — it's a port city along the southeast coastline — when someone decided to make a political or religious statement or something. Sergio was a photojournalist for CNN, so they got to travel a lot. They'd eloped while he was on assignment there. I'm happy she'd found a good guy to marry. I mean, I wish she and my dad had stayed together, of course, but she wanted to see the world...and she got to do that with Sergio." She looked down at her hands. "Everybody says I look more and more like her every day. I'm glad for that."

"Then she must have been a beautiful woman. Freckles and all?"

Cari smiled shyly. "Freckles and all."

Tristan made sure their conversation soon moved to more pleasant topics. Cari shared how she wanted her father to ask out one of his vendors, a sweet woman he talked about every time she brought camping equipment to sell in his store. Tristan told Cari about his parents and grandparents and life in England. The dangers at hand were forgotten...at least for now.

The neckline on Jenny's silk blouse revealed plenty about her assets, and her jeans-and-stilettos combo accentuated curvy hips and legs that went on for a mile. The goateed young man at the valet booth was a goner as soon as she approached him.

"I have only one question for you," she cooed. "What time do you want me to get you off tonight?" She playfully corrected herself. "I'm sorry, I mean what time do you get off tonight?"

The man's eyes sparkled as they roamed from her face to her chest and back again. "Officially at two, but I can take a break any time you say the word." He leaned in and added in a whisper, "And you can get me off all night, if you want."

She swept her freshly manicured nails across his tuxedo shirt, lingering at the buttons. "Can you come make sure my car is parked correctly? I mean, if you don't mind."

The man responded loudly for his co-workers to hear. "Yes, ma'am. We take pride in ensuring our guests are taken care of." As they walked toward the parking lot, Jenny caught him winking at a few of the other valets, who in turn gave him wide, knowing smiles.

When the two returned to the lobby, the valet's face was still flushed and one of his shirt buttons was undone, and the grin on his face told his colleagues what he'd been doing. Jenny kept her cool, blew a kiss to the other valets, and sashayed back over to the elevator and up to her room. Now all she needed was for Saunders and Lopez to follow through with their plans to visit the casino.

The night was young and the future uncertain; it didn't take any convincing for Cari to agree to the Seven Feathers Casino. The light drizzle outside prompted Tristan to valet park, and they soon found the room where the slot machines spun noisily. It took only a few minutes and twenty dollars before the cigarette smoke began to burn Cari's eyes, and rather than bring their last evening together to an early end, they opted for a lounge area where a show would be starting soon. They ordered drinks and were relieved to find the room was devoid of smoke. Their conversation resumed where it had left off at the restaurant, and Cari laughed openly at the tricks Tristan had played on Gemma when they were children.

The noise level was enough that they had to sit close and lean in to each other as they spoke, which Tristan was relieved to find Cari didn't seem to mind. They enjoyed their light conversation and people-watching—the tables around them were occupied by other couples, as well as middle-aged men who seemed to have slipped off their wedding rings for a weekend of alcohol, gambling, and flirting. Most of all, though, they enjoyed simply being together.

"Excuse me, sir?" A young man with a cropped goatee leaned toward Tristan. "Are you the owner of a black Lexus with Washington plates? Here's the valet ticket. Does it match?"

Startled, Tristan reached into his pocket and pulled out the claim ticket, its numbers the same as what the valet showed him. "Is there something wrong?"

"A slight incident, sir. I'm terribly sorry. It seems we might have been responsible for a dent in the front bumper. Could I bother you to come check? We may need you to fill out a report. If one of our valets is at fault, we'll surely reimburse the cost of repair."

Tristan looked from the young man to Cari. "I'll be back in a moment." His gaze was intent. "Don't leave here. If this is going to take longer than a few minutes, I'll call or text you."

Cari's eyes were wide. Tristan hadn't meant to scare her, but he wanted to be sure she didn't wander off on her own, especially in a place unfamiliar to both of them.

"Of course...I'll stay right here." She offered a smile that failed to hide her concern.

As Tristan left the lounge, he turned once more to be sure Cari was safe. Then he followed the valet out the front doors to the parking lot.

Cari picked at the moist napkin under her beer. She hadn't had a Coors Light in ages, and she liked that she was already feeling a light buzz. She smiled again as she recalled the stories Tristan had been telling her. He and Gemma had a close relationship, and Cari was glad her neighbor had thought enough of her to want to set her up with Tristan.

A few minutes passed before she felt the familiar vibration of her cell phone. The car situation must have been worse than Tristan expected. She opened her phone and, once again, was unnerved to see a single letter:

U

But this time, it was immediately followed by another message from the same unfamiliar number:

Think about it

Cari furrowed her brow. She whispered the mystery messages she'd received to herself. "I...C...U...Think about it." A moment passed and her heart began to race. She clapped her hand to her mouth. *I see you.*

But who? Someone must be watching her right now. She swept the room with her eyes, and turned her gaze toward the entrance to the lounge. Tristan was still outside with the valet. She knew she shouldn't react; she was safe as long as she was in this room full of people—even if they were all strangers.

Aleynekov had found her. Maybe he'd intercepted Tristan outside, and he was in danger as well. She closed her phone for a moment and took a deep breath. She had to keep herself from panicking.

"Hey! I thought that was you."

Cari jumped in her seat as she turned around.

"God, I know this town is small, but this is getting ridiculous that I keep running into you!"

It was that guy, Ben, the one from the basketball game and the grocery store. Cari instantly wondered if somehow he'd been the sender of those texts. Ben pulled out the chair vacated by Tristan and sat down, a genuine look of concern on his face. "What's wrong? You look like you're about to pass out. Are you okay?"

"I...um...I need to get out of here." Cari began to stand on unsteady legs, but faltered.

"Whoa, whoa." Ben stood as well and eased her back to sitting. "Wait a minute. Just relax. What's going on? Are you here by yourself?"

"God...um...no." Her eyes flew to the lounge entrance and then back to Ben. "Tristan's outside with one of the valets. Some, uh, some problem, I guess, with the car or something."

"Okay. That's okay. It's started to rain, so maybe he's delayed a little. How about I just sit here with you until he comes back? Will that be okay?"

Cari searched Ben's eyes. He really seemed concerned about her. But he was a stranger. "Yeah. I need to call him — make sure things are all right."

"Let me get you another drink. It'll calm you down." He laughed. "Will you be okay if I just go to the bar right over there?" He pointed to the counter about twenty feet away as he stood. "I'll be back in a flash. If your boyfriend comes back in the meantime, I'll deliver your drink and leave. Deal?"

Cari nodded and got her phone out. She called Tristan, but there was no answer. As the voicemail prompt ended, she said, "Hey, it's me. You've been gone for close to ten minutes. Silly me, but I'm getting worried. Let me know what's going on." She kept her voice light, not wanting to alarm him if he was in the middle of a serious situation with Ethan's car. She was safe, she reminded herself, as long as she remained where she was. If Tristan didn't call or text in another ten minutes, she'd contact Mark.

Ben returned with two beers, placing hers on a fresh napkin. As she raised the bottle to drink from it, he clinked his bottle against it. "To new friends!"

She gave him a half-hearted smile as she took a long drink. He really was being very sweet. "So, do you come here to gamble a lot?" she asked, hoping small talk would pass the time.

Ben grinned. "No, but I might start. I won three grand in just the past few days."

As they chatted, Cari felt the racing of her heart subside as her second beer began to infiltrate her mind and nerves. She glanced toward the doorway a few more times as Ben talked.

"Gotta ask you, are you always this nervous being by yourself, or am I just bad company?"

"No, I'm sorry," Cari said. "Tristan and I...We've been, um..."

"Oh, never mind. Relationship issues. Not my business," Ben said, raising his hands in mock surrender. "But if the two of you don't work out, I'd love to take you out for that coffee I offered the other night."

"No, it's nothing like that." Cari knew she had to be careful what she said. She didn't know this guy. While she appreciated the flirtation and him sitting with her, she needed to stay focused on what was taking Tristan so long and who had sent those texts. Concentration, however, was becoming more and more of a challenge. She pushed the nearly empty bottle of beer away and ran her hand across her forehead, her nervousness sneaking back to the forefront of her thoughts. "I...I need to call...call my cousin..." She opened her phone and saw that Tristan had sent a text.

Bad dent.Bbck soon.Stay put

Cari checked the number. Her eyes were having trouble in the lounge's dim light. It didn't...didn't seem right. Errors. She saw errors. So unlike Tristan. Had he simply typed the message too quickly or was he trying to let her know he was in trouble?...Or that she was in trouble? Her hands began to shake and she lost her grip on the device, dropping it to the floor.

Ben quickly leaned down and scooped it up. "No, you're not calling anyone."

His voice was sweet, but his eyes had suddenly changed. He looked at her differently now. He leaned in and spoke quietly. "Your boyfriend is just fine. You need to stay with me now, Ms. Lopez."

"Wha...?" Cari couldn't complete even this single word. The room was beginning to swirl a little. She squinted to keep her focus on the man beside her. "I never told you...my...my last name. How...? I need...I need...Tristan..."

"Never mind him for now. You'll see him later."

"I...don't...don't understand." Once again, Cari tried to stand, but this time her legs wouldn't let her, and she plopped back into her chair. "God, I'm...I don't feel well...I...Tristan..."

Ben wrapped his hand around Cari's wrist and held it firmly against the table. "I. See. You. Think about it."

As drunk and sleepy as Cari now felt, panic still surfaced at his words. She couldn't inhale enough oxygen. "You...? You...sent..."

"Yes. And you're going to stay quiet and not bring any attention to us. Do you understand?"

"I...But...I don't know what you're talking about. I need to find..." She could hear her voice, slow and slurred. "I have to... have to leave."

Ben popped his phone open with one hand while still holding her wrist with the other. He pressed a few buttons and began to play a short video for Cari. "You're going to listen to me so there's not any trouble."

Cari's vision was blurry, but she was able to make out the images on the tiny screen: Tristan getting into Ethan's car with a blond-haired woman and driving away. He had left her behind. "What's going on? Why would he —? Who is that with Tristan? I…I need to call —"

"Now, listen closely. You're probably feeling pretty dizzy at this point, am I right? I put something in your drink to make you that way, so you're going to cooperate and not cause problems. Behave as we get up and leave and I won't have to give you more. Do you understand me, *honey?* We're going to leave here as a happy couple. You've had too much to drink, and I'm going to help you out to *our* car. You play nice with me, and I'll bring you to your precious Tristan." He kissed her cheek. "Ready to go, sweetheart?"

Cari's eyes welled with tears, but she slowly nodded. Ben pulled her to standing and put his arm around her waist. As they reached the lobby, her legs buckled, and Ben lifted her into his arms. She heard him mumble something to passers-by about too much alcohol…just married…thanks for the concern…The last thing Cari remembered was drifting off to sleep, longing for one man as she was carried away in the arms of another.

The anger in the voices around Cari roused her slightly. She blinked a few times, regaining some ability to focus. She was in a musty living room — not very big, perhaps like a log cabin. The sound above her?…Heavy rain hitting a thin roof. She sat sideways, leaning against something warm. She was on someone's lap. The rhythmic breathing and strong arms around her soothed her. *Tristan…* But then she heard Tristan's voice from across the room. It was that man Ben she was leaning against. Her attempt to move away from him only prompted him to wrap his arms more tightly around her.

"Don't worry, honey. Everything's going to be fine," he said as he brushed his chin along the top of her head.

"Let her go." Tristan's anger resonated in his voice. "She has nothing to do with this."

Cari raised her eyes enough to see Tristan sitting on a dingy yellow sofa. The woman with the blond hair sat with her legs curled under her as she cuddled closely to him. Tristan's arm rested across her legs like they were a couple. The woman laid her head on his shoulder. "We don't want to cause anyone any trouble, Tristan, sweetheart. Once you and I are back in Sofia, things will all work out."

"I said let her go. Now. She and her family know to stay quiet and what'll happen if they don't."

The blonde caressed Tristan's face and kissed his cheek. "We'll see...Just trust me, all right?"

"Look, Evgenia, I'll get you what you're—"

"Wait a sec." Cari felt Ben shift as he spoke. "Who's Yev-whatever? Her name's Jenny, idiot."

"Are you sure?" Tristan challenged, one eyebrow raised. "I met this woman months ago in a bar in Sofia." He turned to her. "So, which is it now? Jenny or Evgenia?"

The blonde smirked and nestled closer to Tristan, making Cari uncomfortable. "I go by many names, love. To you, though, I'll always be your Evgenia." Then she said something in what Cari guessed was Bulgarian. Tristan responded in the same language, surprising Cari. Then the blonde turned Tristan's face toward her, said something else, and Tristan kissed her deeply. Cari closed her eyes and let her head drop against Ben's chest.

"So, what am I supposed to do with Ms. Lopez here if you two are off to Bulgaria?"

"She's already drugged," Tristan replied after the lengthy kiss. "She won't remember any of this. Drop her off somewhere her cousin can find her. We'll be long gone."

"Or," the blonde responded with a smirk, "consider another option. You've already given her enough Rohypnol to last the night, Ben. Go ahead and enjoy the situation while you have the chance."

"No. Don't complicate things further." Tristan's voice was firm, and Cari opened her eyes, trying once again to see him clearly, to understand what he was saying.

"Oh, come on, baby. You and I are going to have our fun tonight. Why ruin it for them?" The woman looked at Cari. "You're in for a good time, too, honey. Ben's quite a pleasure to be with; you won't regret it...that is, if you remember any of it." She laughed lightly as she reached into a canvas bag on the floor in front of her. "Here, Ben," she offered as she pulled out a pair of handcuffs and tossed them across the floor. "I believe these are yours?"

Cari's heart raced, but her mind was floating in and out of consciousness. This woman was encouraging Ben to take advantage of Cari, and Tristan wasn't doing anything to stop it. "Nooo…" Cari's protest was weak as Ben maneuvered to standing with her limply in his arms. She glanced at Tristan, who gave her an icy stare. "Why…?" she called out to him, but Tristan shifted his gaze to focus only on the blonde, and the two nodded at each other. Cari turned her head toward Ben's chest and closed her eyes as tears of helplessness began to fall.

Chapter 29

Nikos watched as Lopez and Pritchard ambled out of their cabin on Friday morning. No way in hell was he going to follow them. He'd had enough of monitoring them this closely. He knew where they were going to be at night; none of the trails in the area were long enough that the men would need to sleep elsewhere. They'd be back at dusk every night until at least Sunday, guaranteed.

His frustration at being cooped up was soon relieved, however, by a call from Grigor.

"Vlad's here, and I'm either going to kill him or myself before day's end."

Nikos laughed. "Oh, come on, he's not that bad, is he?"

"Have you heard his English? What the hell was your father thinking, sending him here to finish the Saunders situation?"

"What?" Nikos began to pace the limited floor space of his cabin. "Where are you?"

"My apartment. I'm still in Seattle. But Vlad's insisting that we head south to where Evgenia and her hired gun are tracking Saunders."

"We can't have Vlad in control of this situation. No way. The guy's not stable."

"That's why I called you. What do I do? I can't keep stalling him or he'll take off on his own. Your father wants this over with."

"Has Evgenia located Saunders?"

"So I've been told."

"I was planning on ditching my assignment here anyway. My father won't be any the wiser. Ronaldo Lopez is out hiking with — get this — the father of Evgenia's new assassin boy-toy."

"What?" Grigor laughed.

"Ironic, eh? But their kids don't know each other. Geez, things would have blown up way before now if that guy Ben Pritchard had already known his target." He snickered. "The dad hasn't got a clue what his son does for a living. It was almost comical listening to him drone on about his kid. But these two will be in a set location for the next few days, easy to track down again if needed. Don't tell Evgenia or Josef, but I'm going to get on the road, get to wherever Saunders has been cornered. Get the location from Vlad and text it to me, but don't leave yet. I want to get there before you and Vlad do — maybe take care of things before he goes all crazy. Give me a few hours' lead if you can."

After finalizing plans with Grigor, Nikos ended the call and quickly accessed the information he needed from the program on his phone. Then he packed up his gear and began his trek south.

When Cari woke again, she was in a dimly lit room, lying on what felt like a lumpy cot. She coughed at the musty smell and could hear only the sound of a ticking clock nearby. As much as she'd hoped, this was not a dream. She was not in her room at the inn.

She shivered — from being drugged or feeling cold, she wasn't sure. As she tried to get into a warmer fetal position, she realized her right leg was restrained at the ankle. *The handcuffs…* "Hello?" She wasn't sure whether she wanted an answer or not.

"Yeah. I'm here." It was Ben.

"What…did you…do to me?" Cari's head pounded, and her stomach felt a little iffy.

"What? Oh, you're cuffed to the bed. Can't have you running off, you know."

"No, I mean…I mean…more than that. I'm…I'm cold…I can't stop shaking."

"You're probably coming off the drug I gave you. That's all." He paused. "It's almost time to give you another dose."

"No…please…don't." Her voice quivered. Cari wouldn't be able to fight Ben. Pleading with him would have to work.

"I'm only following orders. It's for the best," he replied as he got up and pulled a sheet over her. "That's the best I can do for now to get you warm. You're stuck here until I'm told otherwise, and you need to forget that Saunders asshole. He's bad news."

Cari rolled over to face Ben as he retreated to a battered armchair a few feet away. Hot tears began to roll down her face. "How could you do this? What kind of beast are you?"

Ben sat up. "Hey, I'm not the one hanging out with a murderer who steals millions for a laugh."

"What? What are…you talking…about? Tristan?" Cari could hear her voice slurring, her words coming out slower than she wanted.

"You probably can't imagine that he's like that, can you? He's been all nice and sweet to you, hasn't he?"

"I don't understand…Tristan…He's…accountant—"

"Yeah, I bet he's an accountant! He'd have to be to take care of all the money he stole from the Bulgarian government. Maybe he didn't kill that guy himself, but he paid someone to do it for him."

"No…" Cari was confused. Ben was twisting the events from the past few months. "Tristan…there were…two sets of…of books… Aleynekov…"

"Yep. We're talking about the same guy, and Aleynekov's pissed. Jenny told me all about what Saunders did when he was in Bulgaria."

Cari closed her eyes for a moment. *Jenny…the woman sitting with Tristan…He was kissing her…She called him "sweetheart"…*

"She knew him over there…"

"Evidently." Ben suddenly stiffened. "He said her name in Bulgaria is Gaynia or something like that. They're both from there, I guess. They've got a history."

"They were kissing…" Cari said softly. "I didn't know…I didn't know…" Her mind flashed back to the look on Tristan's face when she asked him why he wasn't helping her. His eyes were cold, uncaring, dead. He was with this other woman, caressing her, discussing going back to Bulgaria with her.

Tristan had lied to her—lied to Ethan, his sister, everyone—this whole time. Cari couldn't think, wouldn't allow herself to think. She shifted her body toward the foot of the cot, pulled her legs and arms protectively to her chest, and allowed sleep to swallow her once again.

The Stoneciphers and Stoddards were cleaning up the porch from another night of chatting, bringing their glasses and plates back into the kitchen, when Ethan received a text:

cari w/ me – want more time together –
heading 2 coast – contact u l8r

Ethan read the message three more times before showing Mark. They shared a knowing look and gathered Gemma and Ann.

"Where would they be going?" Gemma asked. "Are you sure your car—"

Ethan patted his wife's leg as she snuggled next to him in the living room. "The auto guy checked it from top to bottom. There's no tracking device on there."

"Do you think they've been found?" Ann ventured. "Do you think something's wrong?"

"Hard to say." Ethan scrubbed his jaw as he read the text again. "Something's not right…but I can't put my finger on it. He's cryptic at best, and he's not answering when I call." He looked over at Mark. "Have you tried to call or text Cari?"

"Yeah. Nothing. I left her a message, though, to call me ASAP." Mark stood and began to pace the room. "Shit."

"We could all be jumping to the wrong conclusion, couldn't we?" Gemma offered. "Maybe it's exactly as he sent: They want more time together before he gets on a plane to London tomorrow. You can't blame them for that."

"God, I hope you're right." Mark let out a long sigh and went outside. Ann followed, leaving Ethan and Gemma in the living room.

"I'm worried, Gem." Ethan shifted to wrap his arm around his wife. "Something about that text…"

"Have you tried responding?"

"I asked him to text me. So far nothing. Could be a cell tower thing, though. There aren't too many towns between here and the coastline, so cell reception is probably pretty low."

Gemma kissed her husband's jaw. "Let's give them a few hours, shall we? We've got to stay positive…I've got to stay positive."

"Yeah, baby, I know."

"With Cari gone for the night, might I join you in your room? I don't want either of us to be alone."

"I'd like nothing better." Ethan pulled Gemma closer and rested his head on hers as they sat in silence.

The duct tape that bound Tristan's hands behind his back severely limited his movements. Sitting stock-straight in a wicker chair was straining his back, and his legs ached from being stationary too long. There was no getting comfortable, and Evgenia was fast asleep on the sofa across from him. If he could only stand, he might be able to get to the door and escape. Trying to gain balance, however, proved impossible.

"So what's your plan?" Tristan decided if he couldn't escape and wouldn't be able to sleep, he wasn't going to give Evgenia that luxury. "Hey, wake up!" He glanced at the digital clock on the stove in the cabin's open kitchen; it was nearing six in the morning.

"*Molkni…*" the blonde replied in a grumble. "Can't you see I'm trying to sleep?"

"And can't you have a heart enough to let me get some rest myself? You want me to cooperate with you, but that's going to be severely hindered if you continue to deprive me of sleep."

"If I cut the tape, will you *then* shut up? You can't leave. You know that. I'll kill that whore you were with the moment you try to get away."

"I've promised to do whatever you say. I proved that to you last night, allowing you to stick your tongue in my mouth and resisting the temptation to bite it off."

"You kissed me better that night in Sofia, you know," she countered.

"Christ, don't remind me."

"What? We had a good time, didn't we?" Evgenia now sat up on the sofa, raking her fingers through her hair. "We make a smart match, you and I. If you'd only kept your nose out of my father's business, he might have grown to accept you into the family. Of course, the way things have turned out, it seems that may be forthcoming after all…"

"Your father?" Tristan furrowed his brow. "Wait. You're Aleynekov's daughter?" It felt like he'd been kicked in the stomach.

"Evgenia Aleynekova," she responded with a smirk. "You never asked my last name; I never offered it. It seemed better that way at the time." She winked at Tristan as she clicked the blade upward on a box cutter and began slicing at the tape on his wrists. "If I remember correctly, we didn't waste much time talking…"

"I was too drunk to remember much beyond the nightclub."

"Oh, you were pining about how your girlfriend didn't understand you, how lonely you were. You really were quite pitiful. If you hadn't been so damned attractive, I might have let you pass out in an alleyway instead of my bed."

Tristan peeled the duct tape from his wrists as he strained to find the memories of that night—to no avail.

"Of course, I *had* to have you once I knew your connection to dear old dad." She let out a short laugh. "It's quite a rush to sleep with the enemy, you know."

"I didn't tell you anyth—"

"No, you didn't. You didn't reveal what you were doing, just that you worked for Carson. I checked with my brother to confirm everything." She paused. "You know my brother well, don't you? Nicky spoke so highly of you."

Tristan shook his head quickly, as if to awaken himself from sleep. "Nicky?…You mean Nikos Dobreyev?…He's your brother?" His eyes widened. "He's Aleynekov's son? Christ…"

Evgenia smiled. "Yes, it's all in the family, isn't it!" Her face became somber for a moment. "He hated what he did to you."

"What part? The lying…the double-crossing he was doing—?"

"The stairwell."

Tristan's world swirled wildly around him. He stood and began to pace, his right knee aching with every step. Nikos had been by his side at the hospital, he'd kept his parents and Gemma informed, he'd mailed that ever-important package…"Oh, God."

"Yes," Evgenia continued. "When my father assigned that nasty task to one of our, let's say, 'heavy hitters,' Nicky knew he had to go along to keep things from going too far."

"I trusted him. Christ, I trusted him with everything," Tristan muttered.

"He respected you, considered you a friend, Tristan. He truly felt horrible for what he did to you."

Tristan scrutinized what Evgenia had told him. She didn't appear to know of her brother's involvement in mailing the accounting documents to the United States. But Evgenia's revelation about her brother and father brought new concerns. His heart began pumping wildly at the thought that what Ethan had received might be blank pages, that Nikos might have kept the papers for himself. If that were the case, what was keeping Tristan alive? What secret game was Nikos playing by beating Tristan to a pulp, but not giving the incriminating documents to his father?

"Where is Nikos now?"

"Watching your whore's father."

"Stop calling her that. She's only involved in this because of my mistakes. She doesn't know about most of this, and she certainly hasn't been in contact with her father. I wouldn't allow it in order to keep him safe."

Evgenia tilted her head, studying him. "Smart move. And I must say the little tramp — is that better? — is an improvement over that bitch you dated in London. I can't imagine what you saw in her."

Once again, Tristan was taken aback by the mafia's infiltration of his life. "God, you're not hunting down her too, are you?"

"No, not anymore. She was actually pretty easy to get rid of."

"What are you talking about?" Tristan knew he had to keep his anger in check, but it was becoming increasingly difficult.

"Relax, sweetheart, she's alive." Evgenia plunked back down on the sofa and looked up at the ceiling, feigning innocence. "But...I did have someone visit her, tell her how prudent it would be if she didn't see you anymore. Didn't you notice a change in her demeanor?"

Tristan knew Melanie's feelings for him had waned, but he'd attributed her coldness to his lengthy absences.

"She never cared for you, Tristan. You must know that. If she had, she wouldn't have moved out the moment it was suggested. She followed my instructions *precisely* after your little accident in the stairwell. I'd already sent her photos of the two of us together that night, but Grigor's visit convinced her you weren't worth fighting for. She was a weakling. She was smart, though. I'll grant her that.

She never asked a single question about me or what had happened in Sofia. Good thing, too, or she might have discovered too late that her car's brakes weren't working some night."

"Is she in danger?" Tristan asked angrily.

"We're still watching her and a few of your colleagues in London. So far she's not stepped out of line. She seems to have taken Grigor's warning seriously, but we'll see."

Tristan stood quietly, taking in all Evgenia had revealed. One night's indiscretion had triggered the events that played out over the last few months. "Does your father know about our night together?"

"God, no!" She blew out a breath. "He'd never have let me track you here if he'd known I held a personal stake in the matter."

"And so I ask you again: What's your plan?"

"Easy. You get me those papers Josef wants, we fly to Sofia together to deliver them, and then perhaps, I don't know, you'll consider staying on there…with me."

"*Consider* staying on? Like I'd have a choice?"

Evgenia got up and began heating a pot on the stove. "Tea?"

Tristan shook his head.

"Suit yourself." She moved about, getting out a coffee mug and finding a drawer with utensils.

"Do I have a choice, Evgenia?"

"Certainly. Of course your decision may impact what happens to Ms. Lopez. But again, I'll leave it up to you whether you want to join me in Bulgaria or not." She gave Tristan a sweet smile before returning to prepare her tea.

A quick rap on the door snapped both their heads toward the cabin's entry.

"It's just me, Jenny," the muscled man said as he came inside. "Got any food I can give Cari, or do I need to run to the store?"

"Where is she?" Tristan growled. "God help you if you hurt her!"

"Calm down. She's sleeping just fine."

"What did you do to her?"

Evgenia came up beside Tristan and hugged his arm lovingly. "It's okay, honey." She kissed his shoulder. "Ben's trustworthy, and he's *very* caring in bed. I'm sure she's fine."

Ben scoffed. Evgenia pulled Tristan to the sofa again and sat comfortably next to him, a sarcastic smirk on her face. She placed a hand on his shoulder, caressing it. "Why does it matter?" she asked softly. "You're not with her anymore."

"I never was with her. I'm telling you, she has nothing to do with any of this. Let her go."

Evgenia's eyes opened wide, and she tilted her head to look directly at him. "Oh, my God." She sputtered a laugh. "You're in love with her!"

"No," Tristan replied through gritted teeth. "Not at all. She's collateral in all of this, someone who stuck her nose where it didn't belong. Just let her go. We'll go to Sofia and work things out with Josef, but leave her alone."

Evgenia leaned away from Tristan and tapped her chin with her index finger. "I don't know...I think she's far more important than you're admitting. How much does she know, Tristan?"

Tristan had to think quickly. Might involving Cari, making her vital to Evgenia's plan to get the documents back, help keep her alive longer?

He sighed, hoping to look convincing. "She's an accountant as well." That was at least partially true. "The documents I have are encrypted so they can't be deciphered if they get into the wrong hands. She knows enough to determine where the money's been sent." He hesitated. "I gave her a copy of the documents as well—with the same stipulation: If she's killed, the papers will be made public."

Chapter 30

Ben stayed by the door, watching the other two and hating how Evgenia flirted with this guy who'd butchered a man to death, for Christ's sake. She rose from the sofa and went to her purse on a nearby table. She pulled out two prescription bottles and handed them to Ben. "Remember what I told you about dosages? Get Lopez to take the Valium now. That'll keep her in just enough of a stupor that we can still get information from her. If she fights you, or if I send you the go-ahead, force her to take the rest of the bottle." She turned back toward Tristan, who watched her intently. "I'm not sure you're telling me the truth, sweetheart. I need to think about this."

She leaned over and kissed him while reaching into her back pocket, extracting his phone. "Let's make sure your family is pacified a little while longer so I can find out how much our little accountant bitch knows." She sat beside Tristan as she turned his phone on. "Ben, grab what you need from the pantry and go back to your cabin. You have Lopez's phone, right? Make sure it's on so you can send a text to anyone snooping into where she is."

"But, Jenny, what about—"

"What, Ben? I've given you specific directions," she snapped. "Now go."

Ben glared at Evgenia. "May I have just a moment of your time? *Please?*"

She sauntered over, adopting a sweet smile as she approached him. "I'm sorry for sounding so harsh, baby. I'm just tired," she whispered as she caressed his face.

Ben pulled her close, wrapping his arms around her waist. "What about us? I miss you already."

Evgenia sighed. "We've got to finish this situation, Ben. Josef is counting on us." She nestled into his embrace. "When all of this is over, we'll be paid a lot of money and can take a vacation to some private island. How does that sound, hmm? For now, though, I have to get Saunders to cooperate. He's told me the documents are hidden in Bulgaria, and he's only willing to give them directly to me. You understand, don't you?"

"I don't like how you act around him."

"I admit that Saunders and I have…a history," Evgenia said. "But I've got to use that to our advantage. I don't like it either, but we won't be gone long, and this will be over soon. Keep to the plan, Ben, and it'll pay off—literally—very soon. Now kiss me like you mean it, will you?"

Ben obliged, making sure he got her to moan in pleasure so Saunders would understand very clearly that Jenny, Evgenia, Delilah, whatever she called herself, was with *him*.

Cari awoke to Ben plunking items down on a table across the room. "I brought a couple cans of soup," he reported. "That's all I could get my hands on."

"Where's Tristan?" Cari's slurring had subsided, but her head still pounded from the combination of beer and whatever drug she'd been given.

Ben coughed out a short laugh. "Forget him. He's on his way to Bulgaria."

Cari raised up and leaned on one elbow as she worked to focus on Ben and her surroundings. "Bulgaria?"

"Those two are heading back home." Ben opened and slammed shut various drawers in the small kitchen, finally procuring a can opener and setting to work on preparing two bowls of soup.

"Can you undo the handcuffs?"

"What?" Ben asked, distracted by his task. "No. Why?"

"It's either that or…um…I have to use the bathroom."

Ben huffed and walked over to the end of Cari's cot. He dug deep in his front pocket and pulled out the tiny key. "There's no way to escape through there, if that's what you're thinking," he said as he unclasped the cuff. A line of blood stained the mattress where Cari's ankle had been resting. "You must have moved around a lot in your sleep. Does that hurt?"

"As if you care," Cari mumbled. "Just let me go pee, will you?" She stumbled as she stood, her equilibrium off. Ben reached forward to steady her, but she slapped his hand away. "Don't touch me."

"Hey," Ben replied as Cari slammed the bathroom door closed. "I'm not the reason you're involved with that asshole. You hooked up with him all on your own."

Cari looked around the small room, ignoring Ben's comments. He'd told her Tristan and that woman were going to Bulgaria...Tristan had abandoned her. *I was such a fool...I bought all of his lies...* She took a deep breath to keep from crying. She was on her own now and had to get away from her kidnapper. A look around the bathroom proved what Ben had said: there was no way out other than the door through which she'd entered. When she returned to the main room, Ben was pulling the bowls of soup out of the microwave. He set them on the small square wooden table. "Here. Eat." He pulled out a chair, sat, and stirred his soup.

Cari stood still for a moment, staring first at the bowl he'd scooted toward her and then at Ben's face.

"It's not drugged. I promise. Look, I'll switch bowls if that'll make you feel better."

Cari just shook her head as she slumped down in the chair across from him. "I'm not hungry, and I sure don't trust you."

"Whatever," Ben replied smugly. "I'll let you sit there until I'm done, but then I have to cuff you to the cot again."

"Why? Why can't you just let me go? I won't tell anyone—"

"You're staying right here, and that's that." He grunted and returned to his soup. Cari didn't want to push him for fear he'd drug her again, so not another word was spoken. She simply sat in the chair and watched her kidnapper, ignoring pangs of hunger as well as thoughts of Tristan and how he'd ruthlessly left her. Her focus was now on finding a way to escape.

Tristan waited until after Ben left to use the bathroom. Evgenia gave him an evil smirk and kept a gun pointed at him while he relieved himself, giving him no privacy whatsoever.

"You should have some tea or something," she said casually when they returned to the living area. "It's not that bad."

"I need to know Cari's alive," Tristan replied.

"Keep your pants on — or would rather have them off? It's up to you, love," she said coyly.

"I need to know if she's alive, you bitch. You've made her the bargaining chip? Well, so have I. I'll get you those damned papers only when I know she's safe. If she dies, or that bastard has already killed her, you and Josef will get nothing."

"You think that intimidates me? You think I won't just call my colleagues in London to take care of your parents? Hell, I could head over to that inn you're staying at. Ann? Was that her name? She and I got along famously the other day when she gave me a tour," she said softly. "Or I'll just pop them each in the head, one by one, until you agree to cooperate." She gazed at the gun in her hand, seemingly mesmerized by it. "You know I prefer poison, of course. Don't want that pharmacy degree going to waste, do we? Daddy Dearest paid a lot of money to make sure I was well-educated for the family business. But...we're getting tired of this, Tristan. Poisons can be unpredictable, sometimes taking longer than I have time for." She smiled sweetly. "Besides, a gunshot to the head is quick and painless. We wouldn't want them to suffer, now would we?"

Get a plan going or you'll lose everything...and everyone. "The only ones who can help are Cari and my brother-in-law Ethan," Tristan announced.

Evgenia looked at him in surprise.

"Cari understands what to look for and can help Ethan translate it so your father will know what everything means. You can keep us all separate," he added. It might help to involve Ethan only remotely so he could also possibly access help. "But I need proof that Cari's okay." Tristan thought for a moment. "I want to see her — "

"Impossible. Don't take me for a fool, Tristan."

"No, set up video surveillance on her. You can keep me here, and you can keep her locked up wherever you've got her. Ethan can get the docume — "

"He knows where they are?" Evgenia stood up. "Where?"

"Don't take *me* for a fool, either, Evgenia. The documents are… accessible within a short period of time. I can get them, but you need to prove Cari's not dead before I'll do a damned thing for you."

Evgenia paced, her finger tapping her chin again. After a minute passed, she stopped and turned to Tristan. "Webcam. I've got a laptop I'll set up here and a video camera I'll have Ben set up there. Satisfactory?"

"Call him now or the deal's off."

She punched numbers into her cell, and Ben was back at the cabin within a half hour, the two of them rifling through a large black suitcase Ben had brought from their car. Before Ben left, Tristan called to him. "Focus on her feet."

"What?"

"You heard me. If you've got her drugged and she's sleeping, she won't be moving around too much. I won't have the proof I need unless you focus on her feet."

When Ben got the call to go see Jenny, she'd told him to give Cari two of the Valiums. He didn't feel comfortable drugging her again, but he didn't share his doubts with Jenny. Cari had begun to plead with him, and he knew her being handcuffed to the bed would keep her from escaping or getting any kind of help. So he just gave her a stern warning that he'd make her take the pills if she tried to get away.

She nodded compliantly, lay back down on the cot, and allowed him to cuff her to the bedframe again. This time, however, he wrapped a cloth napkin around her left ankle, hoping to minimize the chafing the metal cuffs had already caused on her other leg. Remembering her shivering, he once again draped the thin sheet over her. When he returned to the cabin nearly an hour later, Cari had rolled on to her other side, now facing the room, and was fast asleep.

And then he understood Saunders's strange request. At the end of the bed, the sheet rose and fell rhythmically, as though Cari were tapping her foot to a song. Suddenly the sound of the wall clock seemed to grow louder—that was the rhythm she followed. There was a distinct clicking sound as the second hand struggled unsuccessfully to pass the minute hand. The clock was stuck at 3:04. Ben checked his watch — half past seven — and proceeded to set up the video camera Jenny had given him, balancing the mini-tripod on a nightstand next to Cari's cot. Once it was in place, he called Jenny. She confirmed that Tristan could see Cari's foot moving.

Before hanging up, Ben stepped outside the cabin so as not to be overheard. "When will you be back?"

"When I tell you I'm back," she said curtly.

"What the hell?"

"You need to stop questioning everything I do."

"So, what about the whole we're-in-this-together thing, huh? You're flying off to God knows where, pawing a guy you have a 'history' with, and frankly, I don't like it. You're with *me*, damn it."

Jenny's voice was suddenly icy. "No, Ben, *you're* with *me*, doing what I tell you to do. Remember what I told you, baby. Don't wear out your welcome, or you'll find the consequences very unpleasant."

"I thought we were doing this as a team," Ben argued. "What? Now you're hot for Saunders? Where does that leave me?"

"Lucky to be alive, given how you're speaking to me. Now stay with Lopez, and don't you dare challenge me again."

"What's that supposed to mean?" Ben walked farther from the cabin's front door, his voice no longer hushed.

"It means you're in deeper shit than you realize, sweetheart. You'll do exactly what I tell you or your family will pay the price."

"Family? What the — "

"Chloe's, what, almost two?" Jenny's question was clearly sarcastic. "It'd be a shame if she was left an orphan. Or maybe your sister and her husband will wake up one morning and Chloe will be missing from that new big-girl bed Talia just got her."

"Oh, my G — "

"Oh, yeah. I know your sister. She and I are great friends. We met at the gym weeks ago." She gave a sarcastic laugh. "She likes me so much, she even wanted to set me up with you. Ironic, isn't it?"

"You bitch!"

"Like I said, Ben." Jenny's voice once again became ice cold. "You're in deep. You do *exactly* what I tell you, you don't question me, and you don't do something stupid like calling Talia or the police."

"Shit. Who are you, the freakin' mafia?"

"Pah!" she responded. "That's such an ugly word. *We*…you, me, Tristan…are part of what I prefer to describe as *entrepreneurs* with global investments."

"Entrepreneurs who threaten and hurt people? That sounds a hell of a lot like what mafia guys do, and if that's the case, count me out right now. I'm not—"

"Be quiet, Ben. You agreed the moment we left Seattle that you'd help me."

"Yeah, help you do what's right. You told me Saunders was a killer and a thief. How much of that is true?"

"Well…" Jenny paused. "I may have exaggerated the situation."

"So is Saunders really part of this Bulgaria shit? Does he work for Josef too?"

"In a way, yes. But he's in this too. Don't be fooled into thinking otherwise. He went a little wayward for a brief period, but we're back together, like we should be." She paused, and Ben imagined she was touching that bastard again. "Oh," Jenny added, as if enlightened, "and if I decide that Ms. Lopez is no longer necessary to us, you *will* kill her and dispose of the body. Do you understand?"

"What the hell? I'm not some kind of assassin!"

"Yes, Ben, you are. And you'll be paid well, just like you have been for all the other tasks you've done for Josef." Jenny switched to a sickly sweet voice. "Why do you think I hired you? Your skills with a gun are nearly as good as mine."

"I play paintball, you bitch!"

"And you play to win. You're insane when you go after your target. I'm counting on you to turn on your death-to-the-enemy persona when I tell you. And do you know what'll happen if you don't?" She laughed. "I won't stop with Talia and Chloe. I'll find other people important to you." She once again reverted to her serious tone. "You or Lopez get out of line with me, and both of you will bear the guilt of my revenge. My colleagues are able to make things look like unfortunate accidents—drug overdoses, car accidents, house fires—but you'll know you were to blame." She paused. "Now get back to watching Lopez. Oh, and feel free to let her know how *nice* it would be if she'll kindly cooperate." The call went dead, and Ben just stared at his phone.

Chapter 31

Vasily sipped his tea, chatting with Nadia about her plans for the day. Although she'd asked if he wanted to join her, he politely declined, citing business dealings that needed his attention. Another half hour passed before she began her errands and he was finally able to make a phone call.

"*I hadn't heard from you,*" Vasily said. "*But I also haven't heard of any bodies floating in the river, either. I did make myself clear, da?*" He heard a long sigh from the other end of the line.

"*Da. It's in progress. Remember, this is just as important to me as it is to you.*"

"*Do you need my help?*" Vasily asked. He realized neither his anger nor his frustration was going to ensure the outcome he needed.

"*No, I've got things under control, but there's the issue with Alexei.*"

"*Where is he?*"

"*Still in Sofia. But he needs to be protected. Can you arrange papers for him when he comes to the States?*"

"*You take care of this little favor for me, and I vow to ensure safe passage for Alexei to wherever you say.*"

"*Thank you. I'll be in touch as soon as I can. Ciao.*"

Ben's mind raced. The mafia was something he'd seen in movies, not in real life. And this Jenny-Evgenia woman now expected him to kill someone? God Almighty, he'd *kidnapped* someone for this nut job! Should he call his father? No, Jenny had warned against him calling anyone. *Chloe...baby Chloe...* Ben paced the gravelly ground in front of the cabin. *Think, Ben, think!*

He had to get out of here without Jenny knowing. He could wait until she and Saunders went to the airport, but what if she insisted he kill Lopez before she left? He glanced toward the cabin. Cari Lopez — the woman he'd drugged and kidnapped — was a pawn in all this too. Didn't matter. He needed to protect his family; they were his top priority. He had to get out of there, get his family far away from this hellish situation he'd put them in. Ben went back inside the cabin, desperate for an escape plan that would work.

All Tristan could do was maintain his icy stare. He knew Cari's life, as well as her father's, was in peril, but his parents, sister, and Ethan were equally threatened. And now it appeared this man, Ben, was an unwitting accomplice, with his own family also in danger. Evgenia had them all in her grasp. Tristan had to end this nightmare. She hadn't restrained him again, demanding instead that he text Ethan about decoding the documents. She'd checked his message to be sure he wasn't sending some kind of SOS. He was careful as he typed, knowing Evgenia wouldn't hesitate to blow out his kneecaps with that gun she had tucked in her waistband. Once the text was sent, Tristan returned his focus on Evgenia. Physically, he could take her, but the gun made that a dangerous move. He'd have to get to her psychologically.

"If I join your family, what's our role? You and me, I mean." Tristan adopted a gentle, if not curious, demeanor with her.

"You mean besides being back in my bed?" She laughed. "You know you passed out that night, right? Not that I didn't try my most seductive moves on you, mind you! You were just too out of it from the Rohypnol."

"Ah," Tristan said, choosing to remain calm, aloof, at the confirmation that he'd been drugged that night in Sofia. "I wondered about that. I'm usually able to handle my liquor better than that."

He tilted his head, eyeing her with interest. "You didn't trust that I might like you *without* a little powder in my drink?"

Evgenia scoffed. "Don't give me that shit. You were pitiful! Whining about that Melanie woman. God, I was patient with you, you know."

Tristan faked a laugh. "I was pretty bad, wasn't I? Good Lord, I'm sorry. I wasn't very good company for anyone. And I was too blind to see the beautiful woman I had in front of me."

"You're playing games with me, Tristan, I can feel it," she said with a suspicious smile.

"All I'm saying is I recognize that I didn't give you a fair chance."

Her smile disappeared. "And now that you know about me... about my family? Given what you know now, would you have wanted to be with me?"

"Let me turn it around," Tristan responded softly. "What was it about me that you wanted?"

"Freedom," she said immediately. And for a moment, Evgenia's eyes showed a hint of tears. "I thought you could offer me freedom."

They were quiet for a minute. Tristan went to the kitchen and started another pot of water for tea. He knew she was feeling vulnerable after that revelation. He was breaking through, but she was like thin ice, and he had to be very careful how he stepped.

"Where did you learn to speak English without an accent?" A change of subject seemed appropriate. "Even in Sofia, I thought you were American."

"My father made sure his children were educated in boarding schools around the United States," she said as she sat down on to the sofa, hugging a pillow to her chest. "Nicky and I spent most of our childhood away from our parents. I guess in retrospect that was good for us and necessary for him. It kept us safe from the mafia world until we were ready to join it—there'd be no saying no to Josef Aleynekov! So by the time we understood what Daddy Dearest did for a living in his off hours, he'd made sure we were already involved. Nicky was pushed to get an accounting degree at Columbia University and was then hired to help with our father's private investment accounts." She paused, taking a long breath. "I got my pharmacy degree from the University of Houston in Texas and was often asked to provide dummy prescriptions for Father's friends. He'd whine about how Bulgarian doctors didn't have access to the best medicines, and he introduced me to people who worked a pharmacy black market. I was helping legitimately sick people, so I overlooked the illegality of it all. Even Grigor, a Romanian my father adopted, got his IT degree and learned to speak American English with a minimal accent."

"Josef was a long-term planner."

"He was calculating and manipulative," she replied stiffly. "He didn't care who he hurt as long as his business ventures were profitable and kept out of the public eye."

"And so you thought that meeting a foreigner might be a way out for you?"

She sighed. "Maybe. I knew I'd be putting any man I was with in danger. I wanted you to be different. I wanted you to not care what my father did...how evil he is." Tristan watched Evgenia discreetly sweep two fingers across her cheekbone under her eyes. "I thought," she said softly, "you'd be the type of father a man should be."

"You met me at a bar and immediately started planning our family?"

"Not exactly," she said, her voice quiet, hesitant. "I hoped you could be the father my son, Alexei, deserves."

Chapter 32

Ethan hadn't slept, and based on the tossing and turning he'd felt beside him all night, Gemma hadn't either. Something was wrong. He could feel it. He'd left his phone on just in case Tristan called or texted, but so far nothing. He considered calling Vasily, wondering if the Ukrainian had any inside word on Aleynekov's directives regarding Tristan and the documents, but he didn't want to tell him Tristan and Cari were currently, well, missing. He'd just have to keep trying…

Around noon, Ethan finally received a text:

> In negotiations with Aleynekov regarding the accounts.
> I need you to analyze the documents I sent as quickly
> as possible. Seconds count!! Start calculating skewed results.
> Ongoing status awaits confirmation. Accounts have
> aberrative financials internally. Assume the general
> allowances specific across calculated errors within.
> I'll be in touch again soon.

He read the message four times, but it left more questions than answers. He didn't have an accounting degree, but he'd taken a few courses that required him to analyze expense reports and such. However, even he could tell Tristan's text rambled incoherently — he'd even made up the word *aberrative*. None of it made sense, yet this was all Ethan had to go on.

He got the hidden envelope from the bookshelf and brought it to the kitchen table where Ann and Gemma had gathered. He copied down the message on a piece of paper so they could work together to decipher Tristan's directions. With a deep breath and a reassuring nod from the others, Ethan sliced open the envelope and took out the contents.

"You have a son?"

Evgenia smiled shyly. "Alexei. Yeah. He's a good boy too."

"Where is he?" Tristan was intrigued and pleased that Evgenia wanted to talk.

"He's in Sofia. He stays on the compound. Nannies take care of him, but he'll be off to boarding school next year."

"My God, how old is he?"

"Twelve."

Tristan nearly spit out the mouthful of tea he'd taken in. "Twelve? But you're —"

"Going on twenty-nine, yes. I was sixteen when he was born."

"You were just a child yourself."

"But not so innocent. I stayed in Sofia during the pregnancy, and my mother helped me a lot when Alexei was born." She paused. "He brought happiness back into our family...until my mother's death just a month after his birth." Evgenia pushed the pillow off her lap and stood. "Did you make enough tea for me?"

"Yes, certainly," Tristan responded. "Help yourself." He waited patiently for her to continue, but when a minute passed in silence, he ventured a safe question. "Where will he attend school?"

"Somewhere in Boston, I think. My father has people checking out a few places. He knows enough basic English to do well, but it's important for him to learn some American idioms and things to ease the language barrier when he arrives in the States."

"How often do you see him?"

"Enough...I guess."

Tristan noticed Evgenia was purposefully not looking at him, nor was he able to see her face. She was keeping her emotions in check, and Tristan would have to respect that if he wanted her to continue the conversation.

Then he made a mistake. "Has Josef told you what he wants Alexei to study at university?"

Evgenia spun around, her eyes wild. "*I* decide what's best for my son. Do you hear me? That's *my* job! I won't have him doing my father's bidding, and I won't have him getting involved with the mafia."

Tristan raised his hands in surrender. "I'm sorry. I didn't mean to offend—"

"That man is done ruling my life. Once I'm finished with this mess you dragged us all into, I'm going back to Sofia and taking Alexei far, far away from the Aleynekov influence."

Tristan just sipped his tea, wondering how his parents would have reacted had he or Gemma had a child at such a young age.

Evgenia absently stirred her tea. "I can't have my son be in this dysfunctional...*thing* people refer to as a family."

"Then why do you do what your father wants?" Tristan asked gently. "I know to some extent he's forced you to do things, but it seems in some cases you've been willing. I'd guess you may have even killed for him."

Evgenia glared.

"I don't need to know, nor do I *want* to know, any details. I just see...I just see so much anger."

"I have every right to be angry!"

"Of course," he reassured her. "Christ, I can't imagine—"

"That's right. You can't." Evgenia seethed. "You can't even begin to understand anything about my life."

"I can see that you need to start over. Start a new life with Alexei."

"You could be a part of that. Help me figure things out, help me raise Alexei to be like you."

"Evgenia, I—"

"I know I've been horrible to you. I've been a horrible person for a long time." She sat on the sofa and looked down at her tea as she continued. "If I guarantee that you, your family, and the people you're with will be safe, will you come with me to Sofia? At least meet Alexei? You'll fall in love with him right away...and, you know, maybe someday you'd come to care for me too..." Her voice trailed off in a whisper.

Tristan sat beside her, his hands folded in front of him as he rested his elbows on his legs. "I *have* to know the people I care about won't be endangered—ever. You know that's why I kept the copy of the bank accounts; it's been the only way I've had to protect them."

She broke away and walked across to the kitchen. "Just like your family is your priority, Alexei is mine. As long as he's in Sofia, my father controls everything. I will do whatever it takes not to jeopardize being with my son. If my father tells me to kill you or anyone else or I'll never see Alexei again—"

"You'll do what you have to," Tristan finished for her. "I'd likely do the same."

"I hate my father."

"So do I. He's an evil man." Tristan allowed the conversation to end there, choosing once again to watch the video feed of Cari. Josef Aleynekov controlled everything, all right—even people he'd never met and had no reason to hurt. Tristan had learned a lot in his talk with Evgenia, and she seemed to have a vulnerable side. Perhaps this was the start of a peaceful solution to all of this.

He'd always said he could be bought. This price—going into hiding with Evgenia and her son—would be worth it if Cari would be set free and the others would be safe. He let his gaze get lost on the computer screen, and he was glad of the momentary quiet…until he realized Cari's foot hadn't been moving any time he'd looked in the past hour.

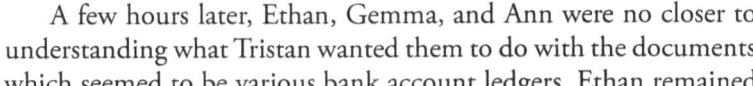

A few hours later, Ethan, Gemma, and Ann were no closer to understanding what Tristan wanted them to do with the documents, which seemed to be various bank account ledgers. Ethan remained at the kitchen table, poring over everything; Mark had stopped by the inn after school, but he soon had to return for basketball practice.

"I'm missing something here, I just know it," Ethan said.

"Still no answer when you call either cell?" Ann asked as she started another pot of coffee.

"None. And neither of them has—" Just then, Ethan's phone vibrated. Once again, however, the message was cryptic.

Agencies counted minimal income. Aggressively study
Moldovan assets. Go after Lithuanian sales associates.
Max Avram kept accounts, falsified profit bids.
Remember, seconds count!!

Ethan ran his hands roughly through his hair. "God, Tristan, what the hell do I do with this?" He looked over at Ann and Gemma.

"He's obviously asking for my help, but it's like he's…I don't know… like he wants me to read between the lines or something."

Gemma had been busily writing down the second message and now compared it to the first. "He's writing like one accountant talking to another. He must know you don't understand this — this jargon he's using." She paused, and then she circled a part of each message. "Funny. He repeated this phrase 'seconds count' from the first message."

"And he put the exclamation points again too," Ann added. "Is he telling us he's in trouble? That time is of the essence?"

"Maybe," Ethan said with a sigh. "But it doesn't help if I don't understand what he wants me to do."

"Let's find the name Max Avram and the Moldovan and Lithuanian accounts," Ann said. She spread out the documents, and Ethan grabbed a few to scan as well. "Anything?" she asked after perusing the papers in front of her.

"I found statements from a bank in Vilnius, but there are no Lithuanian sales associates' names anywhere in these papers. And there's no assets column for any of the Moldovan accounts — and there are seven banks listed from that country."

"Wait a minute," Gemma said in a near-whisper. "Seconds count… seconds count." Then she quickly circled the second word in each short sentence. She blew out a breath. "No. That's even more confusing."

Ann looked at Gemma's circles and grabbed the paper with the first message, circling single letters instead of words. "Oh, my God." She scribbled wildly and studied the page for a few moments. "Oh, my God, Gemma. You were right. He's hidden a message in his text. It starts after he tells us seconds count." She looked at Ethan and Gemma and read, "Take…No, taken…Two…Cab — cabins… Help…Cari.'"

"The other message!" Ethan cried out, but Gemma was already frantically circling letters.

"Got it! 'Going…To…Sofia…Save…Cari.'" Gemma looked up at her husband, dumbfounded, and began to cry. "God, Ethan, what do we do?"

Ethan pulled her into his arms and ran his hand up and down her back, soothing her sobbing. "We'll find them. We'll find them, and we'll save them."

Chapter 33

Ben slouched at the kitchen table, filled with anger at being betrayed by Jenny, fearful of what she would do to his family if he resisted her demands. He opened his phone to reread the last message from his sister, desperate to contact her to be sure she was all right. Then he switched to the Internet, checking news back home. As he scrolled to the bottom of the screen, his eyes widened. "Oh, my God."

This can't be connected to me, it just can't.

The article he'd spotted told of an SEU student who had been beaten and left for dead. Kevin Lamb...Chameleon. There were no witnesses and no suspects, but Kevin was in pretty bad shape. *Jenny... God, did Jenny do this?*

Kevin Lamb was a total asshole, but Ben never wanted him killed. He stood and began to pace as he ran his hands through his hair. Jenny knew Ben hated Kevin...and Kevin had warned him about...about that picture that looked like her. Maybe the mafia found out about that. He quickly switched back to texting, bringing up the message and attachment Kevin had sent him. Varuud Zakharov...Russian guy... apparent suicide although police were investigating. He'd worked at Cari's apartment complex.

Ben returned to the current news article about Kevin and continued reading.

"In other university news, esteemed professor Dr. Jonathan Lassiter was found hanged in his home. According to initial reports, Dr. Lassiter may have been involved in a burglary on the campus last weekend.

Police have not found any link between the professor's death and the attack on the university student..."

Ben's heart was racing now. He went to the St. Eustachius web site and searched for Jonathan Lassiter. *Expert in international finance...written three books...has presented at conferences around the world and...worked with post-Communist countries over the past two decades.* It wasn't too much of a stretch to connect Jenny to this guy too, and he wondered what he'd done that had gotten him killed.

"Jesus..." Ben said as he sat back in the chair. "Too many coincidences. Jenny's had a hand in all of this, I just know it." He blew out a long breath as he wondered what it would take for Jenny to decide that Ben should die too. "This has got to end."

He looked at the wall clock, forgetting it was still stuck...just like Ben. Its clicking hands mesmerized him as he considered his options. God, what a mess he'd put himself in.

*   *   *

"Well?" Evgenia's mood was souring again. "Is your brother-in-law going to turn over the documents?"

"Not yet," Tristan said. "I'm having him decipher them first. Karl Tresk encoded them when he discovered all the embezzling and laundering your father was doing. I figured out what he'd done, and I made copies once I knew what all the numbers and entries meant. That information isn't directly on the documents, but any decent accountant will spot the discrepancies quickly. Ethan's not an accountant, so I'm telling him what to look for. He's smart, though. He'll figure things out."

"Encoded or not, my father wants those documents back. Why does he need to do anything? You need to get those papers from him so we can get back to Bulgaria."

"I highly doubt your father wants to have to bring in another accountant. He's already in danger of the wrong people finding out what he's done." Tristan hoped his explanations would continue to seem plausible. Evgenia had read his texts before he was allowed to send them. Now it was up to Ethan to figure out what Tristan was trying to tell him. "Wait. I just got a text from him."

Evgenia grabbed Tristan's phone before he could read the message, and his heart began to pound. If Ethan had deciphered the texts,

Tristan hoped he hadn't responded openly to the hidden messages. She read it aloud and then tossed Tristan his phone.

> Understood. First things first: When income levels lowered, transfer results yielded total outcomes.
> Financials included no deductions.
> Could Albanian banks indicate nuances somehow?

Tristan looked at the second letters, but it was gibberish. Then he reread the message: "First things first." He looked at the first letters of every word and read the hidden message silently: *Will try to find cabins.* Tristan sighed. Ethan had understood. They were going to look for Cari and help her.

Minutes later, another text came in, and once again, Evgenia read it first. "God, I'm glad I didn't go into accounting! Here."

Tristan anxiously read the text and smiled.

> Calculating assets. Lithuanians leveraged Ignalina Nuclear!
> Gather Vilnians aren't seeing industrial links yet?

Calling Vasily. "Makes perfect sense to me," Tristan replied. "Those Lithuanians are dangerous, aren't they!" He decided to play up Ethan's message. "Is Josef dealing with nuclear power plants now?"

Evgenia scoffed. "I don't know, and I don't care. My father's greed seems to know no bounds. If buying or selling nuclear energy is his thing now, so be it."

Tristan relaxed just a little. Evgenia was completely unaware of the ruse, and Ethan was getting help from someone who understood Josef and how organized crime worked. His main worry, however, was Cari and whether she'd survive the day, let alone this whole ordeal. They were still in danger of being killed. As long as he could continue to play these hidden message games with Ethan, though, he'd be buying time. He needed to delay getting on that plane to Sofia, because he knew in his heart that the moment he arrived, he'd be a dead man.

A few hours passed, and it was nearing four in the afternoon. Tristan had barely looked away from the laptop, watching Cari sleep. Evgenia's accomplice had repositioned the camera so it was focused on her shoulders and head. Cari had shifted a few times, thus dispelling Tristan's worries that she was overmedicated or dead. Still, though he knew she was resting and appeared to be unharmed, apart from the drugs, he worried for her safety.

"Has that brother-in-law of yours confirmed he'll deliver the documents?" Evgenia asked. Tristan's latest text to him had no code. It simply provided Ethan with directions for dropping off the envelope, along with a warning that Gemma would be the next target should anything go awry.

"Yes," Tristan replied. "And he knows not to challenge the situation. I'm counting on you to keep your promise, though. I go to Sofia with you, and you leave my family and friends alone. You'll order Cari's release as soon as we reach the Portland Airport and make sure that goon she's with knows not to harm her." Tristan stood to stretch his legs, his right knee particularly, and went for another cup of tea. "Have you worked out how you'll get your son away from Josef?"

Evgenia sighed. "It'll be dangerous. He's used Alexei as a way to control me all these years. And Alexei looks up to him like he's some kind of hero." She let out an exasperated breath. "God, if he only knew the truth."

"You won't tell him, though, will you?"

Evgenia seemed to think for a moment and shrugged. "No. At least not until Alexei is old enough to understand the decisions I've made over the years that kept me from him. I've been a horrible mother."

"What does Nikos know about all of this?"

"God, nothing. He was away at boarding school when I got pregnant. My father insisted he stay in the States for nearly two years, told him it was good for him. Truth was, no one wanted Nicky to know Alexei was my child. When our mother died, Nicky was told she'd died giving birth to Alexei. Nicky wasn't even allowed to attend the funeral; Alexei was nearly two when Nicky was finally allowed to come home."

"And you never told him. Why?"

"What good would it do? I guess I've always wanted to protect Nicky as much as I want to protect Alexei. Some things are better left unsaid."

Tristan could see Evgenia was done talking for now, but he'd once again learned more about the Aleynekov family. It made him miss his family that much more. When he returned to the sofa to watch Cari, the camera's focus was once again on the lower end of the cot. He realized he too needed some rest. Nothing would be happening until Ethan delivered the package later tonight, so Tristan laid his head on the back of the sofa and let his eyes close for just a little while.

Chapter 34

Vasily Shevchenko had been on his way back to his apartment in Vancouver when he received Ethan's frantic phone call. His Bulgarian colleague's misdeeds had expanded farther than he'd realized. While Vasily knew first-hand the extent to which the mafia would go to protect its assets, he had never approved of innocents getting killed. Ethan and his family were innocents, and more than that, Vasily knew Ethan to be a good and honest man. He provided his best advice on the current situation and assured his American friend he'd take care of things. Upon ending that call, he immediately made another.

"*I need to know your progress,*" he said in Bulgarian.

"*I've got everything planned. Your demands will be met very soon, I promise.*"

"*I'm sorry for asking you to do this. I don't like asking for anyone to be killed. Will you be doing it yourself or will you direct someone?*"

There was silence for a moment. "*You don't really want me to tell you, do you? Isn't it better for all of us if certain things remain understood yet unsaid?*"

Vasily pulled into the parking place in front of his apartment, turned off the car, but stayed inside. He sighed heavily before speaking again. "*When this is done, I want out. Permanently. Can you arrange that?*"

"*Nothing is ever guaranteed, but I can assure you I will send out a directive that you and your family are not to be contacted. No one has crossed me yet. People know not to challenge me if they want to stay alive.*"

There was another short pause. *"In the meantime, may I ask as to the progress of my request?"*

"Alexei's new identity is being secured as we speak. No one will be able to find him. Just let me know when you need everything to take effect."

"I'll be in touch soon. Ciao."

Vasily got out of the car and looked up to the large front window of his apartment. Nadia was inside, likely preparing a cup of tea for him. He would do anything—*anything*—to keep her safe.

Tristan woke with a start and immediately looked toward the laptop. There was no movement at the moment, but he knew sometimes Cari slept soundly enough that her foot didn't twitch. He sat up and looked around, spotting Evgenia reading on a garish recliner just inside a small bedroom off the kitchen. He waited a few minutes, then rose silently, wondering if he could make a run for it. Although Cari's location was unknown to him, he figured she wasn't far. Ben had been back and forth between the two cabins pretty quickly. She could be right next door for all he knew.

"You'd risk your parents' lives? Or your sister's?" Evgenia asked casually as she got up from her chair. "I saw you eyeing the front door, Tristan. I'm not stupid. Neither are you." She rummaged through the kitchen cabinets. "There's oatmeal." She read the package. "Shit. It's expired, but it'll have to do. Want some?"

Tristan planted himself on the sofa again, waving her off. "No." He returned to watching the monitor. Still no movement. After another twenty minutes without so much as a single twitch, he began to worry. "Let me call Ben, please. I need to check on Cari."

"For someone claiming to not be in love with her, you certainly behave otherwise."

Tristan glared but said nothing. He held out his hand, and she gave him her cell.

"This is Ben." The response was calm, matter-of-fact.

"It's Tristan."

"You've got free rein over Jenny's phone now?"

Tristan ignored him. "I…I haven't seen Cari's foot move in nearly a half-hour. Would you mind—"

"Yeah, uh, about that..." Ben's voice changed from clipped to what Tristan could only describe as slimy. "She's, um, well, let's just say she didn't take too well to the amount of Valium in her system. I was going to text Jenny in a few minutes but, well, I've been outside staking out a good place to bury the body. Can you put her on for me? I need to—"

Tristan snapped the phone shut and threw it at Evgenia as he stood and rushed toward her. "She's dead! Your goddamn poison killed her!"

Evgenia pulled out her gun and directed it at Tristan. "You back off right now, or so help me, I'll kill you right where you're standing."

"You killed her," Tristan raged. He continued to advance on Evgenia despite her warning. "God damn it, you killed her..."

Evgenia crouched, grabbed her cell near her feet, and backed up slightly. She quickly redialed Ben, keeping her gun on Tristan. "What happened, you idiot?"

Tristan repeatedly opened and clenched his fists, trying to regain his composure. He listened as Evgenia spoke on the phone.

"Did you try to revive her?...Did you check for a pulse on her neck and her wrists?...Jesus, Ben, I can't believe you let this happen...Don't you dare question me! I told you how many pills and how often she had to take them... *That* many? Oh, my God! You screwed up!...Yes, damn it, you need to bury the body!...Is the spot far enough away from the cabin?...Good, a tarp is good. Wrap her up tight in it. We don't need coyotes digging her up...Do you need Tristan and me to help you?...Don't get flip with me, Ben, it was a simple question!...Okay, okay...Call me when you're done." Evgenia looked at Tristan. "This wasn't supposed to happen, Tristan. Not like this, not now."

"Oh, you were going to have Cari overdose once we were on our way to Sofia, then?" Tristan seethed. He stood firm, and Evgenia still held the gun, ready to fire.

"No. I gave you my word. I was going to set her free. Jesus..."

"I want to see her..." Tristan took a step toward the door. "I need to see her so I can tell her family."

"No, Tristan, you can't. It's better you and I not know where she's buried. If the police ever tie us to this, it'll be to our benefit to—"

"*I've* got nothing to hide, Evgenia. I can't wait to tell the police that you and Ben—"

"You do that, and I promise you your parents will be dead within twenty-four hours, do you hear me?"

"Not if I can help it!" Tristan lunged at his captor, taking her by surprise. He smacked the gun out of Evgenia's hand, and it skittered across the floor, hitting the far wall. Evgenia immediately put her hands up in front of her as she backed herself against the kitchen counter. "You don't shoot your victims, Evgenia. Even I know that. You *poison* them." He wrestled her until he was behind her and had her arms bound within his. She struggled but could not break free. "Come on, *sweetheart*. You want me with you? You want me with you forever? What else have you got in that bag of yours?"

"Tristan," Evgenia pleaded as she struggled. "Tristan, stop! You need to calm down."

He shifted his grip so he could rifle through her large black purse on the kitchen table. "Xanax...Percocet...Rohypnol...Vicodin... What's this? Is this cocaine?" He dug further. "No more Valium, hmm? I guess all of these will have to do." Tristan dragged Evgenia to the sink, where he filled a glass with water. "It'll be so tragic," he said. "They'll find us—lovers who committed suicide together. The autopsy should find a little bit of everything in us, don't you think? What would you like to take first? Which one will take the edge off?"

"No, Tristan!" Evgenia pleaded, still unable to break from his grasp. "This won't save your family."

"Staying with you, trusting you—let's be honest, that's not going to save them either. But when my body's found, those documents will be distributed and your father's days will be numbered." Tristan struggled to open one of the pill bottles with one hand, finally resorting to smashing it on the counter, its contents scattering across the laminate, a few pills dropping to the wood floor.

"Let her go. Now." Tristan and Evgenia looked up to see Nikos standing in the doorway, his gun pointed at them. "Do it, Tristan. Let her go."

Chapter 35

Ethan shrugged nervously in his blazer, trying to loosen the sweaty feel of it on his shoulders as he paced the lobby of the casino. He'd nearly had to fight off Mark as he got in Ann's SUV, but none of them knew whether they were being watched at the inn. He'd been told to go to the Seven Feathers Casino alone, and that's what he was going to do. It'd been risky enough when they sneaked off to Mark's office to make two more copies of the documents. They hadn't seen any people or cars between the inn and the school, so they were hopeful no one had been spying on them.

Evgenia Aleynekova's voice still echoed in his head—a mix of sultry and evil—as he looked around the lobby. Although he'd been surprised by her phone call, and the revelation that she was Aleynekov's daughter, he'd memorized her instructions exactly. "At precisely nine fifty, you will make sure the second elevator is empty. You will place the envelope inside and to the left, press the button for the second floor, and then step back to let the door close without you inside. You will leave the casino. If you try to interfere in any way, you'll be endangering your entire family. I'll call the inn at precisely ten ten to speak to you. That gives you twenty minutes to get back. If you do not answer the phone by the third ring, I will consider you in breach of our oral contract. Do you understand?"

This woman hadn't had any kind of Eastern European accent. Ethan had asked Vasily about her earlier, and he'd said Evgenia had been educated in the United States but didn't offer much else. Vasily had promised to make a few phone calls to find out who else might be involved in Tristan's and Cari's kidnappings. He'd also warned Ethan not to try to outwit the Aleynekov family. They were killers who would not hesitate to act on their threats, he said.

Ethan had assured Aleynekov's daughter he would follow her instructions. He was thankful she'd not mentioned anything about other copies he might have. It would have been a technicality, to be sure, but he didn't want to have to lie. Mark had found secure places at the school and in the basement of the community center to hide the two additional envelopes of information. Now, as Ethan waited to put the envelope in the elevator, he watched every person who walked by and studied each face, focusing on those who got on either elevator, wondering if one of them would be waiting to collect the package in his hands. Wondering if any of them knew where Tristan and Cari were and if they were still alive.

"Jesus, Nicky! Thank God you're here," Evgenia said as she composed herself, now free from Tristan's hold. She wouldn't have been able to fight him for long in his enraged state.

"I wasn't…interrupting anything, was I?" Nicky replied with a sideways smile as he looked at the kitchen counter, pill bottles and pills scattered everywhere.

"How did you know where I was?" she asked as she scooped up the mess.

"Easy." He sauntered in and looked around, one hand holding his gun, the other casually stuffed in the front pocket of his jacket. "Tristan's BlackBerry must be in here somewhere. That GPS is a beautiful thing."

"Shit," Evgenia spat as she dumped the pills in the trash can and returned to the kitchen table. She pulled the phone from her purse and turned it off.

"No, no. You'd better consider yourself lucky, Evie. Vlad's on his way. Dear father's orders. He wants this over with," he said flailing his gun at Tristan. "Now."

"Vlad's crazy!"

"Exactly why I asked Grigor to slow him down enough so I could get here to warn you. He'll take out all of us if we're not careful."

Evgenia softened. "Grigor's coming too?"

"It'll take all three of us to keep Vlad from taking over." Nicky ambled into the kitchen as Tristan, hands raised in surrender, backed away. "Got anything to drink?"

"Just tea. Help yourself," Evgenia offered as she scooped her gun from where it had landed. "You," she said to Tristan, "go sit on the sofa."

Tristan obliged only after giving her a look full of hate.

Nicky busied himself with a cup and saucer, glancing at Tristan and then his sister. "So, Evie, why the gun?"

"Carolina Lopez died a few hours ago. Overdose."

"What?" Nicky's voice filled with anger. He turned away from the tea before pouring it. "Was that on Father's orders?"

"No," Evgenia said. "My error…or Ben's. I'm not sure."

"Damn it. Where's the body?"

"My God, you two are just like your father." Tristan looked at them. "Heartless. Cruel. Evil to the core!"

Unfazed, Nicky poured his tea and took a seat at the table. "Tristan, you just don't understand our life. The Aleynekov dynasty… we can't escape it. We can't deny it or refuse to accept orders or even turn ourselves in to the police." He paused, letting out a heavy sigh. "You were my friend, Tristan. That friendship was real."

"You had a bloody strange way of showing it, beating me within an inch of my life that night. And then—" Tristan sputtered a laugh "—then you stayed by my hospital bed for weeks, getting to know my family. My family! Christ, they adored you, Nikos! They trusted you and were so thankful that you, of all people, were my one friend in all of Bulgaria." He flailed his arm as he continued. "And then, then you have me followed to the States. You have that poor girl murdered simply because you or Ben or someone else mistook her for my sister. Jesus! My sister and Ethan! You've dragged them all into this." He balled his hands into fists. "When is this going to end? Are you going to kill all of us? Will you be satisfied then?"

Nicky looked at Evgenia, eyebrows raised.

"He was in love with her," she offered.

"You're right, Evgenia. I *was*. And I never got the chance to tell her!" Tristan yelled. "I never got to apologize for…for betraying her trust in me." He jumped up and headed for the door. "I have to see her. I have to see for myself what happened to her."

"No!" Evgenia yelled as Nicky interceded, grabbing Tristan to keep him from getting out. "You can't, Tristan. It's over. She's gone. Nothing you do now will change that."

She pulled a roll of duct tape from a large black canvas bag in the kitchen. "I can't let you go to her, Tristan. Nicky?" She looked at her brother as she gestured to the chair where Tristan had been restrained the night before. Soon, they had him secured again. Struggle as he might, Tristan would be unable to escape. Nicky returned to his cup of tea, sipping it slowly while he appeared to canvas the room.

"Do Grigor and Vlad know where we are?" Evgenia asked.

Nicky nodded as he swallowed. "Yeah, they're about an hour behind me, not much more." He paused. "So what's the plan?"

"Everything's going to have to change. Lopez is no longer a bargaining chip," Evgenia replied, chancing a look at Tristan. "And now all of you are showing up." She checked her watch. It was just before nine. "Ben needs to get to the casino. He's scheduled to collect the documents." She glared at her brother. "He'd better not screw *this* up."

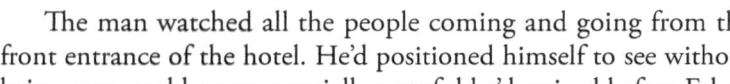

The man watched all the people coming and going from the front entrance of the hotel. He'd positioned himself to see without being seen, and he was especially grateful he'd arrived before Ethan Stonecipher. Stonecipher would pace a little, sit on a side chair a while, lean against a wall near the elevators, and then repeat the cycle.

He was early—they both were. Come nine thirty, the man would take the staircase near the back entrance and lurk near the elevator on the second floor, waiting for its doors to open. The envelope that would be inside was the key to this whole situation.

It was a waiting game, but that was okay. He was good at waiting.

"What happens to me when you get that envelope?" Tristan asked.

He kept trying to shift his shoulders. Evgenia could tell the binding on his wrists was tight.

"Am I still going with you, Evgenia? Still want me to take on fatherly duties?" His sarcasm wasn't lost on her, and for a moment, she let Alexei's face invade her thoughts. *Soon, baby, I'll be home soon.*

Nicky's laugh irked her. "'Fatherly duties'? Jesus, Evie, you're planning a family with a guy who just tried to kill you?" He glanced over at Tristan. "With good reason, I have to admit."

"I'm just trying to focus on Ben and Vlad and Grig — "

"Your sister assures me I'll love her son as soon as I meet him," Tristan said loudly, cutting her off. Evgenia shot him a deadly look, but he only smirked.

Nicky raised his eyebrows, looking back and forth between them. "Son?" he asked. "You two only met a few months ago."

"Oh, I'm sorry, Nikos. I forgot your sister hasn't — "

"Shut up, Tristan!" Evgenia screamed.

"No, no, *Evie*," Tristan responded mockingly. "I'm sure your brother would love to know about Alexei."

Nicky made a scoffing sound. "Alexei's our little brother, Tristan."

"Evgenia," Tristan said coyly. "Don't you think it's time he knew the truth? He's a big boy. I'm sure your story of teen motherhood isn't so uncommon in Bulgaria, is it?"

Nicky scowled. "What? What's he talking about?"

When Evgenia didn't — couldn't — respond, Nicky drew toward her. "Are...are you saying *you're* Alexei's mother?" He paused. "But... Mother died from complications from his birth..."

Evgenia sat on the sofa and gestured for Nicky to join her. When he sat, she shifted to face him. "Oh, Nicky. I didn't want you to know. You were away, so it was easy to lie — to protect you from everything. She hated Father, hated her life. It was bad enough that I knew what she'd done; Father refused to accept her death as anything but accidental. Alexei had been born only a month earlier, so it was easy to tell the media she'd died in childbirth. He'd never allowed her outside the compound, so outsiders didn't know to question it."

"So, Alexei..."

"Is *my* son."

Nicky stood and backed away. "What the hell? So for the last, what, twelve years, you've kept this from me?" He ran his hands through his hair. "My God, does *Alexei* even know?"

Evgenia shook her head.

"Well, I certainly would have understood and stayed quiet. And yet you kept it from me? You were, what, fifteen, sixteen when you got pregnant? Jesus, Father must have had a field day with that one!" He let out a sarcastic laugh. "Did he put a hit out on the poor idiot you slept with?"

Evgenia kept her head down, focusing on her clasped hands. She'd never wanted to discuss this with Nicky. She ignored his question.

"Wait a minute." Nicky pointed an accusing finger. "Is it Grigor?" He turned away in disgust. "That bastard! He wormed his way into our house and into your bed? My God! Well," Nick sputtered, "Father obviously forgave him. No wonder he treats that immigrant like family!"

"Grigor's a good man," Evgenia offered timidly.

"He's a cold-blooded assassin, Evie," Nicky countered. "What a family tree we've got, eh?" He stopped for a moment. "So…Mother's death? Had she also had a child?"

Evgenia hesitated, giving her brother a longing look before shaking her head. "No, Nicky. She…she killed herself." She let the words sink in. "Father didn't want you to know. That's why he made up the whole story. That's why I agreed to keep what happened a secret. You were doing so well in school, living here in the States. We were devastated, but we didn't want you to have to feel all that pain too."

Nicky dropped into one of the kitchen chairs and buried his head in his hands. "We've got one messed up family…" He sighed heavily as he turned toward Tristan. "So where do you fit into this lovely scenario?"

"Tristan said he'll escape with me and Alexei—"

"In return for my family's safety."

"Father will never let that happen," Nicky said. "He loves that boy. You two leave with him and I'm telling you, Tristan, every person you care about, one by one, will be shot at point-blank range until you return. Guaranteed." He looked at Evgenia. "What were you thinking?"

"I want to be free of him!" she cried. "You do too. You know it. You wish he were dead just like I do."

"And what about Grigor? A father has rights, you know."

"Grigor knows how I feel and knows it would be best for Alexei to be as far away from the Aleynekov influence as possible. He's willing to stay with Father. He accepts life in the mafia."

Nicky turned to Tristan. "This is no life for you, though. How can you even consider such a sacrifice?"

Tristan shrugged. "What choice do I have? This is the price I have to pay for the decisions I made…the price I have to pay to keep my family alive. I can only try to—"

"To what? Be happy? Make a life for yourself on the run?" Nicky shook his head in disbelief. "You don't know what you're signing up for." He stood and walked to the far wall, his back to the others. "If—no, make that *when*—you're caught, you'll both be back in Josef Aleynekov's control. That is if he doesn't have you killed, of course. But he cares enough about Alexei that I doubt he'd murder the poor boy's mother." He paused before flopping back down in the kitchen chair. "There's got to be another way, Tristan. Jesus, you were my friend. I know you don't believe that, but I don't want to see you killed, nor do I want to see you forced to join my family. Spouses and significant others in our family don't last very long…"

"Mila was a good woman, Nicky," Evgenia offered. "I'm sorry for what she did to you."

Nicky shot his sister a look of shock. "What do you mean? Her death was accidental. You know tha—"

"No, Nicky. I know the truth," she said gently. "I know she took too many pills on purpose."

"No!" Nicky yelled. "She…she was tired…she didn't realize what—"

"She left you a lovely note explaining why she couldn't live any longer. I assume you destroyed it, like she asked."

Nicky stood so quickly the chair toppled to its side. "What note? Why would I destroy—"

"No more lies, Nicky. It's time I told you the truth." Evgenia gestured for her brother to come sit with her again on the sofa. "I helped her write the two notes, Nicky. I provided her the directions on how many pills to take and when…I helped her die."

He'd no sooner sat down when he shot back up, tears in his wide eyes. "You what? How…how could you? Why would—"

Evgenia took in a deep breath. This was something she'd hoped never to tell a soul, certainly not dear Nicky. "She was pregnant."

"My God! You bitch!" he cried. "You bitch! You killed my wife… You…you killed my child…I…I was going to be a father?"

"No, Nicky," she replied. "You were going to have another sibling." When Nicky's face screwed up in confusion, Evgenia continued. "It wasn't your child. It was Father's."

Chapter 36

Ben's heart beat so fast, he thought it might burst. He was careful of his driving, maintaining a speed just at the limit. He glanced at the passenger seat of Jenny's BMW, just to make sure the thick envelope was still there. Addressed to Ethan Stonecipher, it was covered with a bunch of Bulgarian stamps and had obviously been opened, then sealed again with wide clear tape. He had no desire to open it. He wasn't even sure he wanted it in his possession. He gripped the steering wheel, checked the rearview mirror for the hundredth time, and continued his drive north, out of Canyonville and out of this hell he'd gotten himself into.

When he reached Roseburg, he stopped to refuel and check his phone. So far there was nothing from Jenny wondering where he was. Once the gas tank was full, he pulled into a parking spot in front of the little convenience store and composed the first of two text messages.

Call me ASAP. Go 2 Mom n Dads w/Chloe. STAY THERE.

He said a quick prayer that his sister would contact him soon. Jenny might already have someone watching her house — or his parents' place. He had to hope Talia going to their parents' home wouldn't raise any suspicions. If anything were to happen, they might stand a fighting chance if they were together.

Then Ben got out the scrap of paper with Mark Stoddard's cell number on it. He opened the glove box, retrieved one of the untraceable phones he'd used to send Cari the single-letter texts, and typed a quick message.

Ten minutes later, Ben was on the highway again, heading straight to his family, hoping to God they were still okay. Where they'd hide and for how long, he didn't know. He had the next few hours of driving to figure that out.

Nikos's mind swirled with disbelief. "Mila...and Father?" He shook his head. "No, she never would have done that!"

"You're right," Evgenia agreed, "she wouldn't. She was raped, Nicky, repeatedly over a number of months. Every time you were away."

"No...no...Father wouldn't— "

"Yes, Nicky." She paused for a long moment, seeming to search for words. "That's why he kept sending you on stupid little errands out of the country for weeks at a time—so he could have access to her. He wanted more sons. Mother was gone, and Mila was young and pretty."

Evgenia moved to approach him, but he motioned for her to stay back.

"It wasn't until Mila was pregnant for the third time that I discovered what had been going on," she continued.

Nikos looked up to see Evgenia nodding.

"Yes. She'd deliberately miscarried twice."

"But why didn't she come to me? Why didn't she tell me?" Tears brimmed in his eyes.

"You know Father," Evgenia replied. "Mila knew her family would be in danger if she even hinted at what was going on behind the iron gates of the Aleynekov compound. But Father thought the miscarriages were just that—he had no idea she was doing anything and everything to end the pregnancies." She stepped a little closer, but this time Nikos hadn't the energy to wave her away.

"She wanted to have children, but she wanted to have *your* children, Nicky." After another pause, she continued. "Then one day, she asked to meet with me. It was then that she confided what had been going on. She wanted me to give her something to end the third pregnancy...and her life."

Now Evgenia seemed to have tears in her eyes.

"Nicky, it was the hardest thing I've ever done, but we both knew Father wouldn't stop...He would continue to rape her...continue to keep you from her." She let out a sob. "She didn't have a choice… so I helped her. I helped her write the notes, helped her take…take the pills…even when she was getting tired…and she…she begged me to make her swallow more."

Nikos gritted his teeth, not sure whether to stay still or kill his sister.

"She hoped you'd never find out she'd been pregnant with Father's child. But he knew, or at least he suspected it. That's why he was so angry. That's why he accused her of committing suicide and banished her from the family. That's why he didn't want an autopsy, Nicky! Think about it—you would have discovered she was pregnant…and you'd have known it wasn't yours." Evgenia took his hands in hers. "Before she died, she thanked me. She *thanked* me for helping her… for taking the risk in helping her die."

Nikos pulled away and slapped Evgenia across the face so hard she fell to the floor. Tristan jumped, nearly toppling over in his chair.

"You killed my wife."

"No, Nicky," Evgenia said through another sob. "I rescued her."

Tristan stayed silent through the revelations of the Aleynekovs' dysfunctional family. There was nothing he could—or should—say to either Evgenia or Nikos, but he found he actually felt bad for them, for what their father had done to them. He'd known Josef was evil and uncaring, but he never would have guessed he could do something so heinous to his own family.

Nikos had slumped to the floor near the front door, his head in his hands. Evgenia had decided to put on more tea and busied herself in the kitchen. Tristan stared occasionally at the laptop. He'd closed the lid, unable to look at its screen showing where Cari's foot had been, the sheet now and forever still. He'd failed her. He'd promised to protect her, keep her safe, but he'd let her down—he'd let her die. He'd never forgive himself. He'd never forget the look on Cari's face as Ben carried her out of the cabin, drugged and crying. He'd never be able to explain why he'd had to let her go.

He deserved to live the rest of his days in hiding with Evgenia or working for her father. Given what he'd done, he wasn't sure he *could* ever face his family—or Cari's. Perhaps it was for the best that they'd never hear from him again.

The sound of a car outside interrupted his self-loathing. Nikos and Evgenia pulled out their guns and were ready to shoot until they heard Bulgarian at the door. Like Nikos earlier, the two men entered without knocking.

"Ah!" the shorter man said, his smile full of rotted teeth. "*Znachi hvanahte nashia maluk pakostnik, a?*"

The second man — taller and more muscular — gave the first a disapproving look. "Speak English, Vlad. God knows you need the practice if you're going to be working here." Tristan now knew this he must be Grigor, Alexei's father.

"Eh…you catches our leetle trouble…person, eh?"

Grigor rolled his eyes before extending his hand to Nikos. "When did you arrive?"

"Not too long ago," he replied.

Nikos kept his head down, probably because didn't want his wearied face seen too closely by his colleagues. Evgenia had kept the tragic story secret until tonight, so it didn't seem likely they'd want it shared with the others. Tristan had been the instigator in revealing who Alexei's mother was to Nikos. He decided this time, with these men, he'd keep his mouth shut.

"So, where eez papers we comes for, eh? And where eez womans wits curly hair?"

"Vlad, *molkni*," Grigor said. Then he looked at Evgenia. "Have you got the documents?"

Evgenia took a deep breath. "They should be on their way. I've got the American I hired getting them." She checked her watch. "Shit. I need to call him and the guy who dropped them off." She grabbed her phone and started for the small bedroom.

"So, what did my father tell you? Why did he send you here?" Nikos asked.

"Eh," Vlad said. "He knows I cans do za job." He stepped further into the cabin. "I needs a beer."

"There is none," Nikos said curtly. "And your services aren't needed here. Evie and I have things under control."

"What you means? I no sees womans wits curly hair. I no sees papers."

"The woman is dead," Evgenia said, turning back to the others and closing her phone. "It's just Saunders now. He agreed to give us the documents, and he's agreed to come to work for the family as our lead accountant."

Tristan kept his surprise at her explanation from showing on his face.

"No, no, no," Vlad replied with a sneer. "I am hires to kill him."

Evgenia stepped forward. "You'll listen to *me*, Vlad."

"Pah! Enough wits all ze talking."

In a flash, Vlad pulled out a gun and aimed it directly at Tristan. Grigor and Nikos both reacted with guns of their own, but Evgenia lunged in front of Tristan as Vlad fired.

"Don't!" she screamed. Her body slammed against Tristan's chest, and they toppled backward. Tristan heard a second shot, and one of the men crumpled to the floor.

"Evgenia!" Nikos was gently pulling his sister off Tristan. "Oh, my God, Grigor, she's bleeding so much!"

Tristan lifted his head to see Vlad slumped over just beyond his feet.

"We've got to get out of here," Grigor said calmly. "Those shots could have been heard." He pulled Evgenia from Nikos's arms and into his own. "Let me have her. You need to deal with Saunders. I don't care what you do. We both know neither you nor Evie wants him killed, and frankly I don't give a damn if you want to let him go." He looked directly at Tristan. "We were all in danger because of what Josef was doing. Anyone he was cheating could have found out and come after us. For that, I'll give you your life back. But you know what'll happen if you tell anyone anything." He turned back to Nikos. "As far as Josef's concerned, we'll…we'll talk later about that."

Tristan watched the long exchange of glances between the two men, and he remembered what Evgenia had told her brother. "*Grigor's a good man.*" Perhaps he'd be a good father to Alexei someday.

"I'm going to turn you so I can cut off the tape," Nikos said. Tristan tried to help by shifting his shoulders. "Heed Grigor's warning, Tristan, or my father will come after you. You won't get a second chance." As Nikos helped Tristan to his feet, he continued. "I don't know how else to make things right for you." He paused. "I'm sorry about Carolina Lopez."

"And I'm sorry about your wife." For all the hatred Tristan held for the Aleynekov family, he now knew Evgenia and Nikos had never had a choice. Josef was the source of the evil in that family. Tristan could get his life back...eventually...but Nikos and Evgenia were destined for pain and hatred and lack of control.

Tristan nodded and looked down at Evgenia, her breathing haphazard and her shirt soaked with blood. Then he turned and left the cabin, not looking back even once. He found Ethan's car parked in the leaf-covered circular driveway. Had it been only a day since he'd been kidnapped from the casino parking lot? The key had been left in the cup holder. Tristan started the vehicle, maneuvered it around the other two cars, and drove down the muddy road to find the other cabin—and Cari's body.

Ethan paced the living room floor. Aleynekov's daughter hadn't called. Had the envelope been picked up? *My God,* Ethan thought, *what if it was picked up by the wrong person?* Gemma sat on the wing chair by the fireplace, her legs pulled up under her.

"Can you...can you call anyone to check?" she asked softly.

"No." His response came out more harshly than he'd wanted. "I'm sorry, Gem, I just...I don't know what else to do. I followed her directions precisely." He began pacing again. "Everything they've done up to now has been so exact, so calculated. Something's wrong. Something went wrong, and I don't know what to do about it."

Not even a quarter mile down the winding dirt road, Tristan spotted another cabin. The rain had now been reduced to a drizzle, but it had washed away any evidence of tire tracks or footprints. The place looked abandoned, but Tristan held out hope that he'd found where Cari had been. *Where she'd died...*

He got out and wrapped his arms around himself, bracing against the cool, wet wind. He cautiously went up the steps to the cabin, listening for Ben or anyone else. He opened the cabin door and entered. "Hello?" With no response forthcoming, he proceeded farther inside and closed the door behind him. He found dirty dishes in the sink and freshly opened soup cans. Someone had been there recently. As he looked around the rest of the open room, he saw it: the video camera still focused on the end of an old, rusty cot.

Tristan approached the cot, a dingy sheet draped loosely across it, and a wave of emotion hit him. He'd left her—left her to die in this filthy cabin. He imagined what her last hours must have been like and felt bile rise in his throat. Tristan turned and ran from the room, vomiting on the ground just past the front porch.

"My God, what have I done…" he cried. As he wiped his mouth across his sleeve, he was filled with a new resolve. He would find her body and bring it to her family. They deserved to know what happened. Cari deserved a decent burial. And Tristan…Tristan knew he'd never be forgiven. He'd never forgive himself. The least he could do was find her, take her home.

Returning to the passenger side of Ethan's car, he rummaged through the glove box and found a small flashlight. It wouldn't provide much light, but it was better than nothing. He wandered the grounds around the cabin, looking for freshly thrown dirt. Her grave had to be somewhere nearby.

With each turn and each new pathway between the trees surrounding the cabin, Tristan encountered nothing but leaves, branches, and fallen trees. He expanded his search wider to no avail. After nearly an hour, the flashlight gave out, and Tristan returned, forlorn, to the cabin. He was soaked through from the lingering rain and droplets that fell from the trees.

Inside the cabin, he looked through drawers and the single closet for a blanket or towel he could dry himself with, but the only thing he could find was the sheet that had covered Cari.

He hesitated at first, as if disturbing something sacred, but Cari was gone. Nothing was going to change that. Tristan peeled off his wet shirt and scooped up the sheet. As he swung wide to pull it from the bed, he dislodged something heavy, and it hit the floor with a thud. He looked down and furrowed his brow: a metal-and-plastic wall clock.

The face of the clock was open—no plastic cover. One could manipulate the hands directly. It began to tick, its movements like spasms as the second hand got caught trying to pass the hour hand. Tristan watched, mesmerized by the way the long metal piece rocked back and forth, its end bent slightly outward.

He looked back at the cot, confused. Why would a wall clock be under the sheet? Slowly, with a glimmer of hope flaring in the deepest recesses of his mind, he placed the clock back on the cot, face up with the twitching second hand reaching skyward. He put the sheet back across the bed, just as he'd found it, and backed away, shocked. He cautiously moved around to the back of the video camera and looked at the scene through the camera's lens.

Sure enough, the second hand's rhythmic movements under the sheet were exactly what he'd seen on the laptop. Had Cari created this ruse? Could she have escaped?

Tristan grabbed the sheet and his shirt and ran from the cabin, overjoyed by the possibility that Cari—wonderful, beautiful Cari—was still alive.

"Cari! Cari, can you hear me?" Mark called through the rain and thunder. Ann was right behind him, shouting Cari's name as well.

"Where is it? Where's this cage you're talking about?" Ann asked as Mark helped her down the slippery pathway to the edge of Canyon Creek.

"Up ahead," he responded. "God, I hope she's there." He cupped his hands over his eyes, keeping the rain out temporarily. "Give me the flashlight. Stay there—I've got to get in the river to see inside."

Mark stepped carefully into the water and felt an immediate shiver he couldn't control. He waded toward the burrow under the tree where he and Cari had played as children, the flashlight aimed straight ahead. "Cari? Honey, can you hear me?"

Once he reached the vertical roots, he pulled himself closer and looked inside the little cavern. "Jesus! Ann, I found her! Get the raincoat and bring it to the edge of the river."

He maneuvered his upper body into the cage while standing hip-deep in water. "Cari, it's Mark. Come toward me, baby, let me get you out of here."

Slowly, a shivering, soaked-through Cari moved toward the cage's opening. "I…I can't move my legs very well," she said through chattering teeth.

"It's okay. Just get close enough, and I'm going to carry you out of here." He reached in and gently pulled her toward him until he was able to slip her between the roots and into his arms.

"You…you found me," she whispered as she wrapped her arms around his neck. "Thank you."

Mark could hear the low rumble of the SUV as he climbed clumsily out of the water. Ann was ready at the river's edge and draped the raincoat over Cari's body. She led the way up to the car, and as soon as Cari was in the front seat, Ann gently removed her wet jacket and wrapped blankets over her.

"God, can we get her clothes off? She's so cold," Mark said.

"No," Ann replied. "It's best not to move her too much. We'll just keep her as warm as we can for now. The hospital will take care of her clothing." Ann then adjusted the vents and heat setting as Mark got in the driver's seat. Then she hopped in the back, and they sped down the dirt pathway to the main road and then onto the highway north. Ann called emergency services, who patched her through to Mercy Medical in Roseburg. "Take exit one-twenty-five. They'll be watching for us at the Emergency entrance." Upon hanging up, she called Gemma. "We got her."

An hour later, Gemma sat by the inn's fireplace and sighed. "I just wish we knew where Tristan is. I'm glad Cari was found, but...I was so hoping they were together." She paused. "We don't even know whether Tristan is ali—"

"No, Gem, don't go there. Your brother is clever. He'll find a way out of this."

Another half hour passed without a call or text from anyone. Ethan eventually sat down with a book, pretending to be interested in it for Gemma's sake. At a little past eleven, his cell phone rang. Mark was calling.

He first gave an update on Cari: she was suffering from hypothermia and dehydration. She'd need a few days in the hospital. Ann would stay with her around the clock. Mark was in his car, heading back to Canyonville to gather things for both women.

"I need to confess something to you," Mark said. "I, uh, I had you followed to the casino."

"What? What the hell?" Ethan was livid. "What were you thinking?"

"Calm down. I sent my DJ friend to keep an eye out for you and to hang around after you left, hoping maybe he'd see who picked up the envelope and could track him."

"God, Mark, that was risky."

"But not necessarily unproductive. He got a good look at the guy who walked out with it, and he tailed him for a little bit. He went north on the interstate, but he lost him about eight miles up. I'm sorry, man. Do you think he was going to where Tristan is?"

"Hard to say. Tristan told us they were in two cabins. I would've thought they were near each other. Maybe I was wrong."

"Well, Cari's pretty out of it. She may know more, but we won't be able to ask her for a while. I should be there in a half-hour or so. Keep me posted if anything happens."

Ethan ended the call, looked at his wife, and sighed. "I'm afraid all we can do is wait and hope."

Ann had dozed off a few times but stirred whenever a nurse came in to check on Cari. She studied the faces and names of the staff, wary of anyone unfamiliar and worried the mafia could have followed them to the hospital. It was nearly two in the morning. Mark had called when he'd arrived at the inn, and she'd asked him to stay there for the night. The storm had left the roads dangerous. One of the nurses had provided her a change of clothing—hospital scrubs two sizes too big—and a blanket. She'd manage for the night and see her husband in the morning.

She was falling asleep again when she heard Cari stir, and she came to her side immediately. "Hey, there. You feeling better?" she asked with a smile.

Cari coughed and nodded. "Thirsty."

Ann readied a Styrofoam cup with water and a straw and brought it to Cari's lips. "You gave us quite a scare."

Cari smiled crookedly as she swallowed and gestured she'd had enough. "Scared me too." She coughed a few more times, and Ann brushed her curls from her face. "Thanks for coming to find me. How did you know where I was?"

Ann pulled a small folding chair close to Cari's bed. "Mark got a text. All it said was 'cage,'" she said with a shrug. "He just knew, I guess."

"He remembered..." Cari whispered.

"Tristan remembered? Did he send the text? Honey, where is he?"

The peaceful look on Cari's face disappeared in a flash. "No. Not Tristan. He left me. It was Ben who sent the message. He promised he wou—"

"Ben? Who's Ben? And what do you mean that Tristan left you?"

Cari took a deep breath. "Ben was with the Aleynekovs. He thought Tristan and I had cheated Josef Aleynekov. He...he kidnapped me." Ann started to interrupt, but Cari stopped her. "No. I mean, yes, he kidnapped me, but he didn't know what was really going on."

"He still did something illegal, Cari! God, you could have died out there. The river's expected to rise another foot at least. How could he—"

"I went there on my own, Ann. He let me go. He found out they were planning to kill me, and he let me go. He's actually risking his *own* life now. I gave him Mark's number so he could tell you where I was." She paused, a tear running down one cheek. "And he did."

"But what about Tristan? Where is he?"

Again, Cari bristled. "On his way to Sofia. He and this woman who tricked Ben. They...they knew each other from before...from before he got attacked." She looked straight at Ann. "He was in on this the whole time, Ann. He tricked all of us—he even lied to his own sister."

"That...that doesn't make any sense, Cari."

"You didn't see the look of pure hatred on his face, Ann. When I begged him for help, he just glared at me with dead eyes. I've never seen anyone look so evil, and I'll never forget how he betrayed me... with...with that woman." She pursed her lips as more tears slid down her face. "I hope he's happy with himself. He chose the mafia...he chose her instead of me." Ann could see Cari trying to control her emotions, but as she wrapped her arms around her, Cari finally gave in to deep, painful sobs.

Chapter 37

Grigor carried Evgenia to the sofa, easing her down gently and keeping his emotions in check.

"It's pretty bad, isn't it," she said in a whisper.

"Yeah..." he replied. "You know we can't—"

"I know." She tried to inhale but winced in pain. "You killed that bastard, right?"

"Of course. And I'll make sure his body won't be found until it's just a skeleton."

She smirked lazily. "I loved you. Did you know that? You were the first boy I ever kissed."

"There was no keeping me from you. You were such a flirt, even way back then," he said. "And I loved you too."

Evgenia smiled for a long moment, but then looked directly at Grigor, clenching the sleeve of his shirt in her hand. "I need...I need to talk to you...about Alexei..."

"He's a smart kid, just like his mother."

"Grigor, I—"

"And he's got that sharpshooter eye like you too. Josef's been having him practice on rodents on the compound. Did you know? I've seen pictures, Evie. He's good—"

"Grigor, please. I don't...want him...raised...by my father."

"Would you believe I've already started making arrangements for him?"

Evgenia cocked her head. "Arrangements?"

"I knew Josef was getting ready to send him to the States. I've been planning an abduction—a safe one, of course—so that I, well, *we* could free Alexei from this life." He paused, looking at her uncertainly. "Do you know Vasily Shevchenko?"

Evgenia shook her head slightly. "Only the name. Ukrainian, yes?"

"Yes. He lives in Canada now. He was...he was creating a new identity for Alexei...as a favor to me." Grigor smiled. "I was going to surprise you once everything was in place, but, well, I guess it's important for you to know now."

"Grigor..." Evgenia coughed and winced again. She closed her eyes tight, and tears brimmed along her lashes. "Grigor, I need you to know..."

"It's all being arranged, Evie. Alexei will be safe."

"Grigor...he's...he's not your child..."

Grigor placed a gentle hand on Evgenia's face, wiping away tears, brushing her hair from her forehead. "I know," he said. "I've always known."

"But you—"

"I kept the secret for your sake, and for Nicky's sake. God, I even tried to keep the truth from your mother." He gazed at Evgenia. "But she knew. Somehow she knew what Josef had done to his own daughter."

"Nicky can never know! You can't tell him, please, I beg you." Evgenia's strength was leaving her. Grigor knew he had just moments left.

"I'll never tell a soul." He paused. "Nicky will be a good father, won't he."

"Do you think he'll be willing? He thinks you're Alexei's father."

"Like I said, I'll make all the arrangements. Nicky wants out of this life too. I'm sure Vasily can arrange a new identity for him as well. They'll have a good life, Evie, don't you worry." He smirked. "And I'll find a way to check up on them too. I kind of liked being Alexei's father, even if it was all a lie."

"Alexei can never know the truth either," she said softly. "Promise me. Promise me, Grigor..."

"You have my word." Grigor leaned down and kissed Evgenia's forehead, lingering, remembering, and when he pulled back to look at her, she was gone.

"Gemma?" Tristan opened the door to the inn tentatively. "Ethan?"
"Tristan!" Gemma bounded across the living room and into his arms, her sobs immediate. "Oh, God, Tristan! You're here! You're alive!"

Tristan held his sister tight, so thankful to be free, so thankful she was unharmed. "Where is everyone?" He hesitated, afraid to ask the question he most needed an answer to. "Where's...where's Cari? I...I couldn't find her. I tried...God, is she here? Did she make it back?" He began to pray silently as Gemma continued to embrace him. "Gemma? I need to know if...I need to know about Cari."

Gemma pulled away from Tristan but stayed in his arms. "She's... not here. She's in hospital."

Tristan's heart leaped with joy, and he embraced his sister again. "Thank God she's alive...she's alive. Where is she? I've got to see her!"

Ethan came around the corner from the kitchen and immediately pulled Tristan into a hug. "Christ, Tristan, are you okay? I got your messages but...but we had no idea where to look for you. Are you safe now? What happened? Did Aleynekov's people follow you here? That woman...she's got a copy — "

"It's over. We're not in any danger. But where's Cari?" Tristan asked again, ignoring Ethan's barrage of questions and glancing from his face to Gemma's.

Ethan adopted the same pensive look as his wife. "She's going to be fine." He clapped Tristan on the back. "God, man, you're soaked to the bone. Let's get you warm, and then we'll fill you in. And you need to tell us what happened to you!"

"No," Tristan countered. "What's wrong? What happened to Cari?"

"Come upstairs, Tristan," Ethan insisted, and he didn't speak again until they were inside Tristan's third-floor room. "We got back from the hospital not ten minutes before you arrived. She nearly died, Tristan. It was pure luck that Mark and Ann found her in time." Ethan sat on the edge of the bed as Tristan began to change his clothing. He hesitated before continuing.

"What happened, Tristan? She said you left her to the kidnappers. She said you'd lied to us all and that you were on your way to Bulgaria." He sighed. "I've got to hear your side of things, because the story she paints of you isn't the person I know. She's full of fear and hatred for you, says she never wants to see you again. Ever."

Tristan's shoulders dropped in defeat. She was right to feel betrayed, because she had been. He'd promised to keep her safe, and he'd abandoned her when she was in the most danger. But he needed her to know that between the lies, everything he'd done was to save her and their families.

"She doesn't know the truth," Tristan said somberly. "I need to tell her the truth."

Grigor was still sitting by Evgenia's body when Nicky returned. He nodded and silently went outside to give the siblings their last time together. Nearly a half-hour passed before Nicky joined Grigor on the porch.

"Will you—" Nicky began to ask.

"Of course. I'll find a nice place farther up the mountain at first daylight. Don't worry. I'll take care of cleaning up things here too. Don't call your father. Let me handle that. Jeez, I've got that bastard Vlad to get rid of too. Help me get his body in the trunk, will you?"

Nicky nodded. "In a minute. Thanks for being so quick. Otherwise it could have been a real bloodbath in there." He took in a deep breath. "I want to raise Alexei," he announced.

Grigor smiled, pleased by Nicky's decision. "I was going to suggest it." He looked out at the trees, dripping with the last of the raindrops. "I'm not the father type. You, though, I think you've got it in you. Alexei's a good kid. Hell, he looks more like you than me anyway. No one will ever guess he's not yours."

Grigor relayed the conversations he'd had over the past few days with Vasily Shevchenko, promising a secure transfer of the boy to Nicky's protection. He avoided eye contact as he spoke. "I'm also planning a newsworthy event in Sofia. It should take care of things once and for all, including the issue of those stolen documents." He winked at Nicky, knowing he now understood just enough to be satisfied.

Tristan had slept well, given that he'd been awake for most of the past forty-eight hours. When he came downstairs to the kitchen, Mark and Ethan were at the table drinking coffee. Ethan greeted him with a smile, but Mark only glared.

"I'm heading out," Mark said to Ethan. "Be back around noon."

Tristan helped himself to coffee and noticed the pile of papers on the counter—his documents. "Were these not delivered last night?" he asked, suddenly concerned.

"I, uh, made a copy," Ethan confessed. "The originals were delivered to the casino as instructed—and picked up, from what I understand."

"Good," Tristan replied. "Thank you." He sat at the table and took a long drink. "That woman…the woman who called you…I, I don't think she survived." Tristan explained the events from the morning's early hours and how he left, rather than escaped. "Her accomplice probably has the documents. It's up to them to sort it all out. Nikos Dobreyev, my Bulgarian colleague—"

"He was the one who gave us updates when you were attacked, right?"

"Yes. He was also one of the attackers." Ethan's eyes went wide, but Tristan continued. "He's Aleynekov's son. He had little choice in the matter, but he has promised me he's going to tell his father I'm dead—and Cari's dead—so they'll leave us alone."

"But it's not over, then," Ethan countered. "What do we do? Have an official funeral or something? I don't want Aleynekov coming after you, or any of us, again, especially if he's got those papers."

Tristan patted Ethan's arm. "I know. I think we've got a little bit of time to figure things out. Nikos and this other man, Grigor, seem to want this over too. Otherwise, they could have just shot me and buried me in the woods. They've warned me, though, not to stir up any more trouble—and I won't! Mum and Dad know nothing, and I'd like to keep it that way, for a little longer, anyway."

After a moment Ethan retrieved the documents from the counter and splayed them out on the table. "Are there really hidden codes in here?"

Tristan smiled. "Not to an accountant's eyes, no. Karl Tresk knew what he was seeing, and he'd relayed enough information in his initial report that I knew what to look for." He leafed through a few papers and stopped at one of them. "Here's a place where the funneling of one set of money into three different accounts was pretty obvious. Perhaps that was what tipped Tresk off. I don't know. Ultimately, we're talking about nearly half a billion dollars that was misappropriated from Bulgarian government accounts, but Josef was also cheating some of his so-called 'investors' from other countries. They were all looking for ways to launder money and were getting rich, so I don't think any of them realized how much they *weren't* getting."

"But these account sheets —"

"These account sheets provide the clues as to where the actual money is." He flipped through the various papers. "Lithuania, Albania, Ukraine, Canada, and the US have most of it. And Aleynekov maintains various accounts in Bulgaria, of course." Tristan selected a sheet of paper. "This is the one that has me the most curious, though." He tapped it with his finger. "I'm willing to bet this is where Josef's got most of his share."

"So what happens now?"

"I'm going to see if I can prove my theories and find a way to return as much of the money as I can to its original, intended destinations."

"Might you need some help in such an enormous undertaking?" Ethan asked tentatively.

"I'm not sure you've got —"

"Not me," Ethan interrupted. "Vasily Shevchenko."

Chapter 38

Four days later, Cari was finishing out St. Eustachius University's spring break at her father's house. Her ankle had nearly healed from its ordeal in Oregon. Before leaving the hospital, she'd gotten Mark and Ann to agree to stay mum about the kidnapping. Cari simply told her father she'd been visiting them and had been hospitalized because of dehydration. Her father lectured her about taking better care of herself as he picked her up from Mercy Medical and drove her to his house Sunday night, and she listened politely.

It wasn't unusual for Cari to spend a portion of her spring break with her father. She tended to visit any time the university was closed. His house and the hardware store were in Kirkland, across the 520 and about twenty-five minutes northeast of the university. Cari had grown up there, and when she came to visit, she stayed in her old bedroom, which her father had transformed into a pleasant guest room.

She was glad to be away from her apartment. Ethan and Gemma were certainly home by now, and Tristan would, of course, be with them. Cari had learned from Ann that Tristan hadn't gone to Bulgaria, and the danger they'd been in was essentially over. Her ankle had improved, but her heart had taken a heavy beating and would need longer to heal. She wasn't ready to see any of them.

The first few days in Kirkland, she'd borrowed her father's truck and gone to the university. She and Jazmyn got together and exchanged stories, with Cari lying her way through hers. Kevin Lamb remained hospitalized and would likely take the rest of the semester off. The police had had no luck finding whoever attacked him, and Cari figured they probably never would.

The university was actively seeking a replacement for the late Dr. Jonathan Lassiter. The police and university administrators hadn't revealed anything publicly about why he'd killed himself, but Cari felt relief nonetheless. They discussed proposing to the accounting department that Dr. Kruger be added to Jaz's doctoral committee and Dr. Ujamwe be added to Cari's. Both women, then, would be working with the same professors.

Cari's dissertation topic remained undecided, but she'd saved her notes and links to online articles about money laundering. Now that Tristan was out of the picture, he'd be unable to sway her from pursuing something she'd genuinely found intriguing. She'd keep her promise and focus her research on areas of the world unassociated with Bulgaria or Josef Aleynekov. Fortunately—or unfortunately—there were plenty of other places and people around the globe involved with organized crime and money laundering. She had a lot of resources to cull and would soon prepare an abstract for Dr. Kruger that summarized her plan.

Cari spent Wednesday at her father's store, Seattle Outdoor Supply, as one of his employees had called in sick, and Cari volunteered to help. Weekdays weren't too busy with customers, but vendors' deliveries kept them active as they replenished outdoor building supplies and camping goods. Cari cruised the aisles, familiarizing herself with the stock, and she smiled when she saw the boxes of rope ladders. She stifled her desire to tell her father how hers had come in handy when she'd had to escape over the apartment balcony.

Early in the afternoon, her dad called Cari to the outdoor portion of the store. "Hey, there's someone I want you to meet."

Cari approached to find her father talking to two men. Behind them was a truck with "Pritchards' Fence and Post" on the side. When she saw the younger man's face, she froze for a moment.

"Honey, come here. This is Gary Pritchard," her father said, coaxing her closer. "He's the guy I went hiking with."

Cari continued forward, her eyes locked on the younger of the two men. He was obviously as shocked as she was.

"Cari?" Gary said as he extended his hand. "It's nice to meet you. Your dad told me all about you." As they shook hands, he tilted his head to the left. "This is my son, Ben."

Ben shook Cari's hand as well, and she blushed.

"Hi," he said.

Cari's father watched the exchange and smirked. "You two — do you already know each other?"

Cari recovered quickly. "Uh, yes. We, um, we met at the university. I, I met him through one of my students...Kevin." Cari stared at Ben, hoping he'd catch on.

"Well, small world, huh?" Gary said with a laugh.

"I was actually hoping to run into you, Ben," Cari said pointedly. "Got a few minutes?"

The fathers waved them off with a wink and a smile. Cari had Ben follow her to the far corner of the fenced lot. "Wow..." Cari stumbled for words as she turned to face him.

"Yeah. Who would have thought?" He paused, shuffling his feet and stuffing his hands in his jacket pocket. "So...you, uh, doing okay?"

Cari gave him a weak smile. "You saved my life." When Ben furrowed his brow, she continued. "The text. The one you sent my cousin."

"But I could have killed you too," he added. He looked off to the side. "God, I belong in jail for what I did. And to think, my goal is to go after people like them, and instead I stupidly ended up *with* them!"

"I'm okay, Ben," Cari said softly. "I'll be fine. Besides, bringing this to the police could put us and our families in more danger with the mafia."

"I took that envelope," he said, fear now in his eyes. "What do I do with it? I panicked when I left the casino. I had to be sure my family was okay. But then Jenny never called."

"I think she's dead."

"Oh." He paused. "And Saunders?"

This time it was Cari who looked away as she spoke. "They let him go." She knew tears would come if she lingered on what happened. "So..." she said, changing the subject. "You work for your dad, huh?"

"It's temporary. Just saving up so I can afford college without having to take out any student loans. I'm a debt-free kind of guy." He smirked. "How about you? You back at St. Eustachius?"

"I will be next week. I'm staying with my dad for spring break. Tristan is staying at the apartment next to...well, you know." She looked down. "I have no desire to see him ever again. I'll be back to work next week, but I'm going to try to avoid seeing him when I'm at home. You know…"

"Understood," Ben said with a smile. "Come to think of it, I did kind of ask you out for coffee when we first met. You're not possibly…?"

Cari looked at him sympathetically and chanced a glance over to her father. Ron and Gary were still talking, but now faced her and Ben. "I…I don't think so. It's not that I don't appreciate—"

"No, I get it," Ben replied.

"I just…I need to focus on finishing my degree. I've got a deadline and a lot of work to catch up on from being away and—"

"Hey," Ben interrupted. "I get it." He smiled. "But if you're still single when you get done, I'm not so proud that I won't risk rejection a third time."

Cari laughed. "Sure. And you know I'm at the university. If you end up applying there, let me know if I can help with anything. It's a good school."

"Thanks," he said. "I guess I'd better get back over there. God knows they're talking about us." As they separated, he added, "I'll see you around, okay?"

Cari smiled. "Yeah, I'll see you around."

After spending much of the week with Vasily Shevchenko in Vancouver, Tristan returned to Ethan and Gemma's apartment on Friday. Gemma informed him that, no, Cari hadn't been home. She'd only left a voicemail with her neighbors asking them to get her mail for her, noting that the mailbox key was in her kitchen, and saying she'd be back by the weekend.

Despite his disappointment with the news about Cari, Tristan managed a smile when Gemma asked him about his time with Shevchenko. She'd just made some tea and invited him to grab a cup and join her on the balcony.

Once seated, he released a long sigh and gazed out toward the woods behind the apartment. "Well, I must say we were very productive. Ethan was smart to recommend I work with Vasily. The man had been a deputy finance minister in Ukraine before joining the private sector in his own business ventures so he not only understood accounting but was familiar with many of the banks and businesses listed on the various ledgers."

"Is that how he and Aleynekov knew each other?" Gemma asked.

"Yes, they met years ago, when the fall of Communism had brought various former Soviet countries together to work through the monumental tasks before them. Vasily admitted he was eager to experience the financial fruits of capitalism, but he'd never intended to be involved in money laundering. He thought he was making sound investments. He even had his own accountants vouch for Aleynekov's transactions and business deals. He'd profited greatly, but that's what was supposed to happen to investors dealing with a great deal of money."

"Yet he never suspected Aleynekov and others were acting illegally?"

Tristan snickered. "I asked him the same thing. He said he figured a few rules were being bent here and there, a few laws being overlooked, but, honestly, that's the way the game is played. Everyone wants minimal expenditures and maximum gains."

He paused to sip his tea and explained how he'd shared the account documents with Vasily, and between them they were able to identify the routes of nearly four hundred million dollars of the missing money. Vasily was still well-connected with various banking institutions and key players in European investment circles, and he and Tristan eventually devised a way to essentially reverse some of the transactions. In other cases, they devised new dummy corporations which, in turn, donated their funds back to where they'd been stolen from. No one was the wiser because so many of the accounts weren't for real businesses anyway. Unless Josef was monitoring the bank statements daily, he too would be unaware that monies were slowly being funneled to their originally intended locations. And because Karl Tresk had coded the accounts, Josef would need a highly skilled accountant to decipher everything before he'd truly know he'd been had.

"Vasily was highly amused by the whole thing," Tristan said, "and so proud of what we accomplished. 'We gets that bastard, eh?' he said."

"My heavens, I hope so," Gemma replied. "Josef Aleynekov deserves every rotten thing that happens to him." She reached over and grasped her brother's hand. "You did the right thing." After a moment, she asked, "What about those people who died...and the others?"

"I don't know," Tristan said. "Vlad died in the cabin, I'm sure of that. I can't imagine Evgenia survived either. She took a bullet square in the chest. The mafia do well not leaving any traces, so I'm guessing Nikos and Grigor cleaned things thoroughly. The two of them may be back in Bulgaria at this point. Vasily was pretty cryptic about what role he'd play in the aftermath of all this. I got the feeling, though, that Nikos and Alexei will be safe. God knows, with a family like theirs, they deserve to be free of all of it. I just hope Josef believes I'm dead and this is truly over."

Gemma shooed Ethan and Tristan out of the apartment after breakfast, urging them to go for a walk while she cleared the dishes. They set off on the path Tristan and Cari had taken the night he'd arrived.

"Vasily and I have been able to account for all but thirty-three million dollars," Tristan said.

"Out of?"

"About five-hundred million."

"Jeez…" Ethan said with a sigh. "That was a lot of work you did, then."

"I'm just glad he was willing to meet with me. You were right about him, Ethan. He was Josef's victim just like the government agencies."

"So what next?"

Tristan considered his answer before speaking. "Well, as much as I'd like the bastard to be seen by the world for the criminal he truly is, Vasily feels this will keep me safe. There's no way Josef can retake the money we've channeled back into all those accounts without someone asking questions. And if any of the mafia people who were cheated look closely at their books, they'll notice the discrepancies and be able to tie things back to Josef and the Bulgarian government."

"No appended report, then?"

Tristan laughed. "I've written the accurate version in my mind many times over, believe me." They walked a little farther before he spoke again. "Have you heard from Cari?"

"She doesn't want anything to do with you, Tristan. I'm sorry," Ethan replied.

"What about Ann or Mark?"

"They're on her side. They saw how bad off she was when they found her. She could have—"

"I know, Ethan," Tristan said, his voice full of emotion. "I *had* to make that decision, to allow that man to take her from me. God, I relive that moment, that look of fear in her eyes, every day. I can't close my eyes without seeing her face and knowing I risked having her killed at his hands."

"He's the reason she's alive," Ethan replied. "She said he never hurt her. He let her go. He let Mark know where she was." He paused. "She said he was roped into this, that he was just some guy trying to make a living, hoping to go to college—he's from the area. Bottom line, Tristan, Cari sees you as a traitor and says that guy risked *his* life to save hers."

Tristan rubbed the back of his neck in frustration. "I need to see her, Ethan. I need a chance to talk to her, to tell her what really happened before I go back to England and never see her again."

"I don't know, man." Ethan sighed. "I'll do what I can, but I can't make any promises."

"If I can just talk to her, she'll understand. I know she will."

They circled back to the apartment in silence. When they arrived at the foot of the stairs, Tristan pulled out his cellphone. "The man who helped Cari—Ben, I think. Do you happen to know his last name?"

"No, why?"

"Never mind. I was just curious." He searched for a number and nodded at Ethan. "You go ahead. I'll be up in a minute."

As soon as Ethan went inside, Tristan called Vasily. "I've thought about your proposal," he said. "I know what I'd like to do with the money you offered."

"So you'd be able to finish out Dr. Lassiter's classes for the semester?"

"Yes, sir," Tristan replied, looking at the group of men seated around the long conference table. "I looked at his syllabi online in preparation for this interview. I've taught similar courses in the past, and my research background is quite similar."

"You realize this would be a temporary position. We'll be doing an official search for a full-time replacement, which you can, of course, apply for as well," Vincent Hunsinger said. Tristan had retained the business card his daughter Ashley had given him when he visited Cari's class, and he'd contacted him two days ago.

He'd been just as pompous in person as Tristan had found him over the phone. Still, he was glad to be given an interview on such short notice. Hunsinger was head of the university's Board of Directors, and Tristan could feel his discerning eye on him, as if he were being evaluated as a potential son-in-law rather than a prospective employee.

"Yes, certainly. I understand." Tristan gestured toward the papers in Henrik Swanson's hands. "I've included my vita, and I'll contact the University of Manchester to have them forward my transcripts if you'd like."

Dr. Swanson smiled. "You've come to our rescue, Dr. Saunders. I think you'll find St. Eustachius a wonderful place to work. Do you have any questions before we commence with the official paperwork to get you hired?"

"Just one. Do you allow spouses to be employed at the school, particularly in the same department?"

"We're a small university, Dr. Saunders, a family community, if you will," Dr. Swanson replied warmly. "We can certainly consider your wife's vita and see if there's an appropriate position available."

The professors, seemingly satisfied with the interview, began to gather their paperwork. Hunsinger, however, began flipping through his copy of Tristan's application. "I'm sorry, I...I thought you said you're not married."

Tristan knew he'd never mentioned his marital status, nor did he note it on his application. This was information Ashley had provided.

"I'm not, sir. But I hope to be soon."

Chapter 39

Getting back to work had been therapeutic for Cari. She'd been glad her schedule didn't coincide with either Gemma's or Ethan's, as she still wasn't ready to face them...or Tristan. Cari had been counting down the days until she was pretty sure Tristan would be on his way back to England and forever out of her life. Only then would she be ready to talk to Gemma about all that had happened.

She'd stayed with her father through the previous Saturday, and upon returning home for the first time in two weeks, kept herself busy cleaning her apartment and running errands to restock her fridge and purchase household items. In among the mail was a large envelope containing the precious documents Aleynekov had wanted. Ben had sent it, along with a note wishing her well. He'd included his home address in Poulsbo, his cell phone number, and a reminder that the offer for a cup of coffee remained, any time she wanted to give him a call. She tucked the note in her address book and hid the documents in a file containing papers she'd written during her doctoral courses.

It was hard not to glance at the Stonecipher's' apartment each time she came up the stairs and remember the day she'd come home to find Tristan Saunders asleep at their front door. And once she started remembering, her mind wouldn't let it go. Cari tried to ignore the memory of laughter and embarrassment as she strolled the aisles of Safeway, and she stopped herself from making scrambled eggs one morning, knowing it would only remind her of him. She didn't want to think about how right it had felt waking up in her neighbors' apartment with him, or how she'd thought that was the start of a romance.

Instead, she forced herself to remember his cold eyes the last time she'd seen him. That image could erase the good memories like acid poured on a picture. She needed to forget him. She needed to forget how wonderful things had been, even when they were running from what she thought was a common enemy. She needed to forget how his kisses melted her, how his touch had made her feel safe, protected, loved.

Cari knew she'd fallen in love with him, or at least with the Tristan who'd made her laugh and blush and feel confident about herself and her future. But those cold eyes—they'd quickly bring her back to the reality of his lies. She'd been mistaken to think he'd cared for her at all. Soon he'd be back in England, and she'd be better able to move on with her life.

Articles she'd printed in Canyonville now sat among various books about money laundering, all scattered across her dining room table. She'd developed a decent synopsis for her study and would be meeting with Dr. Kruger next week. With each article she read, she wondered if Josef Aleynekov was involved in similar activities within his circle. It was amazing how easily millions of dollars could vanish and how difficult—and dangerous—it was for police agencies to track it down. Cari was invigorated, though, by her research. If Dr. Kruger approved the topic, she could easily complete her dissertation within a year. In light of all she'd been through over the past few weeks, this alone made her smile.

Most of her students at St. Eustachius, including Mr. Failing Senior, had completed their projects over spring break, and class time was now spent presenting and critiquing them. Cari knew the students would benefit from evaluating their peers, seeing for themselves the benefits of budgeting, and looking into investing at a young age. Even Cari gained a few practical ideas from her students' presentations.

As expected, Cari learned Kevin Lamb would be given an incomplete for each of his classes while he recuperated. By the time she'd returned to campus, his attack was old news among the students. Dr. Lassiter's suicide, however, still cast a pall over the accounting department. His office door remained closed, and little was said about the person they'd hired to replace him for the remainder of the semester. The other professors, especially Dr. Swanson, were less chatty with the graduate assistants. They held their office hours, taught classes, and went home with no more than essential conversation. Outside of interacting with her students and exchanging hellos with Dr. Ujamwe, Cari barely spoke to anyone while on campus.

Spring was blooming in Washington State, and the trees on Bainbridge Island were full and green and beautiful. Cari spent her daily ferry rides across Puget Sound with whatever article or book she'd grabbed off the dining room table and a pack of sticky notes ready to mark significant paragraphs and diagrams. She was returning to her old routines, free of any thoughts about Tristan.

On Thursday afternoon, she arrived at her apartment at her usual three forty and was halfway up the stairs when she saw Tristan. Three weeks earlier she'd found him asleep at the Stoneciphers' door; this time he was awake and sitting in front of hers.

She hesitated, contemplating turning back around and heading to…anywhere but here. Instead, she straightened her shoulders, adjusted her satchel, and continued up to her door.

"Cari, I—" he began as she reached the landing.

"Let me pass." She wouldn't, couldn't, make eye contact with him. She needed to remember his cold eyes so she could get over him.

"I just want to talk to y—"

"I said let me pass. You're blocking my way."

"I need—"

"*I* need you to move. Now." She stared straight ahead at the shingles, still refusing to look at him.

"Please," Tristan said. "Let me have just five minutes. I'll be gone tomorrow. Five minutes. That's all I ask."

"No." *Damn it!* She could feel tears brewing.

"I had to let him take you away."

"Jesus, Tristan. Don't you get it? I don't want to see you. I don't want to talk to you."

"Five minutes, Cari. That's all. Please."

"Get off my porch, or I'll call the—"

"She was going to poison you if I didn't let you go. She was going to make you take things that burned you from the inside out. She showed me the—"

Cari dropped her satchel to the floor, leaned against the wall, and crossed her arms. "So instead you sent me with the man who drugged and kidnapped me from the casino. The look in your eyes that night told me everything I need to know, Tristan." She glared at him, choosing to let a tear roll down her cheek. "I've never seen anyone so full of hatred. Ever."

"That hatred was real, but it wasn't toward you. It was self-hatred. I hated that I had to let you go to save you. I hated that I broke my promise to keep you safe. I hated that I didn't — couldn't — find some way to fight back."

"No, instead you decided to make out with your Bulgarian girl-friend." Cari huffed. "Funny, when we were talking about previous relationships, you kind of failed to mention her." She threw her hands in the air. "Doesn't matter. Wasn't my business anyway."

"I kissed her because she had a gun to my stomach. If she'd shot me, I wouldn't have had any chance of helping you at all."

"Enough. Good story, Tristan," Cari said as she collected her satchel and walked back down the stairs. "Thanks for sharing. I've gotta go."

She heard him start down the stairs after her. "I'm telling the truth. I did what I had to to save you."

"Why did you bother? I was 'just someone in the way,' wasn't I?" she called back to him.

"Who told you that?" he said as he caught up with her.

"Ben. He told me that's what you said to that woman."

Cari headed toward the path, knowing he would follow. As much as this was hurting her, she realized she needed closure. She knew she could get him to reveal his true intentions and all of his lies. He could con his sister maybe, but Cari wasn't going to be fooled.

"I said what I did to buy you time."

"Excuse me? Telling her I was in the way was supposed to help me?" Cari scoffed and picked up her pace as they rounded the first corner toward the trees.

"No," he said with a heavy breath. "I had to tell her that to keep her from knowing the truth."

"Ah! The truth. And what truth might that be, hmm?"

Tristan looked away, not answering.

"Is the truth that elusive for you now? You get so used to telling lies that it becomes difficult to do anything else? Come on, Tris — "

"She was looking for a reason to kill you. If I'd admitted what she could already see, she…" He sighed again. "She knew. She knew…"

This was getting frustrating. "What are you talking about, Tristan? God, you're talking in circles."

"She could see…that I was in love with you."

Cari stopped. She turned to Tristan in disbelief. "So, let me get this straight," she snapped. "You had something going with her in Bulgaria, you're going at it in that cabin, and I'm — "

"You didn't hear what I said to her," he replied angrily.

"Uh, no, because something else you didn't tell me was that you could speak Bulgarian."

"I understand a decent amount of the language and know a handful of phrases at best, some of which are profane and degrading. When she saw you were awake, she told me to kiss her like your life depended on it, and if I didn't, she'd kill you." He paused. "I called her…well, the basic translation is that she was not a woman of any worth, like gutter trash. I also pledged to kill her if she hurt you."

"But the look you gave me after that…"

"I didn't know what else to do. I couldn't even move from beside her. I had to hope to God that, that Ben wouldn't…do anything to you. I had to hope doing what Evgenia asked would buy you your life and time for me to figure things out."

Cari began to walk again. She didn't want him to see her tears. "I thought I was going to die."

"I thought you had," Tristan replied, following. "That's what Ben told me, you know. He told me you'd died of an overdose. When I was freed, I went to find you — your grave. I…God, I thought I'd lost you."

"Tristan…I don't know what to believe or what to think." Cari looked hard at him. "You became so different in that cabin. I believed you were willing to let me die."

He looked down at the ground in front of him. "But…but you know that wasn't the truth, don't you? You did hear what I said, yes?" He glanced at her for a moment. "I know I'm at fault for the hell you went through, but along the way I fell in love with you. Between the lies, that's the truth. And I'm not expecting anything in return. God knows I don't deserve it." He took a deep breath. "I leave for London tomorrow," he said. "I just wanted you to know how I feel and that I'm so terribly sorry for what I put you through."

Cari said nothing and appreciated that Tristan didn't push her. When they'd returned to their apartment doors, she simply said, "I need time to process everything." Then she slipped inside her apartment and cried.

"Tristan!" Ethan called from the living room. "Gemma! Come quick." The two joined Ethan as he focused on breaking news out of Bulgaria. "Look…"

The scene was Lake Pancharevo, southeast of Sofia. The reporter, looking chilled even with a wool scarf over her coat, spoke with a British accent. "Authorities have confirmed the identity of the body discovered last night as Bulgaria's Minister of Finance, Josef Aleynekov, who, along with his two grown children and younger son, had been reported missing nearly a week ago after a family outing. Thus far, only the Minister's body has been located. Given the depth of the lake, experts say drowning victims are often never found. One of the rescue crew I spoke with indicated Mr. Aleynekov may have attempted to swim to shore, which would explain why his body was recovered. Yesterday, deep sea divers confirmed finding the wreckage of the small fishing boat registered in his name, but bad weather has continued to impede the search for the other family members. Sources close to Aleynekov said it was not unusual for him to take long weekends away from his high-stress job, and Lake Pancharevo was a favorite spot. An autopsy will be performed, but right now, foul play is not suspected. Mr. Aleynekov served as the country's…"

Ethan muted the television and he looked at Tristan. "What do you think?"

Tristan sighed. "They won't find evidence that he was murdered, if that's what you're saying. And there won't be any pictures of Nikos either. Josef kept Nikos's true identity well hidden; that's why CWF never knew that he was really an Aleynekov. My guess is Grigor either ordered Josef's death or took care of it himself. This story also takes care of accounting for Evgenia's death and allows Nikos and Alexei to assume new identities." He gazed first at his sister and then Ethan. "Grigor followed through. He's ended this."

"What does this mean for you?" Gemma asked. "For all of us and Cari?"

Tristan straightened his shoulders. "Grigor promised me we wouldn't be touched unless we reveal any documents. Despite the fact that he's a killer, I think we can trust him to keep his word as long as we keep ours." He smiled and pulled his sister into a hug. "I think it's finally over."

Cari had barely slept. Her conversation with Tristan had gone differently than she'd planned. She'd wanted to have reason to hate him, but as she replayed what he'd said, seeing his perspective on what had transpired at the cabin, she softened. Maybe he was telling the truth. Maybe she'd been wrong after all.

Slowly, other happier memories of her short time with him began to push away the image of his cold eyes. His games to get to know each other, his soothing music, his help with her dissertation — he *had* been caring. And when they'd kissed, there was something more than just physical attraction. They both felt it. Hadn't she admitted to herself already that she'd fallen in love?

And now he'd told her he was in love with her. She'd been caught so off guard she'd not known how to respond. Cari had tethered her heart to believing he'd never cared for her. She just needed him to go back to England so she'd never see him again.

She drove to the university for her ten o'clock class in a haze. He was leaving…and she was in love with him. No matter how many times she attempted to convince herself otherwise, she loved him. Gemma had texted her that morning, informing her that Tristan's flight was at four twenty-two, "just in case you wanted to know."

More students presented their projects, but Cari had trouble concentrating. When class was over, she went to the graduate assistants' office and flopped down on one of the overstuffed chairs, her mood growing more and more melancholy.

"Hey!" Jazmyn said from the copier. "How are the presentations going?"

"Huh?"

"Your students' projects? How are they?"

"Oh," she replied with a sigh. "Fine. The usual. You know."

Jazmyn walked over, her brow furrowed. "Girl, you doing okay? You look like your cat just died."

"He's leaving." Cari's eyes welled with tears as she whispered the simple words.

"When?"

"A little after four this afternoon."

Jazmyn sat down on the sofa near Cari's chair. "And…you don't want him to go."

Cari's lip quivered at she shook her head.

"How do you feel about him?"

Cari looked at Jaz and let the tears run down her cheeks.

"Oh."

Another graduate assistant entered the room, and Jaz glared at him. "I'll come back later," he said and retreated quickly.

"And how does he feel about you? Has he said anything?" Jazmyn continued, again looking at Cari.

"He told me he loves me."

"Okay, well, if you two want to be together, then why on earth is he leaving? Why are you here instead of at the airport having some Lifetime Movie Channel love-story moment at the gate?"

Cari shook her head again. "I didn't tell him."

"Why not? God, Cari, if you love the guy, it'd be kind of nice for him to know before he jets off across the ocean, don't you think?"

"I just…I didn't know how. I was so angry with him…and…and now he's leaving." She wiped her eyes with the back of her hand. "I guess…I don't know…I guess I was too afraid of the implications. I mean, come on, the guy lives in England. Long distance relationships—"

"Can work if you're willing to try! Jeez, Cari, if he's going away for good, then what's it going to hurt to tell him the truth?" Jazmyn stood and faced her. "Come on. Let's go."

"What?…Where?"

"The airport. If you're going to be a sniffling mess for the rest of the semester, let it not be because you regret not taking the chance." She reached for Cari's satchel. "Come on."

"Jaz…"

"Let's put it this way. Either you tell him, or I will. I'm going to the airport to find him with or without you. It'll be easier if you're there since I don't really remember what he looks like, and the paging system is just plain embarrassing."

Cari sputtered a laugh. "You're going to be buying me a very nice bottle of wine and helping me commiserate later. You know that, right?"

"If I'm right about this, I'll be buying you the bottle of wine to celebrate."

Cari's insides churned as they walked out to Jazmyn's car. Her friend's enthusiasm was contagious, and Cari couldn't help but feel hopeful that Tristan would open his arms and heart to her.

"Do I dare text him?" she asked. "I mean, that way if his response seems to indicate it's not a good idea, we can turn back and hit the nearest liquor store."

"Stop," Jaz said, turning for a moment to look at Cari as she waggled a finger. "From everything you've told me over the past week, he's just as bummed about how things ended as you are." Jazmyn paused before unlocking the passenger side of the car and shrugged. "Go ahead. Keep it light. Don't tell him you're on your way. Just, you know, maybe see if he wants to stay in touch."

"God, this is crazy." Cari typed and backspaced, typed and backspaced, until she sighed and passed the phone to Jazmyn. "What do you think? Sound okay?"

"Hope you have a safe trip home?" Jazmyn scoffed. "Nope. Redo. You gotta hint that you've got feelings without...without really revealing them."

Cari deleted the message and started over, once again typing and backspacing repeatedly. "How about now?"

"I'd like it if we stayed in touch," Jazmyn read. "Seriously?" She deleted the message and looked at Cari. "Okay. Forget what I said before. Talk to me. What bothers you the most about him leaving?"

Cari's eyes brimmed with tears, and she turned away. "I never got to tell him that I forgive him." She sighed. "I'm sorry that I stopped trusting him, that I assumed the worst about him and was unwilling to let him explain." She looked down at her hands and picked at her fingernails. "I'm sorry I didn't get to tell him how much I... how much I enjoyed being with him and how he made me laugh. God, he even made me want to work on my dissertation again! He's a good guy, Jaz. He'd shown me all these things that were good about him, and I let one, well, one pretty bad thing erase everything else."

"All right, then...Send." Jazmyn said as she pressed a button on Cari's phone and handed it back to her. "Now, let's see if he replies."

"What? Oh my goodness, Jaz! What did you do?" Cari called up her texts. Jazmyn had typed much of what she'd just said. "Oh, my goodness..." Cari said again in a whisper. "What did you do?"

Minutes passed like hours until Cari's phone buzzed. She read the text quickly and turned to Jazmyn. "It's from him," she said with fresh tears and a smile. She blurted out a sob and handed Jaz her phone.

It's me who's sorry. I wish I'd had one more chance
to be with you. I'm hoping when I return to the States
you'll perhaps be willing to see me?
If yes, you can be sure my return will be soon.

"On to the airport?" Jazmyn asked with a smirk.

"Yes!" Cari pulled her friend into a hug. "As fast as your car will get us there!"

Ethan had insisted Tristan eat before boarding the plane. They settled on Dish D'Lish in the main concourse of the airport so they'd have one last chance to talk before Tristan entered the secure area.

Tristan could hardly contain his smile as he re-read the message from Cari. "Did you or Gemma put her up to this?" he asked.

Ethan raised his hands. "Not me, brother," he replied. "Although it wouldn't surprise me if Gemma reminded her that you're leaving. She's still convinced you two are meant for each other." He returned to sipping his coffee, a sly grin on his face. "Are you going to tell her about the job offer?"

"No...not yet, anyway. I mean, you know I haven't even informed my boss at CWF." He paused. "It's going to be a whirlwind trip. You'll need to have a bed ready for me upon my return. I'll be sick with jet lag."

"So, you're going to extend your leave of absence and—"

"Exactly. It leaves the door open to return to England if, well, you know..." He took a drink of tea and wiped his mouth with a small napkin. "This job at the university is only until mid-May. That gives me time to figure out where I'm meant to be. There's not even any guarantee they'll hire me on for the fall semester if I want to stay. It's still very up in the air."

"Well, as much as I know your parents want you home, Gem and I would love to have you here. You know that."

"My immediate plans will all depend on wheth—" Tristan's phone buzzed, and he nearly gasped as he passed the cell to Ethan. "You don't suppose…"

"Where are you right now?" Ethan read. He looked at Tristan. "Answer her. You're in the main concourse of the airport."

Tristan hurriedly typed, making a few errors and corrections before sending the text. "God, it would be…amazing if she…" He finished the last bite of his salad and wiped his mouth again. While Ethan gathered the trays and went to the trash can, Tristan scanned the concourse. His phone buzzed again.

Can you wait for me? I'm almost there.

Tristan knew exactly how to reply:

For you, I'll wait forever.

Epilogue

"**A**re you ready?" Tristan asked as he popped his head in to the graduate assistants' office. "Our flight leaves in four hours, but I don't want to chance any delays."

Summer break had arrived. Tristan found Cari in her usual place on the sofa, a mess of papers sprawled across her lap. "Oh! You're back!" She scooted the papers to the side and stood as he approached. "How did it go? You were in there forever. They must've been impressed. The students loved taking your classes!"

Tristan smiled, wrapped his arms around her, and lifted her off the floor. "Looks like you're stuck with me for at least another year."

"I knew it, I knew it, I knew it!" Cari squealed. "I knew they'd hire you! This is fantastic!"

"Yes," he said, putting her down but keeping his arms around her waist. "It also means I'm going to be all over you to get your dissertation done, Ms. Lopez!"

"You can be all over me any time you want to, Dr. Saunders, dissertation or no dissertation," she said. She slapped his chest playfully. "Let's get going. I'm hungry and want to grab some lunch before we leave."

Tristan's trip home two months earlier had been just long enough to tender his resignation with Carson World Financial, visit his parents, and pack his belongings. He placed some larger items in storage, and day-to-day essentials were either put in suitcases or shipped to the States.

He'd adapted quickly to St. Eustachius and was welcomed by the faculty. Dr. Ujamwe had taken him under his wing and even invited him and Cari to his home for dinner. The transition for the students had been positive: Tristan's lectures were similar in content to Lassiter's, but as students commented, much more interesting and understandable.

Even though their schedules were different, Cari and Tristan rode to work together each day. Tristan planned his lectures and PowerPoint slides while waiting for Cari, and Cari worked on her dissertation while waiting for Tristan. Ashley Hunsinger had been staying on campus longer as well and hadn't missed another class. Once in a while he'd find the girl waiting in the hall after his classes, ready with some inane topic of conversation. He always breathed a sigh of relief as soon as he was rid of her.

Now that the semester was over, Cari and Tristan were taking an extended trip to England. She'd never been to Europe, and Tristan had an entire itinerary planned of places he wanted her to see.

On their way to the airport, Cari turned to Tristan. "Did you hear people talking about the scholarship?"

Tristan gave her a sly grin. "Yes. They seem as intrigued in accounting as the rest of the campus. It's quite a generous donation."

"They won't be able to trace it to Vasily, will they?"

"No. He's been doing this kind of thing all over the world for many years. He's good at keeping his donations anonymous. Besides, it's not the first time a university has received scholarship money. It's fairly common."

"Half a million isn't common, at least not for a small school like ours."

Tristan smiled. "*Ours.* I like how you said that."

"Me too."

"And I talked with Dawn in admissions about looking for Ben's application. I mentioned not so subtly that he'd be a great candidate for one of the full scholarships. And I was honest in saying I really only know *of* him — he's not a friend or even an acquaintance." Tristan grinned. "Since it's a brand new scholarship, she said she's going to push things through with Ben's name at the top of the recommendation list."

Cari tilted her head and sighed. "Thank you, Tristan. This means a lot to me."

"He saved your life, and *you* mean a lot to *me*. I'm sure Vasily will be pleased with the selection as well. He's glad to put some of his ill-gotten gains to good use."

They arrived at the airport with plenty of time to spare. They ate at Dish D'Lish for nostalgia's sake, and then headed to the security area. As Cari walked through the scanners ahead of him, Tristan patted the breast pocket of his blazer and smiled. Inside were surprise plane tickets to Paris and a well-padded velvet jewelry pouch. Tristan had been making these plans since Cari had run into his arms at the airport two months ago.

The top of the Eiffel Tower—the *real* Eiffel Tower—would be the perfect place to get engaged.

Acknowledgments

First and foremost, thanks to the entire staff at Omnific for all that you do. Particular appreciation goes to Jessica Royer Ocken, Kimberly Blythe, and Kayla Watson who worked with me directly to prepare *Between the Lies*. Appreciation also goes to Cory Montagna and Ginny Marston for their medical expertise. I am also grateful for my friends Elena and Drago Dimitrov who translated phrases into Bulgarian, provided insights about places in Sofia and Kiev, Ukraine, and guided me in spelling names properly. I learned a tremendous amount about the mafia from Misha Glenny's *McMafia* (2009, Vintage Books). Finally, my sincere thanks to my son, Drake, for his gun advice and for helping me with some of the major plot twists of this story.

About the Author

Alison Oburia has always had novel plots moving around in her head but has only recently begun to delve into getting those ideas on paper. By day, she works for a major university; by night, her characters take over and the writing begins. *Between the Lies*, loosely based on true events, is her second novel. Alison lives in central Florida with her husband and two sons.

check out these titles from
OMNIFIC PUBLISHING

◄──»Contemporary Romance◄──»

Boycotts & Barflies by Victoria Michaels
Passion Fish by Alison Oburia and Jessica McQuinn
Three Daves by Nicki Elson
The Redhead Series: The Unidentified Redhead and *The Redhead Revealed* by
Alice Clayton
Small Town Girl by Linda Cunningham
Stitches and Scars by Elizabeth A. Vincent
Trust in Advertising by Victoria Michaels
Take the Cake by Sandra Wright
Indivisible by Jessica McQuinn
Pieces of Us by Hannah Downing
The Way That You Play It by BJ Thornton
Poughkeepsie by Debra Anastasia
Burning Embers by Hannah Fielding
Cocktails & Dreams by Autumn Markus
Recaptured Dreams by Justine Dell

◄──»Paranormal Romance◄──»

The Light Series: Seers of Light, Whisper of Light, and *Circle of Light*
by Jennifer DeLucy
The Hanaford Park Series: Eve of Samhain and *Pleasures Untold* by Lisa Sanchez
Immortal Awakening by KC Randall
Crushed Seraphim by Debra Anastasia
The Guardian's Wild Child by Feather Stone
Grave Refrain by Sarah M. Glover
Divinity by Patricia Leever

◄──»Romantic Suspense◄──»

Whirlwind by Robin DeJarnett
The CONduct Series: With Good Behavior and *Bad Behavior* by Jennifer Lane
Between the Lies by Alison Oburia

Young Adult

Shades of Atlantis and *The Ember Series: Ember* and *Iridescent* by Carol Oates
Breaking Point by Jess Bowen
Life, Liberty, and Pursuit by Susan Kaye Quinn
Embrace by Cherie Colyer
Destiny's Fire by Trisha Wolfe
Streamline by Jennifer Lane

Historical Romance

Cat O' Nine Tails by Patricia Leever
Burning Embers by Hannah Fielding

Erotic Romance

Becoming sage by Kasi Alexander
Saving sunni by Kasi & Reggie Alexander
The Winemaker's Dinner: Appetizers by Dr. Ivan Rusilko & Everly Drummond

Anthologies and Singles

A Valentine Anthology including short stories by Alice Clayton, Jennifer DeLucy, Nicki Elson, Jessica McQuinn, Victoria Michaels, and Alison Oburia

It's Only Kinky the First Time by Kasi Alexander
Learning the Ropes by Kasi & Reggie Alexander
The Winemaker's Dinner: RSVP by Dr. Ivan Rusilko
The Winemaker's Dinner: No Reservations by Everly Drummond
Big Guns by Jessica McQuinn
Concessions by Robin DeJarnett
Starstruck by Lisa Sanchez
New Flame by BJ Thornton
Shackled by Debra Anastasia
Swim Recruit by Jennifer Lane
Sway by Nicki Elson
Full Speed Ahead by Susan Kaye Quinn
The Second Sunrise by Hannah Downing
The Summer Prince by Carol Oates
Whatever it Takes by Sarah M. Glover
Clarity by Patricia Leever
Glimpse of Light by Jennifer DeLucy

coming soon from
OMNIFIC PUBLISHING

Reaping Me Softly by Kate Evangelista
Once Upon a Second Chance by Marian Vere
Bittersweet Seraphim by Debra Anastasia
Wallbanger by Alice Clayton
16 Marsden Place by Rachel Brimble
Blood Vine by Amber Belldene
The Winemaker's Dinner: Entrees by Dr. Ivan Rusilko and Everly Drummond
All American Girl by Justine Dell
Divine Temptation by Nicki Elson
The Englishman by Nina Lewis
Tangled by Emma Chase
Corporate Affair by Linda Cunningham